Disruption

Disruption

Mary Withall

Illustrations by Illustrated London News

Matador
9 Priory Business Park,
Wistow Road, Kibworth Beauchamp,
Leicestershire. LE8 0RX
Tel: 0116 279 2299
Email: books@troubador.co.uk
Web: www.troubador.co.uk/matador
Twitter: @matadorbooks

ISBN 978 1788039 482

British Library Cataloguing in Publication Data.
A catalogue record for this book is available from the British Library.

Printed and bound in the UK by 4edge Limited
Typeset in 11pt Minion Pro by Troubador Publishing Ltd, Leicester, UK

Matador is an imprint of Troubador Publishing Ltd

In loving memory of my husband
Petre Withall
and our Kiwi friends
David and Glenys Watt.

Prologue

Edinburgh 1840

The old man was quite clearly dying. She did not think he felt any pain but just to be sure, she leaned across and took up the little blue glass bottle the physician had given her. Disturbed by her movement, he opened his eyes, raised a hand weakly from the coverlet and let it fall. The slightest shake of his head informed her that he was still determined to leave this world in full control of his senses. She slipped the bottle back into her apron pocket and took up the prayer-book from which she had been reading. 'I will lift up mine eyes unto the hills-' her soft melodious voice intoned the familiar passage. She reached the conclusion of the psalm and looked up.

At some time during the past few moments there had been a remarkable change. The skin around his eyes which for days past had been wrinkled and tense with pain was now relaxed and his heavily creased brow of moments before was suddenly smooth. His jaw had dropped slightly to leave a beatific smile playing about his lips. At last he was at peace. For a long time she gazed at the familiar features. In death he had regained the appearance of the man she used to know in happier times. Brushing away a tear she placed the prayer book gently beneath his gnarled and twisted fingers and covered his face with the sheet.

There were piss pots to be emptied, floors to be scrubbed and vitals to be distributed. They had only allowed her father to stay here to die in peace because she had offered to work at general duties with the nursing women. Left now without any means of support she could not give up the work simply because her father was dead.

From beyond the doors to the dingy, overcrowded ward she could hear the sounds of raucous laughter and the click of steel- tipped boots on a stone flagged floor. While people lay dying within, those who should be attending them made merry without.

Suddenly the noise ceased. There was scuffling of feet and a few whispered words before two of the convalescent patients slipped inside and lay down on their pallets, feigning sleep. Two nursing women, red faced and smirking, bustled in and went about their work ostentatiously as if to suggest that the sweat which they wiped from their brows might be associated with honest work.

Jessie knew what this sudden attention to their duties meant. In a few moments the sound of male voices could be heard approaching. The door to the ward was thrown open to admit three professional-looking gentlemen who proceeded rapidly towards a bed close by that upon which lay her father's still warm body.

'A supremely interesting case' declared the leader of the group whom she knew to be the hospital's senior surgeon. 'It took a while to remove the tumour and as you will see, the incision was necessarily extensive and yet the patient lives.'

'Here woman' he addressed her directly, 'remove the bandages if you please. My colleagues wish to see my handiwork!' With chest pushed forward and his thumbs thrust into the pockets of his lavishly embroidered waistcoat, the surgeon oozed self satisfaction.

She hesitated, never having been asked to perform such a function before.

'Come along, my girl' he urged her. 'My colleagues do not have time to wait upon your convenience!'

She began to remove the bandages revealing as she did so a monstrous head wound, the incision carelessly cobbled together with thick cat gut. It was a horrifying sight the shock of which might have caused her to vomit was she not too terrified to do so.

'Not the prettiest piece of surgery, I'll grant you,' the surgeon conceded, 'but gentlemen, the patient lives!'

'With such severe damage to the brain,' ventured the younger of the two other men, 'is there not some impairment in speech perhaps, or sensibility?'

'It is possible,' agreed the great man dismissively. The patient has scarcely regained full consciousness since the operation. 'Only time will tell.'

They began to move away. As they did so, the surgeon addressed Jessie once again. 'Well, don't stand there gawping, Miss. Replace the bandage if you please!'

She gave a neat curtsey and as she retrieved the soiled linen she dared to approach the youngest of the three doctors, he who had show a certain compassion for the patient.

'Excuse me, Sir,' she said, drawing him to one side. 'My father died some moments ago.' She indicated the still form lying stiffly beneath its sheet. 'Pray tell me what I should do about it?'

'Are you not a regular nurse then?' he asked, surprised that she should seek his advice. Women employed by the hospital were seldom as well spoken or indeed as clean as this young girl. He had heard such lurid tales of the behaviour of such women who were said to seduce patients in their sick beds and even to rob the dead.

'I stayed only to help nurse my father,' she explained 'and have done certain other routine work to help pay for his keep.'

The young man, having learned something of the system employed in the maintaining the poorest citizens in hospital, nodded, understanding her plight. 'As for your demised relative,' he said candidly, 'I fear I am only a student, Ma'am. You had best report it to the Matron.' With that, he hurried away to join his superiors.

She bent to the task of replacing the bandages. It was difficult, for the poor creature's head was swollen and misshapen. The activity had woken him and she could see that each movement she was obliged to make caused him great pain. She looked about her, hoping to catch the eye of one of the departing doctors but they were too absorbed in their discussion and had disappeared before she could muster the courage to address them.

She felt in her pocket for the little bottle her father had rejected. Surely it could do no harm to relieve the poor fellow's agony with a little laudanum? She measured a dose into a glass and held his head up so as not to spill the drug as she forced it between his lips. His eyes registered his thanks for her kindness and after a few moments she saw him relax and fall asleep.

Her father's body, having been removed with little ceremony, was conveyed to the hospital chapel there to await its final journey to a pauper's grave. Jessie worked steadily through the afternoon keeping a watchful eye upon the young man with the head wound. Towards evening her patient received a visitor. He was a strong looking man, probably in his early twenties. Muscular and well tanned, she assumed him to be one who worked long hours in the open.

He approached his friend's bedside in trepidation and what he saw there did nothing to allay his worst fears.

'How are you Jem?' he asked quietly, 'It' s your old friend Tam come to see you.'

The patient stirred at the sound of a familiar voice and his eyes sprang open. For a while, the visitor attempted some form of conversation but receiving no response other than the very slightest movement of the eyes, he turned to the girl for an explanation.

'They have cut away a tumour from his brain,' she told him. 'He can neither move nor speak.'

'Is he likely to remain thus?' the young man asked.

'It is not for me to say, Sir,' she replied. 'The surgeon who operated upon him seemed vastly pleased with what he had done, but I believe his satisfaction derived from the patient being alive at all after such an ordeal.'

The visitor returned to his friend's bedside for a few minutes longer but quickly tired of his fruitless attempts to communicate. At last he returned to the woman who was now on her knees in another part of the room, scrubbing the floor.

'I wonder might I ask you to ensure that he wants for nothing?' he begged, handing her a few coins. 'I have business in Aberfoyle during the next day or so but I shall return. Perhaps by then there will be happier news of my friend.'

'Perhaps,' she replied, her tone lacking any conviction.

As the week wore on, the patient showed increasing signs of distress. When he regained consciousness it was to suffer severe pain and more than once the woman was driven to give him further doses of laudanum. In the matron's absence she refilled her bottle from the drugs cabinet. Supervision was so lax that she did not fear discovery. She knew that many of the nurses helped themselves to substances from which they gained certain benefits or relief on their own account.

The surgeon returned and finding his patient still totally paralysed, ordered a second operation to be performed on the following day.

The girl's constant observation of the poor creature had convinced her that although unable to speak, her patient could hear and understand all that was going on around him. When he heard of the second ordeal which had been planned for him, he struggled to make clear to her that he did not want it. She was certain that all he wanted was to be left to die in peace.

She chatted away to him while taking inordinate care to move him as little as possible as she tidied his bed sheets and washed his face. Any lifting or movement of any kind was painful to him.

'What is it? she asked in response to his silent appeal. 'A little more of this is it?' She withdrew the blue bottle from her pocket.

His anxious stare softened in response.

'Very well,' she told him, 'but this will have to be the last.'

She poured a little of the precious fluid into the glass but then, seeing the intensity of his appeal, she tipped out the entire contents of the bottle, holding his head steady as he drank the potion down.

Her intention had been to provide relief from pain, nothing more. Almost at once, he fell into a deep sleep and for a long time his stertorous breathing was the cause of complaints from all those around him. Then, late in the evening, when she was about to leave to go to her miserable lodgings, the irritating sound of his snoring stopped suddenly. In the eerie silence which followed she became vaguely aware of her own heartbeat, while the occasional stifled cough and the creaking of bed boards seemed inordinately loud.

She moved to his bedside, felt for a pulse and finding none bent her cheek close to his slightly open mouth in hopes of feeling the slightest breath. There was nothing at all to indicate that he lived.

She lifted her head and looked around in dismay. The patient's visitor of a few nights before, appeared at the end of the ward and seeing her standing there, hurried towards her.

'What is it?' he asked anxiously.

'I believe your friend is dead,' she replied in a frightened whisper.

The young man repeated her simple tests and was forced to agree. For some minutes they stood silently, side by side, their contemplation interrupted at last by the woman's quiet weeping.

He turned to her, his eyes filled with compassion.

'You must not distress yourself,' he told her, 'You have done everything you could to make his final hours comfortable. Poor Jem would not have wished to live like that, a helpless cripple unable to hear or speak. Surely it is better that he should die?'

Not daring to tell him how she had been instrumental in hastening his friend's demise, she allowed the young man to accompany her to the matron's rooms where she reported the death.

'Och, that will surely vex Mr Thornton,' was all that the matron said. 'He was so proud of his handiwork!'

Jessie wondered if the surgeon, unable to boast that his patient still lived, would blame her for what had happened. If he were to find out how she had administered drugs without permission he would certainly have her dismissed or worse, perhaps arrested. What if he were to accuse her of causing the patient's death? Hastily excusing herself, she bade the gentleman goodnight and left him to arrange for the burial of his friend.

She had reached the front entrance to the hospital and stepped out into the road when she heard a shout and turned to find him chasing after her.

'Please wait, Miss,' he called, 'I wanted to thank you.'

She paused, waiting for him to catch up.

'What of you, he enquired when he had caught his breath. 'What shall you do now?'

'I shall return to my lodging for a good night's sleep,' she told him. It had been a tiring day and its sad ending had taken all her energy. She felt desperately weary.

'You must eat supper, surely?' he suggested.

'I am too tired to eat, ' she told him.

'I insist that you allow me to buy your supper.' There was no denying him. 'I know of an excellent tavern only a short walk from here.'

Ignoring her objection, he took her by the elbow, led her across the street and into a dark alley. Momentarily she feared his intentions, but almost immediately they emerged into a well- lit thoroughfare. On one corner stood an inn with festoons of brightly shining lanterns to welcome them.

Before going in he turned to her. 'I cannot escort a lady to supper without knowing her name,' he declared, his eyes twinkling. 'But first let me introduce myself. I am Thomas Dundas of Eisdalsa in Argyll. Now, may I know whom I have the pleasure of escorting to dinner?'

'My name is Jessie, Jessie Brown', she replied.

He gazed down into her deep brown eyes, marvelled at the lights reflected in the heavy tresses of her rich chestnut- coloured hair, and made up his mind to waste no time in changing her name to Jesse Dundas.

Chapter One

1843

It was a warm evening for April. Ian Bantrie ran his finger around inside his tight collar band fingering the rawness of the skin where the starched linen had rubbed his neck. To be fourteen years old, out of breeches and wearing his new Sunday clothes for the first time had seemed so wonderful when he had arisen that morning. Now, after the tedium of the Sabbath had nearly come to a close he was beginning to realise that being truly grown up at last carried certain disadvantages. He looked along the pew to where his wee brother, Charlie, squirmed on the hard wooden bench beside their mother and envied the child his less restricting smock and knickers. At Ian's side his sister Catherine, ten years old, cool and demure as any woman in the kirk, gazed in rapt attention at the figure in the pulpit, absorbing every word her father uttered. Meanwhile his mother, Judith Bantrie, appeared to be dozing. Her head had dropped forward so that the huge peak of her fashionable new bonnet quite covered her face and she snored gently in rhythm with her husband's droning voice.

Ian grinned to himself as his father's delivery reached a crescendo and his mother came to so suddenly that her spectacles slipped off her nose and her prayer book slipped to the floor. There was a slight scuffle as Charlie, grasping at any excuse for movement, slid down from his seat to retrieve it.

'Consider, my friends, the story of the miracle of the loaves and the fishes.' James Bantrie smiled upon his attentive flock. 'There have been many attempts to explain what actually happened at that great gathering there on the hillside beside the lake of Galilee. Was the amount of food really miraculously increased so that all might eat or was it perhaps that, when Our Saviour began to share out what food there was near at hand, others produced what they had brought with them and passed that around also? What is important to remember is that all in that huge multitude were fed.

Let us now consider the incident in terms of a parable for maybe that was Our Lord's intention in the first place. Let us suppose that the loaves and fishes He distributed are the Word of God. By passing the Word from one to the other amongst all our brethren, by sharing its nourishment with our neighbours, we will find that there is sufficient for all to feed upon.'

The sermon ended at last. Minister Bantrie moved down the aisle and took his place at the door of the Kirk in order to acknowledge his departing congregation. Judith Bantrie gathered her book and reticule and urging wee Charles before her, proceeded to follow in the wake of the good people of Kilmory.

'An interesting sermon, Minister.' Alan Blair Gower, with a forced attempt at camaraderie, shook Jame's hand in a manner as insincere as his congratulations. 'Mind you, there are those who might accuse you of verging upon blasphemy. It is a very confident man who assumes to know what Christ intended!'

'The Lord himself was not averse to converting fact into fiction in order to make a point,' observed James, well aware that his patron disapproved of any new movement within the church to make the gospels available and meaningful to *all* the people.

Blair Gower most certainly did not hold with this new manner of addressing the parishioners in the simplest terms. A little mystery and a lot of fear was what was needed to keep the working classes at heal. If they lost their fear of the Lord where would the discipline of the church be then?

'I would like to introduce my kinsman, Robert Shaw,' he said, rather more curtly. He indicated the stranger at his side. 'My nephew is a man of the cloth, like yourself.'

'Good day Mr Shaw,' James greeted his colleague warmly and smiled.

The other did not smile. He was a pale-faced, lean figure with a long aquiline nose and steely grey eyes, a mite too close together for James's liking. He put forth a limp, cold hand and shook James's without speaking.

‘I trust you are enjoying your visit to Tayside,’ James ventured, ignoring the disdainful attitude of the stranger.

‘More than a visit, I fear,’ the fellow replied. His voice was as chilling as his appearance. ‘There is much work to be done in these parts to restore some control over church matters. Things have been allowed to slide in the more remote villages. We cannot allow this indiscipline to continue I’m afraid.’

James was not sure if he himself was included in this sweeping summary of the state of the church in the district. Dismayed at the man’s unfriendly attitude, nevertheless he tried again to make conversation.

‘Do you have a living in these parts?’

‘Robert has been presented to the congregation at Lawers,’ Blair Gower intervened. ‘His Lordship has been gracious enough to confer his patronage.’

James thought of the many friends he had at Lawers and wondered how they might regard this cold fish who was so very different from the kindly, gentle soul who had been their minister these past twenty five years. There would have been few who would have signed the call for this unpleasant creature.

‘Minister McClure was a fine man,’ James insisted, ‘he is sorely missed by the people.’

‘McClure allowed things to get out of hand,’ Robert Shaw protested. ‘He was slack in collecting dues and spent more time at cottage firesides prattling with the ancients than in his pulpit. It seems he was too busy fussing over his flock to keep abreast of directives from the Assembly. Time has stood still in that parish. Things will change very soon I can assure you.’

As he warmed to a favoured topic, the fellow’s colour improved and there was a spark of passion in those cold eyes. He would likely prove to be a tyrant amongst the simple flock to whom he had been called to minister. There was about the man a great deal of arrogance and self importance, thought James.

Unable to sustain further conversation in the face of the stranger’s rudeness, James allowed a heavy silence to settle between them.

‘We must be getting along,’ Blair Gower blustered, taking his kinsman by the elbow. Then, bowing to Judith Bantrie who had come to stand at her husband's side, he murmured, 'Good evening to you Bantrie, Mrs Bantrie.' He doffed his hat politely and led Robert Shaw away down the path, between the gravestones. The latter did not deign to acknowledge Judith nor did he make any response to James' polite 'Good evening'.

'Worse than I thought,' proclaimed a jovial voice.

Emerging from the gloomy interior of the porch where he had been skulking, not wishing to be involved in any discussion with their patron, William Carswell joined the minister and his family in the gathering dusk.

'They told me he was a sour faced fellow,' he exclaimed. 'No more than a couple of the parishioners would sign his call, yet His Lordship has ignored the entire congregation and appointed him.'

'But why?'James asked. 'The Marquis can be a determined man, I know, but it is not like him to go against the wishes of his people.'

'Money.'

'How so?'

'It appears His Lordship has fallen temporarily upon hard times, some unwise investments I believe. Blair Gower has bailed him out.'

'In exchange for the Lawers living for his nephew?'

'Exactly so'

'What a hypocrite is Robert Shaw,' cried James. 'He condemns a good man like Minister McClure and yet he is prepared to flout all the rules to get a place for himself! He has the impertinence to speak of bringing the parishioners to heal. William, it is high time that something was done about this kind of thing.'

'By the grace of God, it will be, in just another month.' William placed a comforting hand upon James's shoulder and offered Judith his other arm. Together, the three walked down the path towards the lichgate.

'You seem to have greater faith than I in the ability of the Evangelical Party to carry the General Assembly with it,' James sighed.

William Carswell, Apothecary and Elder of St Phillian's Kirk, stopped in his tracks. 'See here, James, you of all people must not lose heart. The time is coming for you take your part in a momentous revolution. Have courage, I shall be at your side to give my support and encouragement.'

'You are coming to Edinburgh?'

'But of course! I do not intend to miss this, the greatest of all General Assemblies.'

Ahead of them, Ian chased his wee brother around the headstones while Catherine walked demurely behind the adults, careful not to scuff her new shoes on the worn paving stones.

*

May is one of the finest month's in the calendar of the Scottish Highlands. The trees and shrubs burst into leaf a week or two later than they do further south but they appear to gain greater energy and a brighter colouring for the waiting. The blossoms are fairer and smell sweeter for the morning dew upon them and the occasional light showers of rain.

The reverend James Bantrie trotted his horse along a rough track, hedged by gorse and broom in full bloom. Emerging bracken fronds lifted their brilliant green heads like so many tiny serpents from the rotting bed of last year's dead foliage and, here and there, the bright blue wild hyacinths were beginning to show. Below the clouds of snowy white blackthorn blossom and in the shadow of each moss-covered boulder, a wild profusion of primroses illuminated the darkest recesses.

Coming at last to the summit of the hill James looked down upon the expanse of river below him and beyond to that vast, ordered conglomeration of buildings which was the city of Edinburgh. A pall of black smoke from a thousand chimneys, hung above the city in the still morning air but even this could not blot out the bright sun which touched the angled windows to be reflected many times over, causing the usually gloomy city to glisten with signals welcoming him home.

James had lived so long in the country he had almost forgotten the thrill which the sight of that sprawling conurbation could give him. With a gentle prick of his spur he urged the big bay mare into a canter and covered the long flat strip of springy turf which capped the hill in minutes.

At last he came to a familiar gully and a deeply furrowed lane which descended steeply towards the river. Sycamore and chestnut trees, already in green leaf and beeches yet to burst their elegant brown buds, bordered the road, obscuring the view beyond. At the foot of the slope he came suddenly upon a group of thatched cottages crouching beneath the cliff on the broad bank of the river. Despite the early hour, smoke arose from every chimney. At the sound of horse's hooves upon the roadway a tousle-headed lad appeared at the door of the house closest to the river. He waved cheerfully to James and then withdrew. In a few minutes a giant of a fellow emerged, his shock of fiery red hair matching that of his young son.

'Would you be wanting the ferry, Reverend?' he enquired, spotting James' tell-tale stock at once.

'Aye,' James answered him, thankful that he would not have to wait to cross.

As he followed James down the slope, the ferryman pulled a rough tweed jacket over his broad, muscular shoulders. ' 'T is gae chilly out on the water,' he explained. 'Even on a bright morning such as this the wind is cold out there.'

'Have you crossed already this morning?' asked James, surprised that others should be abroad even earlier than himself.

'Yours will be the third crossing I have made since sun-up,' the ferryman told him, smiling, 'and every passenger a clerical gentleman like yourself.' He had already taken sufficient coins to feed the family for a week and could afford to be cheerful.

'Who, I ask myself, is doing the Lord's work out there in the hills while all his disciples are down here in the wicked city?' he enquired jovially and James, despite his sore back and weary limbs, was forced to join in with the burst of laughter which followed.

James led the mare aboard the large, flat bottomed vessel which was to carry him across the water. The reflection of sunlight upon the vast expanse of the river Forth, seemed to upset her and it was some minutes before he could get his mount settled into the unfamiliar and somewhat precarious stall provided. The ferryman had already cast off from the shore when they heard a shout and, turning in the direction from which James himself had recently come, they saw a dishevelled figure descending the steep track on foot and signalling wildly for them to wait. With James' consent, the ferryman manoeuvred his unwieldy craft back towards the slipway and tied up again, content to await the approaching traveller.

Red of face and gasping for breath, the additional passenger arrived at last. The ferrymen took his bulging carpet bag and helped him aboard.

'My apologies for causing you to wait Sir,' the newcomer gasped to James once he had settled himself upon the rude wooden plank which served as a seat. 'I was held up along the road and am later than I had meant to be. A further half hour until the ferry returned, would mean I would miss my appointment.'

When he had straightened his coat and dusted off his trousers, it was clear that here was yet another clerical gentleman. James began to wonder what was afoot that so many of his colleagues should be advancing upon the capital a full day prior to the commencement of the Assembly.

'I understand from the ferryman,' said James, 'that a several of our colleagues have preceded us this morning. Can you tell me what has brought so many clergy to the city so early for the Assembly?'

His companion was an older man, of florid complexion. He carried before him a portly belly which spoke of a level of self- indulgence almost unseemly in any member of the cloth. His thin white locks hung loosely to his shoulders and at every turn of his head a shower of dandruff fell about his shoulders covering the dull brownish- black cloth of his jacket in a sprinkling of white dust. His stock was limp and wrinkled and had clearly not seen the inside of a wash tub for many days, the material of his breaches was so thin that his knees were clearly visible through the weave while one of his shoes, dust covered and badly scuffed, appeared to have parted company with its sole.

'Have ye no' heard the call from Thomas Chalmers?' he asked in astonishment. 'A' those who would see an ending of the Patronage Act are to meet in the Tanfield Hall at noon today.'

Startled by the man's openness, James assumed that things had moved on apace since he had discussed matters of common concern with his colleagues at last year's Assembly.

'I set out two days ago and have this morning been on the road since daybreak, just in order to be here in good time for tomorrow,' James explained.

'You'll have come a fair distance then?' the other asked.

'I am James Bantrie, Minister of the parish of Kilmory in Perthshire,' James introduced himself.

'And I am Murdo McLeod, Minister of the parish of Linktown by Kircaldy, at your service, Sir.'

James stretched across to shake hands expecting something limp and sweaty. He was surprised at the firmness of his companion's grasp.

'Tell me, when did the call go out from Thomas Chalmers, to attend this dissenters meeting?' James now enquired.

'It was handed on from parish to parish by word of mouth, no one daring to put the information onto paper. I doubt the message would have reached as far away as Kilmory in time to be of use.'

'Chalmers must be relying on good support from the largest towns if he can neglect to enlist those from the island and Highland parishes,' James observed, dryly.

'Oh, I think you can be sure that he has done his work carefully,' McLeod assured him. 'It was from the Highlands and the Western Isles that the first murmurings came ten or more years ago. He has little doubt about the level of support from that quarter. It is, after all, those remote parishes which suffer most severely from the Patronage Act.'

'By the same token it is the rural parishioners who are the least able to defy their masters,' James, reminded him. 'Their livelihoods depend for the most part upon the goodwill of the patron who is often the sole provider of employment and generally owns the crofts and houses in which the people live. The privilege of selecting their own minister may seem to be a paltry principle upon which to stake the livelihood of their families. Chalmers must take their position into account before commanding any truly drastic action.'

'I feel sure the condition of the remote parishes has already been considered,' said McLeod. 'If not, it seems that yours might be a strong voice in their defence.'

James, wondering whether he would find the courage to speak out should the necessity arise, fell silent. He concentrated his mind upon the crossing, watching with admiration as the boatman, wielding a huge single oar over the stern with apparent ease, conducted his craft through the turbulence in mid stream. At last the ferry glided into calmer waters by the southern shore and the passengers prepared to disembark. McLeod was the first ashore, hurrying up the ramp in pursuit of a lift from a passing cart.

'See you in the Tanfield Hall at noon!' he cried.

*

There had been a goodly gathering of the disenchanted clergy at Thomas Chalmer's meeting of the previous day and on this, the opening session of the General Assembly of the Church of Scotland, hopes were running high that something momentous was about to take place.

Other than the seats reserved for the Members of Council themselves, St Andrew's church was already full. The public galleries overflowed into the halls and stairways of the building and masses of ordinary townsfolk waited in the surrounding streets for word to filter out concerning events within. In a city where most men believed sincerely in the absolute power of God and worshipped regularly every Sunday, matters concerning the conduct of their church were of paramount importance. Businesses remained closed, university classes were suspended and there was scarcely a man or woman in the whole of Edinburgh who did not hang upon every word emerging from the meeting that day.

During the past decade, land clearances by the owners of great tracts of the Highlands and islands, together with the promise of better wages in the burgeoning industrial conurbations of lowland Scotland, had caused the city populations to swell at an alarming rate while the countryside was denuded of what little population it had. In this strange new environment far from the place they had always regarded as home, the new urbanites clung determinedly to whatever they did recognise, fervently maintaining their allegiance to the established Church of Scotland.

The urban churches overflowed to such an extent that the more prominent ministers such as Thomas Chalmers, sought to build new churches, dividing parishes into smaller sectors each having its own minister and body of lay dignitaries. In a few cases, money was found for new church buildings but for many of these additional congregations, an assortment of strange accommodation had been utilised. Abandoned halls and warehouses, school buildings and even ships which were currently unchartered and lying idle in the docks had become temporary places of worship.

Among the wealthy patrons into whose care the State had placed the lives of its parishioners, there was a small number of wealthy tyrants who manipulated laws made in Westminster for the administration of the church, in order to keep the lower orders at heel. When conflict arose between a patron and his people, he could call upon the Civil Authorities to enforce the Law of the land. The Judiciary was, however, as desperate as the clergy to kerb the excesses of patrons in the rural parishes. Judges made the litigation as tedious and expensive as they could in order to discourage these rich and powerful men.Unfortunately many parishes, unable to meet the expense of appointing their own advocate, were quickly forced to give up the fight and the Judges were obliged to find in favour of the patrons.

On this opening day of the General Assembly of the Church of Scotland, My Lord Sheriff of Edinburgh who had at first disregarded warnings as to the degree of unrest amongst the ordinary people, became concerned when he saw the extent of the crowds and hurriedly deployed his inadequate body of lawmen where they might best keep control of the situation. It was in the main an orderly crowd and the interchange between demonstrators and law enforcers was on the whole, cheerful. Fears of a riot seemed to be unsubstantiated and very soon the lawmen were entering into the spirit of the occasion as cheerfully as the rest.

In the body of the church, James Bantrie looked around him for a face he knew. Amongst the rows of empty seats reserved for the Evangelical Party, he spotted his companion of the river crossing the day before and forced a way through the milling crowds to his side.

'Good day my friend,' the older gentleman greeted him. 'I was hoping to speak with you in the Tanfield Hall yesterday but I fear I missed you in the throng. I did however, listen most carefully to your statement and concur with all that you said.'

James had heard, with growing alarm, the more outlandish suggestions for action to be taken against the landowners and city burgers. At last, unable to contain his anger, he had risen to his feet catching the eye of Thomas Chalmers who invited him to speak.

'Gentlemen,' James addressed them, his well practised voice level and clear, 'we have heard some outrageous suggestions in this hall this afternoon. The actions proposed by our colleagues,' he indicated a group of younger clergy who had been particularly loud in their condemnation of State and patrons alike, 'may have some merit in an urban society where a man's wage packet is not controlled by the church patron against whom he proposes to take action. When a minister's only possible source of income and for that matter, housing, is in the hands of a single big fish who also happens to be the patron of the village kirk, he has to think hard before risking the lives of himself and his family on a matter of principle. If we expect that level of sacrifice from ministers as well as from the lay members of our church, we must offer them more than casual promises of protection which we all know, cannot be maintained in every remote parish in Scotland. Those hotheads who advocate non-payment of rents, closure of church buildings and demonstrations which might, all too easily, lead to physical violence against those opposed to the abolition of the Patronage Act, must realise the consequences of such actions and be prepared to give whatever help is needed to defend the people who support our cause. We have heard it said that if sufficient numbers walk out of the assembly tomorrow the Government in Westminster will be required to take notice of our complaints. What if insufficient members walk out? What if the patrons of those who do participate, get to hear of it and have them dismissed? Do we propose to relocate every man who loses his living because he supports our cause?'

He had sat down to loud jeering from the younger element but there were many heads nodding in agreement nevertheless.

Despite warnings such as that from James Bantrie, the vote, when taken was all but unanimous. In view of the size of the gathering and the fact that so many of those unable to be present came from the rural parishes to the west which were most troubled by the terms of the Act, it seemed certain there would be a majority of support for their action on the following day.

Had anyone had eyes for other than the charismatic figure of Thomas Chalmers as he closed the meeting with the strongest words of encouragement uttered that day, they might have noticed a solitary member of the cloth who did not raise his hand like the others, but stood back in the shadows, watching and waiting to see the outcome of the vote. Robert Shaw had taken careful note of the various contributors to the debate particularly the one outspoken minister to whom he could put a name, James Bantrie from a parish on the borders of his own designated living.

Once the vote had been taken and it was clear that the meeting was about to close, the reverend Robert Shaw departed by a side door, mounted the horse he had left tethered close by and rode with all haste to report to his senior colleagues who awaited him, behind closed doors, in an insignificant close behind St Giles Cathedral.

Jame's response to Murdo McLeod's congratulations was lost in the cheering and stamping of feet which greeted the entry of the members of the Council.

These Members of the Council of Churches had met earlier at Holyrood intent upon professing their allegiance to the Queen. There they had been received by her Commissioner, the Marquis of Bute who had then accompanied them to St Giles for an inaugural Act of Worship. From thence, followed by a military escort in deference to the Queen's representative, they had processed to the place of assembly, St Andrew's Church.

The Moderator and his officers filed in and took their places at the front of the church and the pews reserved for the Moderate Party members quickly filled.

James looked around eagerly expecting to see some of those members of the Evangelical party to whom he had listened so intently on the previous day.With the exception of certain of their leaders who were already seated at the front of the church, they had stayed away. He glanced inquiringly at McLeod.

'After the meeting broke up yesterday it was agreed that other than Dr Welsh and Thomas Chalmers and those Evangelicals who are office bearers, members of Council would go to Tanfield Hall there to await the procession of dissenters.'

'But won't that diminish the impact of the walk out?' demanded James.

'Not if the Moderate Party follow Doctor Welsh!' Murdo declared triumphantly.

James was less certain of the outcome than his companion appeared to be. What if these men now filing solemnly into the seats opposite, should fail to rise to their feet when Dr Welsh left the chamber? It would be a pity if the planned procession turned out to consist of no more than those like himself and Murdo who were not Councillors, together with the few gentlemen gathered in the first two pews?

The assembly waited in silence, every man on his feet while the tramp of soldiers marching to a band of fifes and drums could be heard approaching, heralding the arrival of the Queen's Commissioner. To the strains of Her Majesty's Anthem, the Marquis of Bute entered the church in procession and made his way to the throne. Only then did those who had seats, take them. All about him James was aware of comments concerning the empty pews on the left-hand side of the nave and his heart sank.

Then as the Moderator, Dr Welsh, rose to address them, a hush fell over the assembled company.

James glanced along the rows of eager, anxious faces trying to gage the mood of the people. He prayed that there would be a united front. Determined to show his own solidarity with the planned protest, he feared the outcome should others of their colleagues pull back at the last minute.

James was only too aware that in the hall today there were many who valued their own comfortable circumstances too much to jeopardise them for the sake of less fortunate colleagues. There were priests enough who were prepared to indulge those patrons who chose to buy their way into the next world by providing rich stipends for their clergy and by investing their wealth in splendid new churches with rich trappings. As the Moderator called the Assembly to order, James wondered just how many of those who had raised their voices at yesterday's meeting would follow their leader when the moment came.

Being far from home and out of touch with his own parishioners, James, unlike so many of his colleagues in the hall, had received no messages of warning from his church elders, that morning. No one passed on to James Bantrie any of the decisions made last evening by influential, reactionary members of the Assembly. He had no inkling of the retribution to be metered out to those taking direct action to repeal the Act.

Moderator Welsh was not an eloquent speaker like Thomas Chalmers, who had led the discussion on the previous day. His voice was weak and those within the chamber strained to hear his words. His intentions were however soon made very plain:

> *'Fathers and brethren, according to the usual form of procedure, this is the time for making up the roll, but in consequence of certain proceedings affecting our rights and privileges, proceedings that have been sanctioned*

by Her Majesty's Government and by the Legislature of the country, and more especially in respect that there has been an infringement on the liberties of our Constitution so that we could not now Constitute this Court without a violation of the terms of the Union between Church and State in this land, as now authoritatively declared – I must protest against our proceeding further.'

The Moderator called upon those present to accompany him to another place where the Free Church of Scotland might carry out its duties without hindrance. The short speech was listened to without interruption by that vast assembly. Dr Welsh drew his statement to a close.

'... *we now withdraw accordingly, humbly and solemnly acknowledging the hand of God in the things which have come upon us because of our manifold sins and the sins of the Church and nation, but at the same time, with an assured conviction that we are not responsible for any consequences that may follow from this, our enforced separation from an Establishment which we loved and prized, through interference with conscience, the dishonour done to Christ's crown and the rejection of His sole and supreme authority as King in his Church.'*

In the hiatus which followed, the distinguished figure rose to his feet, drew his robes around him and swept out of the silent chamber. Half the members of the Council and in their wake, two fifths of those in the body of the hall followed suit. As Murdo McLeod filed past he cast a glance at James Bantrie. 'Now or never, brother,' he murmured.

James, needing no further bidding, took up his hat and cane and followed. In the gallery overhead, William Carswell noted his friend's departure and determined to be counted amongst the dissenters himself, he also rose to leave and with him many other elders and communicants of the Church. Uncertain what had been the cause of this mass exit, those members of the public packed into the hallways and on the stairs, were obliged to stand back and let them pass.

*

The euphoria created by the demonstration on May 18th, 1843 which was to become known as the Disruption, lasted no longer than the time it took for James Bantrie to return to his parish. On the morning of the 23rd. of May, James had been amongst the first to go to the Tanfield Hall once again. This time it was to sign the Deed of Demission which left no doubt as to his allegiance to the Free Church of Scotland.

James was very concerned about the reaction of his congregation to the news from Edinburgh and considered it imperative that he should return home as soon as possible.

With William Carswell at his side, he embarked upon the homeward journey in leisurely fashion, unaware that James's patron, Alan Blair Gower, had commissioned his own courier to hasten from the Assembly with news of the events.

By the time the two friends arrived home a few days later, Alan Blair Gower had already called together the church elders and let it be known in the parish that what the minister had done was in his opinion, an action against the church which was not to be tolerated. Nevertheless, there were those amongst the Members of the Church Session who wished to hear James Bantrie's side of the matter and insisted that he be invited to preach on the following Sunday, so that he might have the opportunity of explaining his actions to the people.

The church was very full on that evening. James glanced at the one empty pew, that which should have housed his wife and children. He now regretted his decision to leave them at home. He had come to rely upon Judith's silent approbation and missed her comforting presence at his side.

The service progressed normally until it came time for James to deliver his sermon.

In a hushed, expectant atmosphere, he mounted the rostrum and spread a handful of pages upon the lectern. His dedicatory prayer was short and spoken as though between himself and his Maker.

'I shall take my text today, from Revelations iii verse 11: *Hold that fast which thou hast, that no man take thy crown...'* He shuffled his notes and then laid them deliberately aside. Resting both hands upon the lectern he began to speak:

'My friends, first of all I must tell you from my firsthand experience, exactly what happened when the General Assembly met in St Andrew's Hall on the 18th of May.'

He told of the proceedings in a measured voice devoid of all emotion, until he reached the moment when Dr Welsh in a most dignified fashion, lead the dissenters from St Andrew's and out into the street. He described the march towards the Tanfield Hall with the Edinburgh crowds parting to let them through.

'Dr Welsh was followed by Thomas Chalmers our newly elected Moderator of the free Church of Scotland. He is such a charismatic figure that old ladies reached out to touch his gown as he swept past and children were held up to see the great man, so that they might remember the moment all their lives.'

James spoke of grown men weeping and young people, students, not well known for their piety, running forward to join in the procession.

'In putting aside the establishment,' he assured them, 'we will not be disassembling the Church itself but merely removing it to another place and carrying out its duties within a different environment. The building in which we have worshipped tonight, the Manse wherein I shall sleep, the food with which I feed my children, all are provided in part by the establishment and in part by your generous contributions to my stipend. Two days ago I rescinded both. Not because I want to live in penury; not that I do not appreciate the sacrifices which you make so that I and my family may live in comfort; but because the rules under which these things are provided are anathema to the oath which I took at my ordination.

My fate is in your hands and I ask you to consider carefully whether you wish to continue to worship in a house which is dedicated to the aggrandizement of the State secular to the detriment of the true King of Glory whose position as Head of the Church we are, every one of us, sworn to uphold.

Look around you at this fine building my friends. What is it but stones and mortar? This is not the Church. You are the Church and your leader is Jesus Christ and no other. Cast aside the bonds which tie you to an establishment which has moved so far from its initial purpose as to put the will of Parliament before the Will of God. If you follow me, we shall perhaps be forced to worship in the fields, in a barn or tent, wherever we can find shelter, but with God's good grace and through our own endeavours, we shall one day build a fine new church worthy of the name. A Church worthy of Christ the King who is its head, true to its own beliefs and subject to no one's rule save that of our Lord and Saviour, himself. A Church which is truly free!

He paused, his own strong words still ringing in his ears. Suddenly conscious of the stillness surrounding him he glanced at the faces of his friends and neighbours and saw that there was hardly a dry eye in the whole congregation. Suddenly embarrassed by his own fervour, he finished on a calmer, quieter note.

'It is for you to decide how you shall go from here. I shall be at your service during the next two days should you wish to discuss any point with me. The Kirk Session will meet in two days from now when it will decide whether to disestablish or to continue under the rule of Westminster and the Patronage Act.'

He gathered up his papers and looking neither to right nor left, he walked slowly down the length of the aisle and out into the warm summer evening.

*

Two days later, James was summoned before the elders of the kirk.

The chair was taken by Alan Blair Gower, himself. Beside him, revelling in his colleague's discomfort, sat the reverend Robert Shaw.

'I have called this meeting of the elders, Minister Bantrie,' Blair Gower began, speaking as though James's sermon of Sunday evening had never been delivered, 'because of the disturbing rumours which are circulating in the village about your own extraordinary conduct in this disgraceful affair which took place in Edinburgh. To give a professional slant to the proceedings and to provide a clerical opinion upon any matter raised, I have asked the minister of our neighbouring parish of Lawers to be present.' Robert Shaw smirked self- contentedly at the members of Session and James felt his blood begin to heat up.

Blair Gower had chosen to stand to deliver his reprimand. With his thumbs tucked into his waistcoat and his large belly thrust forward as though to emphasise his own importance, he spoke in tones reminiscent of an employer addressing a group of workers on his factory floor. James was incensed that on his own church premises he should be treated as though he were a criminal or a naughty child.

'Forgive me,' he interrupted, 'if I disagree that my conduct was extraordinary or that what took place was in any way disgraceful. My colleagues acted out of the highest motives, and only after lengthy negotiations had failed to change the attitude of the State. The work of the church is a matter for its appointed ministers. Decisions affecting the spiritual well-being of the parish are neither for politicians nor for laymen. We all know that for many years past certain decisions concerning the conduct of the church have been taken on grounds which have little to do with common justice or democracy and nothing whatever to do with the work of God. The action of Moderator West was endorsed by forty percent of the clergy present at the Assembly and it is my belief that many more would have walked out of the chamber had they the courage to defy their patrons.'

'You speak of courage, man. I would call it foolhardiness!' Donald Blair Gower was angry. Maybe it was his own bad conscience which made him assume James's words implied a criticism of his own interference in church affairs. The presence of his nephew at the table was evidence of the extent of his influence in church matters. By great good fortune, the Earl of Stirling had found himself in financial difficulties at the very time when Donald's nephew was seeking a more prestigious appointment. For a thousand pounds sterling, Blair Gower had managed to persuade his Grace to call upon Robert Shaw to take the living at Lawers. Aware that his action had given rise to ill- feeling amongst both his own and His Lordship's parishioners, Blair Gower now cast a glance at the group of elders, daring any of them to interrupt.

'The fact is, Bantrie, the Church elders are not prepared to tolerate a rebel for a priest.'

He raised a hand as though to ward off any protest from James and continued.

'We accept however, that you may have been carried away by the excitement of the moment. It is easy enough to be persuaded by an eloquent tongue when tensions are running high. I am therefore able to tell you that after lengthy and prayerful consideration, we have agreed to accept your public apology and confirmation that you do not support these dissidents.'

James regarded his patron with steely eyes. The suggestion that he might have been led into making such a weighty decision in the heat of the moment was an insult to his intelligence. He glanced around the table at those whom he had thought to be his supporters and saw that not one of them could look him in the eye. Even William Carswell remained silent.

'The poor devil has been got at,' thought James. William, who was the town's only apothecary, depended for his livelihood upon the patronage of the local doctor and of the bulk of the parishioners. The doctor was himself an elder of the Church and of all those gathered around the table, appeared the least uncomfortable in his support of Alan Blair Gower. James wondered how his patron had managed to buy the doctor's good will.

'I will not offer an apology for my actions, Mr Blair Gower,' James declared, fiercely. 'That you expect one shows you to be a singularly poor judge of character. Nor shall I demesne myself by answering your accusation that my decision was taken in the heat of the moment. I shall however, relieve you of the necessity of formally dismissing me for I offer you my resignation as of this moment. You will I trust, allow me the courtesy of one week to remove my property from the manse.'

Not waiting for a response he reached for his hat, forced it firmly upon his head and opened the vestry door.

William Carswell was halfway out of his seat as the minister turned to them one last time.

'I will bid you all good day, Gentlemen!'

*

A large pantechnicon stood outside the main door of the manse with a pair of handsome shire horses between the shafts. As the beasts champed impatiently at the bit, two men loaded an assortment of furniture into the back of the vehicle. The main door to the house stood open and William hesitated for a moment only before entering.

Inside, all was strangely quiet. He had been informed Judith and the children had already left for Judith's parent's home in Edinburgh, but what had become of the servants? Had James dismissed them already? Surely not.

As though in answer to William's unspoken question, a door opened in the rear of the building and Flora McKinnon, Judith's personal maid and long standing companion appeared.

'Oh, Mr Carswell,' she declared, 'what a sad day it is, to be sure.'

'Why Flora, what is happening? Is the Minister leaving so soon?'

'Aye so he is. What a flurry we have all been in these past two days! The other servants were dismissed this morning and a sad parting that was and no mistake, with the mistress not here to see them go.' She sniffed loudly and wiped her damp cheeks on the sleeve of her dress.

'What of yourself, Flora, will you go back to your people also?'

'The Minister has asked me to accompany him to Queensferry, to help the Mistress through this terrible time. After that, who knows? I have been with Mrs Bantrie since her wedding day. I cannot imagine working for anyone else.

'Maybe there will be a place for you when Mr Bantrie finds a new living,' William suggested kindly.

'Oh Sir, I do hope so, I really do. But what am I thinking of. You will be wanting to speak to the Minister.'

She tapped lightly on the study door and hearing a muffled invitation to enter, she opened it.

'Mr William Carswell is here to see you, Sir,' she announced somewhat hesitantly. Not surprisingly, the minister had been very tetchy since his dismissal and she did not wish him to be further upset by any unwanted intrusion.

James Bantrie looked up from the letter he had been writing, put down his pen and sat back.

'Ah, William, you have saved me the trouble!'

He took the half-covered sheet of paper and tore it to shreds, dropping the pieces into an already full basket at his side.

'You were writing… to me?'

'You sound surprised. How could we end a friendship of so many years without a word of farewell?'

With a sigh of relief, Flora withdrew, leaving the two men to mend their broken fences.

'I would not blame you for never speaking to me again,' said William, forlornly. 'There was I, the great man of action, sunk without trace at the first broadside.'

'What pressure did they put upon you, old friend?'

James rose from his seat and ushered William to an easy chair beside the empty grate.

'The lease of my premises comes up for renewal in a few weeks,' the apothecary told him. 'Normally this would be a mere formality but on this occasion Blair Gower was at pains to make mention of the fact that another man has been thinking of setting up in business in the town and has designs upon my shop. It was all very unsubtle, the implication being that if I opposed your dismissal I would be forced to leave also. I am too old to be moving on, James, and too poor to manage without practising my profession.'

'I don't blame you, William,' James reassured him. 'Such a sacrifice on your part would be futile, harming none but yourself and doing my cause no good at all. I went into this knowing full well what the risks might be.'

'Do not doubt it, my friend, but…' He hesitated, wondering if he dared to say more.

'But what?" James demanded.

'I wondered how Judith viewed the situation.'

'I have not discussed it with her. She will comply with my wishes I have no doubt.'

'Take my advice, James. You should give Judith your full confidence from now on. She is a wise woman. You must learn to place more value upon her counsel. You will need all the support she can give you in the months to come.'

James glanced sharply at his friend. It was true he had been less than open with his wife in all this. What if she blamed him for ruining their prospects now he was obliged to seek another living. They might have to go somewhere far from family and friends, perhaps to some remote spot in the mountains. Would she be willing to uproot herself without argument? Would she support him in his act of defiance?

'What are your immediate plans?' William asked. 'Do you have somewhere to store your furniture?'

'I have persuaded Dougal McFarlane, the wheelwright to lend me space in an empty warehouse on the quay in Inverness,' James told him.

'From there it should be a simple matter to have my household goods shipped to any location in the west.'

'That is where you plan to go?'

'I am unlikely to find a living anywhere else,' James told him, 'I am quite resigned to the fact that there will be no invitations from parishes on this side of the country.'

There was a catch in the older man's voice when he said, 'I shall miss you James. You will keep in touch?'

'I shall try,' replied his friend. 'For the moment, I will be at my father-in-law's house from where I will seek information about any vacancies that may be available.

He tailed off as the two men regarded each other one last time. Abruptly, William clasped James warmly, one hand clamped to his shoulder while the other grasped James's in so fierce a grip, it made him wince.

'God be with you, my dear friend!'

William turned on his heel and walked out, unable to bear the parting a moment longer.

James stood back as men arrived to remove his desk and what remained of his furniture. Ignoring a noisy disagreement concerning the weight of the desk and its manner of disassembly, James wandered over to the window in time to see William shambling along the drive beneath the tall chestnuts, pausing every now and again to catch his breath. James wondered if he would ever see his friend alive, again. This miserable business had certainly taken its toll of the unassuming, kindly old gentleman.

Having sent Flora ahead of him by Post Chaise, in charge of those of Judith's personal effects which he knew she would want with her, James set out on horseback once again for Queensferry. He might have covered the journey back to Edinburgh in a shorter time had he not diverted towards the journey's end. Instead of descending to the ferry landing he continued eastward, along the north bank of the River Forth. He was concerned to have something positive to tell Judith, something which would soften the blow of finding herself homeless.

He made his way along an unfamiliar road until he reached the town of Kircaldy where his enquiries led him to the parish church of Linktown. It was a dreich place where the cruel winds from the North Sea swept across the bleak salt flats which provided the principle employment in that part of town.

It was not difficult to find the manse. Apart from the church it was the only sizeable building to be seen amongst the streets of narrow back to back cottages and the dingy sheds and workshops which made up this rambling industrial centre.

Murdo McLeod, recognising his new acquaintance from two weeks before, hurried forward to greet him.

'My goodness, James Bantrie,' he declared. 'I did not think to set eyes on you ever again!'

'Forgive me... 'James hesitated. Weary from the long journey he was unable to disguise the despondency which had fallen on him as he had approached this sorry place. What would Judith say if she was forced to live in a parish such as this? What if there was no place for him anywhere in Scotland?

McLeod was quick to recognise his visitor's fatigue and taking the reins of the mare from James' hand he called for an urchin from a group playing nearby, to hold the gentleman's horse while they went inside. The boy complied willingly on promise of a threepenny piece if he watered the animal as well. James followed Murdo into the gloomy depths of the old stone manse.

The dram of whisky which his host forced upon him, warmed James' chilled, travel weary body, for although it was nearly June, the day was cold with the wind from the east. Soon James felt able to relax in the worn leather armchair his host had provided and his tongue, loosened by the spirit, was relating the happenings of the past few days.

'Aye, it is no' an uncommon story you are telling,' said Murdo when James had finished. 'There are many like you, have been hounded from their livings in just such a manner. The lack of a majority, no matter how narrow the gap between winning and losing the vote, has given the Government the lever it needed to retain the Act of Patronage and ignore the upheaval within the church. In Westminster they can now sit back and let events take their course. If those breaking away from the establishment wish to set up a new church, they must build it themselves and finance it from parish support alone. There will be no subsidy from elsewhere.'

This strangely well informed priest gave no indication of how he came to have access to all the latest news on the topic. James felt confident however that Murdo McLeod was certainly the one to ask about finding another living.

Murdo did not disappoint him.

'Off the coast of Argyll there is a group of small islands where the people depend upon slate quarrying for a living. Much of the area belongs to the estates of the Marquis of Stirling, the parishes being within his patronage, but there is one island which is owned by a consortium of businessmen who have no interest in the place other than what they can make out of it. They contribute a small amount to the spiritual welfare of the people but they take no part in the adoption of clergy, leaving that to the elders of the kirk. It is a broad church, very different in its make-up to what you have been used to. Men have been brought in from all over to work the quarries and while all are Christians, they subscribe to many different sects. The island is called, Eilean Orchy. It is far from being a wealthy parish and the life is hard. Water is scarce and food must be brought in by sea, there being a shortage of good agricultural land in the area. The parishioners are honest folk, free from the machinations of a kind you have known in the past. What is lacking in creature comforts is compensated for by the calm and peaceful atmosphere of the place.'

'You seem to know it well,' suggested James. 'In such a paradise, why do you not take up the living yourself?'

'I know the place well, because I was born there,' he answered. 'I work here, because this is where the Lord requires me.'

This explanation must suffice, for it was all that would be given.

'To whom should I apply for this post?' James asked, always supposing that Judith would agree to his accepting if it should be offered.

'I will write to the church elders on your behalf,' Murdo told him. 'Give me your address in Edinburgh and I will contact you there.'

Chapter Two

James Bantrie never knew what had driven him to seek help from Murdo McLeod that day, but within a few weeks he had been invited to address the parishioners of Eilean Orchy in Argyll and this he had done making the journey on horseback along the well beaten tracks followed by the cattle drovers.

The ferry boats which had carried him across Loch Lomond, Loch Long and Loch Fyne, were his only point of contact with a friendly human face for several days. In the remote villages through which he passed he was greeted with a sullen silence and deep suspicion. Even his clerical cloth was no passport in this wild region where the intimately related clansmen found all strangers a threat. It had been a great relief to reach the end of the drover's road where the waters of Loch Feochan poured into the Firth of Lorn.

Here, suddenly he had felt himself overwhelmed by a sense of history. He experienced a strange frisson of excitement as, when disembarking the ferry which had carried him across the mouth of the loch, he rested a moment upon the very stone on which had be laid the coffins of the kings of Scotland on their way to their last resting place in the abbey precincts of Iona.

He had followed no more than two of the final few miles between himself and the group of islands which were his destination when he began to pass a number of small townships where the houses were tidily kept and the cultivated ground with its neat rigs and furrows indicated a well-ordered husbandry. On the lower slopes well nourished cattle chewed contentedly at the lush summer grasses while high on the hills, sheep wandered into inaccessible colls and crevices in search of the best grazing. His heart began to sing in unison with the sounds of nature. A robin, sparrow-like in his summer garb, trilled from a bush along the way while a chattering flock of oystercatchers made their way across the shore as the tide receded. From high on the hillside the occasional low pitched call of an anxious ewe was answered by the higher tones of some adolescent lamb, old enough now to frolic with his peers and leave his mother to graze alone. How different it was from the harsh rocky outcrops and heather strewn, lonely vastness of the mountains through which he had lately passed.

His path took him along the cliffs to a spot where he could see the islands dotted in the Sound of Lorn. James glanced at the sketch map which Murdo had drawn for him. Ahead of him and near at hand, he could identify Eilean nam Uan which Murdo had told him was an island uninhabited except for a lone shepherd and his flock. To the south, the island of Eisdalsa lay a few yards offshore from the tiny village of Seileachan where Murdo himself was born. To the west a string of islands, triangular rocky outcrops receding into the distance, were the Islands of the Sea while, lying further to the south in the lee of the great mass of Scarba was the largest of that group of small islands, Eilean Orchy, his final destination.

He urged his mare forward along a path which soon dropped away from the sea and took a lower route along a well sheltered valley. He came at last to the place where he was to meet the minister who would be his nearest colleague were he to be accepted by the islanders. Here, so he had been informed, a bed and a meal awaited him before he sailed for Eilean Orchy in the morning.

*

James met his prospective elders in the church, a small stone building under a slated roof. The only lighting was from the tall narrow windows which were adequate on this bright autumn day but would most certainly not suffice in the depths of winter. The building was clammy and cold and there was a distinctly musty smell. James thought of the fine building at Kilmory which he had sacrificed along with his generous stipend and began to feel the first misgivings about his future here.

The elders were led by one Thomas Guthrie who introduced himself as the manager of the great slate quarry which had been gouged from the centre of the island and sustained the population of some three hundred souls. The remainder of the group were the shopkeeper, Galbraith, several quarrymen and an elderly man who introduced himself in a soft highland brogue as the engine minder, Archie McPhee.

This was not an attractive living and it was clear to the islanders that James Bantrie was not just another of that succession of disaffected, slovenly even depraved creatures whom they had been forced to accept as their pastor for years past. Invited to explain his reasons for wanting to work amongst them, James gave an honest account of his participation of the events of May 18th and the subsequent events which had deprived him of his living.

Later that same day the elders invited James to address the entire congregation. The church was packed to hear him and the congregation listened attentively to all he had to say. He finished his dissertation with a short prayer given in the Gaelic language. He had heard the villagers greet one another in the language and thought it could do his case no harm to show them that he too was proficient in their native tongue. At the end the elders dismissed him politely but without indicating what their decision might be.

As Thomas Guthrie handed him into the boat for his return to journey to Seileachan, he thanked James for attending the meeting.

'The full Kirk Session will decide on your appointment, Reverend,' he blustered, embarrassed not to give Bantrie a more definite answer. 'You must understand that we have had our share of inadequates. Our last minister proved to be living with a woman who was not his wife! The people are wary of taking yet another misfit into their midst. We shall consider all you have told us concerning this Free Church of yours. There has been no effective patronage in these parts for many years and much of what you relate has little bearing on our way of living here. It must be left to the parishioners to decide. I will send their findings on to you as soon as maybe.'

*

James returned to his in-law's crowded little house at South Queensferry despondent, fearing that even that uninviting, lonely little parish would almost certainly reject him. Without a flock to tend and with no home to call his own, James became morose and distant. He found himself unable to join in the conversation at meal times and avoided all private discourse with his wife by the simple expedient of taking long solitary walks during the day and reading late into the night in his host's cramped and cluttered study.

For Judith the glamour of the city quickly palled and she found herself more and more concerned with the trivia of living in cramped quarters with parents whom she loved dearly but could tolerate only in small doses. If James did not hear from his Argyllshire parish soon, they would be obliged to find other quarters although where these might be found and how they could be afforded, she had no idea.

She began to pine for that comfortable life which they had lost and despite all her resolution to remain loyal to her husband, she found herself blaming James for their predicament.

As the commencement of the Michaelmas Term approached, Ian began to speak of his anticipated course of study at the University. James remained silent as the boy and his grandfather talked of the great figures whom he would encounter within those hallowed halls, until the name of Thomas Chalmers was introduced.

'Do you think the University will invite Chalmers to take his Chair this session?' the old man enquired of James?

'Why not!' cried James, 'having led so many of his fellows into poverty and deprivation, why should he not continue to enjoy the benefits of his great name? The big fish in this ocean have nothing to fear. It is only the minnows like myself who must bear the weight of their own sacrifice.'

'If that is how you feel, James,' Judith chided him gently, 'you should never have taken so drastic an action in the first place.'

Ignoring her observation, James turned upon his son. 'It is pointless for you to contemplate whom you will be meeting and what you will study. There is no money for you to attend classes this or any other year so there's an end to it. Prepare yourself for working for a living, like other honest men.'

There was a hushed and painful silence. The old people, sensing that matters had come to a head, discretely removed themselves, taking Catherine and young Charles with them. When they were alone with their eldest son, the Bantries faced one another like a pair of fighting dogs.

'Do you dare to tell me that your activities have gone so far as to deny your own son his right to a proper education?' Judith demanded.

'It cannot be helped,' James replied, 'the Lord's work comes before all else.'

By this response he showed that same disregard for her opinions which had always angered her in the past.

'Had it not been for William Carswell's patient explanation of events, I would have been quite unprepared for what has befallen us,' she told him. 'Even he did not suggest that you might so disregard the welfare of your own family as to put your son's chances of a prosperous life in jeopardy. You have been arrogant and selfish in the extreme and your decisions lead me to believe that far from being your closest companion and confidant in all these years, I have never really known you at all, James Bantrie!'

Throughout this exchange, Ian had remained silent. Now he addressed them both with such passion that his adolescent voice wavered between bass and descant with such astonishing results that despite the serious nature of their discourse, his parents found it difficult not to laugh.

'I never really wanted to be a preacher anyway,' he declared. 'That was your idea father, not mine. Don't go telling yourselves that this is some kind of noble sacrifice on my part. When I heard that we might be going to live in the west I was overjoyed. All my life I have wanted to go to sea. Now I shall have the opportunity. I shall find work aboard a fishing boat. Maybe I shall own my own vessel one day.'

Judith's hand went to her mouth as though to prevent a gush of denouncements.

'Nonsense boy,' said his father. 'If we do go to Argyll, and at present I cannot believe at all that we shall, you will be apprenticed to some trade. There are slate quarries. They will need engineers or clerks. Something suitable shall be found. You are a reasonable scholar when you put your mind to it. Such study should not be too difficult for you.'

The thought of her first born exposing his young life to the perils of the sea, made Judith regard her husband with greater respect. So soon after their altercation she found herself agreeing with his every word. She would have supported James openly in his response to the boy but instinct made her draw back. Ian was so like his father. Were both his parents to deny him it would be a challenge he could not resist. She concluded that, for the moment at any rate, there was nothing to be gained from her own intervention in the argument.

There must have been some free thinkers in that congregation on the island of Orchy, for little more than a week later James received a call, signed by all twelve of the church elders. When towards the end of September the minister ushered his little family aboard the fishing smack which was to carry them on the last leg of their journey to Eilean Orchy, he breathed deeply of the invigorating sea air, absorbed the beauty of his surroundings and thanked Providence which in so short a time had lifted him from the depths of despair to a promise of new hope for the future.

Chapter Three

1843

Judith Bantrie viewed with dismay the wild rocky beach where the flat-bottomed slate boat had landed them. Holding the infant Charles close to her bosom to shield him from the salt spray, she squatted upon a metal trunk to wait while James summoned help from one of the cottages. Heedless of the cruel wind, Catherine explored the rock pools left by the receding tide while Ian and Flora McKinnon began the monumental task of moving a mound of boxes and bags of clothing and household necessities beyond the highwater mark.

The surrounding islands to both north and south appeared hilly and colourful. They were covered in yellow gorse, lush green grasses and a faint blush of purple heather. Eilean Orchy however, exploited for more than a century for its harvest of slate rock, was a denuded plain, black with a uniform covering of slate spoil.

Judith, shuddering at the gloomy prospect of their new life, watched disconsolately as her husband disappeared into the distance.

James crossed the level ground between the shore and a rough track along which had been laid a railway line. On it stood some iron-wheeled wagons, the means presumably by which the heavy slate rock was hauled away from the quarry. He followed the track for perhaps a quarter of a mile, arriving at last at a collection of small cottages, the only sign of human occupation in that bleak landscape.

The houses were roughly whitewashed under roofs some of which were slated while others were thatched with heather. A single chimney extended above each roof and the small, unglazed windows set on either side of each door, were shuttered against the elements. Wooden gutters collected rainwater which filled the huge water butt standing before every house.

Leaving the track to make a diversion inland, James passed houses perched along the rim of a single deep pit which had been gouged from the centre of the island reaching down to depths of a hundred feet or more below the level of the sea. On his previous visit the quarry had been a hive of activity. Today there was nothing going on here at all. Not a single person was to be seen. Approaching the church where he had addressed the islanders on his previous visit, he hurried forward hoping to find someone who could tell him what was going on.

The church was of a simple construction, its greater height and steeply pitched roof causing it to overshadow the uniform rows of cottages which crowded together close to the eastern shore of the island. Like the cottages it was built of a combination of hard volcanic rock and slate blocks. Only the rounded door arch and distinctive bell tower which perched above the gable-end marked it as a place of worship.

Beside the kirk stood a dilapidated house, larger than the others and, unlike the remainder of houses in the row, with a slated roof and glazed windows. On his previous visit the islanders had been reluctant to show James over the Manse. Elder Guthrie had hurried him past suggesting vaguely that should he prove to be acceptable to the people, the house would be put to rights before James brought his family to the island. Tentatively he tried the door and finding it locked, took a few steps back to study the house from the outside before making his way back along the street in hopes of finding someone who might tell him where to find the key. The whole place was strangely quiet for a village of close on three hundred parishioners. Where had everyone gone?

He had nearly reached the row of slate wagons again before he spotted the old woman. A small, withered figure she crouched beside her open door huddled against the wind. A woollen shawl was clasped tightly about her shoulders. She smoked a clay pipe which was clamped between toothless gums and held in place by hands twisted and knotted by rheumatism. From inside her house came the sound of childish voices and the occasional whimper of an infant.

'Good day to you, mother,' James called loudly, for he supposed her to be deaf.

'No need to shout, laddie,' she replied, sharply. 'My legs may not function but my ears still hear.' She studied him carefully for a few moments all the while puffing out evil-smelling smoke. Then, removing the pipe for a second time, she concluded, 'You will be the new minister. I heard you speak in the Kirk,' James acknowledged that she was correct. She continued, 'Maybe you'll stay a mite longer than the others.' She paused, thoughtfully summing him up under furrowed brows. 'Just so long as ye dinnie drink and can keep your hands off the women!'

'I was hoping to find someone to help me with my luggage,' he told her, indignantly. 'My family are waiting on the shore. With the tide set to turn, I must remove the boxes as soon as possible.'

'Everyone is away to the funeral on Lunga,' she said, surprised he did not know it.

'Everyone?'

'Oh aye, all except myself and the weans I am minding.'

'Lunga you say? Is there no burial ground here on the island?'

'There is no land to spare for burying the dead in a place where every inch might yield wealth,' she told him, pointing to the edge of the pathway where the profile of the soil could be seen quite clearly. The bed of slate rock was overlaid by no more than two or three inches of soil in which a thin turf with patches of purple thyme and yellow potentilla, struggled for existence.

'When will the men be back do you think?' he asked, remembering the state of the tide.

'Oh, it will no' be long now but you'd best be lifting your things from the beach, all the same. It is the time of the springs. The water will be rising near fifteen feet today.'

'Is there perhaps some form of conveyance?' he demanded, despairing.

'Oh, aye, tak' a barrow from the row, there. The maister will no bother just so long as ye put it back.'

He thanked the old woman and made to return the way he had come, pausing beside a row of assorted wooden barrows in various states of decay. Selecting the most robust of these, he asked, 'The house beside the church. Would that be the Manse?'

'Och aye,' she replied, defensively.

'Is there a key? The door is locked.'

Used as he was to a fawning congregation of respectful ladies and dutiful gentlemen, pious people who respected their minister, he had been surprised by her bluntness. She must have accepted his bona fides however for she answered him without hesitation.

'Oh aye, it will be under a stone beside the door.'

James returned to the shore pushing his barrow before him. He arrived to find that all but the heaviest of boxes and bags had already been placed out of harm's way. Ian and Flora were struggling with one of the metal trunks and as he went to assist them he noticed that his wife was still seated just as he had left her as though she believed there might yet be a choice between staying or returning whence they had come.

He strode across the stony beach towards her and sat down on a nearby rock. He followed her gaze to where a thin plume of black smoke marked the progress of the steam packet *Arran Castle*, which had so lately set them down upon the shore. Even as they watched, the vessel slid over the horizon and out of sight.

'I have located the Manse, my dear,' he told her his tone more optimistic than he felt. 'We must move this trunk now or the tide will have swamped it by the time the people return.'

She looked at him as though awaking from a dream. 'What's that?' she asked.

'The people, they are all away to a funeral on another of the islands. We must move these heavy boxes ourselves. Will you take wee Charles higher up the beach while Ian and I carry the trunk?'

He called the boy to him and together they lifted the heavy metal box. Struggling to keep their footing on the weed strewn rocks, they heaved, slid and levered it above the tide line.

'Pile the lighter bags into the barrow,' he instructed his son. 'The trunk must wait until we can get help.'

Rubbing at his strained shoulders with blistered hands he clambered back across the beach to where Flora was trying to assist his wife to negotiate the rocks. Encumbered as she was by the sleeping child, Judith was finding great difficulty in keeping on her feet.

'Give me the boy,' he said gently, taking the child from her to leave her hands free to steady her passage. 'It's only a few yards.'

Wordlessly she followed him.

Catherine ran to her father holding in her hand half a dozen whelks which she had gathered from the rocks.

'See father, we can have these for our tea!' she cried, excitedly.

Judith, horrified at the thought that they should be reduced to finding their food in such a fashion, snatched at the child's hand causing her to drop the shells which scattered across the beach.

'Don't be so stupid child,' she said harshly, 'It will be a sad day when we are reduced to such commons!'

Flora, bringing up the rear, clasped in her hand her own small valise. Since their arrival she had been too busy working with Master Ian to take much notice her surroundings. Now she viewed the bleak landscape with dismay and began to regret her impetuosity in abandoning her own family in Inverness to accompany the minister and his wife.

The bedraggled group stumbled in procession along the village street. Ian had insisted upon pushing the heavy cart while each of the others carried as much as he or she could manage. James nodded to the old woman as they passed.

'When the men return, will you tell them we're here?' he asked. 'There are still some heavy boxes by the shore which we have lifted out of harm's way.'

She nodded and pointed. James turned towards the south and saw a fleet of small boats in the distance, approaching upon the turning tide. 'They'll no' be long, now,' she replied and settled herself once more with her back to the wind.

Outside the manse James set down his barrow and approached the door cautiously, apprehensive as to what he would find within. He lifted first one then another of the heavy stones beside the step before discovering the key. The lock must recently have been oiled for the key turned easily and when he twisted the brass knob which was ominously green with Verdi Gris, the door swung open with no more than a sigh.

The dim light revealed a dusty interior, apparently long neglected. His heart sank when he saw the few bits of furniture within. Chairs and table were roughly made, the kind of thing found only in the poorest croft. There was a sizeable cooking range before which stood a single armchair whose stuffing was straining through the seams. A wooden settle stood opposite while a pair of long low stools completed the seating. The large deal table, dusty now though showing signs of plenty of scrubbing in the past, occupied most of the remaining space. Apart from a single corner cupboard and a narrow deal dresser, the only storage space appeared to be a cupboard whose door opened alongside the range. What appeared to be the sole provision for washing, a lead lined wooden trough, stood below the window.

This was even worse than he had imagined. Wordlessly, James sank into the single arm chair and placed his head in his hands. What had he done? How could he have condemned his family to such dire poverty? How could he have been so foolish as to give up their comfortable existence, for this? Surely it was not God's will that he should make his family suffer so.

Judith, entering a few moments later, supposed him to be praying and did not disturb his desperate thoughts. She too looked about her in dismay. The room was dark, the windows filthy and the fabric of curtains, furniture and floor coverings stank of dirt and mould. Curiously however the despair she had experienced as she watched their last link with civilisation disappear over the horizon, now left her. Presented with the reality of their situation her immediate instinct was to make the best of what they had, to see what could be done to turn this hovel into a home.

The place had clearly been unoccupied for some time. She shuddered as she brushed away the spider webs which irritated her face and became entangled in her hair. She ran a finger along the mantle shelf and brought it away quite black. Since there was no tap, she supposed that water must be fetched from somewhere outside. She took note of the wooden trough and the bucket beside the door.

Curious to see the adjoining apartments, she pushed open the door into a small dark lobby. Here she came upon a simple staircase which was little more than a ladder gaining access to the loft. Maybe the children will be able to sleep up there she told herself. She began to see that there might, after all, be room enough for everyone.

From the hallway, access could be gained to two further rooms. In the first of these she found a large iron bedstead and, in one corner, a truckle bed too small for anyone but a child. It was not ideal, but wee Charles might safely be left there while she got the rest of the family settled. She sniffed at the palliasse which served as a mattress and decided at once that it must be removed. The heather stuffing must be emptied out and the casing washed before she would agree to lie upon it. The truckle bed contained folded blankets which seemed reasonably clean. Still wrapped in his travelling clothes, she laid the sleeping Charles upon it and rubbed her aching limbs with relief. He was a lusty boy and her back and arms were strained from carrying him so far.

The older children had already climbed up the stair to the attic. Judith could hear them scrabbling about, their excited chatter interrupted every now and again by a scraping sound as some heavy article was dragged across the floor. Their enthusiasm for this strange adventure helped to raise her spirits just a little. Their excitement was contagious.

She sat on the edge of the grubby mattress considering how she might distribute what comforts they had brought with them to best advantage. After a while she remembered the third room and went back into the hallway. The door was locked. Not to be defeated, she ran her fingers along the lintel until they encountered the key.

It was a small square room with a single window which was encrusted with salt on the outside and dust within. She wiped a small corner with her already dirty palm and found that the view from here was of the ocean and the rocky shoreline. Three of the walls were lined with shelves upon which stood an array of books, heavy, leather-bound volumes, dusty like everything else. When she blew away the dust from one cover she found it to be in excellent order, expensively tooled and trimmed with gold leaf; a religious tome of some kind. This was clearly intended to be the minister's study. The desk with its heavily carved chair was set against the window so that anyone seated there could look out upon a glorious view. The furniture was of good quality and would soon polish up using the beeswax and turpentine with which she had come fully prepared. Eager now to set about the task of cleaning and putting things to rights, Judith returned to the kitchen to find that Flora had the stove alight. It would not be long before the worst of the chill atmosphere was dispelled.

James had not moved from his chair.

In the loft above Catherine felt something sleek and furry brush against her leg. She squealed in terror. Armed with an old boot, Ian sought out the beastie. Whether rat or mouse, it had run for cover and in the dim light he searched for it in vain.

The only illumination up here came from a small square skylight glazed in some opaque material which was certainly not glass. There was a timber sarking beneath the slates and the roof appeared sound. While Ian continued the search for animal intruders, Catherine climbed down the ladder. Still shaking from her encounter with the beastie she sought the comfort of her mother's company.

The girl's cry of fear had roused James from his miserable self-accusations. Ashamed of his own inactivity he began to search in one of the bags they had carried from the shore and pulled out an oil lamp which he filled and lit before climbing into the attic himself.

His bright light revealed a very large loft area. There was little headroom for a tall man like himself, but the children might manage here tolerably well. Two wooden truckle beds stood in the middle of the floor, separated by a brass-bound wooden trunk, the only properly manufactured item in the house. This was the only furniture. A large packing case bulging with books and papers, together with an assortment of discarded household equipment, were packed in under the eaves.

On every surface there was a thick layer of dust in which the prints of dozens of tiny feet indicated that Catherine had not been mistaken about there being other occupants in the house. It would be necessary to do something about the intruders before the children could sleep here.

James backed down the ladder and joined Judith in the living room. He was surprised to find that having thrown off her earlier lethargy his wife had already removed her cloak and rolled up her sleeves ready for work.

'Should we not find something to eat before we begin to unpack?' he enquired, not daring to ask her opinion of the place.

'Not one item of our own property will I set out until we have cleaned throughout,' Judith declared. 'Flora, will you bring me that bag please, the one which I told you we might need immediately upon our arrival.'

Flora placed a leather satchel on the table and from it withdrew scrubbing brushes, hard yellow soap, beeswax and rags.

'Ian,' Judith called up the stairs, 'Come down here, at once!' and, as soon as he appeared, 'Go and find us some water, quickly if you please.'

Grubby and flushed with excitement the boy snatched up the large wooden bucket which he found beside the door and went outside without even a murmur of protest.

Judith found herself smiling despite herself. It was a long time since her son had performed any household duties and she might have expected some objection. This willingness to help was quite uncharacteristic. Maybe the unusual experience would prove to have some advantages after all.

Outside in the street, Ian searched for any sign of a well or pump. All he could find was a huge rainwater butt at the corner of the building. It was three-quarters full. He filled the bucket and returned with it to the kitchen.

Judith did not enquire the source of the water. She filled a large iron kettle which she had found standing on the range then poured what remained into a bowl. Flora set the kettle to boil. They would all need tea when the work was finished.

James, anticipating a harsh tirade from Judith at any moment, hesitated on the threshold not knowing where to make a start. He was amazed to discover that far from bemoaning their fate and sitting down to wait for assistance from elsewhere his wife had accepted the challenge and was busy directing the cleaning-up operation. In these straightened circumstances she was already beginning to reveal a side of her nature which he had never witnessed during fifteen years of marriage.

From the day of his first appointment as minister, when he had carried his bride over the threshold of their fine manse in Kilmory, she had lived surrounded by servants, with tradesmen at her beck and call and himself to make the important decisions. From the first it had been accepted that Judith's responsibility was to be no more than the overseeing of the household, the entertainment of James' parishioners and the supervision of his children's upbringing.

While James, now understanding the full implications of his actions, was overcome by a despair which rendered him both anxious and indecisive, Judith took charge of the situation as though to the manner born. In no time she had both James and Flora acting under her orders, scrubbing and rubbing until every surface was clean. The children were dispatched upstairs to clean in the loft, their mother's firm injunction ringing in their ears.

'If you want a place to sleep tonight, you must make it habitable yourselves.'

Excited by the novelty of the situation, Ian and Catherine set to with a will their enthusiasm flagging only when, after an hour or so, hunger pangs drove them down the ladder to see what progress had been made by the adults.

With the dirt banished and fresh lacy cloths covering the table and dresser tops, the kitchen had been transformed. Flora was unpacking Judith's favourite blue and white china and a set of gleaming copper pans which reflected the flames from a cheerful fire. Judith had found curtains, too large for the tiny windows but adequate for privacy. The splash of colour took off the bareness of the walls. The drapes could be made to fit properly later. The slate floor of freshly scrubbed slate was spread with rugs and the chair and stools, now polished with beeswax, gave off a pleasant odour. Covered as they were now by a scattering of brightly coloured cushions, they looked almost comfortable.

James was nailing hooks into the wall to hold a favourite picture when there came a sharp rapping on the door. Flora opened it to a delegation of villagers, each carrying some item of those possessions James had left by the shore.

'Oh, thank you,' Judith cried, relieved to have everything she required to hand at last.

To the bearded figure who appeared to be their leader and who carried on his own shoulders the metal trunk which was the heaviest item of all, she said, 'Would you be kind enough to put that box into the bedroom?'

Looking uncomfortably overdressed in his Sunday best, the fellow heaved the trunk over the threshold and positioned it in the centre of the bedroom floor. He returned to the kitchen, removed his flat cap and nervously smoothed his tousled hair apparently embarrassed in the presence of the ladies.

'You have settled in then?' he remarked rather unnecessarily. 'It was mebbe a bit dusty?' he added, taking note of the rags and buckets and the unruly state of the women's appearance. He had been meaning to muster help from some of the village women to clean the place up a wee bit but had never quite got around to it.

'We felt it needed a little tidying,' Judith replied diplomatically. 'We were just occupying our time until you all returned and we could unpack our heavier baggage.'

James had been carrying in some of the parcels which had been left outside the door. Now he stepped forward and addressed the fellow himself.

'Good day to you, sir. Mr Guthrie isn't it? I believe you were expecting us?'

Relieved at last to be able to speak to the man of the house the visitor turned to James. 'I'm afraid you have taken us somewhat by surprise, Minister.' He held out his hand in greeting. 'Thomas Guthrie it is, sir. Elder of the Kirk and manager of the quarries here,' he explained for Judith's benefit, as he took the hand she now offered him.

James too shook him warmly by the hand while Guthrie was profuse in his apologies.

'How unfortunate that you should have chosen today, of all days to arrive.' he said. 'I am so sorry there was no one here to welcome you.'

'There has been a funeral, I understand?' James asked, dismissing Guthrie's apology with a smile.

'Aye, one of the men was killed in the quarry last week.'

Flora shuddered.

'An accident was it?' she enquired.

'A fall of rock, aye,' he answered.

'There'll be a widow?' James asked, anticipating a need for his services.

'Oh aye, Mrs Dundas and the wee bairns.'

'What will become of them?' Judith exclaimed. She could envisage nothing worse than to be left alone in this miserable place widowed and with a young family to support.

'You must tell me where to find her,' said James, brushing down his coat before pulling it on. He was on more familiar ground now. His professional instincts put paid to his despair.

'Oh, you'll not be going out before you have eaten?' demanded Judith, dismayed.

'It is why I am here,' he replied, taking up his hat and cane.

'Perhaps you will lead the way, Mr Guthrie?'

James turned back to Judith, 'don't wait supper on my account my dear. The children will be hungry. Just put something by for me.'

She nodded, relieved to see him restored to something like normality.

'Thank you for bringing our boxes from the shore, Mr Guthrie,' she called after them. 'And thank your friends!'

Guthrie's companions of a few moments ago had melted away as soon as the introductions had been made. Judith, hoping this would be the last of the interruptions they would have, returned to her work only to be disturbed once more by a light tap on the door. This time it was a woman bearing a large stoneware pot which she held tightly in a cloth. Her eyes searched beyond Judith for somewhere to put it down.

'Och, thank goodness,' she gasped, depositing the heavy dish on the table and sucking each of her fingers in turn to take away the pain.

'That was hotter than I expected,' she explained, laughing heartily. 'It has been cooking away all afternoon waiting on us coming back from Lunga.'

Judith, startled, did not know what to say.

'Maggie McPherson,' the newcomer announced herself. 'I saw Tom Guthrie going off with your husband and thought I would find you here, hungry and wondering what you were going to eat for supper!'

'I am Judith, – Judith Bantrie,' the minister's wife introduced herself. 'This is Flora MacKinnon and these,' as Ian and Catherine clambered down from the attic enticed by the smell emanating from the brown pot on the table,' are my two older children, Ian and Catherine.'

'You have more?' asked Maggie.

'Wee Charles is asleep in there.' Judith indicated the other room and Maggie satisfied her curiosity by peeking at the sleeping child.

'Och, the poor wee soul,' she declared. 'He'll be whacked out by the sea air nae doubt.'

'Mrs McPherson this is very kind of you,' Judith began, hesitantly, 'but this is your own meal, surely? You were not expecting us.'

'It is Maggie, you must call me,' the woman insisted. 'You will have been travelling all day,' she added, generously. 'Your need is greater than ours. Bread and cheese will serve Donald and myself well enough.'

'Oh. I can't have that!' declared Judith.' She lifted the lid, taking care not to burn her fingers, and saw that the pot was full almost to the brim. 'Why, there is sufficient here to feed an army,' she declared. 'What if I lay the table for two extra and you and your husband join us? It will be a splendid way to get to know one another and you will be able to tell us all about the island.'

Pleased at the invitation, Maggie assented immediately and excused herself explaining she must change out of her funeral garb and let Donald know what was happening.

Judith had the children wash their hands and tidy themselves ready to sit down, while she herself went to the bedroom to make some attempt at repairing the damage to her own appearance.

'Where are you going to sleep, Flora?' Catherine asked.

It was something which she and Ian had discussed while they gathered the heather to fill their palliasses from a stretch of level ground beside the shore. Ian had supposed Flora would sleep in the loft with them but Catherine could not believe this.

'Have you no' seen this?'

Flora opened the wooden door beside the range to reveal a narrow bed, set in the wall. 'This is my place, in here,' she told them.

Catherine examined the box bed thoroughly and wished it might be hers. 'With the door closed,' she cried excitedly, 'no one would know you were there at all!'

She considered this for a moment, then said, fearfully, 'I don't think I would like it in there in the dark with the door closed.'

'You don't close the door when you are sleeping, silly,' Ian was laughing at her. The door is just to hide the bed space during the day. Lots of my friends slept in them back home.'

There was an awkward silence. The two children, aware that any reference to their past life distressed their parents, had made a pact never to mention *home* again except when they were quite alone.

While for Catherine the outcome of their father's fall from grace was proving to be a great adventure, to Ian it represented a dramatic change in the future which had been mapped out for him from birth, fourteen years before. When told that he would not be going to university he had fiercely denied that he had ever wanted to become a pastor like his father. This sudden change in their fortunes however had left him stranded in a void with no future whatever to look forward to. He knew he was going to have to find work soon. The most he could hope for here was an apprenticeship with one of the engineers in the quarry. This was what his father had suggested. He fancied fishing as a way of earning a living but he knew his mother would balk at the idea of his going to sea. The sturdy little vessels they had seen sailing these waters on their voyage south from Fort William, had filled Judith with alarm.

'How dare anyone set out to sea in such flimsy craft?' she had wondered.

Ian could not see her agreeing to his sailing to the fishing grounds in any of those boats which had, just an hour ago, carried his father's parishioners back from the funeral.

The children had made themselves ready by the time that Maggie returned with her husband and, there being no hope of James returning for some time, they all sat down to eat.

Flora, looking exceedingly uncomfortable, took her place at the far end of the big table. Whenever anyone requested water, salt, a knob of butter, she was the first to jump up and fetch it. When an opportunity arose for Judith to speak with her out of hearing of their guests, she admonished her gently.

'We are all equal now, Flora. If the children require water or anything else, they must get it for themselves.'

When James had first told Judith of their new circumstances, the one thing she had dreaded was parting with her servants all of whom had been with them since their wedding day. Flora had become more than a maid. She was a friend. When Judith had told her that they would have to part company, Flora had begged to go with the family. 'How will you manage, Ma'am,' she cried. 'You cannot cook and clean and teach the children, all by yourself. I must come with you.'

'But we shall have so little money, Flora,' Judith had protested. 'I could not pay you a decent wage.'

'Have I asked to be paid, Madam?' the woman had insisted. 'My food and a place to sleep is all I shall need. As a matter of fact, Ma'am,' she had added with a smile, 'I am a dab hand at gardening. Give me a plot of ground and I will grow vegetables for the table such as you have never seen.'

Judith had been forced to join in with her good humour. They had agreed that Flora should accompany the Bantries into their new life but as a companion not as a servant. Flora had yet to become accustomed to her changed role.

Their exertions of the past few hours had made them all ravenously hungry. Maggie's stew was excellent, a thick broth containing every kind of shell fish imaginable.

'This is wonderful,' said Judith admiringly. She smiled across at Flora hoping to draw her into the conversation. 'We must get the recipe, Flora. Perhaps Maggie will tell us where to find the ingredients.'

'Och, it is what we most of us cook much of the time. You can gather the shellfish from the shore at low tide,' said Mrs McPherson. 'I will be pleased to show you where to find them.'

'Oh would you really? That would be wonderful!' said Judith with great enthusiasm. Catherine, remembering her mother's reaction to her own suggestion that they cook the cockles she had found on the beach wondered, not for the first time, at the contrariness of adults.

Maggie McPherson rose to her feet and produced from a second bowl a glutinous, porridge-like mixture which she ladled sparingly onto plates and handed one to each of the children.

'It may not look much,' she said, 'but my own children thrived on it. Just try a little and see what you think.'

Ian was reluctant to taste but Catherine, always ready for some new experience, dug her spoon into the unsavoury looking mess and carried it to her lips. She tasted tentatively, took a little off the spoon and then, with a few deft sweeps, emptied the bowl and was asking for more. Ian, taking his queue from his sister also tried the mixture and was soon wolfing it down. When they had eaten alas much as they could manage Catherine asked, 'what is it?'

'It's made from Carrageen, a kind of seaweed,' Maggie told her. This news made Ian turn a little green around the gills but Catherine leaned forward with interest. 'It's delicious,' she said, 'will you show me where to find it?'

'I'll even give you my old auntie's recipe,' said Maggie, smiling broadly, 'if you promise not to tell anyone else!' She laughed, but Catherine took the warning seriously, crossed her heart and swore secrecy in time-honoured fashion.

'I enter my Carrageen dish every year in the competition at the church fête,' Maggie explained. 'I usually win.'

Catherine listened carefully to the details of the recipe while Donald McPherson listed for Ian's benefit, the names of fish to be caught in the waters around the island.

Judith listened to the conversation drowsily, thinking that with her children determined to live off the land in this way they were unlikely to starve whatever else might befall them. In the warmth of the crowded kitchen, her hunger assuaged, Judith felt herself nodding off to the accompaniment of the cheerful voices of her children and their guests. Those fearful thoughts which she had had as she sat on the beach awaiting James' return were quite dispelled by the pleasant company. Within hours they had transformed a hovel into a comfortable place in which to lay their heads. They had good food and warm companionship. What more could anyone want?

She strained to hear James's footsteps approaching, wanting to share with him her new-found peace of mind. Unfortunately the conversation around the table was sufficient to drown out any noise from outside. Exhausted by her labours, Judith found her eyes closing and her head beginning to nod. She could see Flora was anxious to be up and collecting dishes yet fearful of a second reprimand.

Shaking off her weariness Judith stirred herself into action.

'Ian,' she said, 'go along the street and see if there is any sign of your father. Perhaps Mr McPherson will point you in the right direction? Mr Guthrie took him to see the widow,' she explained.

'Och, so Guthrie has made himself known to you already has he?' Maggie enquired, suspiciously. 'How did he seem to you?' she asked.

'He very kindly carried the heaviest of our boxes from the beach,' Judith explained, rather taken aback by Maggie's uncharitable attitude towards the man.

'Then you are highly honoured,' Maggie sniffed. 'Yon man rarely lifts a finger to help anyone but himself,' she added with surprising vehemence.

'Tak no notice of yon woman,' said McPherson who having set Ian upon his way, had returned to his place at the table. 'She listens to too much village gossip.'

Judith was intrigued. In the short while she had spent with Guthrie she had found him shy and maybe a little uncomfortable in her presence but otherwise he was polite enough and certainly very helpful.

'He is in the lap of the bosses,' said Maggie, 'and does nothing which is not of benefit to himself. A man ye dinnie want to cross. And why does he no have a woman? Tell me that. He is a presentable enough fellow. It's no' natural for him to be thirty-five and unmarried.'

'Very soon she'll be telling you about the three wives and seven children he is reported to have secreted about the country,' laughed Donald. 'These women view every stranger as a monster and see hobgoblins under every bed!'

Judith decided to regard Maggie's assessment of the quarry manager as women's gossip just as Donald had suggested. Flora took the lull in the conversation as a cue to get up and clear the table. 'You entertain the guests,' she suggested, boldly. 'Catherine and I will attend to the dishes.'

Pleased to find that at last Flora was taking some initiative in their new relationship, albeit to excuse her compulsion to undertake the more menial task, Judith smiled her thanks. To Maggie she suggested, 'Let us go into the other room. I'd like your opinion as to suitable clothing for the children. It is so damp here I'm fearful they might catch a fever.'

With Judith otherwise occupied, Flora once more exercised her authority this time at the tub. 'You talk to Mr McPherson,' she suggested to Catherine. 'I shall do the dishes myself.'

While Flora worked, Thomas spoke to Catherine telling her about the other children on the island and about the village school which was provided by the Quarrying Company.

*

Ian came quite suddenly upon the edge of the great chasm which had been dug out of the black slate rock of which the whole island seemed to be composed. In the dusk it was difficult to make out the bottom of the great quarry but Ian was able to identify a zigzag pathway cut into the rocky cliff. This must be how the men reached their work. Short ladders reached up to parts of the face where the men appeared to work from platforms fixed precariously into the rock wall. A row of three-sided shelters perched on the rim of the quarry. Each was surrounded by hillocks of waste slate. Here, he thought, must be where the slabs of rock are split into thin sheets and the slates cut to shape. He would not mind learning to do that job, but the idea of climbing down into that huge, yawning chasm, terrified him. Maybe when she saw the place, his mother would agree that fishing was less hazardous work than this.

Ever since their arrival, Ian had been vaguely aware of an unfamiliar thumping sound in the background. Now the noise grew louder as he approached a square stone building, perched on the quarry's edge. Beside an open door sat a grey haired, grey bearded man, his face tanned to leather by continuous exposure to the wind and rain. He puffed away at a long clay pipe as he took his ease in the dying light.

'Good evening, sir,' Ian greeted him, politely.

The man nodded, removed his pipe and blew a perfect smoke ring before answering. 'Aye,' he said. 'You'll be the new minister's son, I'm thinking?'

The lad confirmed that this was so. 'My name is Ian Bantrie, sir,' he answered. 'Tell me,' he asked, 'what is that machinery? I heard the sound of it the moment we landed on the island.'

Always glad to have a new pair of ears to listen to his blether, the old man replied, 'The slate has been dug out of here for centuries and the pit is now more than a hundred feet below sea level. There is a barrier of solid rock between the quarry and the sea but nevertheless water seeps in through cleavages in the rock. Sea water and rain gather in the bottom and must be constantly pumped from the quarry floor.'

Ian shuddered at the thought of working at such depths with the whole Atlantic Ocean just a few feet away behind the rock wall.

'How old do you have to be to work in the quarry?' he asked. Hoping the man would say he was too young.

'Why, the lads begin as soon as they leave the school,' replied the other. 'Some as young as eleven go down to fetch and carry for the gangs blasting out the rock.' Ian, who had recently celebrated his fourteenth birthday, felt positively old. The fellow continued, 'They begin as labourers. The lucky ones attach themselves to a good fireman and learn to do the blasting. That is the best paid of all the jobs. Others are better at cutting the slate. They usually work on the surface.' He pointed to the row of simple shelters which Ian had already seen.

That decided the issue. If he was to work in the quarry at all, he would try to become a slate cutter rather than a quarryman.

'And you, sir. What is your job?' he asked.

'Och, I am the engine minder, just. Too old now to get myself down there,' he indicated the narrow path snaking down into that deep hole in the ground. 'I wish that I had paid more attention to my lessons when I had the chance,' mused the old man. 'I might have become a real engineer instead of an engine minder, too old to work at a proper job. That is what a bright young fellow like you should do.'

Ian thanked him for his advice and asked for further directions to the house of the recently bereaved woman. He was pointed towards a small cottage standing alone, some way from the other buildings. 'My father went straight away to see Mrs Dundas when he heard of her plight,' Ian explained.

The old man nodding over his pipe, murmured, 'She's a poor wee lassie and no mistake.' He took a long, thoughtful, pull at his pipe. 'Aye," he concluded, 'it will be good to have a proper minister again.' He lapsed into silence but as Ian moved away he called after him. 'Tell the minister, if he has any wee jobs need doing about the house or in the church, Angus McPhail is his man.'

Ian waved to show that he had heard, and disappeared into the gloom.

*

Jessie Dundas ran her fingers lightly through wee Tommy's mop of golden curls and replaced a fallen cover tossed aside by the restless child. She kissed him on the forehead, glancing across as she did so at her infant daughter. The baby breathed so lightly that the anxious mother stooped to listen for the tiny gurgle of expelled air which was sufficient to satisfy her that all was well.

At his tentative knocking, she rose from her knees and went to open the door to the new minister.

'I came to see Mrs Dundas,' he said, looking beyond her into the interior of the room, expecting to hear the weeping of women, to see a family gathering perhaps, or at least, sympathetic neighbours.

'I am Mrs Dundas,' she replied, her voice low and refined.

'I am the new Minister; James Bantrie is my name. I am sorry not to have been here when you most needed me. You seem to be all alone at this difficult time,' he remarked. His comment seemed like a condemnation of her neighbours.

'I have the company of my children,' she replied. 'That is all I require.' Nevertheless she stepped back, inviting him in.

He removed his hat and placed it with his cane upon a settle beside the scant fire. Involuntarily he shivered.

'I have allowed the fire to die down,' she said, suddenly aware that the room had indeed become cold. She busied herself with adding a few coals to the grate then came to sit opposite him, crouching down on a creepy stool to get nearer to the flames. She said nothing, gazing as though mesmerised, into the revitalised fire.

He waited, hoping she would speak. When she remained silent he asked, 'Would you have me say a prayer?'

Her reply appalled him.

'Why? What can your God do for me, now?'

'He might give you some comfort; the strength to go on.'

She snorted in disgust. 'Oh I shall go on,' she declared. 'Have no fear of that. I have two young children who need me. Until they can fend for themselves I must go on.'

'Will you allow me to say a prayer on your behalf?' he asked.

'Do as you please,' she replied indifferently. 'Nothing you say can raise my Douglas from his cold grave.'

James took her at her word and quietly intoned the familiar verses, the Lord's Prayer and then, the twenty-third psalm.

Jessie Dundas appeared to pay no heed and scarcely lifted her head during the silence which followed. At last, having said and done as much as she would allow, James fell silent and after a few moments he rose to leave. Suddenly galvanised into action, Jesse Dundas began to fuss with cups and a kettle.

'Will you take a dish 'o tea, now you are here?' she demanded. It was as though his prayers had never been uttered.

Believing, rightly, that despite her protestations, the woman needed his companionship, James resumed his seat.

'Why, thank you Mrs Dundas that would be most acceptable.'

As she worked at preparing the tea, he enquired casually, 'will you stay on the island now that your husband…?' He did not no how to say it.

'Now that he's dead?' she concluded for him. 'I shall stay if only to spite those vicious women who would have me leave!' She spoke with such vehemence James supposed that she must be party to some long standing disagreement with her neighbours. Ever wary of the politics of womankind, he wished he had never raised the subject.

'They did not want me here in the first place,' she went on. 'I was only tolerated because of Douglas. He was born here you see. They are mad, all of them. A tight, clannish people, unwelcoming to strangers.'

'Why stay if you feel so unwanted?' he asked. Despite his apprehension at being drawn into an argument not of his making, he could see that she had a need to talk it out.

'Where else would I go? The children's grandparents are on Lunga. I might go there, but they would deny my existence if they could. They would gladly take the children, but not me. No, my man died in the quarry. The company is obliged to provide me with a dwelling, so here I will stay!'

'Where were you born, my dear?' He tried a softer approach. Perhaps she would warm to sympathy.

'I was born in Edinburgh,' she replied, warily. Too often this fact alone was sufficient to condemn her in the eyes of her neighbours. 'Douglas and I met when he was there, visiting relatives.'

There was no need to mention how they had met. This well- bred minister would not understand the needs which drove a woman to undertake work which was frowned upon by almost everyone with whom she had ever had contact.

'Suffice it to say,' she continued, 'that I rendered his friend some assistance when he was injured. We fell in love and he brought me here to what I thought would be paradise. Believe me Minister, when I say that nothing I experienced in the slums of Edunburgh was as withering of the spirit as the reception I have been given by these islanders.'

'Now I am here, Madam,' he assured her, 'I shall do my utmost to heal this breach and meanwhile I hope that you will befriend my wife, for she too is a stranger to these people.'

'Don't ask me, Sir, I pray you,' Jess answered, 'for to introduce Mrs Bantrie to me, is to condemn her too, to isolation.

'I believe you will find my wife immune to any such suggestion,' he smiled. 'To warn her off would be to invite her to be your very best friend!'

Despite herself, Jess Dundas found herself smiling. 'I believe I should like your wife very well, Sir,' she answered and handed him his hat and stick as he made for the door.

Before leaving he paused.

'Should you need my assistance madam, I am at your service,' he told her. 'Do you have the means to live? Food and coals enough to tide you over?'

'I have what you see.' She indicated a coal bucket, half full, and the remains of a loaf of bread lying on the table.

'I will see what can be done,' he said and stepped out into the night.

*

Thomas Guthrie welcomed the appearance of a new minister after several months without anyone upon whom to lean for spiritual and moral support.

His was a thankless task; trying to hold together a workforce in such difficult circumstances.

Some of his men , those with families to support and for whom the roof over their heads was more important than access to entertainment and a social life outside their work, had been on the island for many years, forming the nucleus of a team. These men comprised a malleable workforce and with their wives, a law- abiding and deeply religious community. The young, single men however were tough, often unskilled and largely itinerate. Their greatest strength lay in their ability to demand a higher wage for a shorter working day. Thomas often wished they might apply their energies as determinedly to getting out the slate.

Quarrying operations were much the same throughout the kingdom, whether the work was in marble, building stone or slate. Even coal miners, having freed themselves from the claustrophobic darkness of the pits, would find their way north and west to Eisdalsa or to the other slate Quarries at Ballahulish and when orders were slack and work scarce, they came to the Isle of Orchy only as a last resort.

With a population containing such a large proportion of young unattached men, Guthrie was hard put to it to keep order. Cut off from normal sources of supply, some of his workers had built a still and produced their own raw and very potent whisky. At the same time, most of the women brewed their own ale in order to overcome the dangers of drinking water which was inevitably stagnant. It was not difficult therefore to see why drunkenness was so often the cause of accidents both at sea and in the slate quarries. With the coming of a new minister to put the fear of hell and damnation into this rowdy element, Guthrie hoped to see a change in the general behaviour of his workforce and a resumption of normal working.

An additional bonus arising from the arrival of James Bantrie proved to be his son, Ian. For a long time Thomas had sought a suitable lad to sign on as his apprentice. Thomas was the only man on the island capable of repairing the steam driven machinery upon which the quarrying work depended. For long he had sought someone with sufficient mathematical ability to take upon himself the difficult subjects of physics and engineering science. The tiny public school run by the inestimable Miss McFadyen, produced scholars well versed in the Bible and in Literature of an improving nature but her curriculum lacked Mechanics and Mathematics, other than simple calculations in money and measurement.

When, a short time after the family's arrival on Orchy, Minister Bantrie approached the quarry manager with a proposal to apprentice his son as an engineer, Guthrie jumped at the opportunity. Soon Ian Bantrie found himself immersed in the laws of physics and mathematical theory of an advanced nature, as well as learning the more practical art of maintaining heavy duty equipment. So closely did he follow his master's every activity, he became known as Guthrie's shadow or just ' the shadow' for short! He was a likeable lad and although they teased him unmercifully, the men did not resent his presence and soon began to treat him more as a comrade than as the boss's mouthpiece they had at first suspected.

When freed from his master's bonds, Ian liked nothing better than to sail with the fishermen on the evening tide, returning in the early hours of the morning to snatch a few hours sleep before the commencement of the working day. While Judith dreaded these expeditions, she said nothing to curb her son's enthusiasm. He was no longer a child to be tied to her apron strings. He must learn to conduct himself in the world of men and besides, she needed the fish he caught to add to their meagre diet.

On the pretext of tutoring the boy, Thomas Guthrie became a frequent visitor to the manse, contriving somehow always to make his appearances coincide with meal times. Guthrie's deferential attitude to herself, which Judith had found so disconcerting at their first meeting, was forgotten once he began coaching Ian at the kitchen table while she and Flora went quietly about their household duties. It was the very astute Maggie McPherson who first suggested that Guthrie appeared more interested in Flora's baking than his apprentice's progress. In contrast with his shy, inarticulate beginnings, the man now positively bloomed in Flora McKinnon's presence.

Catherine quickly found her place in Miss McFadyen's schoolroom, making friends easily with other children of her own age. She required little by way of entertainment other than what was of her own making. Every free minute was spent watching the sea birds wheeling and swooping over the fishing boats when they returned in the early dawning. She sought out, pressed and named the wild flowers which grew in profusion in those parts of the island as yet untouched by the hand of the quarry men. By waiting patiently beside the shore she could watch the otters at play and schools of dolphin leaping in the turbulent currents off the northern end of the island.

When her little brother, Charles, was old enough to be taught his letters, it was Catherine who showed him how to read and write. In his fourth year he learned to count and quickly grasped the elements of subtraction and multiplication. This early education was to stand him in good stead in later days and even when the boy grew to manhood, he would always regarded his sister as his true mentor and confidant.

Judith, having survived the initial shock of finding herself in this remote place and living under conditions more harsh than she had ever known, applied herself to the tasks of a minister's wife. She became a leading figure amongst the women in the community. So firmly did she take a grasp upon the opinions of the womenfolk that none dare criticise her, despite her friendship with the widow Dundas.

Only James continued to fret about their changed circumstances. He could not forget that it was his own reasonable and compassionate interpretation of the rules of his church, together with his rebellious nature, which had brought them to this plight. As one who had forsaken a good living for his principles, James should have been pleased to find himself amongst people who observed the rules of their church so strictly.

In truth, he found the rigid and unquestioning application of religious principles which existed within the permanent population of the island to be less of an asset and more of a hindrance to his work.

The God of the people of Eilean Orchy was a fierce master who would brook no deviation from the rules laid down in the Bible. Sunday was a day for religious observance. Let no man read a newspaper or careen his boat on the Sabbath and woe betide the woman who dared bake bread or wash out a garment. In a community with few women and a large proportion of unmarried men, there was bound to be competition for female favours. Were a girl to be found to be carrying an illegitimate child, the cutty-stool was but the first of her humiliations. To be forced to stand upon a stool before the whole congregation and confess her sins should be punishment enough but the ostracism which followed was sufficient to drive more than one poor lass to take her own life. Better she were dead than that her child should be born without a father. '*Have Mercy*,' appeared to be the one Christian commandment which was lacking in the local vocabulary.

Jessie Dundas, the widow who had been the first of James's parishioners to receive his priestly services, continued to occupy the house which had been allocated to her husband by virtue of his employment in the quarries. From time to time, in order to earn a little money, she took as lodgers one or more of the itinerate workers employed by Thomas Guthrie. This naturally made her the subject of village gossip.

Her unfounded reputation of being a loose woman so angered James that he was at pains to show his own approval of her by the frequent visits he paid to her house and by his insistence upon the parish supporting her family in their dire need. At last he was moved to write a sermon decrying careless talk which was based upon unfounded rumour. This only served to link his name more firmly with that of the Widow Dundas and had it not been for the respect in which Judith Bantrie was held throughout the island, the whispered rumours might well have been given full vent and the minister's tenure placed in question.

Within a year of his appearance on the island, James Bantrie found himself with only a handful of friends in an otherwise hostile environment and with no one to turn to for professional guidance, he took to corresponding regularly with Murdo McLeod in Dundee. It was through his friend that he learned of the expedition which was to change his life and that of his family, forever.

Without consulting Judith, lest any mention of the scheme should cause the opportunity to escape him, James wrote a letter to the address McLeod had given him. Then he sat back and waited for a reply, creating in his mind a new world in which reason would hold sway over bigotry and greed and in which he might worship his God in the manner which he knew to be right.

Absorbed by the goal which he had set himself, James went about his daily round with renewed vigour. Anticipation of a great adventure gave a certain spring to his step and he found he could at last ignore his critics and counter the scepticism with which every one of his proposals had hitherto been greeted by his parishioners. The hang-dog expression he had worn since he arrived on the island now departed. With his head held erect and the old fierceness returning to his piercing grey eyes, James conducted his flock with such vigour that they went in fear of the Lord and no longer dared to voice openly any unfounded suspicions about their neighbours; the gossip which had once so coloured their drab and uneventful lives.

Chapter Four

EISDALSA
1846

Dr Alexander Beaton was awakened by a shaft of bright sunshine which having slipped through a narrow gap in the heavy draperies, fell onto his pillow, making any further sleep impossible. He opened his eyes, groaned, and immediately closed them again.

Last evening's celebrations had begun sedately enough, his mother providing a dinner comprised of his favourite dishes washed down by a splendid Burgundy which his father had ordered especially for the occasion. Sarah Beaton had retired when the meal was over but not before kissing Alexander and telling him how proud she was to have yet another surgeon in the family. She had left the men to their whisky and cigars and the colourful, often crude medical tales which they loved to exchange.

It was the whisky that had done it, Alex decided. Responding to his brother's hearty shout and his insistent rattling of the doorknob, he carefully shielded his eyes before Hugh could rush in and throw back the curtains.

'Hallo, ma wee Bro,' Hugh taunted good naturedly, 'Feeling the after effects of the uisge beatha, are we? You should learn to take more water with it.'

Alexander had had little time, or money, for indulging in strong drink or any other pleasures of the flesh for that matter, during the past six years. He had hardly tasted a drop of whisky since his last night at home when he had visited his father in his consulting room to wish him goodbye. On that occasion Malcolm Beaton had poured him a glass before delivering the homily which he had, no doubt, considered his duty to give to his youngest son.

'In Edinburgh you will encounter all manner of evil from which you have been sheltered hitherto,' he had cautioned, using the tone he normally reserved for his patients. 'I cannot expect you to reject all forms of pleasure but I do ask you to be temperate in your drinking habits and to avoid loose women.' He had cleared his throat nervously at this point and then added, 'for the sake of your own good health.'

Alexander had heeded his father's warning, not for fear of the consequences to his health but because he was determined to let nothing interfere with his studies and his plan which included marriage to the prettiest girl in Argyll. Hugh's jibe had caused him to recall how that very first glass of whisky had burned his throat and brought tears to his eyes. Despite his headache, he smiled at the recollection.

'What's the joke?' Hugh demanded.

Older than his brother by some five years, Hugh Beaton sported a bushy beard whose fiery natural tones could be subdued only by liberal applications of macassa oil. This impressive growth, designed to give him an air of someone older and wiser, was a source of great amusement to all the family.

Not wanting to share his fond reminiscence of his father, Alex deflected his question with another.

'Why don't you get that fuzz attended to Hugh?' he demanded. 'It's like to smother you in your sleep!'

Hugh stroked the facial adornment tenderly. 'You may find it amusing,' he replied haughtily, ' but there is one far fairer than you, who approves of it. For her, I shall wear it to my dying day!'

'Oh, ho!' cried Alexander, 'and who is this unwitting and truly undiscerning creature, might I ask?'

'You will find out, all in good time. Mother has asked her and her family to dinner later in the week. That will be the occasion when all shall be revealed.'

It soon became clear that no matter how much Alexander delved, wheedled or pleaded, Hugh was not going say another word on the subject. With much banter and a good deal of noise, the two young men descended two flights of stairs, reverting to a more solemn attitude only when they entered the breakfast room where their father was already tucking into a pair of Loch Fyne kippers. An edition of *The Glasgow*

Herald, three days old, remained neatly folded on the table beside his plate.

Alexander paused in the doorway, relishing the familiar scene. He recalled how as boys they had waited impatiently for their father to finish reading his paper in the mornings, hoping for him to be called out on some emergency so that they might read some of the more lurid aspects of the news before they were obliged to leave for school. His glance automatically fell upon the front page of the newspaper. The heading which caught his eye tempted him to lift it and read.

NEW ZEALAND COMPANY'S EXPEDITION TO THE MIDDLE ISLAND A SUCCESS!

Mr Kettle reports a suitable site for settlement has been acquired on the Otago Peninsular. Scotsmen are urged to come forward and offer themselves for work in the new colony...

'I had begun to wonder if either of you was ever going to make an appearance, this morning.' Malcolm Beaton grinned at his two sons. He had matched them, glass for glass, the night before, but showed himself to be none the worse for it this morning.

'I'm pleased you have joined us Alexander,' he said in a more businesslike manner. 'We have several important matters to discuss.'

He waited for them to fetch what they wanted from the side table before continuing.

'This arrived this morning, Hugh,' he said, pushing a document towards his older son. 'It was delivered by the Factor's man. From the seal, I would imagine that it is your official appointment!' With a note of satisfaction he turned to Alexander. 'Your brother is to be the new Medical Officer to the Eisdalsa Slate Quarrying Company.'

Alexander, taken completely by surprise, reeled under the impact of his father's announcement. Hugh, the Medical Officer for the quarries? How could this be possible? Hugh had a surgeon's appointment awaiting him in London. His mother had written to him with the news not a month ago. Surely Hugh was never going to remain at home to practise medicine when he had always had his sights set on something far more ambitious.

Conscious suddenly of a lead weight lying in the pit of his stomach, for some moments Alexander remained speechless. When at last he managed to speak at all it was to ask, with apparent composure: 'Have you retired then Pa?'

When they met the previous afternoon, Alexander had seen a marked change in his father's appearance. He had been quick to notice Malcolm Beaton's loss of weight and his pronounced stoop. Then again, when his father had tried to rise from his chair there had been a pained expression on his face which had not escaped the younger doctor's professional eye. What he saw yesterday had confirmed his opinion that it was time to lift some of the more tiring work from his father's shoulders but this had always been his intention, not that of his brother Hugh.

On the long journey home on board the steamer Alex had been contemplating how he might begin to ease his father out of the hard graft of the practice and take more and more of the burden upon his own shoulders. Now, all his resolve had been swept aside by this extraordinary turn of events.

What had happened to make Hugh change his mind? In the months before Hugh had left home to begin his medical studies at the university, he had spent most of his time decrying the merits of a rural practice. *He* was going to work in a big city where there would be a choice of experiences to be gained and wealth to be accumulated from consultations with the rich and famous. No midnight calls and kitchen table surgery for him. A professorship in some university hospital was more in his line!

Hugh's next words stung him into attention. They were such an accurate reflection of his thoughts.

'Father has been suffering from rheumatism for a long time,' he was reminded. 'Now, it seems, the strain has affected his heart. Putting aside any more ambitious plans, I have been obliged to take on more and more of the work of the practice these past months. After much deliberation, I have decided to refuse the offer of a residency in Surgery at St Bartholomew's in London.' He paused dramatically. 'During these past few weeks it has been necessary for Pa to step down altogether. He needs to take a good long rest.'

Hugh's explanation seemed like an accusation. It was as though Alexander was held responsible both for his father's disabilities and for his brother's martyrdom. He had been told nothing of Malcolm's deteriorating condition, his mother had not mentioned it in her letters. How could Alexander have helped in the circumstances even had he known? Until he was properly qualified there had been nothing he could do to assist his father.

'I'm afraid that this tough life has got to me at last,' Malcolm intervened, sensing some inexplicable strain between the two brothers. With unconvincing cheeriness, he continued, 'I have been finding it increasingly difficult to clamber around in the quarries when there are accidents. Night-time voyages to the outer islands, particularly in stormy weather, are for younger men than me to tackle. No, I shall not be sorry to give it all up. I'm looking forward to ending my days husbanding my cattle up in the glen and fishing for salmon in the burn. Mind you,' he added with a touch of his former humour, 'I shall always be happy to provide Hugh with the benefit of my experience.' Hugh's smile in response had little warmth to it. Alex wondered how they would get on together once Hugh began to feel his feet.

Quite unaware of the disquiet which his words had created in the mind of his younger son, Malcolm stretched a hand across the table and gave Hugh an affectionate pat on the sleeve. He concluded confidently, 'I shall be leaving my patients in the very best of hands.'

From as far back as he could remember Alexander had dreamed of the day when, a fully qualified doctor like his father, he would take over the role of Medical Officer in the Eisdalsa quarries. As a boy he had wanted nothing better than to travel the glorious countryside of Argyll accompanying Malcolm Beaton on his rounds.

Before he had left home to begin his medical studies in Edinburgh, Alex had known every man, woman and child in the district. By contrast Hugh, who had spent every minute of his free time sailing in the bay or climbing the rugged hillsides with his friends, had taken little interest in his father's work. His profession had been decided for him at birth. Having accepted the fact, he made no effort to prepare himself for the life ahead of him. He might as well have become a banker or a lawyer so little vocation did he have.

By contrast Alexander, even as a small child, had spent hours seated on the high stool in his father's dispensary counting pills into little boxes.

When he was only five years old he would perch on a chair pulled up for him so that he could reach the deep sink and wash the labels off medicine bottles which were to be used again. While still struggling to read at all, he would try to mouth the names on the labels; Glycerini; Acidi Carbolici; Spiritus Vini Meth.; Sapo Mollis. It had never once occurred to him that he might not become his father's successor. It gave Alexander some satisfaction to know that Malcolm Beaton, despite his infirmities, was determined to retained control over the business affairs of the practice. Hugh might think himself in charge but his father still held the purse strings and while he was yet able, he would be making all the important decisions.

'There are two matters both of considerable urgency, which must receive attention this morning.' Malcolm's tone left little doubt in the mind of the younger brother as to who was in charge.

Malcolm glanced across at his older son as he said pompously, 'In his capacity as official Medical Officer for the district, Hugh must examine and declare dead, a corps washed up on the shores of Lunga, yesterday.'

While the two brothers exchanged a glance, he continued, 'No more than twenty minutes ago a message arrived from the minister on Eilean Orchy requesting medical assistance there. It seems that there has been an outbreak of fever, probably Enteric from the symptoms described. I suppose I should make the effort myself but…'

Alex could not understand why his father did not immediately consider *him* for the task.

'I'll go,' he offered, without a moment's hesitation.

'Are you sure? You don't mind?' Irritatingly, Malcolm looked to Hugh for approval before accepting Alexander's offer.

This only served to increase the younger man's annoyance. Why did Papa not take it for granted that he would be ready to leap at any opportunity to be of service? What had he done, that his father should treat him with the same deference that he might show to some visiting physician here on holiday? Was he not a part of the family team, obviously to be included? Naturally he would go to Orchy. He would do anything to help the old man. Besides, he couldn't wait to try his hand at medical practice on his own!

All he said, in reply, was, 'Of course I'll go, Pa. I'll just nip upstairs and get my bag.'

By the time that Alexander had returned to the surgery, Hugh and his father had already gathered together the equipment and potions he would need. Even in this he was not to be left to make his own decisions.

'The old remedies are the best lad,' Malcolm told him. 'Luke- warm sponging to reduce the temperature. Omit the castor oil. You don't want to end up with a perforated gut. A little olive oil if there is constipation and kaolin and opiates for the flux and the pain.'

Alexander refrained from telling his father how he had single-handed, successfully treated an entire Edinburgh family on one occasion when there had been no tutor from the hospital to advise him. As Alex packed the items one by one into his cleverly constructed canvas case Hugh could not resist a derisory comment.

'Where did you get that museum piece for God's sake?' he demanded.

'It was a graduation gift from an elderly surgeon friend who served in the Peninsular War,' Alexander replied. 'Actually I find it particularly useful. Everything is in its place and easy to locate while the case itself is light in weight. He was only half attending to the advice being heaped upon him. Let the two of them give their instructions. Once he was away on his own he would do as he thought fit. While the others were discussing the merits of one course over another, he slipped a small bottle of sulphuric acid into the bag and fastened the strap decisively.

'I'll be on my way then.' Standing in the open doorway he glanced at the heavy sky and the mounting seas and said, 'It looks as though there might be some bad weather, later. Don't worry if I am not back by evening. If necessary I shall find a bed for the night and return in the morning.'

The Beaton family home was a substantial house of three storeys built of local stone under a slated roof. It stood some four hundred yards back from the main road at the end of a narrow lane. The policies included some five hundred acres of rich pasture at the seaward end of a glen, well sheltered between the two rugged outcrops of volcanic rock, Caisteal an Spullidair to the north and Smiddy Brae to the south.

Malcolm Beaton had arrived in the village thirty years before and on being appointed medical officer, he had been offered the tenancy of Tigh na Broch. It was a house which was suitably superior to those of the quarry workers, on a par with the dwellings of the Quarry Master and the local Manse but modest by the standards being set by more substantial incomers.

Lowlanders, industrialists of every kind, who had made their fortunes during recent wars with the French and the Americans had been buying up large estates in Argyll and building new houses of lavish proportions. In so doing they had ousted numbers of crofting families who had been farming the land for generations. While the country folk flooded into the cities looking for work and a place to live, good agricultural land was being laid to waste, left to become a home to wild animals and game birds reared for shooting. There was evidence of this sad demise in the population even here in Seileach, where the local economy was more dependent upon slate mining than agriculture. Alexander had already noted the absence of several faces familiar in his childhood.

'What happened to the Stevenson's,' he asked Hugh as his brother walked his horse alongside him as far as the gate.

'Emigrated,' Hugh replied, shortly. 'Gone south into England I believe. Wullie McIver and his family sailed for the New World only a month ago. If it were not for the quarries employing such large numbers of people the islands would be quite deserted.'

'Without the produce from the farms, who will supply the quarry workers with food?' Alex demanded. The whole situation seemed set to become a major disaster.

'Grain and potatoes are imported from Ireland, brought here by the slate boats which otherwise would return without a cargo.'

'While our farmers are put out of work,' observed Alexander, 'the quarrymen must pay inflated prices to have their food carried in. What kind of economic sense does that make?' he demanded angrily.

'You have to ask the merchants that question; they are the ones making the profits!' Hugh laughed the matter off but Alexander, already smarting from the events of the morning so far, saw only disaster looming for the people. Perhaps this was not the place for him to put down his roots after all. There must be somewhere in the world which offered a man a more rewarding future than this.

When they reached the shore road Hugh turned his mount to the left. His path would take him up, over the brae, dropping down in a mile or so to the ferry for the island of Lunga. From thence he must travel by road. It was a good few miles to the southern part of that island to where the body had been washed ashore.

Alexander turned right towards the village of Seileach and the harbour where he expected to be able to hire a boat to take him to Orchy. As he walked the familiar road he swung his bag in rhythm with his rapid strides, the effort helping to dispel his moodiness at every step. A storm might well be brewing but the air was crisp and clean and the sea birds wheeling above the cliff, cried out in welcome. He relished the scene, appreciating how much he had missed this view of the sparkling ocean and the islands scattered out there in the Sound.

To his left and only a few hundred yards off shore, lay Eisdalsa. Little more than a mile in either direction the tiny island had been quarried for its slate rock for hundreds of years and boasted some of the deepest pits in the district. Eisdalsa represented the heart of the slate quarrying industry which had sustained a population of three thousand souls in these islands for nearly a century.

The sound of steam pumps working continuously to keep the deep quarries clear of water, came to him across the waves. Since daybreak the men would have been at work chiselling and blasting out the rock, spitting and carrying the product of their labours to the quay while, out in the bay, sailing vessels of every kind waited patiently to be loaded up with roofing slates to be transported around the world.

Since childhood Alexander had wondered about the places to which the Eisdalsa slates were carried. Nova Scotia, the West Indies, such names had enthralled him when as a boy in knickerbockers, he had listened to the seafarers talking of their travels while they smoked their pipes and supped their ale of an evening outside the village brew house. Earlier that morning he had had a moment of madness after Hugh dropped his bombshell. He had been tempted there and then to sign on for that expedition to New Zealand announced in the newspaper. For a man with a good woman at his side it would be a great adventure. What would Annie have to say about taking such a step? She had been waiting six years for him already. She was not likely to accept a further three or more year's delay while he explored the possibilities of life in the colonies. Maybe he could persuade her to accompany him.

A group of sheep wandering from off the hill, scattered to the sides of the road as the post cart approached from the direction of the village in a cloud of dust.

The postie, Euan McDowell, touched his cap in exaggerated salute as he pulled up beside the doctor.

'Is it yourself Alexander Beaton?' he demanded in his deliberate, west-coast manner. 'The great doctor returned to his roots at last!'

Alexander greeted his boyhood companion warmly, glad to see that one thing had not changed since his departure. Inseparable companions from the day they started school, for season after season the two of them had fished from the rocks below Caisteal an Spullidair and bathed in the quiet waters beyond the finger of rocks which marked the northern end of the bay. Occasionally they had even skipped Sunday school and risked a skelping so they might tickle trout in the lochan over the hill.

Visions of his carefree childhood flashed into Alexander's mind as he reached up to grasp his friend's strong brown hand. 'By God it's good to see you Euan,' he cried delightedly. 'I was planning to visit yourself and your parents. Pa tells me that your father is not so good these days.'

'Och, our parents are all growing older,' said the postie. 'Dr Malcolm can talk, the poor wee man. There's many the day I have seen them having to lift him down from his horse, so stiff was he from a wee ride across the hills.'

'He has retired from the practice,' Alex told his friend. Much as it pained him to pass on the news it was important that folk in the village should know who their new doctor was going to be. 'My brother, Hugh, has been appointed as doctor for the quarries.'

Euan seemed surprised.

'But I thought...' He knew how much Alexander had set his heart on working amongst the quarrymen himself, tending the folks with whom he had shared his childhood.

Out of family loyalty if nothing else Alex hastened to justify his father's decision. 'Hugh is the eldest son. It is only right he should inherit the practice.' He tried to sound cheerful and nonchalant about it but Euan knew his friend too well to be deceived.

'Maybe he will not stay after all,' he suggested, kindly.' I understand that his future rather rests upon the whim of a young lady.'

Alex, scarcely attending to what his friend was saying, recalled the day that Euan's father had taken a tumble down the quarry wall and sustained fractures to an arm and a leg. Malcolm Beaton had feared the quarryman would not survive but Euan's father had recovered, although he was never again able to work in the quarries. Rather than pay compensation for his injuries, the Company had given Mr McDowell the Store and the Post Office to run.

'But what's this,' Alex demanded of his old friend, 'Here are you, wearing the postie's cap and delivering the mail when I thought you were bent on a career in the quarries. I felt sure you would have been well on the way to becoming an engineer by now.'

The good-hearted Euan gave a wry smile. 'Work in the store was no problem to my father,' he explained, 'but delivering the mail was another matter all together. Daily exposure to wind and rain caused the old fellow to suffer agonies with arthritis in his mended limbs. I couldn't bear to see him suffer so.'

'But surely if he gave up the shop you could support him on your wages from the quarry?'

'And leave the old man without useful employment? It was a matter of his dignity do you see. He needs to feel necessary to the community. He is well enough while he can remain indoors. Sat on his stool behind the shop counter, he is never without someone to talk to. I do the heavy lifting and he takes the money. It works very well.'

Alex, appreciating the sacrifice his friend had made for his father's sake, knew better than to comment.

'I will call and see your father just as soon as I get back from Eilean Orchy,' Alex told him.

'Oh aye, I heard tell there was fever on the island. It is a bad place to be when the winds are strong and the weather wet but it seems even worse after a long dry spell as we have had this past month. It is lack of fresh water is the problem so they say.' He glanced up at the lowering clouds. 'That is all about to change though,' he grinned at his friend. 'It must be your sour countenance has brought on the bad weather.' It seemed Alexander's solemn expression had not gone unnoticed as he approached along the road deep in thought.

'How is Martha?' demanded Alex, rapidly changing the subject. 'Are we soon to hear wedding bells?'

Euan blushed to the roots of his hair.

'Next month, 'he said shyly. Then brightening suddenly, he asked, 'now that you are home, will you not stand up for me as my groom's man?'

'I'd be delighted,' replied Alex, hesitantly, 'but I may not be here in a month's time. Since Hugh has accepted the doctor's position in the quarries, I shall have to look elsewhere for employment. The practice will not sustain the two of us and my parents as well.'

Alex was still not convinced that his brother meant to remain at home. Probably Hugh saw this as a stop-gap while he waited for another surgeon's post in one of the hospitals. For the moment Alex had a more pressing question which was burning to be asked.

'What of Annie, Euan, how is she?'

Euan looked positively evasive as he answered cautiously, 'I haven't seen that much of her lately. Martha is her great confidant. She rarely speaks to me at all.'

'Oh. Have you quarrelled?'

'Have you not been writing to her, yourself?' Euan knew the answer to be in the negative of course. Did he not deliver every letter and package in the district by his own hand?

'I was busy with my work.' Alex knew it to be a feeble excuse. The truth was that once he left home he had put out of his head all thoughts which did not refer directly to his studies. Annie was a sensible girl she knew how important it was for him to concentrate on his work. They would soon re-establish their relationship once he had met her and told her how much he had missed her.

When Euan did not respond immediately, Alex began to fear that there was something his friend was not telling him. What was it? Surely Annie was not already betrothed or, even worse, married?

'What is it?' he demanded now. 'Is there something you have to tell me?'

'Annie must tell you for herself,' was the stark reply.

Then there was something. Alex resisted the temptation to pursue the question further and in the heavy silence which followed Euan took up the reins and tapped his horse's neck with his long whip.

'I must be on my rounds,' he called back over his shoulder as the post chaise pulled away.

'Will I see you in the tavern one night?' Alex shouted after him.

'Maybe!' His reply drifted towards the doctor on the breeze. Euan's unsatisfactory replies to his questions had left Alex even more despondent. It was with a heavy heart that he made his way to the quay.

*

James's had been reluctant to call in the doctor. His prevarication had angered Judith. He had protested that he could do nothing if the people did not agree to it. What was the point of calling for aid if no one wanted it, he had argued? She knew the people to be stubborn but they were not stupid. There came a time when the old wife's practices must give way to modern science. She was sure that she had been right to insist.

It was their reduced circumstances which had created the rift between them. At first she had supported James's defection from his church, respecting his motives and ready to accept whatever trials his decision might bring upon them. She had been content to get on with their new life as best she could but James's constant apologising for their situation and his monotonous self-deprecation had soon begun to wear her down. This coupled with the reluctance of the islanders to accept them as ordinary members of the community had made her embittered.

While Judith found her former happiness fast fading to hopeless despair, her friend and companion of so many years, Flora McKinnon, had found in this new life the answer to all her dreams, the engineer and quarry master Mr Guthrie. Married for some months now to her dear Thomas, Flora was taken up entirely with her own household and the new circle of acquaintance appropriate to the wife of a quarry manager. Were it not for her children and her friendship with Jessie Dundas, Judith felt she might lose her mind.

Like Judith, Jessie was an outsider in this close-knit community. Thomas Dundas had been one of very few eligible bachelors on the island and there had been much speculation as to which of the island's unwed lassies he would take for a wife. His return, after a brief holiday in Glasgow, with a bride of just one week on his arm had caused shock waves throughout the slate isles. Jessie had never truly been accepted by the women of the community although for Thomas's sake she was tolerated while he lived. After Thomas died she was shunned, particularly when, to raise sufficient money to feed her two children, she had taken in lodgers. The succession of itinerate quarrymen staying in her house set tongues wagging and although there was no justification for it, James Bantrie had been approached on more than one occasion to eject the widow from the church on grounds of adultery. In their isolation Judith and Jesse clung to one another. When Jessie's infant daughter became sick with the fever Judith went at once to her aid leaving Catherine to take care of the household duties in the manse. Little Amy Dundas had slipped quietly away in the early hours while her brother Tommy, also sick with fever, would have followed her had not Judith produced one of Flora's remedies, dried bilberry for relieving the flux. The boy seemed to be out of danger when Judith at last left her friend to cope alone so that she might call her husband to deal with the dead child.

When she returned to the manse it was to find that James, alarmed at the sudden increase in cases of disease, had already called the doctor and was preparing to go to help where he could. She sent him at once to comfort Jessie in her loss while she herself, weary beyond belief, took to her bed. Despite her weariness she found she could not sleep. Pouring a glass of whisky from the decanter left by her husband she drank it down quickly, hoping for oblivion.

At last exhaustion got the better of her and she slept.

She was only half awake and still a little tipsy from the whisky when hours later she answered the door to Alexander Beaton's insistent knocking. The spirits had lowered her reserve and loosened her tongue.

Alexander found it difficult to disguise the fact that the appearance of the Minister's wife had taken him by surprise. A woman in her late thirties or early forties, she had an air of neglected elegance as though she no longer cared about her appearance. She wore black silk where most of the island women would wear woollen cloth or maybe linen in the height of summer, yet the black skirts which hung down to touch the toes of her unpolished boots were rusty with wear and there were tears which although neatly mended, were clearly visible. Her hair was piled high in the crude semblance of an elegant coiffeur but wisps hung untidily around her ears and a comb which had been set to keep the greying locks under control had slipped sideways and remained unchecked.

'Good morning, Ma'am,' Alexander greeted her. 'The Minister sent for a doctor.'

'Oh yes. Will you come in Doctor?' She ushered him into a room with a low beamed ceiling such as was common to the poorer houses in the district. Alex ducked as he entered, surprised to find the manse to be such a lowly dwelling. This was little different from any of the slate worker's cottages.

'I must confess I was expecting an older man,' the woman said, blushing rather prettily. 'When my husband said he had sent for Dr Beaton...'

'I am his son, Ma' am, Alexander Beaton.'

'My own family has been very well since we arrived here,' she explained. 'We have had no need of medical aid, until now.'

'Is your husband available to show me those who require assistance?' Alexander asked.

'He is somewhere in the village just now,' she said waving her arm vaguely in the direction of the window, 'but he asked me to send you along to Mrs McLaughlan first. Her husband is very ill.'

Alexander made for the door.

'Thank you Mrs...?'

'Bantrie, Judith Bantrie. My husband is the reverend James Bantrie.'

He would have left her then but her light touch on his sleeve caused him to hesitate.

'Will you not take a cup of tea before you set to work?' she asked. Starved for so long of contact with those of her own class, Judith would have detained him longer.

'I have delayed too long already,' he told her somewhat brusquely. 'In cases of fever it is necessary to begin treatment as soon as possible.'

Reluctantly she released her hold on him. 'I shall see you again, Doctor, before you leave?'

He bowed his head courteously determined to be on his way. With a sigh, she preceded him to the door and directed him to the McLaughlan's cottage.

As he strode out along the dusty track Alexander wondered about Judith Bantrie. The woman had appeared reluctant to let him go. She behaved like someone who, living alone and suddenly confronted by a stranger, realises her need to communicate with another person after long isolation. Yet he was certain his father had mentioned children in the minister's household and of course there was the minister himself.

He approached the cottage Judith Bantrie had pointed out to him and finding the door already ajar, he bent his head and stepped inside giving a sharp knock as he did so. After the glare of the bright sunlight outside he was obliged to pause for a moment and adjust to the sudden gloom. He found himself in a single-roomed house, sparsely furnished with rough hewn table and stools and, along one wall, a truckle bed in which lay his patient. Pale and sweating, his jaw slack and his eyes glazed over in a disconcerting stare, Jack McLaughlin's intermittent painfully rasping breaths were the only indication that he still lived. Even from across the room Alex could tell that there was little he could do here.

Mrs McLaughlan was bent over the stove attempting to coax some life into a dying peat fire by the addition of a piece of damp driftwood. She lifted her head at his knock and struggled painfully to an upright position.

'I am Dr Alexander Beaton Ma'am,' he told her. 'I understand that your husband has succumbed to the fever. Is it your wish that I should try to revive him?'

She shot a glance at the still figure on the bed and nodded dully. Requiring no further encouragement Alex approached the bed.

The patient was in his forties. His sunken cheeks and wasted frame told their own story of days of pain and high fever.

'What have you done for him? Alexander asked gently, knowing how the goodwives of Orchy would have applied their own ancient remedies.

'I have bathed him to take down the fever,' she indicated a bowl and flannel on a stool beside the bed, 'and I gave him castor oil as the widow Lasky said' The woman was distraught. 'But the pain was so severe and there was blood!' She broke off, too embarrassed to say more.

'In his stool?' The doctor observed no niceties in so urgent a case.

The woman nodded.

'Has he eaten or drunk anything at all?'

'He has taken nothing but water and a little milk these past three days but today he is bringing up even these.'

'Nevertheless you must persist with the water, with a little salt added to replace that lost in the sweating. While even a small portion of the fluid is retained, his chances improve.'

Alexander reached for a flannel left lying in the bowl beside the bed. He wrung it out and gently wiped perspiration from the fevered brow.

'He is very dehydrated,' he observed. He felt the man's thready pulse and noted the distended abdomen. When he placed his hand lightly over the right iliac region the patient cried out, drawing his legs up in agony. Blood in the stool, rigidity of the muscles and that anxious look which Alex had observed previously in his visits to the poorest tenements in the city, these symptoms all confirmed Alex's suspicion that there was no hope for the man. The poisons from his perforated colon were even now pouring into the abdominal cavity. Death would come painfully but soon. He poured a generous dose of laudanum into a spoon and trickled it between McLaughlan's lips.

'He should sleep a little now,' he told the woman. 'If he should wake and be in pain, give him another spoonful of this.' He gave her a small bottle containing sufficient of the drug to see her husband painlessly into the next world.

'Are there others in the family who are sick,' he asked.

Mrs Mclaughlan shook her head but indicated three silent little figures standing at the door. He turned to the children taking each anxious little face in his hands in turn, examining for swollen glands and feeling each brow for signs of fever.

They appeared well, for the moment.

'We do not know what causes the sickness,' he told their mother, 'but I have found that letting a good draft of air blow through the house and using only boiled water for drinking purposes helps to dispel the pestilence. If you have somewhere else for the children to stay, perhaps you should keep them away from here for the present.' He fastened the strap on his medical bag and made to leave.

'Mrs McLean, in the second cottage along, her wee boy is sick…' Mrs McLaughlan murmured. She turned back to her dying husband, taking up a flannel with which to sponge his ashen face, already glistening again with beads of perspiration.

At the second house, Alexander's patient was a young boy of perhaps six or seven years. His skin still carried the tan from long summer days in the open air but beneath the superficial browning was a pallor attributable to the disease and there was about him the look of a wizened, bewildered elf.

'Has he had a high fever?' Alexander asked, feeling a brow which was for the moment, cool.

The mother nodded. 'I have been bathing him in tepid water all night,' she explained. 'The fever broke just before dawn.'

She looked tired. Alexander reached out and touched her forehead. She was flushed but not unduly hot. He attributed her high colour to the work she had been doing, humping buckets of water to and from the stove.

'The boy is constipated?' he asked.

'He has eaten nothing for two days. I did not think it mattered.'

'It is essential to clear the bowels,' Alexander insisted. 'I shall give you an emetic of olive oil and bicarbonate of soda. See that he receives a dose every three hours until his functions are normal. Keep the child warm and quiet. He should recover completely within a few days.'

Before handing her the mixture he took out the bottle of sulphuric acid he had included in addition to his father's prescriptions. Taking care to add only a drop at a time, he added a little to the solution in the bottle. Despite his caution, the amazing heat generated by mixing the chemicals nearly caused him to drop the bottle. He set it on the table to cool a little.

Aware of the mother's curiosity he explained, 'A little trick I learned in medical school, Ma'am. It seems to be effective in some cases.'

Having administered one dose of the medicine himself, he handed her the bottle. 'A spoonful every three hours and your boy should make a good recovery.'

The grateful mother saw him to the door.

'Your husband is he well?' he asked.

Enteric fever was unlike other fevers. It attacked some individuals in a family indiscriminately leaving others untouched. Even dirt and squalor had little significance. When it struck, the disease attacked rich and poor alike. In this it was unlike other fevers, cowpox for example, or measles. These attacked everyone with whom they came into contact.

'My man is well,' the woman assured him. 'He is at his work today, as usual. The sare heid that he took with him is from the uisge beatha he drank last night!'

Alex could not restrain a laugh.

'And you? What have you had to drink these past few days?'

'Nothing but tea, it is all I ever take."

'The boy drinks water, milk perhaps?'

She nodded.

'You would be well advised to boil everything he drinks for a time after the fever passes.'

Alexander repacked his case and moved on to another house which Mrs McLean had indicated. As he worked his way from house to house around the village, he did what he could to relieve the last hours of the dying and advised on the recuperation of those who would make a recovery. In every house he asked the same questions. Those who drank tea, ale and whisky from the island's one illicit still were all quite well. It transpired that only those who drank either milk or water from the rain barrels had been stricken. When he had encountered the disease in the city it was the water that had been suspect. There had been broken stand pipes in the crowded streets and the water pipes had been contaminated by slops from the houses and horse dung from the passing vehicles. What, he wondered, could there be to contaminate the water here?

At last Alexander came across the quarry manager Mr Guthrie and knowing there were no natural springs on Orchy, he demanded to know where the islanders obtained their water supplies.

Guthrie answered defensively.

'If there is trouble with the water, the people have only themselves to blame,' he declared.

Water was just one of many contentious issues regularly brought up by the workers who considered that hauling barrels of water from a spring on the Isle of Lunga constituted a part of the work for which they were employed and should be carried out during working hours for suitable payment.

'There have been squabbles amongst the men,' Guthrie confessed, 'and they have refused to go to Lunga for water. For some while the islanders have subsisted on water from the rain barrels but since this dry spell set in supplies have become very low.'

He did not elaborate upon the fact that water had been drawn from barrels long neglected, from troughs reserved for the cattle and even from cisterns intended for the steam boilers which operated the quarry machinery.

'As I said, they have only themselves to blame.'

He tried not to show his deep satisfaction that his stand against paying the men to fetch the water had paid off. The Company would not have welcomed such unnecessary inroads into their profits!

'It is not clear to the medical profession what is the cause of this disease,' Alexander told him, icily, 'but it is certain that an unclean water supply is associated with its onset. I suggest that you ensure a plentiful supply of fresh water in the future at whatever cost, if you wish to keep your men working rather than languishing in their sick beds. Meanwhile an order should be issued to every household to boil all water which is intended for human consumption.'

*

Dr Alexander Beaton, calling at the suggestion of the old engineman, Angus McPhail, found Jessie Dundas working laboriously over her son. The room was dark and airless, the shutters closed over both windows.

'I understand that your children are sick, Ma'am,' he addressed her. 'I have been visiting several houses on the island where there is trouble and the engineman down the way suggested you might need my services.'

She was a good-looking woman with striking eyes and well cut features. Her strong, sturdily built frame was clearly capable of heavy work. She had indeed been employed at one time in the coal mines of Lanarkshire where she was born. Undernourished as she was now, Jessie appeared gaunt, the wasted flesh hung from her bones giving the appearance of a woman older than her thirty-three years. Dark purple shadows surrounded her deeply sunken eyes and the tiredness of many days without sleep gave the impression that she had given up all hope, submitting to her fate without protest.

'My little girl is already dead,' she told him, wringing out a cloth as she spoke and laying it gently on her son's forehead. Her voice was devoid of all expression. 'My son screams in pain intermittently and then just lies still almost unconscious. I do not know what is worse, the crying or the silence.'

In the dimly lit room he had not noticed a second occupant until the minister rose awkwardly from his knees. He had been saying prayers over the dead baby.

'Ah, Doctor, at last!' The cleric extended his hand. 'I gather your father was unable to come, himself.'

Alex, unwilling to spare a moment of his time in idle and unnecessary conversation, moved James brusquely to one side and stooped down beside the woman, taking her patient's wrist between his fingers and laying his other palm on the hot little brow. He questioned her minutely about her treatment, nodding in agreement with all she had done. The bilberry posit she had administered had been an inspiration. He was not always as dismissive of the country remedies as many of his contemporaries and this was one he had seen used to good effect during his boyhood.

'It was Mrs Bantrie, the minister's wife, who brought it,' Jessie explained glancing guardedly in the direction of her other guest. 'Do you think he will survive, Doctor?'

Alexander continuing with his examination, grunted with concern at some symptoms and with satisfaction at others. He reached into his medical bag and once again drew out the phial containing sulphuric acid. He dropped a little of this into a cup of boiled water and gently lifted the boy's head so that he could force a spoon between his lips. At last he replaced the covers over the boy and turned to her, smiling.

'He seems to be doing as well as anyone could expect in the circumstances, Mrs Dundas,' he told her. 'With such excellent nursing, your son cannot fail to make a good recovery.'

Despite the trials of the night and her extreme weariness Jessie smiled her relief at his words and for a few seconds Alexander felt that the room had shed some of its gloom. Then Jessie turned to the tiny form wrapped tightly in its shawl and her dry eyes filled with tears once again.

'The poor wee thing,' she spoke as of a lost kitten or a pet dog. 'Little Millie never knew her father. She was but three months old when he died. There was always something ethereal about her. It was perhaps that she knew her time was short. Her father will be glad of her company.'

She spoke so confidently of an after life that even Alexander, normally a confirmed sceptic in such matters, felt the glow of comfort her words engendered.

James Bantrie, intending to use this testament of faith as a source of contact, suggested that all three of them should give praise to the Father for saving the boy.

Alexander would have joined the minister in his prayers for the sake of decency but Jessie turned on him.

'Thank Him?' she was almost shouting, 'what has your God done that we should thank Him? He has taken my husband and now my innocent little child. He has destroyed my life! What is there to be thankful for?'

'Your son has survived.'

'Due to your wife's knowledge and my own nursing,' she insisted. 'Do not ask me to give thanks where they are not due.'

Crushed, James Bantrie appealed to the doctor for his support. Alexander, disinclined to be brought into this exchange decided upon a more practical course.

'Will you rebuild the fire, Minister,' he suggested, 'Mrs Dundas needs a cup of hot sweet tea. I will carry the little girl to the mortuary.'

He lifted the tiny bundle in his arms and when Jessie made to protest, he stilled her protest gently. 'It is for the best, Mrs Dundas,' he told her. 'The village people are dealing with the dead. Your little girl is one of many who have succumbed to the disease. I believe that there is to be a mass burial. It will be best if she does not remain here with your son so sick.'

Without further protest, Jessie returned to her sponging of the boy's hot little body, scarcely lifting her head as Alexander carried Millie out of the house. When he returned some time later he found that the minister had rolled up his sleeves, had a good fire going and a kettle singing on the hob. He had gathered up Alexander's instruments and replaced them in the doctor's bag and had collected together all the soiled bed linen.

'The women have set up a communal wash-house to cope with the laundry,' he explained to Alex. 'I shall take this along for them to deal with and then return home. I hope that you will join us for a little breakfast when you are finished here?'

'Thank you Mr Bantrie, I shall join you later.'

Alexander was inordinately pleased that his ploy had paid off so well. The Minister seemed to have benefited from his practical activities. Perhaps if he concentrated a little more upon the provision of material comforts for his parishioners and less upon their souls both his and their lives might be improved. He thought once again of the sad-eyed, hysterical woman he had met at the Manse that morning and believed that he understood her problem better now that he had met her husband.

When he presented himself again at the Manse it was approaching midnight and Alexander was half a mind to spend the night beside the engine minder's fire, rather than disturb the minister and his family. Angus, however, had received strict instructions from Bantrie that the doctor was to be sent on to the manse as soon as he appeared and so Alex found himself once again knocking on the door of the house beside the church.

The minister himself opened to him and when he was ushered into the living room he found a good fire burning in the grate and a table fairly creaking with food. Only when his eye lighted upon the haunch of cold mutton on the table and his nose detected the appetizing smell of stew simmering on the hob, did he realise how hungry he was.

The Bantries gave him a warm enough welcome but he could not avoid noticing how Judith directed all her questions and all her attentions to himself with the complete exclusion of her husband. He thought this was taking hospitality to extremes until he noticed how aptly James handled things and realised that this must be their normal way of living. It was as though these two souls shared nothing in common but the roof under which they slept. It must be a cold bed they occupied at night.

The contemplation of a bed, any bed, brought on the drowsiness he had been fighting off all through the meal.

Judith had been describing the children.

'Catherine you will be sure to meet in the morning. She is a good girl. She will be up in good time to prepare breakfast for us all before she goes to school. Her wee brother Charles on the other hand is a bundle of mischief but a likeable enough child all the same. Our son, Ian, is away fishing. Fergus McLean has taken the *Maid of Orchy* to the outer isles and Ian was invited to go along for the trip. It is a little reward for his hard work. He is Mr Guthrie's apprentice you know and is soon to travel to Cornwall to learn more about the mining trade. We shall miss him terribly of course but Mr Guthrie believes him clever enough to be a proper engineer. He will almost certainly become a mine manager himself one day.'

Her obvious pride in her eldest son reminded Alexander of his mother's very embarrassing monologues about his own merits and those of his brother, delivered usually while entertaining the village ladies at sewing parties at Tigh na Broch.

Although there was little or no exchange between the minister and his wife her prattling kept up the semblance of hospitable conversation until Alexander was no longer able to keep his eyes open. As he nodded off and came to abruptly for the third or forth time, James Bantrie said sharply, 'Judith, our guest needs rest before he makes his homeward journey. Will you retire while I see to the making of his bed yonder. He indicated the box-bed in the corner.'

'It's a little cramped for one of your stature,' he remarked, estimating Alexander's height as more than six feet.

'Don't worry, Mr Bantrie,' Alex assured him, 'I could sleep anywhere tonight and that bed looks uncommon comfortable to me.'

The minister fussed about for a few minutes with cushions and rugs as though reluctant to leave Alex and go to his own bed. Sensing that the man needed to talk Alex opened his medical bag and extracted a flask of whisky.

'I always keep a little by me,' he explained, 'in case an operation is needed.'

When he observed James' startled expression he laughed. 'Not for me, for the patient. It helps you see, with the pain.'

James nodded somewhat relieved to hear Alex's reassurances and fetched a couple of glasses.

As they sipped at the smooth, peaty spirit, James blurted out suddenly, 'You must forgive Judith. It is not her fault you know, the way she is. She was a fine girl when I married her, the toast of the town until I reduced us to these distressful straights. We had an excellent living near Inverness until I chose to abandon it for my principles.'

No one who had been living in Edinburgh three years before could have failed to appreciate the enormity of the step taken by so many clergy when they left the established church to set up their own organisation. Alex had heard of many men of the cloth who had suffered great deprivation for their principles.

'I do not profess to understand the reasons for your actions,' he ventured now, 'but I am sure they were fully justified. A man like you would not take such a measure without good cause.'

'If only Judith would agree with you.' James sighed and downed the last of his whisky.

'Your wife is not behind you in this?' Alex asked. So, this was the cause of the distance between them.

'She says she supports my action, but I cannot help feeling that she resents what has happened to us and blames me for our present discomfort. I am desperate to find a way out of my dilemma. How I envy you, a young man with a profession which knows no compromise, setting out in a new career with the world your oyster.'

Alexander did not feel able to disillusion him. He could not take his mind off the bed which awaited him.

'Perhaps you should consider an even more drastic move,' he said now, yawning as he remembered the snippet about New Zealand in his father's paper. 'You might be better off in the colonies. I understand that there is an expedition being formed to settle in New Zealand.'

He removed his jacket and loosened his collar, indicating his need to rest and at last James took the hint and left him to his bed. The instant Alex's head rested on the pillow, he was asleep.

James, on the other hand, lay awake in the dark. Judith's stiff form occupied the very edge of the bed ensuring that no part of their bodies might come into contact. As he listened to his wife's gentle breathing he thought about Alexander's final words.

A new colony with its own rules to make, far away from the machinations of a society which he had come to despise, why should he not join this expedition? Was this not exactly what Murdo McLeod had advocated three years before?

*

Hugh Beaton awaited his younger brother's return with impatience.

Although his journey across the neighbouring island of Lunga had taken nearly an hour, it took him only a few moments to certify the fisherman washed up onto Garbh Riabhag had died as the result of drowning. There was nothing suspicious about the death. He could sign the report to the Procurator Fiscal with a clear conscience.

When Alexander had not returned by evening he was convinced the outbreak of fever on Orchy must be more than an isolated case. He contemplated taking a boat out to the island himself but at his father's insistence, he agreed to wait until noon the following day before joining his brother. That would mean cancelling the dinner arrangements he had already made with his fiancée. For much of the morning he fretted over the possibility that he might have to postpone his announcement and was therefore very relieved to see Alexander alight from the post chaise at a few minutes before noon and stumble wearily up the drive towards the house.

He hurried out to meet him.

'How was it?' Hugh demanded as Alexander approached. He took his brother's medical bag and half in fun and half from necessity supported him to the surgery door.

'Eleven deaths during the past three days,' Andrew reported. Three were elderly people, one was a father of three and there were seven children. There has been some dispute about who should fetch the barrels of spring water from Lunga and the islanders have been using water from stagnant sources so I have ordered everyone to boil the drinking water until the clean supply is restored. The women had the matter well under control except for their insistence on using caster oil. In almost every fatal case death was due to a perforated colon. I have left strict instructions as to medicaments and dosages, now it is up to them.'

'It has been a long dry summer,' observed Hugh. 'We can expect a few outbreaks of fever under such circumstances.'

'In the city I can see some excuse for it,' his brother replied, savagely, 'but away out here? The cottages are squalid and too small for the numbers housed in them. We all know that Enteric fever is associated with overcrowded cities and mean streets. This outbreak is surely related in some way to poor sanitation and a contaminated water supply.'

'In the case of Eilean Orchy the problem is scarcity of water, pure and simple,' Hugh agreed with him. 'Even when the rain butts are filled, insufficient is collected from the roofs to supply all the island's needs. Father has been telling them for years that a proper underground cistern is what is required, with a funnel arrangement to extend the catchment area. The Company is prepared to spend a fortune opening new seams to extract larger quantities of slate but they are unwilling to spend a penny more than is unavoidable on the comfort and welfare of the people. The proprietors even begrudged the use of undersized slates for roofing the houses until there was a stockpile so large as to be embarrassing. Even then they only offered the slates if the men would do the roofing themselves, in their own time!'

Alexander threw himself into his father's comfortable arm chair and yawned. 'I could sleep for a week,' he declared.

'Did you get any sleep at all?' Hugh asked.

'Only an hour or two, in a box bed five foot long and three wide. I woke up with cramp, my legs being forced up against my chest!'

The brothers were both tall. Hugh grinned sympathetically.

'Maybe you should snatch an hour or two now before my dinner party this evening.'

Alexander groaned. 'Surely you can do without me,' he protested. 'I shall be sorry company for anyone until I have had a full night's rest.'

'It's important to me,' Hugh insisted. 'It will not be the same if you are not there to share my special moment.'

Certain now that Hugh was going to announce his betrothal, Alexander succumbed to his pleading. 'Just make sure you wake me in time to shave and dress properly then,' he said, getting wearily to his feet to go to his room, 'but not a moment before necessary!'

At the door he turned, remembering his brother's own mission on the previous day.

'Who was your drowned sailor?' he asked, wondering whether he knew the man.

'The boat was from Orchy as a matter of fact,' Hugh answered. 'Parts of the vessel were washed up alongside the body. It is almost certain that all hands were lost although only the one member of the crew has been found so far.'

A sudden stab of recollection, alerted Alexander.

'Did you have a name for the victim?' he asked cautiously.

'No,' Hugh replied. 'They had to send to the island for someone to identify him but the vessel was the *Maid of Orchy* and the skipper, a man called McLean. They were debating whether to continue the search for other bodies or to go immediately to the island with the news. Eventually they decided on the former course thinking it best to bring all the bad news to the people at the one time.'

As he had departed from the Manse that morning, Alexander had congratulated Mrs Bantrie upon the healthy state of her family. How cruel of fate to strike her this further blow just when she imagined that she was safely out of the wood. Unable to articulate the utter despair which Hugh's tragic news had caused him, Alex arose from the chair, recovered his medical bag and ascended to the attic bedroom he had occupied as a child.

Unaware of the distress he had caused his brother, Hugh called after him, 'Best bib and tucker this evening, Bro'. I'll see you are woken in time.'

The moment Alexander's head touched the pillow he fell into a deep and troubled sleep and would probably have lain there until morning had not Hugh bullied him awake, shaking him roughly by the shoulder.

'Come on young 'un. It's six thirty already and we dine at seven!'

He observed Alexander's two day's growth of beard and shuddered. 'Hurry up now. We have guests arriving at any moment!'

Reluctantly, Alexander allowed himself to be hustled and chivvied by his brother into bathing and shaving. With his stubble removed he began to feel more alive. He pulled on the fine cambric evening shirt his mother had laundered with care that morning, and took from the wardrobe the dress suit he had not worn since last Hogmanay. With a final glance in the wardrobe mirror, a tug at the collar of his elegantly cut jacket and an unnecessary brush to the silk lapels he descended to the ground floor, satisfied that even Hugh would find nothing wrong with his appearance.

His brother had said he had a surprise for them all. His career was settled so there was only one other disclosure for him to make. It was certain he was about to announce his betrothal, but to whom? Alexander had been away so long he had no knowledge of the eligible females in the district. His mother had spoken of new families arrived in the district while he had been away. He supposed that Hugh's ideal woman was one of these.

Refreshed and curious to know what surprise his brother had in store for him, Alex took the stairs two at a time arriving in the entrance hall just as Hugh's visitors rang the bell. Before Alexander could open the door, Hugh emerged from the dining room where he had been supervising last minute arrangements. He thrust his brother to one side and with an expansive gesture, threw the door wide.

To Alexander's amazement Hugh ushered in His Lordship's Factor, Martin McColl and his wife. Hovering demurely in the background behind her parents, her beautiful face outlined exquisitely by the swansdown trimming to her blue velvet hood, stood Anna McColl.

'You will remember my brother, Alexander,' Alex heard Hugh's voice as though muffled by fog or from somewhere far away. Blissfully unaware of the distress Alexander's unexpected presence was causing to all three of his visitors, Hugh introduced Anna's parents.

'Good evening, Alexander,' Mrs McColl was the first to recover her composure. 'Hugh did not mention that you had returned home. Have you completed your studies?'

Alex took the delicately gloved hand and bowed over it.

'Yes, Ma'am,' he replied, 'I arrived home a few days ago.'

McColl nodded to him, embarrassed. He cleared his throat nervously and said, 'Alexander.' They shook hands and the Factor passed on to where Malcolm Beaton and his wife waited in the room beyond.

'Anna, I don't know if you ever met my brother? Oh, but of course, you must have been at school together, how stupid of me.'

Hugh, five years older than Alexander, had already gone off to Edinburgh to study by the time that Anna and Alexander had begun to take notice of one another. Although the brothers had shared one year together in Edinburgh, Alex as a first- year student had seen little of Hugh who was already walking the wards and taking his final examinations. It was not surprising therefore that Hugh was unaware of Alex's friendship with Anna. Why, he wondered had Anna never mentioned him to Hugh?

Alexander, now utterly dumbfounded by the shock of encountering Anna in these circumstances, was unable to offer any but the briefest greeting. Could this vision of loveliness be that same tomboy who could sail a boat as well as any lad her own age, the teacher's pet who had beaten them all when it came to solving meaningless algebraic equations, the scrawny girl with whom he had romped in the heather and from whom he had stolen his first adolescent kiss? Could this dainty, fair haired Venus be his Annie McColl, the girl who at the age of twelve years he had sworn to marry? Could this be the girl to whom his brother now laid claim?

When they were children she had been party to all his dreams, all his ambitions. When he had had time to think about her at all during his exile in the city, it had been to imagine her going about her parish duties, performing such tasks as any daughter of the gentry might be expected to undertake. He had envisaged her in the role of benefactress, bringing succour to the poor and sick of the parish. He had imagined her as he had known her, striding across the hills with her dogs at her heels or gathering roses in her mother's walled garden close by the castle where her father worked. Most of all he had imagined her waiting patiently for his return. Never in all his imaginings had he seen her as someone else's wife!

They had talked together so often, in those balmy evenings with which the summers of their youth seemed endlessly blessed. They had spoken of the time when he would take over his father's practice and be appointed Medical Officer for the quarries. They had imagined how, as the doctor's wife, Annie would get to know his patients as well as he, roll his bandages and prepare his pills for him, write fair copies of his letters (his own hand was almost indecipherable) and keep the accounts, for she was so much better at figures than he.

What he wanted more than anything at this moment was to gather her in his arms, to caress her fair cheeks, to bury his face in her lustrous chestnut hair and kiss her beautiful mouth. In a voice hardened by disappointment and yearning, all he could find to say was, 'You're looking well, Anna.'

As Hugh solicitously removed her cloak and carried it away, she returned Alexander's bewildered stare and murmured, 'I felt sure you had decided to remain in Edinburgh, that you had been lured away from this simple life. I imagine you to have been absorbed by those sophisticated city circles in which you have been moving all these years.'

He was too tongue tied to deny it.

'For months, I waited eagerly for your letters,' she remonstrated. 'Only my parents know what agonies of despair I went through, waiting for letters to arrive which never came, wondering what I had done to annoy you, to make you so disappointed in me, to turn you away. At last I came to accept that I had been living a childish dream and that all those plans which we had made as children were mere fantasy. The reality was that you had dismissed this backwater from your plans and in so doing you had forgotten my existence.'

Hugh, quite unaware of the tension between them, returned at that moment in high spirits and Anna turned to him with a smile. She placed her hand on his arm in so proprietary a manner they might have been married for years.

'Come, Mama is waiting,' Hugh told her and bent to whisper something in her ear. She laughed, the sweet sound striking a chord in Alexander's memory and twisting the knife in his already battered heart.

Alex approached the coming meal with dread, afraid that by his manner or his words, he might betray his true feelings for Anna. When the time came at last for Hugh to announce the betrothal and for Malcolm Beaton to rise and propose a toast to the happy pair, it was as much as Alex could do to repeat his father's words.

'Anna, Hugh, your happiness!'

He swallowed the drink, nearly choking in so doing and hurriedly excused himself from the company. In the darkness of his own room with the drapes pulled back to expose the night sky, he lay fully clothed upon the bed and nursed his wounded pride. This final blow had determined his future. He must get away, far, far away. Even the other side of the world could not be distance enough!

Chapter Five

Judith Bantrie had spent the hours following Alexander Beaton's departure, in the company of Jessie Dundas. Following the doctor's directions, she had located wee Millie's body in the disused engine house which had been commandeered to serve as a mortuary and under Jessie's direction she had dressed the child in her Sunday pinafore, washed her face and platted her hair. Then they laid Millie in the little wooden coffin which had been hurriedly constructed by the island's only carpenter.

'Ma' wee sleeping angel,' Jessie murmured as she bent to give her little girl one final kiss. She placed a tiny posy of wild flowers at Millie's waist and dry-eyed, she looked on while the carpenter screwed down the lid of the coffin.

It was a simple enough service which Judith had provided for her friend but as they walked out into the stormy night, away from that quiet morgue, Jessie pressed her hand and in a tone so low as to be almost indecipherable, she said, 'Thank you. I do not know what I would have done without your support. It is good to have a friend at such a time.'

Judith was embarrassed by the compliment. She was only too aware of the distance which the other island women had put between themselves and Jessie Dundas and her insistence on supporting the woman had as much to do with her own rebelliousness in the face of island prejudice as any compassion she might have held for the widow.

'I am sure that you would have done the same for me, were the positions reversed,' she replied, rather more sharply than intended.

James returned from visiting some of his parishioners to find Judith crouched disconsolately beside the dying fire. He was dismayed to see that any remaining spark, any of the enthusiasm for life which he had once so admired in his wife, had slipped away. There had been a difference in her for several months past but the greatest change had come since the death of Jessie's little girl. When she became aware of James standing in the doorway she shouted aloud, 'If that should happen to me, if I should lose one of my bairns, I would kill myself!'

'You can't mean that,' he admonished her outburst. 'That is a wicked thing to say.' Distressed as he was himself at the deaths of so many of his parishioners, James was nevertheless shocked by Judith's words.

'You would be putting yourself outside the Lord's protection' he admonished her. 'Besides, what would the rest of us do without you?'

'Jessie is a good woman who has harmed no one. What kind of a God is it that can allow one so gentle to suffer so much?' she demanded.

'That is just what Jessie Dundas asked me, herself,' he replied, utterly defeated. 'I had no answer for her and I have none for you.'

He sat down at the table and buried his head in his hands.

'I have to go back' Judith determined, suddenly. 'The boy needs constant attention and Jessie has been up for three nights in a row.'

'Young Thomas was sleeping soundly when I looked in on my way back,' James protested.

'Nevertheless, I must see if there is anything more I can do to help Mrs Dundas. If I am needed, I shall stay all night.' Judith made no mention of any provision she might have made for her own family. James looked around in vain for a sign that she had prepared a meal for them. With a sigh, he went to the press and took out what remained of the shoulder of mutton which was all they had had by way of meat, since the epidemic began.

As Judith stepped out into the gloomy afternoon, she held on to her hat and gathered her plaid tight about her. The blustery winds following the storm had scarcely abated and the air was chill despite the summer season. Intent as she was upon her mission of mercy, she gave not a thought to James or her own children. Even Ian had been put to the back of her mind. The Dundas boy required beef tea. She would call in at the village store and see what Mr McDowell had by way of meat.

In Judith's absence, James crouched beside the stove searching for an answer to his dilemma. How was he to get his loved ones out of this dire situation into which he had led them? Ian's future was settled. He had already discovered his way of escape. James thrust aside the notion that Ian would be under any obligation to work on Orchy once he had completed his engineering studies. There was no law which said he must return here. There were plenty of other places in the world where a mining engineer might find a living. Catherine was fast approaching womanhood. Soon it would be time for her to marry but how would she find anyone suitable in this awful place? Who among the islanders could provide the life her ready wit and her astute brain deserved? Without a suitable sparing-partner the girl would whither and fade in these prosaic surroundings. She might study of course, become a teacher perhaps, or a governess. She might even marry into one of the families of the landed gentry but how was she to meet such people stuck out here on this desolate island? Outside, the sky darkened and the unnatural gloom of the summer day served only to add to his despair. He leaned forward to place fresh coals on the dying fire and as he did so he became aware of a hesitant tapping at the door.

When he failed to respond immediately, the door was pushed open and Flora stepped over the threshold. James looked up to see that her husband, Thomas Guthrie, hovered at her back. James looked from one to the other of his visitors reading both apprehension and fear in their chalk-white faces.

As the Guthries hesitated in the doorway, James regarded them with a questioning glance. Assuming they had brought further bad news of the epidemic, he ushered them inside and bade them sit down before delivering their message.

'We have terrible news, James,' Flora began, hesitantly.

'It's about the *Maid of Orchy*,' Thomas explained.

James stared at them uncomprehending. What had a fishing smack to do with the epidemic on the island?

'The *Maid of Orchy*?' he enquired.

'Fergus McLean's boat,' Thomas confirmed.

'I know the vessel,' James said, impatiently, 'Ian has gone fishing aboard her. They will be away for some days yet. They have sailed to the outer isles fishing for cod.'

He caught an exchange of glances between his two friends.

'What is it?' he demanded. 'What's the matter?'

'No Minister,' Flora corrected him sadly, 'it seems they never got beyond Scarba. It is rumoured *The Maid of Orchy* foundered in the Corryvreckan, three days ago.'

James shuddered as a cold chill crept over him. He knew full well that a small fishing boat stood little chance of survival if it was sucked into those infamous whirlpools.

'You said rumoured,' he rasped. 'There is yet no proof?'

'The body of one member of the crew was washed up on Dearg Sgeir.'

She watched the dawning of comprehension in the minister's face and then the mixture of agony and anger which suffused it.

'After the first body was discovered and identified, a search was carried out first on Lunga and then once the storm had abated, among the surrounding islands.' It was Thomas who now took up the tale. 'Two more bodies and wreckage from the same boat have been washed up on Scarba. They were discovered this afternoon.'

'Ian?' James demanded in a strangled voice.

Guthrie cleared his throat nervously. 'It's impossible to say. The bodies must have been in the water for a long time and with the rocks...' He could not bring himself to disclose the details he had been given. 'Only someone who knows the men intimately would be able to tell.'

Flora was sobbing.

'I wanted Guthrie to go to identify the body, but they insisted it should be you,' she cried.

'You say three have been found? There is one other still missing. Yes, that must be it. Ian has yet to be found. He must be alive. I would know if my son were dead!'

Thomas pressed a cheap watch and chain into James' hand. 'This was taken from one of the bodies as a possible means of identification.'

James stared down at the inscription which he himself had had engraved inside the case before giving it to Ian on the day he had signed the boy's apprenticeship papers.' *Ian Bantrie from his father. May 3rd. 1846.*

'No!' He mouthed the word. It was not a scream. He threw back his head and with his mouth wide open in a silent shout of protest he clamped his hands over his ears as though to ward off any further ghastly tidings. This was indeed the end of everything. God could have used no harsher punishment than this. Slumping down in his chair, he buried his head in his hands and wept.

Thomas and Flora, unsure what they should do now that the message was delivered, waited silently for him to recover from the shock. They were still sitting there when the pendulum clock above the mantle shelf struck eleven and Judith lifted the latch.

*

It was a blustery day. Under full sail, Dougie McDonald's lugger flew before the wind making the crossing to Eilean Orchy in record time.

'Will you anchor off-shore, Dougie?' Hugh Beaton requested as he prepared to leap ashore. He handed Flora Guthrie off onto the beach. 'I could be some time.'

'D'ne worry, Doctor,' Dougie shouted, 'I'll nae leave ye to spend the night on Orchy.' He shuddered in an exaggerated way, indicating his own distaste for the island. Waving them away, he drew his boat clear of the rocks before dropping a sea anchor and preparing his lines for a spot of casual fishing.

Today the quarry was in operation and the noise from the deep pit in which the men worked, was overwhelming. 'What an atmosphere in which to recuperate from any illness,' Hugh muttered as he followed Flora Guthrie along the narrow path beside the railway track.

'How is Mrs Bantrie?' Hugh asked, remembering what his father had told him of the minister's family.

'She is tired and anxious, of course,' replied Flora, 'but she is determined that the boy will live, just as his father was determined that he had not drowned.'

It had taken a further twenty-four hours of searching along the craggy coastline on either side of the Corryvreckan before a lookout on one of the boats had spotted what he thought might be a bundle of rags and called the attention of their companion vessel. A spy glass revealed that what he had seen was a body. There was nowhere to land the boat safely to recover the corpse and it was a further four or five hours before they were able to reach the spot where they could reach it from the cliffs above.

Ian Bantrie was barely breathing when they hauled him to the top and laid him on a makeshift stretcher. Amazed to find the lad still breathing and anticipating that he would be dead before they could get him to a doctor, they had taken him home to Orchy.

Judith immediately despatched Flora to fetch the doctor from Seileachan and set about saving her son with a vigour and determination which astonished her husband. With Jessie Dundas at her side, she had worked tirelessly for an hour, sponging Ian with warm water while Jessie rubbed at every part of his skin with a rough towel, to increase the circulation. When his skin recovered its normal pink colour they had packed hot bricks wrapped in strips of flannel all around his body and piled blankets over him to keep him warm. The boy's lower leg had been badly shattered and the sharp end of one bone stuck out through the calf muscle in an alarming fashion. There had been bleeding of course but the constant immersion in sea water and the cold had reduced the blood flow to a minimum and it had finally stopped altogether. Jessie's activities to restore circulation had started the bleeding off again. Knowing that it was unwise to move the leg more than necessary, she had packed cotton around the wound as tightly as she could in the hope that the blood would dry and prevent further bleeding. Only when the boy seemed to be breathing easily and his colour had been restored to normal, did the two women cease their labours and sit silently supping the hot sweet tea which Catherine had made for them.

James Bantrie, unable to be of any practical assistance in all this activity, withdrew to the church and sank to his knees in prayer. He had believed his son lost and had blasphemed against his God. Now he must beg forgiveness.

*

His father had already acquainted Hugh with the circumstances which brought Minister Bantrie and his family to Eilean Orchy. In Edinburgh, Hugh had witnessed those scenes of unrest and violence three years before and he knew how strongly some churchgoers felt about the clerics who had abandoned their traditional livings on principle. He did not understand the passions that had moved them to such lengths, but he respected their right to rebel and had refused to participate in the student ribaldry concerning them.

As he and Flora Guthrie neared the manse, the minister's daughter Catherine, came running to greet them. She was dishevelled, her skin pale, her cheeks sunken in from lack of sleep and too much heavy work. When she saw Hugh she stopped and stood defiantly in his path.

'Where is Dr Alexander Beaton?' she demanded. 'Mother wanted Dr Alex. She will be very vexed if she finds he has not come himself!'

'Hush child,' Flora remonstrated. 'This is Dr Hugh Beaton, Dr Alexander's brother. He is the proper doctor.'

'But mother likes Dr Alex,' wailed the girl, 'and so do I!'

Flora would have remonstrated with her again but Hugh dissuaded her.

'My brother was obliged to leave home rather more suddenly than we would have wished,' he explained to Flora. 'Don't worry about the child, Mrs Guthrie she is distressed about her brother's accident.' To Catherine he said reassuringly, 'I feel sure I can help your brother, little miss,' he bent down to pat the child's cheek and received a heavy scowl as his reward.

Despite her disappointment at Alexander Beaton's desertion, Catherine led the way indoors, scolding her young brother as she did so for the untidy state in which he had left his things. Amidst the childish wrangle which followed, Flora ushered the doctor into the poorly lit living room.

They found Jessie Dundas watching over the patient. As the newcomers entered she turned to greet them.

Jessie was stunned. By this unexpected encounter she was transported in an instant to a miserable hospital ward in Glasgow, several years ago. She knew this man. He was that courteous medical student who had been kind to her when her father died. The colour mounted in her cheeks as she hurriedly turned back to her patient, praying the doctor would not recognise her. For his part, Hugh Beaton showed no sign of recognition. Jessie quickly regained her composure but not before Hugh became alerted to her anxiety. He appeared to interpret her reaction to his sudden appearance as concern for the patient.

At last she managed to say, 'It is very good of you to come, Doctor.'

Once it became clear to Jessie that Hugh Beaton had no recollection of their having met before, she breathed a sigh of relief. He may not remember her but she could never forget him.'

'Mrs Bantrie sent for Dr Alexander Beaton.' she said now. 'I'm afraid she will allow no one else to attend her son.'

On hearing her name, Judith emerged from the bedroom. Hugh introduced himself.

'My brother is leaving for Glasgow, on the midday steamer,' he told her. Then noting the despair in Judith Bantrie's eyes, he added, hurriedly, 'but I will be happy to treat your son, Madam, if you will allow me.'

For a moment Judith stared at him blankly then with a shrug, she appeared to accept the inevitable and moved away, leaving Jessie to pull back the covers and expose the patient to the doctor's examination.

Ian lay on the box bed in the corner, apparently sleeping. His colour was good and his pulse was steady. Hugh looked from one to the other of the two women and smiled. 'The vital signs are surprisingly good,' he told them. 'I understand the patient was exposed to the elements for some time?'

'Three days and nights,' volunteered Jessie Dundas. 'He was blue with cold and scarcely breathing when they brought him in. I thought there was nothing we could do for him, but Judith here, Mrs Bantrie, would not accept defeat. She started working on the boy and when I saw what she was about, I lent a hand.'

'You have both done splendidly,' Hugh assured them. 'Now let me examine this leg. Mrs Guthrie tells me it is badly shattered.'

Until this moment the boy had lain with his eyes closed and Hugh had thought him to be sleeping. At the suggestion that his leg was about to receive attention however, his eyes flew open and he stared anxiously at the doctor.

Jessie squeezed his hand reassuringly as Hugh unwound the dressings to expose the injured limb. Dried blood had caused Jessie's cotton bandage to stick to the wound and as the doctor removed it, the boy flinched and the blood began to spurt again.

'There was nothing we could do to straighten the bones,' Jessie explained, 'but we did manage to prevent further bleeding.'

Hugh nodded, relieved to find that no attempt had been made to interfere with the fracture. Further disturbance might have ruptured a main artery and the boy would certainly have bled to death.

Hugh pressed at a point in Ian's groin and the fresh flow of blood ceased instantly.

'Here, place your fingers very firmly where I have put mine,' he told Jessie, easing himself out of her way. 'I must prepare a tourniquet.'

When Judith watched closely as he extracted the thick leather strap from his bag, glimpsing the edge of the bone saw which Hugh had been at pains to disguise. She screamed at him. 'You shall not take his leg. Oh, no! I have not worked all these hours to save him, so that he shall live to be a cripple!'

'Hold hard,' Hugh smiled at her, disarmingly. 'I have no intention of taking away the leg if it can be saved, please believe me. Before I can hope to set the broken bones to rights however I must have the bleeding under control.'

Judith hung her head in apology. Ever since they had carried her boy home, she had been thinking that he would have to spend the remainder of his life minus a leg. She had conjured up pictures in her mind of the mutilated soldiers who begged on the streets of Edinburgh. Even now, with the doctor's reassurance still ringing in her ears, she shuddered at the thought.

While Jessie applied pressure to the point indicated by the doctor, Hugh adjusted his tourniquet. Then he busied himself for some time joining the cut ends of the ruptured artery. Only when he was satisfied that his ligatures would hold, did he order Jessie to release the tourniquet.

They all three, waited with bated breath to see the blood spurt once more but only a trickle of pale yellow fluid seeped from the wound. Now he could examine the fracture from every angle.

It was an untidy fracture of both the bones in the lower leg. The broken ends were splintered with loose pieces of bone lying in the surrounding mangled flesh. The boy was young and until his three-day ordeal appeared to have been well nourished and very fit. With careful manipulation and correct after care the healing should be rapid and successful. The boy should walk again without trouble.

'I'm afraid I can do nothing for him here in bed,' Hugh declared. 'We shall have to transfer him to the table.'

He looked from one to the other of the two women. 'Are there no men available to help me lift him?' he demanded.

'I can do it,' Jessie said and without his instruction took up a position at the lad's feet ready to hold him around the lower limbs.

'He will be too heavy for you,' said Hugh.

'Not at all, Jesse told him. 'It is a matter of knack not strength and I have learned the trick.' With extraordinary ease, Jessie helped him to lift the boy from his bed and lay him on the table.

To get a proper sight of the damage, Hugh decided he would have to open the wound further and requested a bowl of boiling water. Thinking that this might be for cauterisation, Judith flinched but breathed a sigh of relief when she found the doctor had only requested the water to wash his instruments before cutting open the skin. Not all surgeons of the day were as particular, Jessie knew, and viewed him with renewed respect. In that other life, before her marriage, a time she chose never to recall, she had seen some marvellous feats of surgery wasted by the subsequent corruption of the wound with the onset of gangrene, days later.

Hugh was now ready to proceed with setting the broken bones.

'I need some powerful traction to pull the bones apart and set them properly,' he told the two women. 'Is not Minister Bantrie at home? Are there any men about?'

'The men are all at work, in the quarry,' Jessie told him. 'The minister is at his prayers.'

He noticed a note of, what was it, sarcasm perhaps, certainly criticism in her voice. It was clear that Jessie Dundas held little respect for the cleric who had left his wife to cope with their injured son while he made his peace with his Maker.

'I have helped to set bones before,' she announced disregarding her earlier fears that Hugh might recognise her. 'As with the lifting, it is firmness and a certain knack that is needed, rather than strength. Mrs Bantrie and I can manage. Just tell us what to do.'

She was right, of course. He bowed to her common- sense approach and showed the two women where they should take a grip. They stretched the limb so that the bones slid apart. Deftly Hugh grasped the broken ends and rearranged those loose splinters so that when the women eased their grip, the pieces came together satisfactorily straight. The moment when the traction was applied created such excruciating pain that the boy screamed out and then fainted. While he was still unconscious, Hugh bound the bones in place with silver wire and stitched together the edges of the torn flesh, making as neat a mend as he could manage. Where he had extended the wound with a sharp scalpel there was no problem, only the ragged original wound was likely to leave any substantial scarring.

'Hold the leg up while I apply a tight bandage,' he instructed Jessie, regarding her as a competent assistant now that he had seen her at work. When the limb had been made as rigid as possible, he lowered it to the table.

'The leg must be kept immobile for at least six weeks,' he declared looking from one woman to the other. We shall need bags filled with sand to pack against the limb to stop it from moving. Can you manage that?'

Catherine who until now, had watched the proceedings with horrified fascination, was suddenly galvanised into action. 'I can do that, she announced. Let me see to it.'

She rummaged in the wooden chest which contained most of the family's clothing and from the bottom extracted some old pillow cases. An enquiring look towards her mother received immediate assent and she went out to fill the cloth bags with fine shingle from the shore. As she went she called out to her wee brother Charles, 'Here Charlie, this is something you can do. Come on!'

They replaced Ian in his bed and while Jessie tidied up after the doctor, Judith made tea.

Hugh, concerned about the quality of the nursing which would ensure that Ian's leg healed cleanly and that no putrefaction occurred, began to give instructions as to the management of the case.

'There are those who say that a healthy accumulation of puss, aids healing,' suggested Jessie, wondering what his response would be.

'If you had ever experienced the smell of putrefaction in a hospital ward filled with wound and fracture cases, Ma'am, I think you would not say that,' said Hugh, seriously.

'Nevertheless, I have heard that statement put about by at least one surgeon in a very exalted position,' Jessie insisted, 'the professor of surgery at Glasgow Infirmary, no less.'

She realised her mistake the moment she said it. Hugh Beaton must remember her now! What would Mrs Bantrie think of her when she learned that Jessie had once been a ward assistant in the public ward of a hospital? Such women had a low reputation and characteristics were attributed to them that many certainly deserved. She had always tried to keep herself aloof from the worst excesses of these women but anyone who had worked in the wards in those days became tarred with the same brush. Many times she had been branded a slut, a drunkard and much worse, by those who knew no better.

'I wondered where you acquired your skill,' Hugh commented. There had been something nagging at him ever since he had first set eyes upon her. Something about her manner had stirred a faint recollection and now he remembered her. She had asked his opinion as to what to do about her dead father. His initial admiration of her beauty and the respect for her nursing skills had suddenly turned to distaste.

'It is not a pleasant job, nursing the sick under hospital conditions,' he remarked. 'Hardy a job for a lady, don't you agree Mrs Dundas?' His tone was sharp and altogether unfriendly. 'I wonder what could have possessed you to take it up.'

Jessie, her secret now exposed, lifted her head defiantly. 'My father was a veteran of the Peninsular War,' she explained. 'He had a wound in his thigh which never really healed. For more than twenty years my mother dressed his running ulcers and when she died I took over the task. Finally, when I could do no more for him at home, he was taken in to the Infirmary and I did my best to nurse him there. We had no money so I was obliged to offer my services generally as a nurse. When my father died, somehow it seemed the natural thing for me to carry on. Until, that is, I met Mr Dundas.'

Judith was amazed to hear her friend's revelation, not so much for its content as for the fact that in all the time that she had know Jessie Dundas she had never disclosed these aspects of her past life. If the village women had got wind of it, it was no wonder they viewed her with such suspicion.

'Your son will make a good recovery, Mrs Bantrie,' Hugh said, abruptly, ignoring her companion. Then, putting down his cup and taking one last look at his patient: 'I shall call in again in a few days or if not me, then my father.'

Jessie was aware of, but hardly surprised by his sudden change of tone. It was clear that his opinion of her was a very low one now he knew of her background. She had to admire his surgical technique however and as she watched Hugh Beaton making his preparations for departure, she could not help but compare him with his brother. They were both handsome, both skilful men but she felt that there was more humanity about the younger man. How remarkable that there should be two such capable medical men in the one family. Hugh was taller than her late husband with narrower shoulders and a paler complexion. The result, she concluded of long hours of study and of working in the foggy, grimy atmosphere of the city. Like Alexander Beaton, he had the red hair and startlingly blue eyes of the true Highlander and his accent betrayed his early use of the Gaelic language. The soft tones and the sibilant sounds of the west coast still surprised her unaccustomed Glaswegian ear.

There was something more however. Both these young men possessed a self assurance and an air of authority which she admired, but while Alexander was modest in the demonstration of his ability, this older brother exhibited a certain arrogance which she did not admire. While he reached for his hat and went to the door Hugh paused and addressed Judith.

'Your son has been badly injured Mrs Bantrie. Do not expect a quick return to full health. He has suffered from both shock and exposure and must be kept quite and well nourished while his bones heal.'

She nodded, and held the door open for him.

'With Mrs Dundas to help me, I shall manage,' she answered.

Hugh ignored the remark, deliberately refusing to acknowledge Jessie any further.

Jessie could not resist a parting thrust of her own. 'Please wish your brother well when you write. We on Orchy have much to thank him for.'

Conscious of the need to return home before the weather changed again for the worse and stranded him on the island for the night, Hugh stepped outside and with his shoulders bent against the strong breeze blowing in from the sea, he fought his way to the shore.

*

James Bantrie moved across to where his son lay sleeping and looked down on the still form. A strong dose of Laudanum had ensured that Ian had a good night's sleep after his ordeal with the doctor. He looked surprisingly comfortable despite the rigid barricade of sandbags ensuring no movement in his right leg. His colour was much more natural and his breathing seemed as normal. James pulled the covers up to the boy's chin and leant over to kiss his brow. Something he had not done for many a year.

James undressed in the kitchen, hoping to creep into bed without disturbing Judith. He must get a few hours rest before it was time to be up and about his business again. Cautiously he opened the door into the bedroom shivering as his bare feet touched the stone floor. Inevitably the door hinge complained, piercing the silence of night. He felt his way cautiously across the cold, slate flags until his feet encountered the soft texture of the rag rug beside the bed. Lifting the covers, he slid beneath them. As he did so, Judith groaned drowsily and turned over towards him, her arm falling across his chest. In a few moments her heat had dispelled his chill and as he closed his arms about her, her relaxed body snuggled into him, finding familiar hollows in which to fit. It had been a long time since she had allowed him to approach so closely. Welcoming her unexpected advance, James felt his body responding with the ferocity of long abstention.

'Oh, my darling,' he breathed, 'it has been such a terrible time. Thank God you are awake. I could not have born another frigid, lonely night. Not after all that has happened.'

He rose above her. Gently thrusting and encountering no resistance, he penetrated further, deeper, until he was engulfed by her. As he thrust, he felt her response to his own rhythm the agony and the ecstasy combining to rouse him to heights he had not know since the day they had arrived on this beleaguered island.

Judith, emerging from her sleep and for the moment forgetting the terrible events of the past week, felt safe and secure within his familiar embrace and gave to their coupling a passion equalling his own. As he moved inside her, feelings, long dormant, took control of her body. She writhed exultantly and expelled that strange, agonized climactic cry of delight which he had always loved to hear.

It was over all too soon, she rolled away from him to face the wall and lay tense and silent for some time. When at last he turned her towards him and kissed her gently on the lips, he tasted the salt tears coursing down her cheeks.

'Why are you grieving my dearest one? 'He comforted her like a child as he gathered her into his arms once more. 'Our boy is sleeping like a babe. Pray God he will soon be well again.'

'I have treated you shamefully,' she wept. 'All these months I have harboured resentment at the loss of the life we used to have. We must take this as a warning. The only important thing is that we are together, the whole family. We might so easily have lost our precious son.'

'My dearest one, can you ever forgive me?' he murmured, 'I had begun to fear that not only had I lost the love of my God, but that I might have lost you too. You won't go away from me again will you?

She regarded him strangely.

'I have been here beside you all the time,' she replied. 'You did not seem to see me.'

As he lay in the dark, looking up at the ceiling and the familiar damp patch in the corner which was gradually taking shape in the dawn light, he thought about what she had said. In his concern for the low state to which he had brought his family, he had never once consulted either Judith or the children as to their feelings in the matter. Rather than allow his wife to accommodate herself to their new situation, he had spent all his waking hours begrudging every difference, every reduction in their standard of living. He had seen no advantage whatsoever in their position. While she had tried to make the best of their new circumstances, he had been no encouragement to her at all.

He turned to look at her as she slept, more relaxed now than he had seen her for a long time. She seemed to be dreaming, thinking of better times perhaps, for that was a smile which played about her lips.

*

'I have come to a conclusion which will affect all our lives, profoundly.' James noted Judith's doubtful expression and added, hurriedly, 'I trust it will be for the better.'

He took from his pocket a letter he had received by that day's post and with irritating deliberation, spread it on the table before him.

Judith and the two younger children were seated at the table with the remnants of their evening meal scatted about them. Ian lay in the box bed in the corner, propped against his pillows. He was more comfortable now that his bandages had been changed. His recovery had been so rapid that on his last visit, the doctor had suggested a little gentle exercise would be beneficial to improving the muscular strength of his legs, provided he did not attempt to put any weight onto his broken limb. The restricting sand bags had been removed to be used from now on only when he was sleeping. As he stretched his good leg luxuriously he made an effort also to tense the thigh muscles of the injured one. He was gratified to find that he could actually feel a slight movement.

Judith regarded her husband with some scepticism. Since Ian's accident, the minister had been kept busy about his parish duties and despite his resolution to pay her more attention and to discuss matters more fully with her, he had been no less absorbed and introverted than before. Any belief she may have harboured that their relationship would improve after that one moment of reconciliation, had been short lived. While they remained in this fearful place, Judith could see no hope of any change in her life. Thus it was that James's sudden declaration failed to raise more than a glimmer of interest.

Catherine, who held her father in the highest esteem, awaited his announcement with rapt attention while Charles wriggled on his stool, anxious to be outside where he could hear his friends preparing for an evening visit to the shore.

'I have been in contact for some months with a clerical friend on the east coast.' James cleared his throat somewhat nervously, 'The reverend Murdo McLeod has made arrangements on my behalf for our passage on an emigration ship leaving from Greenock before the end of the year.'

Stunned, Judith could only stare blankly at him. Words failed her.

Catherine appeared bewildered, while wee Charles piped up with, 'What's an emigration ship?'

'It is a vessel which will carry us to a new world and a new life,' his father explained.

'To where?' Judith demanded.

'New Zealand. There is a colony to be settled in the South Island to be made up principally of Scottish people and,' he paused for effect before continuing triumphantly, 'to be established by members of the Free Church of Scotland! Imagine it Judith,' he went on enthusiastically, 'a place where we can start afresh; make our own rules; create our own standards without fear of interference from those who would divert our church from its true purpose!'

'New Zealand?' Judith had only a hazy notion of the place. 'Why, that is on the other side of the world and peopled by cannibals. Would you have our children grow up amongst savages?'

'Where we are going, there are very few of the native population and I am assured that they are peaceable folk. They will have no reason to trouble us for the New Zealand Company has, quite legitimately, purchased land from them to build a new town. We shall be made welcome and will, I am assured, live harmoniously alongside them.'

'Who will be aboard this ship?' Judith demanded. There were many horrific tales told of the ships sailing to Australia with their holds filled with the derelicts of the western world, the criminals and the adventurers whom no-one wanted here at home.

'The passengers will all be like us, honest folk seeking a new life. Most must find their own passage money and the fare is not cheap I can assure you. Others will have to find sponsors who can guarantee them work in the new colony. These will be artisans and people with special skills. The women will be school teachers, domestic servants, seamstresses and the like, while the men will be those who can contribute to the construction of the town: carpenters; masons; farm labourers and so on.'

'Presumably you do not count as an artisan, so how are we to afford the fare?' she demanded, coldly.

'That is the beauty of it!' he declared. 'The principal Minister of the Church is to be the reverend Thomas Burns of Monkton, but an additional minister is required to look after a more rural parish up-country from the main settlement. It will be a farming community, much like our old parish of Kilmory. What is more, I am charged with caring for the souls of both crew and passengers on the voyage out, a role which carries with it a family cabin on the main deck.'

Only slightly mollified by his assurances, Judith pursed her lips but said no more. If James had made up his mind, there was little she could do to make him change it. Once again he had gone ahead with his arrangements without consulting her. She remained silent while the children plied him with further questions.

'Will I go to school?' demanded Charlie who was just beginning to develop the small boy's natural aversion to lessons. There was always the hope that in New Zealand schools might not exist.

'Indeed you will,' said his father. 'We shall build our own!'

'Will you have your own church also?' asked Catherine. 'Do the natives go to church, Papa?'

'A church will be built and we shall try to persuade the Maori to join us when they are ready.' He glanced quickly at Catherine, 'We shall not however, force them to come to church. That has been tried before and caused trouble in the north of the country.'

'What will Ian do if he is not to be an engineer, after all?' asked Catherine suddenly.

There was a moment's silence. Then from the bed in the corner, Ian spoke for the first time since his father's announcement.

'Who says I am not to be an engineer? My leg will soon be good as new. The doctor said so, only this morning.'

Once Ian had adjusted to the idea that he was not to enter the Ministry, he had knuckled down to work with Thomas Guthrie with a determination which had amazed his parents. He himself had been surprised to find that mathematics and science were all-absorbing subjects for study. He looked forward most eagerly to the period of training which had been organised for him in the Cornish mines and he was not about to forgo the opportunity which the experience might afford. Just because his father had decided to go off to the far side of the globe, did not mean that he must follow. Soon he would be eighteen, quite old enough to make his own decisions and to take care of himself.

'Of course you must come with us. We shall go as a family,' James insisted, glancing anxiously at Judith. He knew that if Ian refused to accompany them, she would never leave.

'I'm sorry Pa. I must insist.' Ian was adamant. 'Already your actions have thwarted my boyhood ambition to enter the Church. Now I have found something else which I want to do more than anything. I want to be an engineer. My employers have seen fit to pay for my training. You cannot stop me now!'

It was true. Although his wages would be small, when Ian went to Cornwall his food and accommodation would be all found. That was the arrangement made with the Quarrying Consortium who would sponsor him. There was no question of his father having to support him. James was forced to concede that his son was now an independent man with a mind of his own and with every right to make his decisions for himself.

Judith however, would have none of it. 'Much as I loath this place and would welcome any means by which we might leave it, I will not have my family split asunder. Either we all go, or none of us does.'

Without waiting for a response from any of them, Judith stamped out of the room. Astonished at this extraordinary outburst her husband and children remained seated until they heard her slam the outer door.

'Your mother is overwrought,' James muttered, embarrassed at his wife's behaviour. 'She has had much to contend with of late.'

Ian, a little ashamed of his own part in the incident, now apologised. 'I'm sorry, Pa. I was thoughtless. I should have waited until Mama had had a chance to assimilate your proposal. I think it has come as a shock to us all.'

'I too am at fault, 'his father replied. 'I should have broken the news a little more diplomatically. The fact is, I have been so taken up with finding some solution to our problems that when one actually presented itself, I could contain my excitement no longer. I thought you would all be as delighted as I to learn that there is a new and challenging opportunity for us if we have the courage to take it!'

'Oh yes, Father, I want to go!' Catherine cried and flung her arms about his neck to show him he was not alone.

'Me too,' declared Charles who could imagine nothing more exciting than sailing to a place half a world away in a great sailing ship just like the ones which took slate from the quarries to the West Indies and North America.

'I must go and find your mother,' James told them. 'Catherine, clear away the dishes. Let us have everything spick and span when she returns. Let us show her how we can get things done when we all work together.'

Obediently, Catherine began to tidy away the remnants of their meal. After a moment of rebellion, Charles too began to help by ladling water into the great pot beside the stove and placing it to boil. James left them to their tasks and drew on his warm overcoat, for the September evenings were chilly despite the brightness of the days. Noticing that Judith had gone out without her cloak, he took it with him and disappeared into the gathering dusk.

*

James found his wife where he knew she would be, on the furthest point to the west of the island, gazing out over the ocean. Judith shivered in the evening breeze clutching her arms about her in a gesture which seemed designed to fend off all comers. The blue -grey of a darkening sky was tinged with red by the setting sun, and while that huge red orb poised on the horizon before her at her back, the moon already hung low in the eastern sky.

Wordlessly James placed the warm cloak about her shoulders. She did not acknowledge his gesture but nevertheless she hugged the woollen garment to her. Soon she began to feel warmer and calmer.

'I have erred again, despite all my promises,' he admitted. His voice was warm and friendly as she remembered it in the early days of their courtship.

'There is no use my asking for your forgiveness. I do not deserve it. I would have discussed the matter with you, really I would, but I was so afraid that nothing would come of McLeod's promises that I dared not raise your hopes. Now I see that I should have spoken of the possibility at the very least.'

She turned to him, her eyes red with crying, tears still damp upon her cheeks.

'It is not so much that you have gone ahead with your plans without speaking to me,' she claimed. 'I ought to be grateful that you understand my hatred of this place and my need to get away. Rather it was Ian's refusing to join us. That was the last straw! After that terrible night when we thought we might lose our son, I prayed to God for forgiveness for losing faith in Him. When Ian began to get well I could almost believe that He had. It seemed he wanted us to be a complete and united family. Together we can be invincible. Now here is Ian wishing to branch out on his own, telling us he can do without our support.'

'It was bound to happen one day,' said James. 'He could not remain tied to your apron strings forever. After all, this proposed training in Cornwall would have meant we would not see him for as much as two years.'

'Oh I know it is foolish of me,' she answered. 'Cornwall is a long way away, but it is not overseas. If needs be, we could reach him in the space of a few days. New Zealand is months away and the route hazardous. If we leave him behind, we may never see him again!'

'You must think more positively Judith. As an unschooled lad, the boy would arrive in our new country unfitted for any work and having to take on tasks that others could fulfil equally well. As a mining engineer he will be sought after in a territory with untold treasures to be found beneath its surface. Two years in Cornwall now, will make all the difference to the boy's future in New Zealand.'

'You mean he will come out to join us?'

'Why should he not? You'll see. One day he will make all our fortunes!' There was no point in voicing any disquiet now he had her attention. Surely their son would want to follow them, eventually.

Chapter Six

1847

A chill south-easterly wind blew in from the river whipping along narrow streets between the tall tenements and swirling around the ornamental copings of prestigious red granite buildings in the city centre. Holding onto his hat with one hand while he grasped the thick folds of his heavy winter cloak with the other, Alexander Beaton hurried along glancing from time to time at the numbers displayed beside each magnificent portico. Coming at last to the one shown on his paper he climbed three white marble steps to the front door and entered the building.

The entrance hall was dark. Alexander's steps echoed through the vast empty space as he crossed black and white marble tiles to the reception desk and rang for attendance. While he waited his eyes slowly became accustomed to the gloom and he could make out something of his surroundings.

It had once been the elegant entrance to premises of some distinction. The walls, heavily panelled in oak, displayed gargantuan oil paintings of past city fathers. They were all men in uniformly dark clothes with spotless linen at their throats and the decorations of high office on their breasts. A magnificent staircase in white Italian marble rose in a gracious curve towards the upper floors. Its complex iron balustrades supported handrails of red mahogany polished smooth over the years by countless gloved hands. The stair carpet, once deep-piled and a shade of crimson, was heavily stained by years of constant use. It was badly worn in places and several of the brass rods were damaged or missing altogether.

The building carried an air of past opulence now gone to seed, the scent of recently applied beeswax being quite incapable of disguising an all-pervading odour of mould and boiled cabbage.

After some moments during which Alexander had time to regret his impulsive decision and had almost made up his mind to leave, a stocky young man in rusty black jacket and stove-pipe trousers emerged from some dark recess and bustled towards the counter.

'Yes, Sir,' he asked, 'What may I do for you?'

'I have come in response to this invitation,' Alexander told him, placing his leaflet face up on the counter.

'Oh yes? You'll be one of those adventuring gentlemen looking for passage to New Zealand.' Did Alexander detect a note of sarcasm or was the man genuinely impressed with the doctor's aspirations?

'Second floor, third door on the right.'

Alexander approached the flight of stairs.

'Not that way. Take the back stairs, through the door at the end.' The fellow indicated the shadowy area from which he himself had emerged moments before.

At the rear of the building a narrow flight of stone steps led steeply to the upper floors. Alexander reached the second landing and paused for breath before pushing open a swing door leading into a dimly lit passage with offices to either side. While the entrance below had appeared merely neglected, on this floor the building seemed ready for demolition. Plaster mouldings festooned in cobwebs, were crumbling under the dampness which penetrated from above and spread in a dark stain across the ceiling. Green paint had peeled from the walls making strange patterns in the dirty plaster. Some doors stood open revealing rooms empty of all but a few packing cases and scraps of paper while from behind others, the soft murmur of voices indicated some sign of occupation

There was nothing which Alexander had seen so far to inspire confidence in the credibility of The New Zealand Company. Referring again to his paper he stopped before the door he was seeking. On a small printed sheet of paper, stuck to the glass panel he read the words:

LAY ASSOCIATION FOR THE PROMOTION OF THE SETTLEMENT OF OTAGO.

Knocking sharply on the door, he turned the round brass knob and went in.

It was a roomy enough office lit by one large window which commanded a view straight down Glassford and Stockwell Street to the river. One enormous desk, occupying the centre of the room, was surrounded by cupboards bulging with bundles of papers jammed in so tightly that the doors would not close. Alongside stood bookshelves into which were crammed folios and ledgers, heaps of papers and vast leather-bound tomes of all descriptions. The surface of the desk itself was strewn with piles of documents which concealed all but the bald pate and be-whiskered face of the room's sole occupant, a cheerful person of some fifty years and by his dress, a clerical gentleman.

'Good morning. Good morning,' he cried, leaping up and grasping Alexander by the hand. The doctor wondered at the effusive greeting. Were volunteers for emigration so very difficult to find?

'Hutcheson, local secretary,' the fellow introduced himself. 'Do sit down Mr?'

'Beaton, Dr Alexander Beaton.'

Alexander looked about for somewhere to sit. Every available surface was covered.

'Oh, just let me,' said Hutcheson, gathering up armfuls of books from a solid, wooden chair so that Alexander might sit.

'Dr Alexander Beaton you say?' He looked about in vain for somewhere to put down the books and with a sigh consigned them to the floor beneath the window. 'I have known plenty of colleagues called Beaton of course, but I fear I have not heard of an *Alexander* Beaton. So, you are wishing to join our little party to the Southland?'

'I would like to know something more about the expedition before agreeing to join it.' Alexander's desire to get up and go was increasing by the minute. The disorganised condition of the premises and the vagueness of their incumbent served only to convince him that he had made a mistake even contemplating this mad idea.

The enthusiastic Mr Hutcheson ignored Alexander's hesitancy. 'For those willing to take up the challenge it will be a great adventure. Imagine the satisfaction of clearing the land and setting up your own homestead where no white man has been before. Think what it would be like to be there at the creation of a colony able to make its own rules and set its own standards, to inhabit a land where poverty is unknown and where everyone has an equal place in society! Oh, how I envy young people like yourself!'

It all sounded too good to be true.

'The land will be allocated as indicated on this paper,' Hutcheson continued, handing over a sheet of paper and speaking without a pause. He gave Alexander no opportunity to waver. 'You will see that the standard cost is forty shillings per acre but to ensure equal distribution of land for various purposes, allotments are restricted to one quarter of an acre in the town with the opportunity of acquiring in addition, ten acres in the suburbs and grazing land on the outskirts amounting to twenty-five acres. The cost of the entire package is one hundred and twenty pounds, ten shillings!' he announced triumphantly. 'Where in the world would you find a better bargain than that?'

'Where indeed,' Alexander agreed. 'Regrettably I cannot raise a hundred and twenty shillings to buy land, let alone one hundred and twenty pounds! It was not as a land owner that I had hoped to sail,' he explained, 'but in my professional capacity. To be frank Mr Hutcheson I do not have the cost of the fare about me let alone the means of purchasing land on arrival!'

'Oh, I see.'

The cheery gentleman tried unsuccessfully to disguise his disappointment. He had met at least a dozen others this week alone, wishing to work their passage. What he needed were fare-paying passengers willing to sponsor others less fortunate than themselves. Of such as Alexander Beaton, he had plenty.

'Then I fear I cannot help you, not on this trip at least,' he said. 'We already have a Doctor of Divinity appointed to administer to the moral and religious comfort of the emigrants on board ship. The spiritual leader of the new colony is Dr Thomas Burns who set sail in the *Philip Laing*, earlier this month. Our man, sailing with *The Albatross*, will become Dr Burns's assistant in New Zealand and is expected to establish his own parish up-country from Dr Burns's parish of New Edinburgh.'

'I am a Doctor of Medicine,' Alexander corrected him, 'and I was given to understand, by the gentleman who spoke to the public meeting at the Tron Church last evening, that there was a position aboard ship for a surgeon.'

Hutcheson dropped the papers he had been flourishing as he spoke and held up his hands in genuine surprise.

'My profuse apologies, my good sir!' he cried, 'A medical man, upon my soul? Now that's a different kettle of fish altogether!'

'Then the position is still vacant?' Alexander was not sure whether the idea pleased him or no.

'It is indeed!' Hutcheson was almost as enthusiastic as he had been when he thought Alex was to be a paying passenger.

'You will wish to see my credentials.' Alexander withdrew from his inside pocket a leather-bound cylinder containing a number of documents carefully rolled so as not to crease them.

'My degrees in medicine and surgery from Edinburgh, a diploma in midwifery from Glasgow although,' he laughed, 'I cannot see too many seamen having need of such services.'

With only a cursory glance at the documents, Hutcheson handed them back.

'You might be surprised how many births there have been amongst the passengers on similar journeys, Dr Beaton. Four months is the shortest time taken for the trip! There's many a young mother taken in labour who upon setting out was not even aware that she was to give birth! It is said that the children born on board an emigrant ship may well equal the number of infant deaths during the voyage. God's manner of compensation, one must suppose.'

'I trust that is an exaggeration!' Alexander declared, dismayed at the prospect of wholesale deaths at sea.

'It is part of the surgeon's duty to ensure that everything possible is done to prevent sickness and accident but nevertheless, tragedies do happen. Hutcheson seemed resigned to the situation, an attitude which alarmed Alexander yet further.

'Perhaps you should explain more fully, the surgeon's duties,' he suggested. Nothing in the advertisement, nor yet in the lecture he had attended the previous evening, had indicated life-threatening dangers even before arriving in New Zealand.

'You will appreciate that the living quarters are cramped,

particularly for the steerage passengers,' Hutcheson explained. 'The maintenance of cleanliness in the accommodations and indeed of the passengers themselves, are the surgeon's responsibility. Food and water supplies must be inspected regularly and allocated so that all personnel are properly nourished and food is not contaminated. Medical consultations will be held with passengers and crew on a regular basis and it is the surgeon's duty to treat all injuries resulting from accidents on board. No fee will be paid for treatment received by members of the crew but passengers may be charged according to the seriousness of the case and their ability to pay. There is also a question of occupation of passenger's time on board ship. Since idleness and boredom can result in quarrelling and other forms of distress, the doctor is required to draw up schedules for entertainments of every kind to keep the people happy. Regular exercise is recommended and when the weather permits such activities as competitive sports and dancing go down very well.'

'And for all this, I can expect a free passage, otherwise costing at the very most, twenty-five guineas!' It seemed to Alexander a great deal of work and responsibility for the price of a cabin.

'Oh we can be a little more generous than that,' Hutcheson assured him. 'As ships' surgeon, you would be entitled to the normal salary, say thirty guineas for the voyage. In addition, you will receive from the New Zealand Company, one standard parcel of land worth one hundred and twenty pounds ten shillings as I have just described. You will most probably acquire sufficient funds on the journey, amassed from fees charged to fellow passengers, to purchase further packages of land. Some surgeons in similar circumstances in the past have become substantial stake holders from their activities while aboard ship.'

Alexander began to feel less despondent about his prospects.

'What facilities are provided for the surgeon to carry out his duties on board?' he demanded.

'The surgeon's quarters are situated on the main deck, aft, close to the lazaret and medical stores. There is a small dispensary and sleeping cabin where you will have your own accommodation. I believe you will find everything you require.'

'Lazaret? Quarantine quarters? Are they likely to be required?'

Alexander had not considered the possibility of communicable disease aboard ship.

'Always a wise precaution on a crowded vessel,' said Hutcheson, playing down the notion. 'It will be the surgeon's responsibility to ensure that everyone coming on board is examined for symptoms of communicable disease but no matter what precautions are applied, some diseased persons inevitably slip through the net. We are particularly concerned to eliminate those with lung disease and of course, the mentally retarded. In addition, as I mentioned before, the surgeon must supervise all water and food supplies. In fact, should you decide to take the post, Dr Beaton, your first responsibility will be to oversee the proper provisioning of the ship.'

Alexander weighed up the proposition while Hutcheson, to give the younger man a moment for consideration, got to his feet and moved to the window. After a short time he could contain himself no longer.

'Well, what do you say, Doctor? Shall you join us?'

Alexander was still not committed. 'When would you want me to start?' he asked. Perhaps he should take a little longer to make up his mind. He had walked out on his family so suddenly and without any proper explanation. He knew his mother would be distressed at his going even if his brother Hugh would be happy to see him well out of the way.

'Right away would not be too soon.'

Still unable to decide, Alexander looked around the untidy office viewing the clutter with dismay. Was this the atmosphere in which he wanted to begin his working life? Perhaps if his demands were too excessive Hutcheson would make the decision for him.

'Before sailing I shall require a suitable place from which to work, a budget to work to and someone to assist me who knows about the provisioning of ships.'

Hutcheson was not to be put off by these demands. He liked the look of this young doctor and the very fact that he did not immediately jump at the offer of employment showed him to be a man of principle and, he suspected, of high professional standards.

'Help yourself to one of the empty rooms along this corridor.' He noted Alexander's look of surprise and explained. 'Our position here is a temporary one. The building is shortly to be demolished and a splendid new set of offices constructed for the company. Any furniture you require you may take from the other rooms. You met Mr Leny downstairs? Just ask him for what you want. The *Albatross* is lying in the yard at Broomielaw, undergoing a refit,' he continued. 'The First Mate, Mr Wallace, has the task of provisioning. You will be working closely with him. It may be advisable for you to visit the ship and meet him as soon as possible. I will give you a letter of introduction to the captain'

'How many passengers do you anticipate?' Alexander had heard stories of emigrant ships sailing to America with steerage passengers crammed into every available space but that journey took only weeks whereas the voyage to New Zealand amounted to a minimum of four months.

'For such a long journey accommodations must be of a high standard, even for those travelling in steerage,' Hutcheson assured him. 'After all, everyone is a paying passenger even if they are sponsored by others, so all are entitled to the best we can offer. There are berths for two hundred and twenty although it is unlikely that all will be filled.'

'And the crew?'

'A full compliment of thirty is to be catered for. They are all experienced seamen, strong and healthy. It is unlikely the men will trouble you other than with such minor accidents as occur at sea at any time.'

'Your advertisement mentions a sailing date some time in January. Can you not be more specific than that?'Alexander demanded. 'I shall need to travel home to Argyll just once more before we sail.'

'Och, there will be plenty of time for that,' Hutcheson, convinced now that he had found the right man for the voyage, brushed aside Alexander's concerns. His tone changed noticeably however when Alexander requested a small advance on his promised salary.

'I shall require funds to pay for my accommodation until sailing and sufficient money to equip myself for the journey.' He cast his glance down the necessities listed on the sheet he had obtained at last night's meeting. 'As a bachelor, I have lived in furnished accommodations for the past six years. I own no household effects of my own. Sheets, blankets, cooking pots, these are things I shall be obliged to provide for myself, if not for the voyage, at least for use on arrival in New Zealand. There is also the matter of certain personal comforts for the voyage.'

'Yes… yes!'Hutcheson hesitated, emphasising the extreme irregularity of Alexander's request. 'As to accommodation, as soon as you sign your contract you may take up your allotted quarters on board the *Albatross* and mess with the officers in the wardroom. Opening a drawer in his desk, he took out a handful of golden guineas. He scribbled an entry in the ledger which lay on top of the pile in front of him. As he turned the page towards Alexander, he said brusquely, 'It is normal for all gratuities to be paid at the end of the voyage, you understand. There are ten guineas to set you up for the voyage. As Alexander made to lay a hand on the money he added, 'Sign here that you have received the money, if you please!'

Alexander read the entry carefully. This seemed, somewhat unreasonably, to irritate his new employer even further. Finding nothing wrong with what had been written he signed and thereby contracted himself to the New Zealand Company for the extent of the voyage.

*

Having spent the night in a noisy boarding house he knew from his student days, Alexander had slept fitfully and was glad to be up and about early the next morning. On returning to the offices of the New Zealand Company, he quickly decided upon an unoccupied room next door to Hutcheson's, of similar proportions and commanding the same view of Glassford. He went in search of the janitor he had encountered the previous day and found the fellow in the cubby hole he occupied at the foot of the back stairs. Having given his instructions as to the room he had chosen and the furniture he would require, he asked for directions to the dockyard. The janitor introduced himself as Tobias Leny and invited Alexander to call him Toby. He seemed to be inordinately interested in Alexander's appointment.

'Are you to go on board right away, may I ask, Sir?' he enquired, politely enough.

Surprised at his interest but seeing nothing wrong in the question, Alexander answered, 'Why, yes, as it happens. Why do you ask?'

'Oh, it's only that the last gentleman to be appointed surgeon by Mr Hutcheson, took one look at the accommodations aboard ship and turned the job down flat.'

'Oh, do you happen to know why?" Alex wondered.

'It was the 'roaches, Sir, and the rats put the gentleman right off they did.'

'I'm not surprised.' Alexander shuddered. 'I suppose such livestock is almost inevitable aboard ship?' he ventured. 'Would you know of a cure, by any chance?'

'Just one, Sir, take along a good man of your own to look after your personal effects; to take care of the cleaning and the 'orspital laundry and such. A sponsorship, if you know what I mean.'

'Would that I could afford such luxury,' said Alexander. 'Sadly, I cannot pay a servant's wage, let alone find money for an additional passage.'

This confession did not appear to concern the janitor one little bit.

'Did I mention wages or passage money?' he demanded. 'Perhaps I can put you in the way of such a servant, one who would be happy to go along with only the benefit of your name to protect him.'

Alexander knew that he might regret taking on an unknown, yet there was something about this cheeky little man that intrigued him.

'Would this extraordinary creature who is willing to work his passage half way around the world for no wages be yourself, by any chance?'

'The very same, Sir,' the little fellow admitted.

'And why, may I ask, would you want to do that?'

'A small matter of matrimonial promises unfulfilled if you understand me, Sir. The young female with whom I have been consorting has got herself in the family way so to speak and her father, a huge gentleman as tall and broad as yourself, Sir, appears to think that I am the father.'

'And are you?' demanded Alexander, trying hard to sound severe but hardly succeeding.

'Could be, Tobias Leny admitted. But then, might not be; her being somewhat promiscuous if you know what I mean.'

Alexander knew very well. His work in the city's Infirmary had introduced him early to the less salubrious side of life on Glasgow's streets. He wondered why the girl in question did not go to an abortionist if her lover would have none of her. As though reading his thoughts, Toby chipped in.

'It is a Catholic family, Sir, an even greater reason for my not wanting to marry her, me being brought up in the Church of Scotland so to speak.'

'So rather than face up to your responsibilities you want to hide away on the far side of the globe, is that it?'

'It is, Sir, and to prove my innocence in the matter I am willing to put up the passage money for myself.'

'In that case, why not simply sign on as passenger.'

'Ah now, there is the problem. They will take only those who can prove that they can provide useful services to the new colony, men who have skills of craftsmanship, carpenters, masons and the like, occupations which can be put to good use. My experience lies mainly in procurement, if you know what I mean.'

Alexander suspected that he did know exactly what the fellow meant. Thievery, deception and all forms of roguishness seemed more his mark.

'I do not think I can be a party to your illegal entry into the new colony,' Alexander said, shaking his head. He had taken a liking to the man and had no wish to turn him down but how could he be trusted not to destroy the doctor's reputation, simply by association?

'Look at this way, Sir,' said Toby. 'If I am signed on as your servant, I already have my trade so to speak. I assure your, Sir, that you will not be sorry for your decision.'

'There is a month to go before we set sail,' said Alexander. 'If you can make yourself indispensable to me during that time and show that there have been no further indiscretions of any kind, I will take you along as my official assistant.'

Toby thought about this. It would mean a whole month of dodging and weaving to avoid confrontation with an angry father. He had hoped that the ship would be sailing earlier. In the event, Alexander made the decision for him.

'When you have thoroughly cleaned the office I have chosen, and found the furniture I have requested, you may collect my belongings and carrying them to the ship. As I am to take up my quarters there at once I see no reason why you should not do the same.'

He gave Tobias the address of his lodgings and himself made his way to the dockyard where *The Albatross* was lying.

*

News of Alexander's appointment had preceded him to the ship and as he negotiated the gang plank he was welcomed aboard by the First Mate, Arthur Wallace.

'Dr Beaton, is it?' he enquired, holding out his hand and grasping Alexander's with enthusiasm. He seemed surprised to find the newly appointed surgeon to be such a well set up young man of education and breeding. He had anticipated the usual ship's surgeon, a man of little reputation, probably addicted to the rum bottle and knowing the barest minimum of his profession. Beaton would of course be setting up in practice when he arrived in Otago. Perhaps it was this which made him a bona fide practitioner.

'Mr Wallace?' Alexander enquired.

'The very same.'

The mate was an Englishman, a Yorkshire man from his accent. Dark curls protruded from beneath the flat seaman's cap which he wore at a rakish angle. A bushy black beard all but concealed his wide friendly mouth and heavy brows did little to disguise a twinkle sparkling in his eyes. These too were dark, set sufficiently wide apart as to remove the slightest suspicion of menace. Alexander took to the man at first glance and readily returned his friendly greeting.

'Been to sea before, have you?' demanded the mate, leading him forward in the direction of the poop deck. 'It wouldn't do to have a ship's surgeon more sea-sick than his patients!' He laughed in such a way that his whole body shook.

'I grew up on the coast of Argyll,' Alexander explained. 'I have never been on a long voyage but we are accustomed to heavy seas in the Western Isles and I have spent many days, in all kinds of weather, aboard the little fishing ships which ply between the islands.'

The mate nodded, clearly satisfied. They ascended a short flight of steps to the poop deck where Alexander was introduced to the Captain, Archibald McCallum.

Despite the wintry weather, the master of the *Albatross* wore no coat and as he bent over a chart table which had been set up on the deck while the vessel was in dock, his loosely fitting cambric shirt billowed in the wind. His hair was long and fair and blew in a golden cloud around his handsome, deeply tanned face. He stood inches taller, and seemed to be some years younger, than Wallace. Alexander wondered at the method of promotion of these officers. Despite the First Mate's cheerful disposition, might there perhaps be some element of resentment because Arthur Wallace had been passed over for a younger man? In the master's presence Wallace's attitude was more serious and his introductions seemed very stiff and formal.

'Captain Archibald McCallum, may I present our Ship's Surgeon, Dr Alexander Beaton.'

'Good day to you, Doctor. Glad to have you aboard.' The greeting was fulsome enough and Alexander shook the Captain's hand warmly.

Wallace, having completed his duty, departed hurriedly on the pretext of having pressing business to attend to.

'I understand you are joining the ship immediately,' the captain seemed to regard the arrangement as quite normal. 'That's excellent. It will give you a chance to familiarise yourself with the vessel before she fills to capacity with doltish landlubbers who will need shepherding and cosseted until they gain their sea legs. We shall be leaving all of that to you, Doctor. The passengers' comfort will be your responsibility. You will be expected to deal with all but the grossest of their complaints. Be prepared to take a deal of criticism. When people are bored they fill their time finding things about which to make an argument.'

'Have you sailed often with emigrants Captain?' Alexander asked.

'Once only I'm pleased to say. Were I able to refuse this commission I would do so, believe me! However, I have a growing family to support and cannot refuse what is a very lucrative post.'

Alexander was flattered to receive the man's confidence so immediately. He knew very little about life at sea but he could imagine that the Captain's role was a lonely one. It may be that the surgeon was the only officer on board in whom he *could* confide.

'You'll wish to see your quarters and get settled in,' said Captain McCallum. He glanced over Alexander's shoulder and remarked, 'Your man will need to find a suitable shake down in the focsle I'm afraid, but your own quarters are quite private and should be to your liking.'

Startled by the reference to his servant, Alexander turned around to find Tobias Leny waiting at a discrete distance, with Alexander's portmanteau in one hand and his medical bag in the other.

The doctor disguised his astonishment at Toby's presence, with a sharp rejoinder. 'Ah, Levy, what took you so long?'

It was as simple as that. Alex had been concerned that a ship's surgeon arriving on board with his own servant might give rise to some suspicion but here was a captain who seemed to regard the arrangement as quite normal.

Captain McCallum summoned a young lad to his side.

'This is Midshipman Frawley. He will show you to the hospital.'

The Master turned his back abruptly. Considering himself dismissed, Alexander followed the midshipman down to the main deck, and towards the stern of the ship. Toby followed them, carrying the doctor's luggage.

The hospital consisted of a small, square cabin with a desk built in to the bulkhead. On either side a pair of bunks faced one another across a space some six feet wide. A glass-fronted cabinet contained an assortment of bottles, in most cases only partially filled with the liquids and powders commonly associated with the physician's art. Labels were stained. Most were indecipherable. The working surfaces were bare of varnish, sticky and dirty. The once whitened walls of the small cabin were splattered with brown marks, mud or blood? It was impossible to say. Alex shuddered with disgust and commented to Toby, 'You were certainly correct in one respect. This looks like a morning's work with the scrubbing brush!'

He opened one drawer after another in the desk to reveal an assortment of surgical instruments, rusted, bent and blunted. Finally in exasperation, he turned the entire contents of the drawers out onto one of the bunks. They were indeed, a sorry sight.

'Mr Frawley,' he addressed the midshipman, angrily 'be so kind as to ask Mr Wallace to attend me here at his earliest convenience.'

There was no doubting the authority in his tone. The young man hurried away fearing the wrath of this new officer even more than that of the First Mate.

While he waited for Wallace to appear, Alexander opened a second door to the compartment and found himself in a minute sleeping cabin. Cunning use of space allowed for a washbasin and chest of drawers, a small wardrobe for hanging garments, a shelf for books and a mirror for shaving. There was barely room to turn around. The only light came from a small porthole situated over the narrow bunk beneath which further drawers were provided for storage. The bedding smelt mouldy, the floor was filthy and littered with the refuse left behind by the previous incumbent. So much for the 'tidy little cabin,' described by Wallace!

Alexander emerged from the dank hole in which he was expected to spend the next five months of his life as Arthur Wallace appeared in the doorway to the open deck.

'Settling in, are you?' enquired the mate.

'Hardly,' replied Alexander, shortly.

'Is something amiss?'

'I think you could say that. Yes.' came the reply.

Wallace looked genuinely baffled as Alexander took him through the inadequacies of the dispensary and the hospital's accommodation.

'I cannot set sail without a complete set of new surgical instruments and all these,' he indicated the chemicals in the glass cabinet, 'must be discarded.'

'Are you certain?' asked Wallace, doubtfully, 'the previous surgeon made no complaint.'

'In many cases it is not even clear what the bottles contain,' Alex protested. 'I must order new stocks.'

It was a new experience for Wallace to encounter such a demanding surgeon.

'I'll mention it to the Master,' he said, reluctantly. 'Draw up a list of what you need for my approval.'

Alexander wondered how a seaman, be he First Officer or ship's cook, could appreciate what was necessary to equip a ship's hospital but he supposed the fellow must be seen to exert his own authority in such matters, particularly in front of the midshipman. The doctor began to see how he might find the restraints of life at sea invidious and began once again to doubt the wisdom of his decision.

The mate turned away considering the interview to be at an end but Alexander called him back.

'The place must be scrubbed out and fumigated,' said Alexander. 'Who knows what pestilence lurks within these piles of dust and patches of grease.'

Wallace nodded. 'Tell your man to report to the Bos'n for the necessary materials,' he said, indicating Toby. 'I can't spare anyone to help him.'

'But he...' Alexander's protest was cut short by Toby himself, who touched his flat cap and said, 'Aye, aye, sir,' in a manner which suggested previous experience of life aboard ship.

Toby scurried away before Alexander could make any further objection.

The offensive smell of the confined space was beginning to affect both men. Dismissing the midshipman, Wallace invited Alexander to accompany him to the wardroom while Leny cleaned up. Once settled in the rather larger cabin where the officers took their meals and spent their off-duty time, Alexander took the proffered chair ready to hear what his role might be in the days leading up to the ship's departure.

'I understand that you are responsible for provisioning,' he said. 'It seems my own responsibility is the supervision of the foodstuffs brought on board to ensure a healthy diet.'

'That's about it,' Wallace agreed, happier now that he was on more familiar ground. 'For food supplies we use the firm of Macfie, Graham and Company. They have an excellent reputation. Now, if you will allow me...'

He spread out several sheets of paper across the surface of the table.

'This is the list of items normally carried aboard ship. You may of course decide to vary these but I would advise that any proposed change, particularly in the rations for the crew, should be discussed with me first. The Captain would not care to have a mutiny over the provision of the wrong kind of biscuits!' Wallace roared with laughter at his own suggestion, but Alexander sensed that the warning was important and should be heeded.

'There are strict rules laid down concerning the quantities of staple foods allowed per passenger.' Wallace pushed a paper across to Alexander. 'You will see that the weekly allowances are all worked out according to the quality of the passengers.'

Alexander read:

Chief cabin, of prime beef, 2lbs; Fore-cabin, 11/2lbs; Steerage, 1lb.

'I see that the main cabin people receive twice as much, or more, of everything as the steerage,' he observed.

Chief cabin, of raisins 16oz; steerage 4oz.'

Only suet was provided in equal amount and butter not at all to the steerage passengers. So much for any idea of the equality Hutcheson had so emphasised.

'Well, there is something to be said for keeping the steerage folk lean. Their quarters are very cramped.' Alexander's startled expression made Wallace roar with laughter. 'In any case,' he concluded, 'those in the chief cabin pay handsomely for their fare and must be shown to have a little something extra for it.'

'Is there a list of those travelling in the various categories?' Alexander asked.

'The maximum numbers in each class are shown here,' Wallace pointed out. 'We must work on these figures to begin with. Should they be different by the time the supplies come on board, then we have to be ready to make adjustments.'

'Now let us be quite clear,' Alexander was beginning to become confused as to what his own responsibilities were. 'You will order the supplies while I check that the amounts are correct for the numbers travelling and confirm that the foodstuffs are in wholesome condition.'

'That is what's laid down, but as to the amounts and so on, you can safely leave all that to the ship's cook. Just make spot checks to see that what is delivered is of the quality ordered and in a condition to last the voyage.'

'What if the sailing is delayed by storms or damage to the vessel?' Alexander demanded. 'Do we carry emergency supplies?'

'We do not!' cried the mate, amused at such a thought. 'If such a state of affairs presents itself then it will be for you to ration the supplies accordingly.'

Wallace got to his feet, careful not to stretch to his full height lest his head should contact the lowest beams. Alexander, who had already been made painfully aware of the low ceilings, took note of the way the mate stooped his shoulders and decided to adopt a similar stance.

'There's paper and writing materials here.' Wallace indicated the desk built in to the bulkhead. 'You might be more comfortable here while your man cleans up. Get your lists of requirements drawn up and we'll see about ordering them tomorrow. The first barrels of salt meat will be arriving later today. I'll see you at six bells in the afternoon watch' said Wallace.

Alex looked puzzled, 'Which is?'

'My but you do have a lot to learn!' laughed the other. 'Three o'clock in landlubber's parlance!'

'It's quite easy, Doctor,' Tobias Levy seemed to come and go like a shadow. As they listened to the mate's footsteps receding along the passage, he spoke as though he had been a party to the entire conversation between the mate and the surgeon. 'The day is divided into four hourly watches, six all told in twenty-four hours. One bell is struck for the first half hour of a watch, two for the first hour and so on to eight bells a half-hour before the change of watch d'ye see?'

'You're very knowledgeable for a janitor,' observed Alexander, dryly.

'Served my time under Admiral Hood while he was yet Sir Thomas Hood, during the French wars that was.' Toby told him proudly. 'I was Captain's steward aboard the *Pallas* when she cut out the French guard ship *La Tapageuse* from the river Garonne.'

Intrigued as he was to discover his manservant might be an invaluable source of information upon matters nautical, Alexander felt sure he would be subjected to further reminiscences if he did not cut the conversation short.

'How goes the cleaning operation?'

'Complete and ready for your inspection, Sir!' Toby gave a mock salute. 'I was wondering what I should do with the chemicals you wish to discard?'

'Over the side with them,' said Alexander. 'Let's make a completely fresh start. You can wash out the bottles and keep them though. We shall find a use for them when the new consignment arrives.'

*

Once Alexander had the hospital and his own cabin cleaned out to his satisfaction, he concentrated upon the stores which were already coming on board. He soon realised how fortuitous it had been for him to live aboard ship right from the start. Deliveries were made at all hours. If, as he suspected, this was to escape the detection of below-standard goods, Alexander was determined to be always on hand ready and waiting to carry out his inspections.

The weeks began to fly past, each day bringing with it some new experience. He quickly learned that he must have eyes in the back of his head if he was to inspect all the foodstuffs before they were stowed away in the hold. Salted and smoked meats and fish must be inspected for smell and taste. It was not above the abattoirs to sell off condemned meat cheaply to the smokeries, but even the best oak-wood chippings could not disguise the scent of putrid beef or lamb and Alexander was quick to recognise tell-tale discolouration. Macfie, Graham and Company might be a reputable firm in the city but they were not above trying to palm off on the ships wheat flour already running with weevils. By the time Alexander had sent back his first half dozen barrels of defective biscuits, the suppliers understood they were dealing with someone determined to accept nothing but the best and they responded accordingly.

Having established his required standards, Alexander felt he could relax his supervision a little and turned his attention to equipping the hospital to his satisfaction. Shown the bill for the materials he wished to order, Wallace blanched but when he dared to query certain items which clearly related to midwifery, Alexander reminded him of Hutcheson's comments about the number of infants born on such voyages and he was forced to agree to the order.

In all this work Tobias Leny stuck close to Alexander always ready to lend a hand, always ready with advice on where and from whom to obtain every item. The little man had become a familiar figure in the focsle. No one questioned his position as the doctor's valet cum sick-berth attendant. Other than an occasional word of recognition of his efforts, the fellow demanded nothing of Alexander.

Each day Toby left the ship at day-break, returning mid- morning to resume his duties in the hospital. When Alexander questioned him on his activities he replied. 'Why bless you doctor, I must continue to carry out my duties at the New Zealand Company offices. How else am I to pay my passage money when the time comes?

So, he was still determined to pay for himself. Alexander felt some considerable relief because as the days passed he had become more and more reliant upon the industrious little man and was beginning to feel that he must himself find some way of paying for his sponsorship. If he could not find all the necessary money, he would at least try to make some contribution to the man's expenses.

When the provisioning was almost completed Alexander found himself obliged to attend the offices in Glassford more frequently. With less than a fortnight to go before sailing, passengers were lining up to sign on and pay their fares. Before accepting any money however Hutcheson insisted they be examined by the ship's surgeon.

In general, the people Alex saw were artisans with or without a family; men whose skills ensured them a steady income so that their womenfolk and children were well nourished. He found little sign of rickets or the dreaded phthisis to which he had been particularly alerted. The young single women who presented themselves were generally less robust and he was obliged to turn down more than one who showed early signs of lung disease.

Inoculation against smallpox also caused Alexander some problems for there were many who protested that they had already been treated. In most cases, they could show the distinctive scar but because he could not be certain of the quality of the serum used Alexander insisted that each be treated again regardless of their protestations. Infants howled and grown men fainted away at the sight of his knife but he pursued his examinations with such punctiliousness that word soon got around. There was no fooling this doctor. Nor was there any chance of bribing him to let by some applicant whose health was suspect.

Towards noon Alexander was alerted to a disturbance in the corridor outside. A mixture of voices, high pitched and deep throated, suggested a family come to pay for their passage. Alexander glanced at the clock. It had been a long morning and he was worried that if he were delayed there would be no one to supervise the final collection of water, one of the last of the commodities to be taken on board the *Albatross*.

The noise abated a little as the company was ushered into Hutcheson's office next door but soon the noisy talk and short bursts of merriment resumed and Hutcheson threw open Alex's door.

'We have quite a gathering for you here,' said the Secretary. 'A cursory examination is probably all that is required.' He fixed Alexander with a stare. His meaning was quite clear. For no reason was this family to be rejected.

'How do you want them, Dr Beaton, one at a time or all together?'

Alexander looked beyond his rotund colleague and much to his surprise, glimpsed the familiar figure of James Bantrie. The minister advanced into the room, paused when he saw Alexander as though trying to recollect, and then smiled broadly. 'Why, upon my soul, if it isn't Dr Beaton!'

He turned back to his companions. 'Judith, my dear, just look who it is! Catherine, you remember Dr Beaton.'

The Bantries looked considerably more relaxed than when he had last seen them. Judith was blooming with good health. Young Charles had grown noticeably and Miss Catherine, wearing a new gown and without the usual schoolgirl's pinafore, was quite the young lady.

Alexander came forward to greet them. 'Mrs Bantrie, a great pleasure Ma'am, I'm sure!'

'Dr Bantrie is to be responsible for the spiritual welfare of the passengers on the voyage,' Hutcheson explained. Turning to James he explained,'Dr Beaton is our ship's surgeon for the voyage out. He will then be staying on in New Zealand.'

'Well, what an extraordinary co-incidence!' exclaimed James. 'There was so little time to talk when we last met. I had no idea that you too were contemplating going abroad.'

'At the time, neither had I,' confessed Alexander. 'The decision was arrived at after our encounter.'

He looked from one to the other of the Bantrie family. One child was missing. The son he had never seen. The one for whom a search had been initiated on the day he left Eisdalsa. He scarcely dared ask about him.

'Is this all of you?' he demanded. He noticed a shadow pass across Judith Bantrie's face as her husband replied.

'Our eldest boy, Ian, is not coming with us.' He glanced at his wife and seeing her lips begin to quiver, he added hurriedly, 'he is to learn mining engineering at Redruth in Cornwall before he joins us in Otago.'

'A very sensible move,' Hutcheson was nodding his head in approval. 'That's what we want, strong young men who are able to exploit the riches of this new land to the full!'

Relieved to learn that the lad had been rescued after all, Alex dared to enquire further, 'He was found safe and well then, after the shipwreck?'

'Hardly that,' Judith spoke for the first time, her voice so low he had to strain to hear her. 'Had it not been for your brother's intervention he would most certainly have been a cripple. His leg was broken and he was exposed to wind and weather for three days.'

'Judith always neglects to mention her own part in Ian's recovery,' James blustered. 'Were it not for her and Mistress Dundas, the boy would have been dead long before the doctor reached him.'

'Mrs Dundas, how is she?' Alexander felt a rekindling of excitement as he recalled the handsome woman with her refreshingly pragmatic view of life.

'See for yourself!' declared James, dramatically. 'She is to accompany us on the voyage!' He turned to where an additional figure had appeared in the doorway.

Alexander felt inordinately pleased at the unexpected appearance of Jessie Dundas. How could she manage it, he wondered? Surely, like himself, she lacked the price of the fare?

As if reading his thoughts, Bantrie explained. 'I have procured for Mrs Bantrie the post of Warden of the single women's cabin. She will work her passage. When we arrive in New Zealand there is sure to be employment for such a resourceful person.'

'Indeed yes,' Hutcheson was nodding delightedly, enthused by this unexpectedly happy meeting. 'Mrs Dundas must be vetted along with other members of the ship's company, before sailing.'

Savouring the promise of renewed conversation with Jessie Dundas, Alexander declared that he would see Mrs Bantrie and the children together, then the reverend Bantrie and finally Mrs Dundas and her son.

'Splendid, ' said Hutcheson, 'Come back to my office Dr Bantrie, I have a word or two for your ears alone.'

He settled Jessie and wee Tommy Dundas on chairs in the corridor and retreated with Bantrie to his own lair.

Alexander could find nothing amiss with either Catherine or her little brother. The sea air and simple country food seemed to have agreed with them. He dismissed them quickly and turned his attention to their mother.

Judith seemed to be a healthy colour and there was a fulsomeness about her which had been absent when they had last met. She was much depressed at that time, he recalled, and justifiably worried about her son's whereabouts.

'Run along to Mrs Dundas,' Judith ordered the children when they had stoically endured the small pox inoculation, scratched into their upper arms. When they were alone, Alexander took her pulse, examined the inside of her mouth and throat and bade her unfasten her blouse that he might listen to her heart and lungs.

She seemed reluctant to expose herself.

'Would you like me to call in Mrs Dundas as chaperon?' he asked.

'No, it is not that.' She coloured prettily. 'It is just that I had hoped you would not notice.'

'Notice what, Mrs Bantrie? That you look to be in blooming health?'

'There have been changes. Oh, for goodness sake, why should I attempt to hide it?' She threw all modesty to the wind and exposed her breasts, 'The truth is, Doctor, I am pregnant.'

'I see.'

He examined her carefully, without comment.

'You have born three children successfully,' he said, as she buttoned her blouse. 'Were there any complications on any of those occasions?'

'None at all. In fact, when wee Jamie was born I scarcely knew I was in labour before he arrived, all in a rush!'

'And there have been no miscarriages, no infant deaths?'

'No, none.'

'What do you calculate to be the date of the birth?' he asked and was surprised at her precision when she said, 'The child was conceived on the night we knew that Ian was safe. That was August 16th.'

'So we shall expect the happy event in mid- April.' It was cutting things a bit fine. If the ship arrived on time the baby would be born after their arrival in New Zealand. Any delay could mean a confinement at sea and all the hazards which that entailed.

'Is Mr Bantrie willing to take the risk?' Alexander demanded.

'If he knew, I feel sure he would not be,' she told him, honestly. She saw an expression of doubt cloud the doctor's face. 'This opportunity means everything to my husband, Dr Beaton. Were we to postpone our departure it could be months before he got another passage under such generous terms. Since James decided upon disestablishment at the Disruption, his only offer of a living has come from the Isle of Orchy. I cannot face further years in that God- forsaken place, Dr Beaton, and neither I can I bear to see my husband dragged down because he is determined to stick to his principles. In New Zealand he will have the chance to practice his religion in his own way. I cannot deny him that.'

'So you are asking me to be a party to your deception?' Alexander was torn between his sympathy for her plight and his duty to the husband. 'Dr Bantrie will know sooner or later.'

'But not necessarily before we sail.' Tears welled in those pretty, wide set, startlingly- blue eyes and glistened on her long golden lashes.

'Please Doctor,' she pleaded, 'I promise that I will tell him, just as soon as we are truly out of sight of land and when I do, I shall not implicate you in any way. I shall say that you never asked and I was not disposed to tell you.'

'If I allow you to sail you will adhere strictly to the regime I shall draw up for you? Not neglect yourself in any way?'

'I promise to be good.'

How could he deny her this small service? After all, he was fully prepared for just such an eventuality on board and would most likely attend her even if, as he hoped, the birth occurred after they landed in New Zealand. Was not colonisation all about increasing the population as fast as possible? Bantrie would probably accuse him of being careless in his examination but what of that? No doubt there would be other matters which would slip past him far more obvious than this. He would have to plead ignorance through lack of experience.

All these excuses crowded into his mind as he dismissed her with a list of special items with which to equip herself for even if the child was not born at sea, there was no certainty that the necessities would be available in New Edinburgh.

'We will say no more about it,' he said, smiling, 'until we are in mid Atlantic.'

*

Jessie Dundas seemed to glow with excitement. Her deep brown eyes, almost bovine in their placidity, were framed by thick, auburn lashes, which reflected her richly waving chestnut hair. She had discarded the cambric cap commonly worn by the island women and in its place sported a neat straw bonnet tilted to the back of her head at a saucy angle.

The classic beauty of her ivory skin was enhanced by the bright colouring of her lips and scarcely marred by a swathe of freckles which swept across her smooth white brow and the bridge of her neat little, slightly turned up nose.

Alexander quickly dismissed the child clinging to her skirts. Wee Tammy Dundas had recovered fully from his illness. His slight frame, fever racked when Alexander has seen him last, was filling out well. His colour was good and his skin clear of eruptions.

He cringed when he saw the doctor take up his scalpel, but a soft word from his mother and the child stood stoically while Alexander prepared the smallpox inoculation. His eyes glistened but he did not cry out as the knife cut into his skin and his face was wreathed in smiles when Alex swabbed the place with cotton and popped a comfit into the child's mouth.

'You'll do,' said the doctor, rubbing his fingers through a tumble of curling brown locks. 'Run along now and join your friends while I speak with your mother.'

He led her to the window to see more clearly and with a professional air examined the glands of her neck, glanced into her mouth and found no sign of infection in her throat. Heart and lungs appeared to be functioning normally.

'Do you have any persistent cough?' he enquired coolly. Her reply was in the negative. He ticked off the next item on his list of questions. Hers was a robust constitution due he suspected, to the clean air and the outdoor life of the island she so despised. He doubted if her health had been this good when she had arrived on Orchy from the Glasgow slums.

'I understand you are to control the single women's quarters?'

She watched carefully as he carried out the inoculation process with a professional skill, developed from considerable practice during the past few days.

'Yes, Mr Bantrie was kind enough to speak for me. You don't know how grateful I am to him for giving me this chance. I thought that I was doomed to spend the rest of my life on that island.'

'What will you do when we arrive in New Zealand?' Alexander wondered if she had committed herself in some way to the Bantrie family.

'I have a little experience of nursing the sick,' she did not elaborate, 'I can wash and sew and care for other people's children. Maybe there will be some boarding house or hostel where I can get employment. Who knows? It will be a fresh start away from prying eyes and evil tongues with too little to occupy them.'

'If you are keen to learn about medical matters maybe I can help you during the voyage.' Alexander leapt at the opportunity to spend time with her. 'I fear we shall all be looking for ways in which to occupy ourselves.'

'We shall see,' she answered, flattered that he should think her worthy of his teaching. 'I shall of course have my duties to attend to. I understand that it is no easy task to keep the young unmarried women under surveillance.'

It was the first time he had heard her laugh. It was a hearty sound, lacking all restraint. Even had he wished to he could not have avoided joining in with her. They were still smiling as he led her to the door and shook her warmly by the hand.

'I shall look forward to seeing you aboard *The Albatross*,' he said, including the entire company in his remarks as they emerged to join the Bantries in the corridor. Nevertheless, Jessie knew that his words were intended for her alone and the knowledge that the doctor was more than a little interested in her was worrying.

She had been looking forward to this new life as an opportunity to begin afresh. Any link with the past however tenuous increased the danger of exposure. Hugh Beaton had made it only too clear how *he* regarded women of her background. There was little doubt his brother would hold similar opinions.

Chapter Seven

As the day for sailing approached, Alexander Beaton realised that there would be no time for him to return home and take proper leave of his family. He had written to them, of course, and received a long letter back from his mother pleading with him to change his mind.

His father's comments had been brief and to the point. Surprised at his younger son's sudden decision to go abroad, he assumed that there were wild oats waiting to be sown and seemed certain that Alexander would return in due course and settle down in some quiet little practice, preferably in Argyll. Neither he nor Alexander's mother seemed in the least aware of the true reason for their son's sudden departure.

If Hugh understood anything of Alexander's feelings, he made no reference to it. Knowingly or unknowingly he had thwarted his brother's most cherished objectives both by taking over the family's medical practice and by winning the hand of Alexander's childhood sweetheart. His only regret it seemed was that Alexander would be sailing before the date of his marriage to Annie McColl.

The victualling of the vessel was all but complete with only the water-barrels left to be filled. With the enteric fever epidemic on Orchy still fresh in his mind Alexander was concerned to ensure the safest possible supply and spurning the stand pipe at the dock gate which Wallace had indicated, he scoured the countryside for a suitable source of fresh drinking water. He decided finally upon a burn which drained into a wee lochan to the north of Dunbarton. It meant a couple of hours travelling to collect it, but Alexander was adamant that the additional work entailed was necessary to ensure the health of his passengers.

On the first two journeys he had travelled with the hired brewer's dray, insisting upon attending to the operation himself. When however on the eve of departure, he heard Wallace directing Midshipman Frawley to take three men and collect an additional twenty barrels he found he had too many other last minute details to attend to and must allow the midshipman to carry out the duty unsupervised.

'You know the spot where we loaded up before Mr Frawley,' Alexander reminded him, as the young man climbed up beside the driver. 'Be sure to take the water up-stream from any place where cattle have been drinking.'

The youth nodded. If his 'Aye, aye, Sir,' carried the faintest hint of adolescent disrespect Alexander chose to ignore it. To the boy's mind the ship's surgeon was an old woman fussing about clean this and clean that. As he was quick to point out to his comrades, Dr Beaton would make a better superintendent of a bathhouse!

Frawley's working party consisted of a group of very unhappy sailors. Once the dray had pulled clear of the dockyard and was trundling along Hope Street towards the junction with Cowcaddens Road, the men fell into a heated discussion as to how they might fulfil their mission and yet have time for a little entertainment before the night was out. After a while their spokesman, Lachy Stuart, crept forward and tapped the Midshipman on the shoulder.

'Excuse me Sir,' he touched his cap obsequiously, 'the lads and me has had a wee thocht. Here are we, ready to set sail on tomorrow's evening tide and no last chance for a dram or two on oor ane hame soil. 't is a long way to Loch Ard and chances are we'll no' be back before morning.'

Frawley turned around and faced the seaman.

'What did you have in mind Mr Stuart,' he asked shortly, none too pleased himself to be working this evening. The vessel he had served in prior to signing on with the Albatross had today sailed into port and his old shipmates had invited him out on the town. This assignment meant he had been obliged to refuse them.

'Dougie Watts is from these parts,' the man explained eagerly. 'He says he knows of a spring just on the edge of the city which yields the sweetest water in Glasgow. As good as that from Loch Ard any day.'

'Is that so?' Frawley feigned indifference but his interest had been aroused. It would take a couple of hours at most to fill the barrels if the spring Miller spoke of was not far. They could be loaded up by eight o'clock and he would still have time to join his friends.

'Well, Sir, what d'ye say?'

'About what, Mr Miller?'

'Will ye no' consider a wee change o' plan? It is oor last nicht ashore.' Frawley was wavering. Should the doctor hear that his orders had been disobeyed there would be hell to pay. On the other hand, the situation offered certain advantages. If he were to conspire with these men, they would all be equally guilty. The knowledge that he could expose them to the First Officer would surely give him additional authority over them once the voyage was under way.

'Very well,' he agreed, 'Tell the driver where you want him to go. But see here, if word of this gets back to the ship I shall personally find some good reason to see that you all get a taste of the rope's end.'

It was dark when they reached the spot and Frawley was obliged to order lanterns to be lit so that they could see what they were doing. A stone trough extended out from the steep rock face providing a drinking place for horses and shallow steps, wide enough for two men to stand side by side, led up to the rim on one side. Filling of the barrels would be a simple task. After the rain of recent weeks, the water flowed freely from a spring which gushed out of the rocky cliff some eight or ten foot above and tumbled continuously into the stone trough below.

Frawley could see no reason why the doctor should condemn such a likely source of water and, relieved the men's suggestion had proved to be an excellent alternative, he directed so efficient a system of filling and loading the barrels that the operation was completed in record time. As the cart trundled back along its homeward track in good time for them all to enjoy the evening ahead the men talked excitedly and broke into song while Frawley was left to contemplate his next move.

They could not take the water barrels directly to the ship as the doctor might see them arrive and would certainly realise that they had not been all the way to Loch Ard. If they were to escape detection it would be necessary to involve the driver in their scheme. They must keep him and the wagon out of the way until it was the right time to return to the ship.

At Frawley's suggestion, the driver drew up in the yard of the Hollybank Tavern about a mile from where the Albatross lay at Broomielaw Quay. He slipped down from his perch and called Stuart to his side. At the entrance to the tavern yard the midshipman explained in an undertone what they must do. Then producing a handful of coins, he murmured urgently, 'Keep the wagon and the driver with you at all times. Get him drunk. It will help to cloud his memory. I shall return to the Hollybank at midnight and we will complete the journey together.'

'See you at midnight then, Mr Frawley, Sir,' the man said, putting two fingers to his cap in a sailor's salute. He stood watching as the midshipman stepped into the street and turned in the direction of the West End of the town.

*

Jessie Dundas who because of her engagement, had been obliged to come on board ahead of the rest of the party from Orchy, had reported to Mr Wallace on the eve of departure. He passed her on to Alexander with instructions to defer to the doctor in all things. Alexander, certain that her good common sense and authoritative tone would soon have the women sorted if not satisfied, decided to leave the organisation of the single women's quarters entirely in Jessie's hands. In a rush to get everything done his instructions to her were brief and to the point but she seemed undisturbed by his somewhat distant greeting. She listened intently to what he said and went about her business with obvious determination.

From time to time during the following day he caught a glimpse of her gently shepherding a weeping lassie who had recently taken leave of doting parents or being forceful with some more argumentative female who was demanding alternative accommodation. For the most part their paths did not cross and it was to be some time before they had a chance to converse in a more intimate manner.

The passengers began to come on board from early morning and straight away Alexander was called upon to sort out sleeping arrangements which would be acceptable to all. On the lower deck, normally reserved for cargo, wooden scaffolding of good Scots pine supported three tiers of bunks each three foot six in width. These must accommodate two adults or several small children. The bunks were fixed to the bulkheads leaving a space between the bunks some ten feet wide. Down the middle of this was fixed a long table with narrow benches on either side. Above the table storm lanterns, set at intervals of ten or twelve foot, provided the only lighting when the hatches were battened down.

Some twenty or thirty people had already been directed down to the steerage accommodation by the time the doctor and the First Mate arrived on the scene. Baggage lay strew around, single individuals occupyied the table top, several bunks and much of the floor space as they sorted their belongings and argued amongst themselves as to the best location to avoid sea sickness, get air, get light and so on. The mate could see that this chaos must be resolved before further passengers arrived. Having directed Simon Frawley to the gangway to prevent others coming aboard for the time being, he climbed onto the table and called for their attention.

'Ladies and gentlemen, you have been told the rules about baggage. You may have with you in the cabin one bag only containing those items which you need for your immediate use. Each family has been allocated bunk space and if you will consult your joining instructions you will see that parents and children are placed together as far as is possible. The sleeping spaces are labelled so there should be no problem in identifying your own allotted area. Any additional baggage must be stored in the hold and will be charged as freight. There are crew members available to assist you.'

'But there are garments for the warmer weather; things we shall need when we reach the tropics,' protested one florid faced gentleman who in addition to carrying on board too many bags, was wearing several layers of clothing to flout the regulations concerning the quantity of luggage allowed.

'Arrangements will be made from time to time during the voyage for you to visit the hold to fetch additional items from your luggage and reorganise your possessions. I must emphasise however that no one individual may take up space allocated to others, or to common use. For reasons of safety there must be a clear passage from one end of the deck to the other at all times!'

Relying on these early comers to pass his words on, the mate departed while Alexander positioned himself where he could conveniently check off the passenger list and take aside any who had previously escaped his inspection. This way he soon had a small queue awaiting inoculation outside the hospital.

A lady of vast proportions edged her way into the dispensary and settled herself with some difficulty into the seat which Alexander indicated. Behind her, her husband, a wiry individual some six inches taller than she and several stones lighter stood for the doctor's examination. Both appeared to be in good health but Alexander could see that the couple were going to cause some problems. The man was clearly too long for the standard bunk while the woman would have difficulty squeezing herself in let alone leaving room for her spouse. There were children also but they were of an age to fit in anywhere other than their mother's bed where they would be in danger of suffocation.

There was no need for them to point out their difficulty.

'Until we put in at Southampton to pick up the last of our passengers, there will be additional accommodation available,' Alex told them. 'During the first week you may take a bunk each. Maybe by that time we shall have made alternative arrangements for you. It may be that we can give you a berth to yourself Mrs Crawford, but we may have to accommodate your husband in the bachelor's quarters where the bunks are somewhat longer.'

'I could always sleep on the floor,' the man suggested obligingly.

'I'm afraid that cannot be allowed,' Alexander told him, bluntly. 'The deck will, like as not, be awash as soon as we reach the open sea but apart from that the walkways between the bunks must be kept free to allow for the movement of other passengers and members of the crew.'

As the unlikely pair departed there was a sound of scuffling in the passage outside before the door flew open to admit Toby with a small, surly looking urchin firmly held by the collar of his jacket.

'I caught this one skulking in one of the lifeboats,' he said. 'I noticed his family gathered close by paying rather more attention to the boat than was normal and when I went to see what they were looking at I found them feeding the laddie wi' apples while he hid beneath the tarpaulin. Trying to avoid showing him to you I don't doubt!'

Alexander, feeling he should reprove Tobias for his rather high-handed treatment examined the child. Perhaps eight or nine years old, the boy was extremely thin, his eyes deep sunk and his skin grey. Far from being the rascal that Toby had suggested, the boy was dull, listless and his breathing was laboured.

When Alexander told the child to remove his shirt he was startled at the degree of emaciation. Percussion of the chest revealed dullness on the left side and Alexander's request to the boy to cough not only revealed the expected tell-tale sounds but caused him to bring up a quantity of phlegm, alarmingly flecked with blood. It was a most advanced case of pthysis and Alexander knew immediately that he should exclude the child from the ship.

'Where are your parents?' he asked and looked up to see a wide-eyed, frightened little woman gazing in through the still open cabin door. Behind her stood her husband, a burly man with the look of a prize fighter about him.

Alexander ushered them in and bade Toby close the door.

'The boy is sick,' he said. 'You are aware of the rules about passengers travelling only if they are in good health?'

The woman nodded meekly. The man looked defiant. Alexander felt he was going to have trouble.

'Your son has an advanced case of Consumption, a disease which is known to be highly contagious. I cannot risk the lives of the other passengers by allowing him to live in the crowded conditions of the steerage accommodation.'

'But what are we to do?' the woman wailed. 'My husband is a blacksmith. He has sold his smithy. All his tools are packed into the hold. We have given up our house and stripped it of all its furniture to bring away with us. We must sail now!'

'Are there no relatives with whom you could leave your son?' Alexander asked, not unkindly. It was obvious that they had known very well that they were breaking the rules by smuggling a sick child aboard and yet in all other respects they seemed an honest, hard working couple. His heart went out to them.

'My parents are dead and my husband too is an orphan,' the woman told him. 'Eddie's brother has gone ahead to Otago to prepare somewhere for us all to live. There is no one here in Scotland with whom we can leave the boy.'

Tears streamed down her face as she pleaded with him but Alexander's eyes were on the boy himself who at the suggestion he might not be allowed to travel appeared terrified out of his wits. He too began to howl in unison with his mother.

Alexander signalled to the father to accompany him on deck where they might consider the matter in relative quiet. They moved to the rail where they could speak without interruption.

'Now then Mr…?'

'Mackie, Sir, William Mackie.'

'Well, Mr Mackie, while it is my duty to ensure the health of everyone on board, I am not insensitive to the situation in which you find yourself. It occurs to me that it might be possible to house your boy with the livestock out here on deck.' He indicated a row of substantial wooden structures built to house a cow, a nanny goat, four sheep and a breeding sow with a family of a dozen piglets. Scrabbling about in the straw which covered the floor of the pens were a dozen or so chickens while towards the stern were stabled two horses belonging to a Government official who was travelling in the Superior Cabin.

'Now,' Alexander could see the father was about to protest, 'I appreciate that this may seem to be a harsh way to treat an ailing child, but I have it on good authority that cases such as his improve on exposure to fresh air and of that,' he grinned disarmingly, 'he will get plenty out here. More importantly, if he is isolated on deck he will be less likely to infect other passengers.'

The dark scowl had left the blacksmith's face as Alexander spoke. He viewed the buildings with a professional eye finding little in them to criticise. Clearly the crew would wish to preserve their livestock to provide fresh milk and eggs throughout the voyage while also having occasional access to a supply of fresh meat. They were not going to put the animals at risk. The horses stabled aft were valuable beasts. He had already had a word with their groom and having seen the accommodations below for himself and his family had even been envious of their stabling. The boy would be warm and comfortable in the small hay store provided.

'Will they allow it?' he asked anxiously, casting a glance in the direction of the poop deck.

Alexander was none too sure that Captain McCallum would agree to his proposal. 'I can only ask, 'he told Mackie.

He was excited at the prospect of seeing for himself the effect of a sea voyage upon the ailing child. Such treatment was advocated for rich sufferers of the disease. Here was a unique opportunity for him to test the theory for himself. Pthysis was a disease which carried off more people at an early age than any other. What a feather in his cap if he were able to record a happy outcome from such an experiment. It was this argument which he presented to the Captain a few moments later when he was explaining the infringement made by the Mackies and his own solution to the problem.

'The Company rules are quite plain,' the Captain protested.

'I must not knowingly allow diseased passengers on board.'

'Are there such stringent regulations set for members of the crew?' Alexander asked, innocently.

'Well, no. It is hardly likely that a sick man would present himself for heavy duties on a long sea voyage.'

'So there is nothing to demand a certificate of good health from any member of the crew?'

'No. But that is not to say that I am at liberty to sign on someone who is obviously unhealthy.'

'You have not requested me to examine members of the crew,' Alexander persisted. 'Is it not possible that more than one man on board is suffering from disease, especially of a venereal nature?'

'Oh, undoubtedly,' the Captain grinned. 'That is why Mr Wallace advocated an increase in the quantities of mercuric salts and iodide of potassium you ordered!'

'Sir, if I can guarantee that no other passenger will be infected by this child, might I not put him down on the crew list as in charge of livestock? He is not so sick that he cannot be taught to feed and water the creatures. Someone has to do it and maybe there will be times when the men will be otherwise occupied.'

The Captain had children of his own. He was not insensitive to the plight of this unhappy family and more than a little admiring of their determination not to leave the boy behind.

'Oh, very well, Mr Beaton, but he is your responsibility. Sign him on as assistant to your man Leny, although the idea that he should look after the stock is a good one. I leave the matter in your hands.' He paused for a moment before adding, 'If you should write up a learned paper on the treatment will you be obliged to mention the name of the ship?'

'Only if you so wish it,' was Alexander's reply.

'Then we'll wait and see,' said Mc Callum.

*

The Bantries did not appear until late in the afternoon having travelled from the home of Judith's parent's in Edinburgh. As ship's Chaplain, James was given a standard passenger cabin on the main deck which although cramped, at least afforded the family some privacy and gave them direct access to the fresh air. Jessie's son, Thomas, was to share a bunk with little Charles. The single female's cabin was considered unsuitable for a boy of rising six years. They had scarcely settled themselves, stowing personal possessions into every available storage space, when Alexander Beaton appeared to bid them welcome.

'What a shambles!' exclaimed Judith as the doctor closed the cabin door to the overcrowded deck where passengers and those who had come to see them off, were milling about anxiously awaiting the moment of departure.

'It will all settle down when we set sail,' said Alex with more conviction than he felt. The preceding weeks spent aboard ship, albeit tied up to the quay, had given him a certain air of assurance.

'Are all those people sailing with us?' asked Catherine, a worried expression on her face. She had lived all her short life in country places where there was ample space for all. The sheer numbers and the close proximity of their fellow-travellers troubled her.

'The vessel is large enough to accommodate everyone,' Alex assured her. 'Once all is battened down and we are ready for sea you will be amazed at how everyone fits in.'

'My parents insisted upon coming from Edinburgh to see us off,' James told him. 'Seeing the crowds, my mother refused to come on board so will you forgive us if we go ashore for a few moments to bid them farewell?'

'I have my duties to attend to,' Alexander reminded him, 'Perhaps we can meet for a dram or two after we set sail. Remember to return on board at the first bell,' he laughed. 'After all this, it would be a pity to be left standing on the dock!'

He caught sight of the Bantrie family a few moments later in company with a tall, grey-haired gentleman, trying resolutely to keep a merry expression as he spoke animatedly to the children while his wife, a neat little body in dark cloak and a gay red bonnet, made liberal use of her handkerchief.

The doctor experienced a pang of regret that there was no one here to wish him bon voyage. Feeling very much alone and extremely sorry for himself, Alexander retired to his quarters and busied himself with his various duties until the ship got under way. After a while Toby came in carrying the evening papers.

'I thought you might like to see what's likely to be the last news of home for a wee while,' he said, handing the doctor a copy of the Glasgow Evening Courier.

'Very good of you Toby,' he said, laying the paper aside while he continued with his work. 'I'll save it for later.'

As he worked away at his notes he lifted his head from time to time to listen for sounds that the vessel might be getting under way and at last heard the bell warning all those who were going ashore that it was time to leave. Last minute messages and cries of farewell were lost in the turmoil as the crew turned to and set a short sail, giving what assistance they could to the barges whose task it was to tow the vessel out into mid stream.

Resisting the temptation to join the passengers on deck, Alexander picked up the paper and gave the close printed public announcements and personal messages on the front page only a cursory glance, before turning to the news items on the inside pages.

One heading immediately caught his attention.

CHOLERA STRIKES AGAIN

The medical Officer of Health for the Glasgow City Council has described recent deaths from the old enemy, as having reached epidemic proportions in one quarter of the city. Our readers are advised to avoid visiting the Milngavie district. Affected households will be fumigated and the contents will be burnt by the official scavengers to avoid any further spread of the contagion.

Congratulating himself for having had the foresight to fetch water from outside the city boundary, Alexander searched for further reference to the epidemic but found none. Thankful that they would soon be well away from such problems he folded the paper and feeling the movement of the ship beneath his feet he went on deck to take one final look at Glasgow. The ship was already some yards from the shore. Passengers were crowded against the bulwarks and occupying every vantage point from which to take what for many would be their last glimpse of home.

On the dock the crowds were beginning to thin. Some of the spectators began to run alongside the vessel as slowly gathering way, she moved down-stream. Those remaining continued to wave disconsolately until their loved ones were out of sight. Alexander could see James Bantrie's parents who had been left isolated by the departed onlookers, and beside them, surely he was not mistaken, the familiar figure of his brother Hugh, clearly over- heated and out of breath. He must have only just arrived.

With a pang of disappointment Alexander waved and saw Hugh catch sight of him. Then he too began to wave wildly. He shouted something which Alex was unable to make out and began to run along the quay, still shouting. Alex could only wave in response, immensely cheered to have someone to send him on his way after all. At that minute he became aware of James Bantrie at his elbow holding out a thick wad of correspondence with Alexander's name scrawled across the outside, in Hugh's almost indecipherable hand.

'Such a pity,' said James. 'Your brother arrived only moments before the last bell for boarding. He thrust this package into my hands and bade me wish you a fond farewell from all the family.'

Alexander stepped forward and waved and waved until Hugh became a minute figure in the distance. Only then did he turn back with a lump in his throat, intending to thank James Bantrie. Considerately, the minister had already withdrawn.

*

There were four letters each bidding him farewell in their own way. His mother's, was full of loving words and fond memories of his childhood and his father's a homily on how to behave in order to maintain the standards of a gentlemen even in the primitive situation in which he might find himself in New Edinburgh. The third letter was in a firm round hand more akin to the schoolroom than to that of a grown woman about to be wed.

My Dear Alexander, soon to be my Brother-in-Law,

Hugh has an appointment in Glasgow to see the lease holders of the Lunga quarries about medical care of their men. If he is offered the business, it means that the practice will double in size. I do hope it will not mean too much work for the poor dear to cope with. Anyway, this sudden call to the city means that he may have a chance to see you in person before you sail. If not, maybe he will get these letters to you by pilot boat or something.

Now Alexander Beaton, what can I say? Shall I reprove you for not delaying your emigration until you could toast me at my wedding? Shall I remind you of your broken promises to write to me in the past? How much I once longed to hear from you. Just a few words would have done.

Do you recall how we used to share our dreams of the future? How you would be a famous surgeon and I would be a country doctor's wife, keeping a motherly eye on the community?

I shall always remember when I was no more than five years old, how shocked my mother was when I talked of nursing the sick in some great hospital in the city. It was many years before I understood why she was so distressed! It is so unfair that men are the ones to be the doctors. What a pity it is that to be a nursing sister in a hospital one must either take Holy Orders or be considered little better than a whore! No wonder my mother was so distressed!

Some of those dreams we once shared are already fulfilled. I shall be a doctor's wife and you are to practise surgery, even if it is only in a remote corner of the Empire! Was this departure for a foreign clime always part of your plan, I cannot recall? If you must go away, why should it be to New Zealand? Why not Africa or India, somewhere where the British are well established and used to being in charge? Travel to and from these places is frequent and without incident but New Zealand is such an untamed, savage land, filled with so many unknowns.

So, my dear brother-to-be, soon you will be thousands of miles away on the far side of the world, while I shall be writing the labels on the bottles, pacifying the mewling infants and calming the anxious mothers. I do so admire the way your mother seems to know what is to be done when patients come to the door in the doctor's absence. She has promised to teach me all about the healing herbs her mother used to gather and make into medicines and ointments. It will be like going back to school but I am so looking forward to it.

Promise you will remember to write to us when you reach the shores of your new homeland. I shall look forward to hearing of your adventures. Who knows, perhaps one day I shall have a beautiful, dusky native maiden for a sister-in-law? Wouldn't that cause a stir in the parish if you brought her home with you!

Our love goes with you to your new Eden. God speed.

Your loving sister-in-law to be, Annie.

Alexander read the letter through again and again, searching for some small indication of regret, some hint of remorse. The thoughts she expressed were as childlike as the neat round hand that had written them down. It appeared that Annie was more concerned about the trivia of her new life, than she was about the man she was to marry. She was in love with the idea of being the doctor's wife, not with Hugh himself. What of Hugh? Was he to be satisfied with any wife just so long as she was presentable, knew her place in society and fulfilled all the accepted functions of a doctor's spouse?

He turned to the next letter, this one from Hugh, himself. Alexander was not to know until later what Hugh had to say. He had read no more than the opening sentence before Jessie Dundas and her little boy came to stand beside him at the stern rail. She looked a little weary, her clothing crumpled and her hair in disarray. The women must have been more difficult to settle than he had supposed they would be.

Jessie had begun the day in a neat black dress and snow white pinafore, her lustrous dark tresses firmly entrapped in a severe bun at the nape of her neck. When, earlier on, he had watched her going about her duties she had impressed him with her efficiency and her authoritative manner. In the fading light, he studied her more closely. Wisps of hair had escaped to soften the outline of her face. Deepening shadows blunted the sharpness of her well-chiselled features and she wore a cheerful, almost relaxed air.

'At last I begin to feel the adventure has begun!' she cried ecstatically and bending down to gain wee Tammy's attention, she pointed out the place on the north bank of the Clyde where she had been born, thirty years before.

'See Thomas, where that great rock stands out in the river? It is called Dunbarton Rock. When I was wee girl, not much older than you, my brothers and I would bathe in the river from that little beach. Do you see?'

'Not the cleanest stretch of river,' observed Alexander, 'considering the amount of household and industrial waste that must find its way into the waters of the Clyde by this time!'

'We thought nothing of that,' she retorted. 'For us it was our only playground and we came to no harm from it.'

She stared wistfully into the distance and as she did so her expression altered becoming harder and more resolute, just as it had been when they had first met on the Island of Orchy.

She had never mentioned that she had brothers. He had understood her to be all alone in the world.

'Where are they, these brothers?'

The ship was under full sail. The barges had discharged their duty and departed and with the tide turning and the evening breeze blowing westwards off shore, the *Albatross* moved smoothly and swiftly down river towards the sea. It would be some time before the evening meal was ready. Alexander looked around for somewhere where they could sit and spied a stack of wooden rafts firmly fixed to the bulwarks.

'What are these?' demanded wee Tammy.

'They're in case we are shipwrecked,' Alexander told him. 'Should the ship founder, they would be cut adrift and thrown overboard for people to cling to.'

'Oh I hope we shall have a chance to use them!' the boy cried excitedly, dancing up and down and running to peer over the side, marvelling at the great distance between himself and the surface of the river.

Jessie shuddered. 'Hush Tam,' she said reprovingly, 'don't say such things. You don't know what you are talking about!'

'This is a fine strongly built vessel,' Alex tried to reassure her as he settled comfortably beside her on their makeshift couch. 'Her crew are all picked men who know their business. I do not think we shall come to any harm.'

She remained silent, his interruption having broken the thread of her recollections.

'You were telling me about your brothers,' he reminded her, gently.

'If you are sure you want to hear it.' She seemed hesitant.

'But of course,' he assured her, anxious to learn all there was to know about her.

'My mother bore four children who survived beyond infancy, my three brothers and myself. I was the second child, older than my twin brothers by five years. I think there may have been other siblings born dead or who did not survive for more than a few weeks. They were never spoken of.'

Alexander nodded, understanding. The high incidence of infant mortality was an accepted fact amongst both the poorest and the wealthiest in the land.

'My mother was weak after the birth of the twins' she continued. She never completely recovered, soon becoming a permanent invalid. At the age of ten I was left in charge of the household. My father was a schoolmaster, an academic who knew nothing of the practicalities of running a home.'

'When Danny, my older brother, contracted Diphtheria he was so ill that my father called in the local physician who bled him to release the ill humours and purged him relentlessly to clear the bowels. Dan had been a strong boy full of vitality. It was clear that he was wasting away fast. We could only look on while he choked and struggled for breath. At last he simply faded away.'

She paused, remembering the incident as though it were yesterday. Instinctively, Alexander took her hand to comfort her. She did not shrug him off.

'As if this was not enough for us all to endure,' she continued, 'no sooner had Danny been interred than the twins contracted the disease, simultaneously. This time I insisted that I would take care of them without calling in the doctor.' Glancing at Alexander apologetically, she explained, 'He seemed to have done more harm than good.'

Alexander nodded.

'My own professor of medicine was wont to say that some surgeons are too keen to interfere heroically; to rush in with leech and bleeding cup before finding out what is the trouble.'

'I sponged them down and fed them thin gruel until their throats were so closed over that they could not swallow,' she told him. 'A neighbour brought my mother Peruvian bark which she had ground up and made into a tincture. It took down their fever but made them vomit and gave them the flux. They grew weaker and weaker. I do so wish they had left me alone to take care of the boys in my own way,' her eyes filled with tears as she continued. 'They would have got better I know they would, but my mother insisted in pursuing the treatment. On the third day, they were both dead.'

Once again she paused in her narrative and Tammy fidgeted, bored with the adult's conversation.

'Why don't you go and find James,' she suggested. 'He will surely be back in his cabin by now.'

The child scampered off and Jessie, settling herself more comfortably, continued,

'Strangely, after their death my mother recovered her strength and we three lived quite normally together for a few years. Then my father's old war wound which had never healed completely broke out again becoming severely ulcerated. Mother nursed him until her own health once more deteriorated while I took on the whole burden of Father's work in the schoolroom. I had to. We needed what little income I could earn.'

It was clear that Jessie was steeling herself to tell him the next part and Alexander was inclined to bid her cease, since the story gave her so much pain. Having started, however, she intended to finish.

'At last my mother died and I was forced to give up my teaching post.'

She stopped suddenly, unwilling to reveal that she had accompanied her father to the infirmary. She would have to admit to rubbing shoulders with those coarse women of low morals and ill repute who were normally employed to clean the wards and provide what few comforts were available for the sick.

Leaving out the most damning part of her narrative, she ended the story abruptly. 'While I was caring for my father during in his last days, I met my future husband. It was as though God knew that I was going to be alone in the world and provided a fresh champion for me.'

'You were happy then, when he took you back with him to Orchy?'

'Thomas Dundas was a good man, faithful, brave, hard working, everything a woman could hope for in a husband. If only those island women had not soured our life together. They hated me because I was an outsider. I suppose there were young females who had had their eye on Dougie, who knows? They never accepted me as one of themselves.'

Alexander squeezed the hand which had, all this while, lain limply in his own.

'This is a new beginning for you,' he told her. 'I for one shall do all in my power to make the next stage of your life full and happy. Whenever you are free to do so, you must come to the dispensary and we will study together for I am assured that anyone with medical knowledge is to be welcomed in New Zealand.'

'I should like that,' she told him. 'Maybe I shall have an opportunity to assist you with nursing the sick on board should need arise.'

'I think it will not be necessary,' he replied, almost wishing that it might be so. 'I intend to enjoy this voyage. I shall make the most of the opportunity to read some real literature for a change in place of all those serious medical tomes. Should the need arise, however,' he added hastily, 'I shall remember your offer.'

Chapter Eight

The Albatross had one more port of call before leaving the United Kingdom. Among those coming aboard from this southern city was the party headed by Sir Tristram Wimborne whose family seat had been for many generations, situated in the county of Hampshire. With the family fortunes at a low ebb and a threat of bankruptcy likely to blacken his name amongst his socialite friends, this gentleman had decided to try his luck on a clean slate, elsewhere. His party was small consisting of himself, his wife, his manservant and his wife's personal maid. They were to occupy the grandest passenger accommodation available.

At the age of eleven Nellie Parker had been placed in the household of Sir Tristram Wimborne as a tweeny maid, rising before dawn to lay and light the fires in all the rooms and carrying endless cans of hot water up and down stairs. She had been at the beck and call of the lowliest member of the servant's hall throughout the day and would fall exhausted into her truckle bed beneath the eaves at ten o'clock but only after all the fires had been stoked for the evening.

Within ten years she had progressed to become at first, parlour maid and then lady's maid to the Wimborne's elder daughter. During in all that time she had been allowed, on alternate Wednesdays and every second Sunday in the month, to visit her parents and the growing collection of siblings who occupied the one roomed cottage she called home. Otherwise there were no holidays and there was no opportunity to experience any life other than that within the boundaries of the Wimborne's own estates. When Her Ladyship's personal maid had refused to travel to New Zealand with her mistress Nellie had seized the opportunity for advancement without hesitation.

Life aboard the *Albatross* represented an independence she could never have imagined. Once her mistress had dismissed her from her duties she was free to roam the ship, participate in the activities provided for the entertainment of all and listen to the talk of the other passengers. This ranged from the reasons for their departure from Britain and those politics of the day which had decided so many of them to seek a different kind of life elsewhere. She listened also to speculation about the hardships these adventurers expected to encounter in a new and untamed land.

Until now Nellie had seen little hope of her life ever changing. She could see herself washing out My Lady's small clothes, combing My Lady's hair and gathering up My Lady's discarded garments until the day she died. She could dream however. Perhaps the day would come when some knight in shining armour would sweep her away to a life of infinite luxury. There were no half measures in Nellie's experience. She knew of only two kinds of existence, the poverty of the tiny cottage by the canal where she was born, its timbers stinking of rot and the plaster peeling from damp walls and the grand houses in London and Hampshire where she had spent her working life. She had no intention of returning to the former and if to remain in the latter meant spending the rest of her days acceding to the orders of Lady Wimborne and her kind, so be it.

In the single women's cabin she listened to the talk of those brought up in middle class families, the daughters of merchants, clergymen, doctors and teachers who were themselves well read and aspiring to salaried positions as governess, nursery nurse or schoolteacher in Otago. Then there were the women who had run hostels or taverns or who had kept house for aged parents, all of them prepared to undertake this adventure to find something better, something new and exciting.

There had been no opportunity for contact with members of the opposite sex in the Wimborne household. Nellie was no ignoramus however for in her former existence there had never been a shortage of female servants to put her on the right path to understanding the ways of gentlemen. She had been warned early on of such of the Wimbornes' male visitors who might seek their night time pleasures in the servant's quarters and she had observed at first hand the treatment meted out to any serving girl who got herself in the family way having succumbed to such advances. So far she had managed to steer clear of anything which might take her out of the comfortable situation she had carved for herself.

The butler and footmen employed by Sir Tristram had been for the most part venerable gentlemen, married and with daughters of Nellie's age. Fred Weeks, Sir Tristram's personal manservant, was a younger man but he displayed no interest whatsoever in women quite the opposite in fact. The gardener's boys of her own generation were always destined to be just that, garden boys without prospects. Aboard ship however, provided she could escape the eagle eye of Mrs Dundas, Nellie found herself almost daily in conversation with young gentlemen of a very different calibre, particularly the younger officers.

She was a pretty girl who made the most of her assets. She gave her lustrous chestnut brown hair a hundred strokes of the brush every night before sleeping, something she had learned to do for her mistress. She plucked at her bushy eyebrows to make them thin and seductive and would curl her long lashes over the handle of her button hook so that they swept upwards in a delicate curve and down to lie prettily on the peach bloom of her faintly coloured cheeks. Her nose, which was lightly dusted with freckles, turned up just sufficiently to give her a saucy air which was compounded by the twinkle in her light blue eyes and the faint laughter lines about her mouth.

From time to time Lady Wimborne handed down items of dress she could no longer squeeze into and Nellie had amassed a considerable wardrobe of good quality clothes. She was handy with a needle and had managed to convert her mistress's fashionable although rather fussy gowns into something which, while more appropriate to a lady's maid, nevertheless retained the cut and fall of a couturier's model. To the young men aboard the Albatross, she was delicious. In the officer's mess there was great competition to see who would be the first to gain her affections. Mr Midshipman Frawley wasted no time at all in staking his claim for he believed he knew just the way to gain her attention.

He approached her one morning when she was busy at the tub, enduring the cold winter winds with fortitude as she scrubbed away at her mistress's fine linen. She held up a pair of lacy drawers and uttered a cry of despair. The dirty mark she had struggled for several minutes to eliminate remained untouched.

'Madam will give me such a wigging,' she declared to her companions. 'She does not appreciate the problem we have washing in salt water. See, the soap will not lather and the rubbing stone is wearing away the cloth. Everything will be in ruins before we reach New Zealand.'

She rang out the garments, twisting them ferociously to remove all the water, and hung them to dry. As she rolled down the sleeves of her plain working dress her hair fell forward onto her face its neat curls having been dislodged by her energetic activities. She tossed the heavy locks out of her eyes and found herself staring into the smiling face of Mr Midshipman Frawley.

'Here, let me carry that for you Miss Palmer,' he said, removing the empty water jug from her grasp.

They ambled slowly along the deck. She was weary after her morning's activity while he was anxious to prolong their meeting.

'I could not help hearing your complaint about the sea water,' he said casually. 'We have on board a special kind of soap which works better than the ordinary lye soap you are using. Would you care to try some and see how you get along?'

'Anything must be an improvement upon what we have been using,' she replied, viewing her reddened hands with dismay. 'The idea of a sea voyage was most appealing when I first heard of it,' she told him, 'but no one suggested one's clothes were going to be ruined and one's hair would become unmanageable.'

With an enchanting little toss of the head she shook out her imprisoned locks so that the glorious mass of curls tumbled down around her shoulders. Julian Frawley took a quick look around to ensure that there were no prying eyes, put down the jug and drew her towards him. As he pressed her into the shadow of the poop deck he accepted her invitation to examine what a mess the salt air had made of her hair.

'Well, well now.' he said, stroking the chestnut curls which were indeed sticky with salt,' I am sure that I can do something about that for a price.'

'What price would that be,' she asked, coquettishly.

'Just this,' he said and bent to kiss her full on the lips. She feigned surprise and blushed prettily.

'And what do I get for that?' she asked.

'Follow me.'

Passengers were permitted to collect their supplies of drinking water at specified times of the day from the hold, which was approached through the steerage cabin on the lower deck. For occasional drinks, a barrel was constantly on tap outside the mid-ship house. Mr Frawley however took Nellie by the hand and led her down a companionway usually forbidden to passengers. He opened a heavy door into the forward hold where the chain locker housed the anchor chain when the ship was at sea. Here, additional space had been created by Mr Wallace to store those additional barrels of water which Frawley himself had collected the night before the ship left Glasgow.

'This is the emergency supply,' Frawley explained to the girl. 'No one knows about it but myself and the First Mate, plus a few of the men who carried it down here. Provided the ship is not delayed there is every chance that this water will never be needed. If you promise to come here only in company with myself I shall see to it that you get all the fresh water you need to wash that pretty hair of yours.'

He grabbed at her in the darkness and kissed her again, this time so passionately she thought she would not be able to breathe.

She pushed him away.

'I think maybe the price is too high!' she suggested.

'Come on, just one more kiss and you shall take away a whole jug full of fresh water that you may use for your own purposes.'

'Oh, all right then,' she gave in, perhaps a little too easily for this time he pushed down her loosely fitting bodice to expose the top of one tantalising breast whose soft white flesh he brushed with velvet lips.

Nellie felt that her knees would melt. She knew she should not allow it and yet she did not want him to stop. She closed her eyes in expectation of the delights to come.

Not too fast, Julian Frawley warned himself. This was no dock-side whore he was dealing with. He must proceed with caution and give her just enough to want more. He drew back, kissed her on the tip of her turned up nose and tapped her well padded rump.

He filled her jug from one of the barrels and handed it to her.

'We must not be seen leaving here together,' he warned. 'Follow me and keep quiet.'

He led the way up the ladder to the open hatch, she following on, carrying the jug carefully so as not to spill one precious drop of water.

At the top of the companion ladder he paused, looking to right and left to make sure the coast was clear. The officer on the poop deck was preoccupied with his charts and the helmsman had his back towards them. He waved her on, watching as she darted across the white-stoned deck to slip past the door to the Chief Cabin.

At that moment, Fred Weeks stepped outside, also carrying a water jug and seeing her there he called out to her.

'You must have anticipated her Ladyship's need, Nellie.'

Without asking, he took the freshly filled jug from her and replaced it with the empty one he was carrying. 'Run along and fill that one too if you please Nellie, and bring some more limes from the galley. The mistress is calling for her midday refreshment.'

Muttering indignantly to herself, Nellie descended to the lower deck and went to fetch the allocation of water which was dispensed at midday. She could hardly use this jug for her own purposes now. She supposed she would have to wait until she could persuade Mr Frawley to take her to the chain locker again.

While she waited in line for her jug to be filled from the barrel, she passed her fingertips across her lips which were still tingling from the pressure of his kiss. She blushed as she anticipated what might happen the next time she went with him to fetch water.

*

Catherine had brought with her a small reading book, some pencils and the remains of a block of drawing paper from which several sheets had already been removed. She wished she could bring the child new things, but this was all she had until the time came for them to visit the family's heavy luggage stored in the hold. Feeling somewhat ridiculous, she tapped at the stable door before opening it and looking inside.

Philip Mackie lay on his straw-filled pallet gazing up at the light filtering through cracks in the rough planking. For some while he had been making out in his head the pictures formed by the intense lights and shadows of his little cell and wishing he could find a way to put down what he saw on paper. He could only wish he had the materials and indeed the expertise, to do so.

'Hallo,' Catherine called from the doorway. 'May I come in?'

'I don't know,' he raised himself on his elbows and levered himself into a corner of the bunk as if to get as far away from her as possible. 'The doctor says I must not get too close to anyone. I am ill, you see.'

'I know,' she told him. 'I have permission to come and talk to you for a while, if you want.'

At the start of the voyage Philip had been starved of human contact. Most days he saw no one except Jessie Dundas, when she brought him his food or came to wash his face and hands. Soon however Sir Tristram's groom who looked in each morning to see that the horses were in good order, began to find a cheery word for the invalid. Unfortunately, his visits were short and usually taken up dealing with the needs of his four-legged charges. As Philip had become stronger from the regular meals and the copious supply of fresh air which his new quarters provided, the boy was able spend more time on his feet and take an interest in the animals about him.

By the time the ship docked in Southampton, the boy felt sufficiently strong to help muck out the beasts and prepare their fodder and soon the pigs and chickens were looking out for him when feeding time came around. The groom showed him how to use a curry comb and was soon leaving much of the work connected with the horses, to him.

'Ye'll no want for an occupation in New Zealand, I'm thinking,' the man observed after a while. 'You'll mak' a fine farrier like y' faither, when y're a mite bigger.'

In the solitude of his lonely bed the child examined his wasted limbs comparing them with the broad shoulders and iron muscles of his father and knew that despite the groom's encouragement, there was no possibility that he would ever be a blacksmith. If it were possible, he would prefer to continue to draw pictures and conjure up poems in his head. He could not write them down for he had never managed to learn to write in the few months which he had spent in school during a childhood so frequently interrupted by sickness.

Since he had come on board the *Albatross* Philip Mackie had become accustomed to being on his own, appreciating the silence and the absence of sibling rivalry which at home had always interfered with his most intimate thoughts. Unusually for a boy of his age, he preferred his own company and was generally reluctant to share his space. The animals however kept him warm at night and the gentle rustling of straw and the soft blowing through the horses' velvet nostrils were his lullaby as he drifted into sleep.

At first he was suspicious of Catherine's claim to want to help him. His first instinct was to register annoyance, regarding her presence as an intrusion. Curiosity overcame apprehension however when he spotted the book tucked under her arm. 'What's that?' he asked.

'It's a story book,' she replied showing him the cover and handing it out to him. He took it from her, his eyes devouring the charming wood engraving of fairies at play beside a stream, white water tumbling over moss covered rocks and tall trees bending to meet their own reflections in the water.

'How do they do that?' he asked, enthralled.

'I believe it's called a wood cut,' she replied, not entirely sure herself. 'You carve out the spaces you want left white and then ink over the wood. The impression you make is your picture.'

She wondered that he had seen nothing like it before. He studied the picture, enthralled, trying to work out how anyone could make such an intricate design so skilfully.

'I wondered if you might like to borrow the book, to read it' she suggested.

'Can't read,' he replied. 'Never learned.'

'But you must be ten years old at least!' she cried in disbelief. 'Did you not go to school?'

'Yes, once. I didn't like it,' he dismissed the subject, bored with the discussion and returned to admiring the picture.

'I could teach you to read,' she suggested, not to be rejected so arbitrarily.

'You can read to me if you like,' he suggested. That was the one thing he had liked about school. The teacher had read a few chapters of a story about a man shipwrecked on a desert island. He had always wondered what happened in the later chapters.

'Of course I'll read it,' she said, delighted to have gained his attention at last. 'I can sit here in the doorway. The doctor can hardly object to that.'

'I thought you said you had his permission to come here,' said the boy. Despite being unable to read, he seemed extraordinarily astute in other ways.

'Mrs Dundas said she would talk to him about it,' Catherine explained hastily. 'I have no doubt he will agree to my being here.'

If she sat by the open door, she could not share the book with him and therefore would not be able to suggest he try read it himself. The excitement caused by her sudden appearance and the argument which had followed had tired Philip. He handed back her book, lay slumped against the stable wall and closed his eyes. She glanced at him anxiously. The doctor would certainly not approve if her presence made the boy ill.

'Shall I begin?' she asked tentatively.

'Of course, I'm listening.'

The book contained a collection of stories by the Brothers Grimm. Although they were about fairies and hobgoblins they were sufficiently gruesome to satisfy the requirements even of a ten- year- old boy. Catherine's brother James loved them all and many of his own fantasy games were based on tales of princesses locked in towers and children eaten by wicked witches.

She began to read. By the time she had finished the first story, Philip was snoring gently.

'I'm sorry I bored you,' she whispered, not wanting to wake him. She supposed that the sleep was what he required and was not offended. She stepped inside and laid the drawing book and pencils at the foot of his makeshift bed before creeping away. Perhaps the drawing things would keep him amused until she came again.

*

It was no more than five days later when, at four bells in the early morning watch, Alexander Beaton was called to attend Lady Wimborne. The woman was suffering from severe stomach cramps, had vomited twice within the hour and had a severe case of diarrhoea.

The overly dramatic description of her symptoms relayed by the manservant Mr Weeks, caused the doctor to suspect that this summons in the middle of the night was a false alarm. Nevertheless, he drew on his shirt and trousers and hurried along to the Chief Cabin. Supposing sea sickness to be the most likely cause of the lady's malady Alexander was disturbed to find her flushed and running an inordinately high temperature. With each muscular spasm of the abdomen her legs were drawn up to her belly and she moaned faintly. It was clear that her pain was quite as excruciating as Weeks had described.

His rapid examination left little doubt in Alexander's mind that Lady Wimborne was suffering from a serious condition of the bowel. He set about immediately to try to alleviate her symptoms but there was little he could do except administer opiates for the pain and fluids as rapidly as the patient could take them in. He called for the galley hands to get a fire going so that bricks could be heated and packed around her and sufficient tepid water provided for the continuous sponge baths which would be required to reduce her temperature. Weeks was dispatched to rouse Mrs Dundas while Sir Tristram who, on hearing Alexander's diagnosis, was beside himself with fear, was confined to his day cabin to ensure that the disease should not be transmitted to others in the ship.

When Jessie arrived, she exchanged a few brief words with the doctor before getting to work.

'I have every reason to believe this is a case of cholera,' he told her. 'We shall treat this as we did the enteric fever, but I fear that the prognosis is a poor one. With your assistance I shall administer saline solution anally, but I fear it will do little to restore the body fluids.'

With a minimum of instruction, Jessie set about preparing the sick room for the treatment which was to follow. Once she had taken over the care of the patient Alex was free to question Sir Tristram and later, Weeks and the maid, about what Lady Wimborne had eaten and drunk in the past few days.

'My wife drinks only tea and plenty of the lime- flavoured water which you yourself, advocated,' Sir Tristram assured him.

'Never touch the stuff myself,' he declared, pouring a generous dram of whisky from the glass decanter at his elbow and swallowing the better part of it in one gulp.

'As for food,' Weeks intervened, 'My Lady eats very little. Everything other than dinner is prepared by myself.' This was said in a manner defying Alex to suggest there might be anything amiss with the man's cooking. 'One would suppose that if it were yesterday's dinner to blame you would have other patients,' he concluded.

Alexander had already reached the same conclusion. He sent Weeks for the First Officer and an inspection of all the sleeping quarters was made to find out if there were others on board suffering from the same condition. Mr Wallace came back with the good news that, other than a certain amount of nausea due to the rolling of the ship, they were after all making their way through the Bay of Biscay which is notorious for its heavy seas, everyone was quite well.

The *Albatross* had been at sea scarcely a week since leaving Southampton. It was always possible that Lady Wimborne had brought the condition on board with her. Alexander prayed that it might be so.

'We must be thankful that the Wimbornes have so little contact with the rest of the passengers,' Alex told Jessie as they worked together to reduce the raging temperature of their patient. Uncomplaining, Jessie removed soiled bed linen and spread clean sheets provided by Weeks from her ladyship's generous supply. When Weeks offered to take away the sheets for washing, she stopped him. 'They will need to be steeped in lysol and then boiled,' she told him. 'You may watch what I do the first time, then we'll see.'

Alex could not help but smile at the way she had taken command of the situation. Her duties in the women's cabin had given her a certain authority which she exercised with determination, albeit with a ladylike discretion.

Her unexpected efficiency in dealing with matters however gave Alexander cause for speculation. As he continued with the routine tasks of managing the case he considered the problems of laundering were the disease to spread throughout the ship. He tried to sort out in his own mind what steps might be taken to limit the damage to passengers and crew alike.

Alexander had seen the devastating effects of Cholera when completing his training as a physician in the poorer quarters of Glasgow. He was aware that the greatest danger to the patient was from dehydration. Body fluids were being lost constantly at a rate which could not be compensated for by imbibing further liquids. It was usual for the patient to deteriorate rapidly until the kidneys failed and death ensued and so it was with Lady Tristram Wimborne. Despite the best efforts of Alex and Jessie to alleviate the symptoms, all they could manage was to allow the woman to die in peace under the influence of large doses of laudanum.

During this period of frenzied activity in the Chief cabin, the First Mate kept an anxious eye on the remainder of the passengers and the crew, on the alert should the disease break out elsewhere. It was with great relief that he could report to Dr Beaton at the end of each day that all was well.

Following Lady Wimborne's death, the passengers gathered silently on deck for the burial service. There was a eulogy delivered by Sir Tristram himself followed by prayers conducted by the Chaplain, Dr Bantrie.

'Brethren, we have seen the hand of the Lord at work here. While he has seen fit to take our sister Winifred from our midst he has in his infinite wisdom seen fit to spare the lives of others on board this ship. We must thank Him for his great mercy and pray that he will deliver us from all the evils which might beset us now and in the unknown future that lies ahead.'

Jessie Dundas, her hands firmly upon her little son's shoulders lest he dart away in the throng, commented in a sotto voice, 'and thanks also to Dr Beaton for taking matters in hand to see the disease did not spread.'

Her remark was directed at Judith Bantrie who, despite her fervent loyalty towards her husband, was of a similar opinion. Her only comment was, 'with help from you my dear. With your help, also.'

Knowing the officers would be wearing their best uniforms, Tobias had seen to it Alexander too was appropriately attired for the funeral. Today he wore the suit in which he had greeted the passengers on the day of departure. Toby had brushed it carefully, folded it into a linen bag and stowed it carefully in a locker to be unearthed solely for this solemn occasion. As James Bantrie's sermon droned on, Alexander found himself feeling in his pockets for some form of diversion. His fingers encountered a stiff envelope which he withdrew cautiously, hoping no one would witness his transgression. Recognising his brother's hand, he recalled the letter as yet unread, which he had received as the ship drew away from the quay in Glasgow. He slipped out the contents and began to read.

My Dear Brother,

I hope I shall be able to deliver my news myself but should I be delayed and cannot catch you before you leave, I trust you will receive this somehow. I have recently spent a few days at the Edinburgh infirmary renewing acquaintance with some of the staff. I took the opportunity to make some enquiries about a certain widow, Mrs Dundas, whom you may have come across on your visit to the Isle of Orchy. When she assisted me in setting the Bantrie boy's leg I felt sure I had met her before, while I was a student in Edinburgh. I have now confirmed she was indeed nursing the sick in the infirmary, which is where I must have encountered her. Well, you know what a reputation such women have. She is certainly not a suitable companion for respectable society. Imagine how distressed I was to learn she was to accompany the Rev. Bantrie and his family to New Zealand. Perhaps you will find a way to warn Mrs Bantrie of the danger she puts herself in associating with such a woman and of course you yourself should keep your distance. You don't want to blight your reputation in a small community where the truth is most likely to come out.

Here's wishing you well old fellow! Think of Annie and I in our mundane surroundings while you charge through the untamed wilderness placing your footprints where no man has been before!

Alexander read the letter twice, unable to fully absorb his brother's further comments for the anger rising in his breast. The insufferable prig! What did Hugh know of Jessie? He had met what, once, twice at most, knowing nothing of her circumstances. Yet he felt compelled to besmirch her reputation in this way. Alexander had to admit he had wondered at Jessie's ability to carry out sickroom duties with such skill. Now he understood. It was no wonder she was such an excellent nurse. He had certainly witnessed some unsavoury characters amongst the nursing staff during his student days, but he could not believe Jessie would have associated with such women. If anything was amiss Judith Bantrie would surely have found it out by now.

He glanced up to see both women staring at him, wondering no doubt why he was not attending to the ceremony. He smiled briefly in their direction and screwed the letter into a tight ball. As Lady Wimborne's body slid silently beneath the waves, Hugh's letter followed it over the rail. Its contents would never be revealed to anyone.

Sir Tristram retired to his cabin to mourn with his whisky bottle for comfort and with Weeks in constant attendance. Nellie Parker with her services no longer required, found herself free to enjoy life as never before. That there would be no employment for her in the Wimborne household once they reached New Zealand troubled her little. She was confident Providence would provide for her, one way or another. Her best solution would be to find herself a husband and while there were plenty of eligible young bachelors to choose from, she determined to make the most of her opportunity. Since Mr Frawley had already shown an interest she decided to concentrate her attentions upon him.

Thereafter she proposed several trips to the chain locker in his company returning each time, her hair just a little awry and her cheeks charmingly pink, carrying a jug full of fresh water. She would take her prize straight away to the canvas bathhouse which had been rigged on deck for use by the ladies. By using it immediately to wash her hair and rinse out her small clothes there was no chance that the other women would guess that she as not using salt water. In her heart, she knew that what she was doing was wrong but Julian Frawley had assured her that the ship was making such good progress there was little chance that they would be late arriving at their destination. How vexed she would be if they were to reach Otago with the chain locker full of barrels of unused water and her fine linen underwear in tatters.

When her cabin companions asked how she managed to get her clothes so clean and keep her hair so fine and silky, she explained it by showing them the bar of special soap which Frawley had given her. In answer to their pleas to borrow the amazing product she would say that she could not allow anyone else to borrow it because she had only the one bar and she wanted it to last for as long as possible.

After a week when there was no sign of further cases of cholera developing, Alexander declared the danger past. His explanation was that Lady Wimborne contracted the disease before embarkation. Cross infection had been avoided and there was nothing further to fear.

Chapter Nine

As the vessel drew nearer to the Tropic of Cancer, the weather improved and the passengers spent much more of every day on deck. Catherine was allowed to sit outside with Philip Mackie for hours at a time and at last was able to begin teaching the boy to read. He had resisted at first, preferring to draw his pictures or to watch the sea for the occasional sighting of a school of porpoises or sea birds flying far out from land but he was a bright lad and at last, with Catherine's persistent urging he began to master the principles of reading. He was soon devouring the contents of any book he could lay hands on but found the most inspiring stories in Catherine's own small copy of the New Testament. What he read inspired his drawing and soon his sketch book was full of illustrations of the tales he had either read for himself or which Catherine had read to him.

The invalid' s unexpected appearance on deck with the voyage well under way, caused some eyebrows to be raised. The other passengers knew the rules about taking any unhealthy person on board and the recent scare over Lady Wimborne had raised fears of any kind of outbreak of disease.

Dr Beaton was obliged to make a statement that the child's condition was no longer acute and that the disease could not be transmitted to others if the rules he had laid down were observed. It was the fact that he was conducting an experiment which might be beneficial not only to his young patient but also to other sufferers of phthisis which put a stop to their murmurings.

By the time the ship had crossed the equator and the passengers had celebrated in time – honoured fashion, little Philip Mackie was as rosy cheeked as any child on board, his sputum was no longer flecked with blood and his tiresome coughing had ceased altogether.

Although he still felt it unwise to allow Philip to mix with the other passengers in the confined atmosphere below deck, Alexander saw no reason why the boy should not now amuse himself in company with other children in the open air. Tommy Dundas and Charlie Bantrie, by now the firmest of friends, took it upon themselves to provide for his entertainment. They taught Philip to play deck quoits and a game of deck draughts at which both had become very proficient during the voyage but as little boys will, they were soon looking for something more adventurous.

It was a warm, sultry afternoon. The tropical sun beat down relentlessly upon the decks causing the planks to shrink and the corking between to loosen. Morning and afternoon, Captain McCallum ordered the deck to be swilled down with sea water to prevent the planks from opening up. It was a job with which the boys liked to join in, soaking themselves and everyone around them.

In the aftermath of this frenzied activity, they lay now in the shadow of the main mast, contemplating the spider's web of rigging above their heads and speculating on the chances of their being able to climb to the crow's nest.

'It's not difficult with the mainsail furled and the t'gallants double reefed," declared Charlie Bantrie trying to impress his comrades with his seaman's talk. 'I've watched Mr Frawley. He climbs up there as easily as if he were running upstairs.'

'It's very high,' observed Tommy Dundas, comparing his short fat little legs with Charlie's longer, stronger, ones.

'Would you go if I did?' asked Philip calmly.

The others stared at him.

'You can't go up,' said Charlie decisively. 'You're not well enough. What if you were to get stuck and couldn't get down?'

'I might be weaker than you two,' said Philip, 'but I'm older than Tommy and taller than you, Charlie. I should be able to manage all right.

'It's no good, 'said Tommy, suddenly frightened at the prospect of the climb but unwilling to admit it. 'Someone will see us and make us come down before we reach the top.'

'Not if it's dark,' said Philip.

'That's right,' said Charlie, 'we'll go up this evening while the adults are having their party' He had listened to the conversation in his parent's quarters that morning, over breakfast. There was to be a 'crossing the line' ceremony at which James Bantrie was to act as master of ceremonies. His mother would be singing and playing the mandolin while his sister would be doing one of her recitations… ugh! The very thought of listening respectfully while Catherine rattled through all thirty-two verses of Gray's Elergy in a Country Churchyard was too much to bear thinking about!

The Captain had had an awning rigged across the well of the main deck and here, by eight o'clock in the evening, the ceilidh was well under way. When Judith got up to sing, Alexander Beaton regarded her with a professional eye. She was looking better than he had ever seen her. This latest pregnancy had enhanced her appearance and she was positively blooming. He wondered idly what Bantrie had said when she told him she was to have another child. Did he rant at her he wondered, for taking such a risk as to put to sea when she knew there was a chance the birth might occur before they reached New Zealand? The minister had said nothing to him on the matter and Alex assumed that because Judith was looking so healthy James had accepted the situation and decided not to make a fuss about it.

The boys kept to the back of the audience, feigning interest for the first ten minutes or so before quietly slipping out of sight behind the long-boat which was kept amidships and used for ferrying people ashore when the *Albatross* was anchored in port.

They paused at the foot of the main mast and stared upwards through the jungle of ropes and spars to where a few feet of sail were spread to catch even the lightest wind. The Captain had put on extra canvas during the day but even the breeze which had got up at sundown was insufficient to move the ship along at more than a few knots.

It was now quite dark except for the bright pool of light surrounding the improvised stage in the well of the main deck. Otherwise, only an occasional lantern swinging from a corner of the superstructure, provided illumination to interrupt the inky blackness of the night sky.

'It'll be easy as climbing a ladder,' said Charlie encouragingly, seeing Tommy Dundas's worried expression, 'You'll see.'

'It's very dark,' said Tommy. The younger boy stared fearfully into the rigging and shivered though the night was warm and still.

'It'll be all right, kid,' said Philip taking a firm hold and pulling himself up into the rigging. Philip did not fear the climb itself so much as the wrath of Dr Beaton, should he start a coughing fit on the way up. He felt well and strong now and capable of anything. If only he could reach the crow's nest it would prove to his parents and everyone that he was no longer an invalid.

'Well, come on,' he said. 'What are we waiting for?'

If Charlie was at all worried about their exploit he showed little sign of it. As he watched the heels of his two companions disappearing into the gloom above his head he called out after them, 'I shall be a midshipman like Mr Frawley, just as soon as I'm old enough to go to sea on my own.' He hauled himself onto the wooden bulwark, grabbed at a ratline and began to climb.

Julian Frawley had singled out Catherine's brother for special attention, teaching him all manner of nautical terms and showing him how to tie knots that would not slip and to splice the loose ends of rope together, neatly. It was little wonder that young Charlie admired Mr Frawley above all the men on board. Julian Frawley for his part enjoyed the company of the youngster for he was a bright little boy and generally required telling only once. Besides which, his friendship with the lad gave him access to Charlie's sister when he needed help with his own studies while at the same time giving Miss Parsons little cause for concern about the direction of his more amorous attentions.

Tommy Dundas, following hard on Philip's heels, was concentrating on the climb and had little breath to spare for responding to Charlie's announcement. Too terrified to look down, he followed Philip's lead, placing his foot on each of the ropes as his friend vacated it. Above the sound of Philip's heavy breathing and occasional short dry cough he could hear the comforting noises of Charlie coming up behind.

About halfway between the deck and the crow's nest, Tommy paused to catch his breath. 'Just a minute,' he called out, not wanting Charlie to bump into him. He looked down to see how close they were and found himself staring straight into Charlie's upturned face. Beyond his shoulder, Tommy could pick out details of the deck below where there were isolated pools of light. A few couples were taking the air between dances, a group of men played cards beneath a lantern suspended from the wall of one of the animal pens while the helmsman, whose only light came from the illuminated face of his compass, stared straight ahead, ever on the alert for danger.

For a moment Tommy's eyes focused on the shadowy figures then he turned his gaze upon the swaying rigging and the pitching bowsprit and his head began to spin.

'Come on. Get a move on,' called Charlie impatiently.

'I can't move.' Tommy's limbs had suddenly become leaden. He was terrified.

'Of course you can. Don't look down,' commanded Charlie, recalling Mr Frawley's words about the climb to the masthead. 'If you look down you'll get giddy and fall. Hold on tight, I'm coming up to get you. Stay still and look straight ahead until I reach you. Hang on!'

Tommy tried to do as Charlie said. At last he managed to tear his gaze from the whirling deck below and instead stared into the blackness ahead. At first he saw nothing but a blur of spars and masts and flapping canvas. Then he found he could see beyond the pitching foremast to what lay ahead. Was it a trick of the light he wondered or could he really see a shadow on the port bow rising up from the surface of the sea?

Charlie had climbed up beside him. 'Come on,'

Charlie urged, 'One step at a time.'

Tommy felt his foot lifted and placed on the next rung above. ' N o w let go with your right hand and reach up. That's it.'

Despite a strong urge to resist climbing higher, Tommy found himself moving steadily upwards towards the crow's nest.

'Look up to the landlubber's hole. Do you see it, straight ahead of you?' Charlie's disembodied voice came to him out of the blackness. He looked upwards and saw the stars through an opening in the narrow platform which was now just a few yards above his head.

Charlie had often watched Mr Frawley reach this point and, spurning the easy route, climb out and over the rail onto the ledge but he knew that those who were not such expert seamen were able to go up through the hole in the decking.

With agonizingly slow movements Tommy moved on, hand over hand, grasping at the ropes above his head. From below, his friend steadied his feet.

It was all very well Charlie helping him to safety up here, Tommy thought, but they still had to get back down again. Trying not to think about the inevitable descent he reached up and made a grab at the edge of the landlubber's hole. Mustering all his strength, he pulled himself through the hole to sit on the edge of the platform with his legs dangling.

'Well, come on then,' called Charlie, 'Give a fellow some room.' Tommy clinging, limpet-like to the guard rail, finally hauled himself up onto his feet.

Philip, with his back hard against the mast, was staring back the way they had come his attention arrested by the ship's wake. The waves created by the movement of the hull broke in a shower of luminescent spray which rolled away to either side, disappearing into the blackness of the ocean. The music of the band, rising up from the deck below, blotted out the gentler sounds of the sea.

Tommy turned in the opposite direction to see if he could make out the shadow he had noticed earlier. Charlie, pausing for a moment before making a final grab for the crow's nest, nearly lost his footing at the little boy's sudden cry of alarm.

'Look there! That's rocks, ahead. See the white where the waves are breaking? That shadow must be land and we're making straight for it.'

For a few seconds the two older boys could only stare into the darkness ahead. Then, as their eyes also became adjusted to the dim light above the horizon they too cried out in alarm.

It would mean disclosing their position and facing punishment for their escapade but Charlie knew what had to be done. He lifted his hands to his mouth to make a megaphone and shouted. 'Land ho! Rocks and cliffs on the port bow!'

Steeling himself to look down over the rail, Tommy saw the people still wandering to and fro, unheeding, on deck. The helmsman stared ahead into the darkness unable to see at sea level what they could make out from this height.

Charlie tried again.

'Hallo there! Officer of the deck! Land ahead!'

The boy's high pitched shriek at last alerted the helmsman. They saw him glance upwards, peering into the rigging. He called the officer of the deck over to him and a large lantern was produced whose beam was directed towards them. Both men stared upwards searching for the source of the hullabaloo. Deciding that what they had heard must be the cry of sea birds or maybe a trick of the wind, the helmsman returned to his duty while the officer consulted his charts. The ship's position was clearly marked on the sheet calculated by Mr Frawley who had brought it up to date when he had made his final readings towards the end of his watch. According to the midshipman's calculation, they were ten miles to the east of the Azores, the only islands within a thousand miles.

Fearing now that their warning had been ignored, the children raised their voices in unison. This time their shout coincided with the ending of a dance and in the momentary silence which followed even the passengers heard their cries.

Judith Bantrie, with a mother's instinct, looked around anxiously for her son. Neither he nor Tommy Dundas were anywhere to be seen. She caught hold of Jessie's sleeve.

'It's our boys, ' she said. 'I know it is.'

Jessie too looked up in horror. She could see nothing in the darkness, but she could make out her own son's voice amongst the others. She forced a pathway through the milling passengers, all now alerted to the crisis.

'Please, let me through,' she cried, 'My son, my little boy, he's up there!'

She almost fell into the arms of the First Mate who had come on deck to discover what all the fuss was about. Still holding the distraught woman who appeared on the point of collapse, he shouted instructions to call out the captain and alert the watch below. Those younger officers who had been joining in the dancing, stepped forward to await his instructions.

Wallace glanced down for a moment into the white face of the woman who had reached out to him for help. Needing to be free of her and yet not wishing to cause further distress, he glanced around him at a sea of faces, some fearful, many hot from the dancing and ready for further excitement and spotted Alexander Beaton.

'Take care of Mrs Dundas, Doctor,' he said gruffly and thrust the widow into Alexander's arms.

'Mr Frawley, to the look-out, fast as you can. Mr Cuthbertson, go with him, get those children down from there.'

Hot headed and devil-may-care they may be, but both midshipmen were more agile and faster than their superior. While Wallace would have preferred to get the boys down himself, he knew the children would feel less intimidated and more ready to respond to the orders of his younger officers.

As Frawley and Cuthbertson climbed rapidly towards the masthead, the boy's cries became more and more desperate and Wallace began to wonder if, far from being a childish prank, their warnings were genuine. He ran to the foremost part of the bridge and stared into the night sky.

Alexander, his strong arm holding Jessie firmly around the waist, watched the midshipmen as they climbed the rigging. He could feel Jessie's heart beating rapidly against his own breast and moved her gently into the light so that he could see her face more clearly. He noted her strained and anxious expression. Poor woman, she had already lost both husband and baby daughter, could the Lord be so cruel as to take Tommy also?

'Don't worry,' he said quietly, squeezing her hand comfortingly. 'The men will get them down.'

He felt her begin to relax and would have led her to a seat but she insisted upon remaining in a position to watch every moment of the drama being enacted above their heads.

Julian Frawley arrived at the masthead a few seconds ahead of his companion and climbed up through the lubber's hole to join the boys on the crowded platform. Hoarse and almost speechless by now, Charlie grabbed his arm and pointed.

Julian stared into the night sky and for a few seconds saw nothing. Then he too gasped in horror. Ahead of them and less than a mile to port, he too could make out the white tops of breakers and beyond, the dark outline of tall cliffs. For a second there flashed on his mind's eye a picture of the chart he had so lately updated and he felt a cold chill travel down his spine. The mistake was his. He must have miscalculated!

The night was quite still now. The scant breeze hardly sufficient to flap the sails, yet the ship was still under way and yawing to port. There could be only one explanation for the movement, she was being carried along by a current, one which was taking her on a collision course with the shore.

'Land ho!' he shouted, 'two points off the port bow and closing!'

Sudden activity below assured those at the masthead that their warning was being acted upon at last.

'Get these lads down from here,' Frawley ordered his junior colleague while he himself took a more careful bearing on the rocks ahead and called again to confirm his previous estimate of their position.

Philip and Charlie were quick to respond to Mr Cuthbertson's order to climb down through the lubber's hole and make their way to the deck. Tommy took one step towards the hole and froze.

'I'm sorry,' he wailed, 'I can't do it!'

'Of course you can,' urged Frawley, anxious now to have the child down below where he stood some chance of survival should the ship strike. 'You've already done the hard part. Going down is easy.'

'I'll go first,' Cuthbertson persuaded gently. 'I'll steady your feet from below.'

He slipped through the hole, took a firm hold of the rigging with one hand and reached up to tug gently at the child's boot.

Tommy swallowed hard, tentatively lowered first one foot and then the other and went down through the hole. A few yards from the masthead a further cry from Frawley was answered from below and without thinking, Tommy looked down to see who was calling. Once again the spinning deck held his attention. He lost his footing, ran in air struggling to regain it and seemed like to lose his hold on the ropes altogether. This was no good. They would never get down to the deck at this rate. Cuthbertson climbed back up beside the boy.

'Look, young'un,' he said, 'this won't do. We haven't time to mess about. I'm needed down below. Grab me around the neck and get you foot around my waist, I'll carry you.'

'Oh no, I can't! 'sobbed the child.

'You have to… come on.'

Tommy made a grab for the officer's neck and hauled his leg across the man's back locking it tightly around his waist.

'Now the other leg.' Cuthbertson felt the weight of the boy on his shoulders and adjusted his grip on the rigging. 'All right, let go the rope… now!'

For one terrible moment Cuthbertson thought the child would let go with the wrong hand but he held fast, clinging to the midshipman's neck so that the poor fellow thought he would choke. The next second the boy had his arms locked around Cuthberstson's shoulders.

'Now hold on tight,' he ordered, 'because I need both my hands for the ropes.'

The child clung on like a monkey to its mother and Cuthbertson lowered them both to the gunwale where willing hands stretched out to take the boy.

While this small drama was being enacted in the rigging, all was frenzied activity on deck. The longboat had been moved and was already being lowered over the side. Two more boats had been launched and were waiting to pull away with tow lines fixed amidships.

Captain McCallum stood on the poop directing operations.

'Set royals, and topgallant Mr Wallace and any other sail you can cram on. We must try to get her on a starboard tack. To the bosun he cried, 'Free the anchor chain and be ready to drop as a last resort!'

With his megaphone to his lips he addressed the passengers.

'I must keep sufficient skilled seamen aboard to work the sails,' he told them, 'but I also require strong men to man the boats. This is a matter of life or death, gentlemen. Now then, who will take an oar?'

Several of the men who, only moments before had been dancing a reel beneath the awning, stepped forward and were directed to take up their positions, among them Alexander Beaton and James Bantrie.

'I can't allow you to go, Doctor,' said the First Mate, 'you may be needed here on board if she strikes.' He made no objection however when the Minister climbed into the longboat alongside the cook and the Captain's steward. There were still places to be filled in all three boats and Wallace looked around him, desperate for volunteers.

Suddenly, Jessie Dundas, who all this while had been standing close beside Alexander and holding on to Tommy so firmly the child squirmed in her grasp, turned to Judith Bantrie. Placing Tommy's hand in Judith's she murmured, 'take care of him,' and stepped down into one of the two smaller boats. Her move encouraged others of the unmarried women to follow and then, shamed by the sight of women seated at the oars, men who had hitherto held back, came forward also. Among them was Sir Tristram Wimborn and because he refused to let his master out of his sight, Fred Weeks.

The Captain had ordered more canvas to be bent on in hopes that, with the small boats to hold the ship off the land, the slightest wind getting up might fill the sails sufficiently to shift her onto a different tack.

The little boats fanned out on the starboard side and with tow ropes taught, they fought to hold the *Albatross* off the rocks. The breakers were now clearly visible, even from the boats.

Jessie was seated amidships. She grasped her oar with determination, scarcely noticing the pain when after a short while hands which had been softened by the idleness of recent weeks, became blistered and raw. At first she had felt strong and well adapted to the situation for she was used to rowing. On Orchy, after her husband's death, she had been obliged to row herself across to Lunga for supplies and had plenty of experience of handling a small boat in a heavy sea. Today the waters were quite calm and should have presented no challenge but the boat was heavy and they had been working against a fast-flowing current for a long time. Her arms were tired now and as she reached forward to make each stroke of the oar, every fibre of her body screamed in agony.

Those around her were faring no better. Two rows in front she could see the back of James Bantrie's head, slightly balding she noticed with some surprise. His hair was ruffled and his neck was red, the muscles bulging with his exertions. At his side was one of the young single lassies she had taken under her wing. She was proud to see that two further women from her cabin had volunteered to take an oar. Alice Montgomery was a governess whom she had always regarded as a prim, unfriendly person and beside her, was the rather coarse, always cheerful, Mary McBride, who had confessed to keeping a bawdy house in the east end of Glasgow. It was an odd combination and yet the two women worked well together and as they strained on the oars they sang to keep the rhythm going. Soon all on board were joining in and despite the discomfort she felt, Jessie found herself enjoying the adventure.

Mr Midshipman Cuthbertson at the helm called out the strokes, trying to get his motley crew to pull together. With his back to the Albatross and his eye on the breakers ahead he alone was able to see how little headway they were making against the current.

Those on board wrestled tirelessly with ropes and canvas bending on sail to collect every breath of wind which might carry the vessel across the current and out of harm's way. Julian Frawley, having remained at the lookout until relieved by an able seaman, now directed a group of sailors as they worked frantically bending on a foresail in a last desperate attempt to capture the slightest breeze. When all was made ready under the midshipman's command they began to haul on the sheets. To the disappointment of those passengers still crowded on deck and hoping for a miracle, the additional sail which crept to the masthead flapped ineffectively in the still air. Their collective sigh of disappointment almost immediately gave way to cheering as the great sheet of canvas caught a sudden gust of wind, shook, making a sound like a whip-crack and then billowed out, shifting the direction of the vessel quite noticeably away from its suicidal course. The excitement was short lived however. The wind dropped as suddenly as it had arisen and the Albatross was picked up once again by the current, the ship's boats quite unable to hold her on her new course.

Another hour passed. The breakers were now within two or three hundred yards and it seemed certain that the ship was going to founder.

As dawn approached the sky lightened but instead of bringing some relief to the weary passengers and crew the sight that met their eyes only deepened their conviction that all was lost.

The cliffs in their path were near vertical, some three hundred foot in height, dark and menacing. The beach beneath them was no more than a narrow shelf of rock upon which even the grey Atlantic seals had some difficulty in finding a comfortable perch. If the ship were to founder those persons cast into the sea would stand no chance at all of survival. The Captain knew it, the men knew it and many of those who stood helplessly by could see that their case was hopeless, yet no one dared voice such fears.

Aboard the *Albatross* some of the passengers fell to their knees in prayer, while in one of the boats James Bantrie chanted the words of psalm one hundred over and over again, keeping the oarsmen rowing together.

Those straining at the oars could not see how close they were coming to the rocks but in each of the boats, the man at the helm urged his crew to pull away while saying nothing to alarm them and disturb the rhythm of their strokes.

Another sudden puff of wind from off the land filled the sails and shifted the ship sideways. The helmsmen in the boats were taken by surprise; the tension on the tow ropes slackened for an instant and the advantage was already lost. The vessel swung back on her old course. Shouts of encouragement turned to cries of despair from those on board. By now every man, woman and child not occupied in saving the ship was leaning over the rail urging the rowers on.

Then as though in answer to their prayers, a second puff of wind filled the sails causing the great foresail to bulge forward over the bowsprit and the vessel shifted a full point to starboard. This time the boat's crews were ready and rapidly restored tension to the tow ropes to make the most of the change of course. The boats pulled away steadily until even the least experienced of those on board could see that the direction of the *Albatross* had altered and that beyond the edge of the cliff, clear water was in view.

Their joy was short lived however for now those on the poop deck could see that they were not out of danger yet. As the cliff fell away into the sea a long skerry of sharply pointed rocks continued westwards for several hundred yards. Waves could be seen breaking over some of the rocks but it was clear that an even greater danger was posed by those lurking beneath the surface.

Now clear of the land and with the wind filling the generous spread of sails the ship began to increase speed. In a short while she would be sailing right across that treacherous tail of rocks.

'Make ready the anchor,' shouted Captain McCallum above the roar of the surf. The bosun stood in the bows with mallet poised to strike loose the pin when an even stronger gust than before whipped around the point, filling the topgallant and causing the ship to heal right over almost running down the nearest of the small boats as she turned. Now the bowsprit was pointing to clear water, the skerry fell away to port and the ship continued to pick up speed. The crew of the longboat, together with one of the two smaller boats, at once cast off their tow ropes and rowed themselves out of danger.

The third boat, which moments before had narrowly missed being mown down, was now being pulled under by the bows her tow rope caught beneath the keel of the *Albatross.* The little craft, hauled tight against the mighty hull of the mother ship, tipped into a vertical position with her stern uppermost, spilling her crew into the water. Those fortunate enough to be thrown clear were able to swim away from the *Albatross* and tread water until the other boats came to the rescue but the remainder, caught in the undertow, were keel- hauled to their deaths.

Shouts of alarm arose from on deck as the women saw the boat in which their husbands had been rowing suddenly overturned and her crew struggling in the waves. Judith Bantrie watched in horror as James, initially thrown clear of the boat now struggled in the water. He was no swimmer and quickly began to give up the fight. She saw him wave one hand as though in farewell and then sink beneath the waves. In that instant a great yell arose from those on deck as a slight figure, that of a woman, also disappeared reappearing a moment later with the minister in her grasp. Working with her legs, her arms tight about James Bantrie, Jessie Dundas was making towards the rescue boat. Reaching it, she gave up her burden but refused to climb aboard herself. Turning back to the scene of the capsize she spotted another arm raised in despair and with swift strokes she made for the two women she had been seated behind for the past few hours. Alice Montgomery was on the point of exhaustion and it was only the support of her companion that kept her afloat. Mary McBride was no swimmer, but she made up for it in determination. She intended to keep them both alive for as long as was necessary!

'Can you manage alone if I take her from you?' gasped Jessie, coming up alongside the two women. Mary willingly passed over her burden to Jessie and scarcely waiting to see that her companion was now safe, she struck out for the longboat which was standing off some fifty yards away. As Mary came alongside she looked up into a sea of friendly faces while strong arms hauled her on board. They laid her on the boards and one of the seamen began to press on her ribcage, forcing out the water she had swallowed.

'Right, that's it then, its back to the ship for us. Ready lads?'

Lachy Stuart at the stroke position raised his oar ready to return to the ship. Julian Frawley was seated at the helm, the strain of the past hours clearly showing on his pale young face.

'We shall return to the ship when I give the order!' he yelled at Stuart. Then to the crew of the longboat, he called, 'hold your oars until the woman returns.'

'Ready, row,' commanded Stuart, ignoring the midshipman's order.

'Steady the oars,' screamed Frawley, watching the perplexed expressions of his crew.

Whose orders were they to obey? Lachy Stuart was a hard man to cross. They hesitated.

'Ready, pull,' shouted Stuart and all the oars dipped into the water.

Frawley held fast to the helm, still refusing to throw it over and turn the boat back towards the ship. Still under sail, the *Albatross* had covered several hundred yards while the rescue was taking place. Although the captain was fighting to reduce sail and slow her down, he must keep the ship under way or she would be swept back towards the land.

'Turn the boat, Mr Frawley.' Lachy Stuart, sitting only inches in front of the midshipman, snarled at the young officer. 'Either you do, or I'll take the helm from you.'

'But the women!' Frawley cried.

'Fuck the women. They're as good as dead anyway.' He continued to hold the young midshipman's gaze.

'Do it man,' he commanded.

Frawley threw the helm over and the boat turned slowly into the waves until she was facing towards the ship.

'Now then lads, pull!' As Stuart put all his strength behind his oar, the rest followed suit.

Frawley, white faced, stared over their heads towards the *Albatross* where, almost bereft of sail, she wallowed in a trough with only her bare topmast visible in the mountainous seas. For a few seconds Mary McBain experienced only relief that she was safe, but then realising that they were returning to the ship without Jessie, she thrust aside comforting arms and sat up.

'Why have you stopped searching,' she cried. 'There are more to be saved. Mrs Dundas is out there with another woman. You must pick them up!'

This final burst of energy was enough to cause Mary to slip into unconsciousness from which she scarcely recovered until she was lifted on board and found herself in the hands of Dr Beaton. She opened her eyes and looked about her, anxiously.

'Jessie,' she whispered 'Jessie Dundas… did they find her?'

'Hush,' said Alexander, the word choking in his throat. He examined the patient, his mind only partly on her shallow breathing and dull sounding lungs, still partly filled with water. He had watched the two remaining boats hauled on board and counted the survivors as they were carried in to him. With the living attended to he went to check on the dead; those they had recovered. Each body had been carefully wrapped in a blanket so as not to offend the living. With trembling fingers he removed the first covering to reveal the face of Sir Tristram Wimborne, his cheeks now white and flaccid, the full mouth and bulbous nose tinged with blue. The next corpse was that of Sir Tristram's manservant, Fred Weeks, faithful to the last.

A third body lay a little apart. It was a slender figure with one delicate ankle partially exposed. His heart sank. This must be she.

Steeling himself against the inevitable sight which would meet his eyes when he lifted back the blanket he grasped the woollen covering and peeled it back. It was the body of the little seamstress who had rowed beside James Bantrie.

Alex had met her only once when she had first come on board. He remembered how frail she had seemed then and how grievously she had taken leave of her parents.

Where then was Jessie? Had she been drawn under the keel like the helmsman, Mr Cuthbertson and those others unable to resist the undertow? That young woman in the hospital, she had said something which sounded like Jessie. Perhaps she knew what had happened.

He hurried back inside the dispensary and shook the girl who was on the point of sleep. 'Mrs Dundas… you were with her in the boat… what happened?' he demanded.

'She took Alice from me. I had been supporting her you see, but I was nearly done. Jessie took her from me, told me to make for the longboat.'

Then she had not been sucked under. She was a good swimmer. She might still be alive and waiting to be rescued. Alex ran out on deck and up onto the poop. With all sails set the ship was under way and the island of Tristan da Cuna whose northern cliffs had so intimidated them for so many hours, was slipping past on the port bow.

'You must go about,' shouted Alexander. There are two women still out there. They were alive and swimming strongly some time after the boat capsized!' He knew he was exaggerating but he could not let it go now, not when she had been reported as still alive. She was a strong, determined woman. She would not give up easily.

'You must go back!' It was a command that Captain McCallum could not ignore. Turning to Mr Wallace he ordered the mate to take in sail and drop anchor. He ordered the longboat hauled out once more and called for volunteers amongst those members of the crew who previously had stayed on board to work the ship. They were all exhausted but not a man amongst them refused to go to the aid of Mrs Dundas. As the boat was lowered over the side, Dr Beaton stepped on board.

Wallace called out, 'you Doctor?'

'I may be needed immediately,' Alexander shouted back.

Wallace nodded, understanding perhaps more than Alexander himself realised.

It took the longboat twice as long to return to that fateful shore than it had taken the *Albatross* to steer away from it. The men bent to the oars, the helmsman kept his eyes on the approaching skerry and the dangerous rocks below the waterline while Alexander stood in the bows, scanning the wide expanse of ocean for some sign of the two women.

A strong breeze had got up during the past hour. How they could have done with it hours earlier. Now it was more of a hindrance than a help. It scurried across the surface of the sea whipping the tops of the waves into white seahorses and creating a spume which obscured anything floating there.

Suddenly Alexander spotted something on the far side of the skerry. It was large, flotsam of some kind. Part of the lost ship's boat maybe... He drew the attention of the helmsman who steered the longboat through a narrow channel between rocks left exposed by the retreating tide. The rowers commented on the sharpness of these rocks, recalling how the *Albatross* had slipped across the skerry at this point. Had she touched bottom they wondered? If so, had she been holed? They would know soon enough. Some of the men raised their eyes anxiously to the distant vessel they regarded as their home. She still rode comfortably at anchor more than a mile away.

As they drew closer Alexander could see that what he had spotted was indeed a large portion of the hull of the lost boat, all that remained after being dragged below the keel of the *Albatross*. It was a sizeable piece of wreckage, the obvious thing for someone to cling to if they had been left stranded in the water. He raised his hands to his lips and shouted. 'Ahoy there! Is anyone out there?'

There was no sign of movement.

He called again. Now the men rested their oars, hoping to hear a call or to see some sign of life.

Alexander was almost ready to give up when he saw a small movement. Something white fluttered for an instant on the upturned hull and was gone.

'There's something there, I know there is!' cried the doctor. The men took up their oars again and rowed with renewed vigour. The helmsman took the boat around the piece of wreckage and there on the far side they saw the two women, lying across the keel of the boat, half in and half out of the water. One seemed lifeless and could already be dead, but the other raised her head as they approached and made a feeble attempt at a wave.

'Jessie... oh my dear! Hang on we have you.' Alex continued to call out encouragement as the men caught hold of the wreckage and secured it to the boat. Eager hands reached out to draw the two women into the boat and the men waited while Alexander, fighting against every instinct, went first to the governess, Alice Montgomery, to ascertain that she was alive though barely so. He wrapped her in blankets, got one of the men to chaff her skin to encourage the blood to flow and gave him a flask of brandy with instructions to administer small sips only until she revived.

Only then did he turn his attention to Jessie. Someone had already placed a blanket around her shoulders and persuaded her to lie down as best she could in so small a boat. He knelt beside her, taking her wrist and feeling for her pulse. It was weak but steady. He rubbed her wrists to encourage the flow of blood and her fingers began to gain a little colour. With the renewed flow came the pain and she cried out. He gathered her into his arms with soothing words, while someone else rubbed at her bare feet and legs. He gave her brandy to revive her and then sips of water. The action of taking anything by mouth was painful to her for her lips were caked in salt, swollen and split. Soon the warmth and the comfort of Alexander's arms calmed her and she dozed. The helmsman ordered the men to their oars and the little craft, gaining speed with every stroke, made her triumphant return to the *Albatross* in record time!

Chapter Ten

'This escapade might well have resulted in the death of any one or indeed all of you, you understand?'

The captain sounded ferocious and the three boys quaked. There had been talk on the lower deck of their being placed in irons, made to walk the plank, receive a kiss from the cat-o'-nine tails and other unspeakable punishments. The lower deck had been merciless in its prophecies.

'I demand your promise that you will none of you attempt such a foolhardy exercise again!'

'I think you may be assured of that, Sir,' said Minister Bantrie, speaking for the boys. He and Charles had already discussed the matter prior to their summons to the captain's cabin. Charles rubbed at the softest part of his anatomy and flinched when his fingers touched the spot where his father's leather belt had left its mark.

'I'm very sorry, Sir,' he said quickly. 'It was my idea and I understand now that it was a stupid thing to have done.' He hung his head so that he did not see the amused glances exchanged between his father and the doctor.

Philip, not to be outdone, stepped forward.

'It was my idea, Sir,' he protested. 'If anyone is to be punished it should be me.' The blacksmith, Mackie, placed a firm hand on his son's shoulder and nodded solemnly.

'While I can only agree with you, Sir, that what the boys did in climbing to the mast head was foolish and might have lead to the injury or death of those sent to retrieve them, we do have two things to be grateful for.'

'Two?' asked the captain, puzzled.

'We were given warning of the danger we were all in,' said Mackie and my boy, who was almost too sick to walk when he came on board, was one of the climbers.'

Alexander nodded his head in agreement. He had examined Philip since the escapade and pronounced him none the worse for the experience.

Little Tommy Dundas hung his head, his eyes brimming with tears. He was too terrified to speak up.

'I believe the lads have had sufficient of a fright to deter them from climbing into the rigging again, observed Alexander Beaton. The three white faces turned to him, gratefully.

'Well...' the Captain appeared to be struggling over his decision or was he merely trying to suppress his amusement? At last he continued. 'I feel that I must set against this crime the fact that had you not been at the masthead last evening and had you not been sufficiently sharp-witted as to appreciate the danger, the ship would undoubtedly have foundered. That being the case it is doubtful if any of us would have survived. Every soul on board this ship owes his life to you boys. For this reason I shall not after all, keel haul you, nor shall I be marooning you on a desert island.' The children's startled glances indicated this was one punishment even the Lower Deck had not considered. Their bleak countenances became wreathed in smiles when he added, hurriedly, 'I have too much concern for the natives. I want you to remember this however; had any one of you fallen from the cross trees it would have been I who would have had to face the wrath of his mother and I am far too frail a creature to meet such a daunting challenge.'

Even wee Tommy Dundas understood by now that Captain McCallum was joking. He brushed his sleeve across his tear- stained face and laughed with the others.

'Cut along now,' said the captain, 'and try not to get into any more mischief before dinner.'

Needing no further encouragement, the boys fled leaving the hastily convened court to disband in its own way. Feeling out of place in this gathering with an embarrassed touch to the forelock, the blacksmith also departed. The ship's officers and the minister breathed a sigh of relief.

'A dram, gentlemen?' Captain McCallum summoned his steward who handed around well charged tumblers of whisky.

'I think our toast should be to the memory of Mr Midshipman Cuthbertson and those passengers who lost their lives in saving ours.'

The men downed their whisky in silence, each remembering some special moment during those arduous hours in which every man, woman and child aboard had had his or her part to play.

'I shall hold a memorial service tomorrow for those lost at sea Chaplain, at six bells of the forenoon watch. Please see that the passengers are made aware. Thank you gentlemen,' he concluded but then, as an afterthought, 'A moment of your time, Doctor, if you please.'

They took the captain's abrupt dismissal kindly. The man had endured far greater agonies of mind than any of them could ever know. Now he must sit down and write a report of the incident for his employers and, far more difficult, a letter of condolence and explanation to the parents of his gallant midshipman.

While James Bantrie silently followed Mr Wallace out of the captain's day cabin, Alexander Beaton remained seated.

'What of our survivors, Doctor?'.

'Fortunately the water was not too cold so the effects of immersion upon those rescued soon after the capsize are not serious. As you saw for yourself, the Chaplain is well recovered, as are those who were rescued with him. The ladies who were adrift for several hours are in a different case. Miss Montgomery would most certainly have died had not Mrs Dundas held on to her for much of that time. I cannot praise your matron enough for her fortitude and determination. Whether or not Miss Montgomery makes a full recovery will depend upon her not encountering any further distress or deprivation before the voyage ends. She is badly sunburned and the damage to her lungs may be permanent. Only time will tell.'

'And Mrs Dundas, what of her?' The captain demanded.

'She is recovering remarkably well. Given rest and quiet I believe she will be fully restored in a week or two.'

'Thank God for that,' the captain breathed a sigh of relief. 'I would not want to lose such a woman. Did you hear how she rescued Bantrie and then went back for the governess? How it was that the bosun failed to pick her up that first time I shall never understand.'

Alexander, who had asked himself a dozen times how it was that the man in charge of the longboat had neglected to go back for the two women, was charitable with his explanation.

'A decision had to be made to return to the ship while his survivors were still living, or to risk their lives while searching for others who were most likely already dead. I do not think he had any other choice.'

'Maybe so,' said McCallum and then added. 'That's a very generous conclusion, Alex, considering the circumstances.'

Alexander looked up sharply. What was this? First Wallace and now the captain had indicated that he took something more than a professional interest in the widow Dundas. Were his feelings for Jessie so obvious? While he had never even hinted to the lady how much he admired her, it seemed others had already observed his attachment. Maybe he should speak to her now, before someone else did it for him!

He took his leave of the captain and made his way to the hospital where he had insisted upon keeping Jessie and her companion under close observation.

The governess lay in a drugged stupor, the only way in which Alexander could ensure the woman did no harm to herself. Whenever she regained consciousness, she screamed as though still enduring the torment of the past hours and struggled to get outside on deck. The semi-immersion under a blazing tropical sun and the conviction that she was about to die, had played their part in her disorientation. All he could hope for was that she would calm down eventually and perhaps regain her sanity.

Jessie had been dozing. She was aware of the doctor's presence however and painfully opened her sunburnt lids as he bent over her and felt her brow.

'Well,' she demanded, 'will I recover?'

'Undoubtedly,' he concluded, smiling. 'Now madam, if you believe by languishing here like some maiden in a romantic novel by Miss Austin that you will receive special attention from me,' he paused to give greater effect, 'you are absolutely right.'

'And Alice?' She tried to lift her shoulders off the pillow to see the figure lying prone on the other bunk.

'She is comfortable.' He eased her gently back upon the pillows. Hours of exposure to the unrelenting sun had burned the skin from her shoulders and the sudden pain from contact with the coarse linen caused her to cry out. Instantly filled with remorse he clutched at her one undamaged hand and kissed the back. Then, turning it palm up, he kissed it again.

'Forgive me, my dear. I didn't mean to hurt you.'

He remained silent for a few moments while her pain subsided.

'Perhaps I should give you another dose of laudanum,' he said. 'Sleep is the only therapy I can recommend at present.'

Sensing that he had more to tell her, she resisted the temptation to accept instant oblivion. She smiled up at him and waved away the proffered medicine glass.

'Perhaps later,' she croaked, her throat dry and painful.

'You were very brave,' he said, 'but you must promise me not to risk your life in such a way again. Now that I have you safe I do not intend to lose you.'

'I am a good swimmer,' she struggled to speak. 'Those others were unable to help themselves.'

'Had you let the men pull you aboard once you had taken James to the boat you would not be lying here in my hospital now.'

Jessie glanced across at the other bunk. 'Alice would have died. You would not have wanted that.'

'Of course not, but I couldn't have born it had you not been found.'

'Who would you have to keep the womenfolk in order without me?' Her swollen lips curved into a grimace as she tried to smile.

'Who cares about the women? They are big enough and silly enough to take care of themselves! Don't you understand Jessie, I am trying to say that I love you, that I know now, having so nearly lost you, that I cannot live without you. There will be difficult times ahead when we reach New Zealand. No doubt it will take great courage and fortitude to survive. No one knows what obstacles we shall find to overcome but I know now that I can face anything our new land has to throw at us provided I have you by my side.'

As though to fend off his proposal, she answered, 'naturally we shall all remain together, you and James, Judith and the children. Have we not already agreed that we shall set up our homes close by, wherever we decide to settle?'

'But I want you to be my wife, Jessie. Think of it, our children will be the first generation of white New Zealanders. Doesn't that make you proud just to think of it?'

She wanted to accept him. Despite the soreness in her shoulders she wished she could reach up so that he would take her in his arms but she held back. How could she allow him to make such a terrible mistake? What if he were to find out that she had been a servant in a hospital ward, so lowly a situation that there were those who considered nurses to be in the same category as women of the night? Many of the women she had worked with were indeed no better. Hugh Beaton, Alexander's brother, knew about her. He had guessed at her occupation immediately on the one occasion when she had met him. Her professional treatment of Judith's son Ian had been her undoing. He had guessed at once where she had acquired her skills. Had Hugh already mentioned her in his letter to Alexander? Had he already warned him off? Surely not or he would not have been speaking to her in this way.

She shook her head, much as it pained her to do it and her words sounded all the more harsh for the dryness in her throat.

'I cannot marry you, Alexander. Our worlds are too far apart.'

'But that is nonsense. Where we are going the laws both secular and moral will be of our own making. Who is to say who or what is right or wrong other than we, ourselves?'

'Nevertheless, your career will depend upon your reputation. I could not live with the thought that I might in any way stain it and hold you back by so doing.' She coughed with the effort of speaking and he reached for a glass of water holding it to her lips as she sipped.

'How could you or anything that has happened to you in the past, stain my reputation?' he demanded, dismissing her fears. 'What you say only confirms that you do indeed love me since you care so much for my reputation.'

Wearied by the talking and seeking release from the mental torment his words had unleashed, she lay back against the pillows and closed her eyes.

'I am ready for the medicine now,' she said.

He took the tiny glass and held it to her lips.

'You shall not get away this easily,' he assured her. 'I shall ask you again when you are better.' Then with melodramatic fervour, he added, 'I will not be denied!'

'What about Tommy?' she wondered, her lids already heavy with the drug.

'Tommy? Why, naturally, he shall be brought up as one of my own What else would you expect?'

He didn't know if she had heard his answer for she was already asleep.

*

'How many barrels?' the captain demanded, ashen faced.

'About half seem to have been contaminated,' Wallace answered.

Scraping the hull across the jagged rocks below the water line had caused the ship to spring a small leak in the after hold where the main body of fresh water was stored. Several barrels had been contaminated by sea water and would have to be discarded.

'How do you estimate our situation? Do we have sufficient water to get us to New Zealand?'

'I calculate that with careful rationing and using the additional barrels stored in the chain locker, we shall have sufficient to get us there but a delay of even a few days could prove disastrous.'

'If the leak were worse, I might go about and put in to Cape Town for repairs. That could add another month to the voyage.'

'The pumps have control of the leakage and a pitch and canvas patch is being constructed as we speak,' Wallace assured him. 'We are dealing with a strained rather than a punctured hull and I have no doubt that the patch will get us home to Scotland before the ship will need to go into dry dock.'

'I hope you're right Mr Wallace, I really do.' Captain McCallum dismissed the First Mate with a nod and then just as Wallace grasped the door handle, he called him back.

'Best send the doctor to me right away Mr Wallace. He can draw up plans for rationing water and I will announce them after the funeral service.'

*

James Bantrie was badly bruised and clearly tired after his adventures. Nevertheless, he had a sermon to compose before morning. He read through what he had written, referred to his concordance once or twice and made some alterations to the script.

'How are you feeling now dear?' Judith looked up from her sewing and regarded him anxiously.

'It was bad enough pulling at the oars for all those hours,' he replied, unconsciously rubbing his hands together to relieve the pain in his blistered palms, 'without being ignominiously cast into the sea just when we were about to return to the ship in triumph.'

'At least you are safe now,' Judith observed, relieved to have him back with her in the privacy of their cramped little cabin. She looked white and strained. The adventures of the previous day had left her completely drained.

'Are you unwell my dear?' James asked solicitously. He made a conscious effort to study her face and was somewhat disturbed at what he saw there. 'You have been such a picture of good health these past weeks that it is a shock to see you looking so poorly.'

Perhaps now was as good at time to tell him as any. She put down her sewing with studied care and smiled across at him.

'I am a little tired,' she confessed, 'but no more than is to expected in my condition.'

Although she had been wearing loosely fitting garments ever since they had arrived in the tropics, Judith had taken little trouble otherwise to disguise her pregnancy. As a result it seemed that everyone on board had noticed that she was expecting a happy event. Everyone that is, except her own husband.

'Do you think you are perhaps putting on rather too much weight, my dear?' he asked, not responding to her hint. He studied her charmingly full bosoms and the somewhat less attractive thickening about the waist as though seeing both for the first time. There was little chance that any of those tight -waisted ball gowns she had insisted upon packing, would fit now even if she had the opportunity to wear them.

'Come to think of it my dear you do seem to have changed shape more than somewhat. Not to say that it detracts from your good looks of course,' he hastened to add, 'Far from it.'

As a young bridegroom, he had taken great pride in his wife's slender figure. Now that he himself was having greater difficulty in bending to put on his boots and struggling to do up his trouser buttons it was little wonder that his wife was also putting on a little fat. She was still lovely in his eyes. He was reminded of those other occasions when she had temporarily altered in shape. He stopped what he was doing and stared at her. 'Judith, you are pregnant!'

'At last,' she cried, delighted not to have been forced into telling him, herself. 'I thought you were never going to notice.'

'When is the baby due?' he demanded anxiously. His momentary delight was now clouded with concern. What if the child were to be born before they landed in New Zealand? It did not bear thinking about. He had read of the large number of mortalities in infants born on such voyages and Judith, what of her? What if the birth should prove to be more difficult than those others? He hated the whole business, the discomfort for his wife, the anxiety for himself and the distress caused to the other children when their mother was long in labour. Surely Judith was too old to bear more children?

'Does Beaton know?' he demanded, suddenly.

'He would be a poor physician if he did not,' she replied cheerfully. 'Yes, I consulted Alexander soon after we sailed.' She did not dare reveal that Alexander had wanted to prevent her from sailing altogether but had allowed himself to be persuaded otherwise.

'And what is his opinion?'

'That the child will be born after we arrive. He has promised to deliver me, himself.'

'Let us pray that the ship is not delayed.'

This was just one further anxiety to add to his already overburdened conscience. The family cabin, shared with their children and the Dundas boy, together with the narrowness of the bunks, had put paid to any possibility of sexual activity during the voyage. To fit them all in Charles and young Thomas bunked together while Catherine shared with her mother. James, who was a tall man although stockily built, filled every inch of one narrow bed space. It was hardly to be wondered at if he had not observed his wife more closely during the past weeks.

James began a calculation in his head. Once they had decided upon emigration there had been too much to do to spend time enjoying pleasures of the flesh. When he thought about it, the last time he and Judith had been together had been the night when Ian was brought home after the shipwreck. Why that must be all of what five or was it six months ago? If that were so, they should have two full months in which to reach New Zealand before her confinement. He prayed there would be nothing more to delay their journey.

*

James read out the names of those who had lost their lives. 'Of the crew, Mr Midshipman Cuthbertson of the New Zealand Company and Able Seaman Miles and of the passengers who so gallantly took an oar on our behalf, Sir Tristram Wimborne, gentleman, and Frederick Weeks, manservant.'

Nellie Parker shed a tear for Fred. She had never been friendly with him exactly, but he was a likeable enough fellow and had kept an eye out for her wellbeing ever since her ladyship died. Now she was all alone without employment and with nothing in the world to live on once she left the ship. The tears flowed even more freely now they were for herself.

'The Lord has seen fit to take these our brothers from us,' James was getting into his stride now.

Judith watched his face, knowing what a great strain he was under. He had suffered a battering in the boat the previous day and was not totally well after a disturbed night. He had been exceptionally harsh in his handling of Charles yesterday, his mood owing more to his exhaustion than to the boy's misdeeds.

Catherine hung upon her father's every word while her brother Charles fidgeted and cast a glance along the row of assembled passengers, catching the eye of Philip Mackie where he leaned against the wooden structure which housed the pigs.

Despite the congratulations heaped upon them by their fellow-passengers, the boys had been particularly subdued since the incident off Tristan da Cuna. They had taken the captain's words to heart and were unlikely to get themselves into such trouble again. Truth to tell, they had all three been terrified out of their lives and could hardly believe their good fortune in having got off so lightly.

'As we travel into the unknown there will surely be others who will give their lives that the rest may survive. That has always been the way of mankind. Banding together against adversity gives the whole a strength which one individual may never achieve. Friends, we must take heart from this lesson which the Lord has taught us. In the new country which is to be our home there will be few enough experts such as doctors, teachers, priests, masons or carpenters to serve a community. No doubt we shall be widespread and in some cases isolated as some settlers venture further into uncharted territory. Each one of us must carry into the wilderness what knowledge and skills we possess that they may be passed on to others. In this manner everyone can be equipped for the tribulations to come. The Lord Jesus Christ did not have with him a band of ready-made preachers to help him do his work. He took His disciples from all places and every walk of life. You are the new disciples, brothers and sisters. Ingenuity, initiative and leadership are the qualities expected of you in the days to come. You must take the opportunity while you are still together, here aboard the Albatross, to learn from each other what skills you will need when we arrive in Otago. Read your Bibles now, while you have the leisure to do so, talk to one another, express your ideas freely. It is for these freedoms that so many of your clergy have walked away from the old ways of the church. It is for this that they have abandoned a Church ruled by a State which keeps its activities secret from the community it serves. Do not doubt that you will be tempted to revert to the old ways. When you find yourselves out of contact with your priests, out of touch with neighbours who set standards you find hard to meet, you must not be persuaded from the path of conscience. Keep the faith and strengthen your spirit in the name of the Lord our God.'

The hush which had fallen upon those gathered on the deck was like a soft woollen pall hanging above the ship. No sound disturbed the silence save the comforting creak of timber and a whisper of soft breezes in the rigging. 'We now commit our brothers to the deep…' In the absence of any corpses, James Bantrie was obliged to intone the prayer for those who have died at sea. From up in the bows a piper played his sorrowful dirge, while some of the women cast into the waves dried flowers which they had carefully carried on board to remind them of home.

Tommy Dundas clung to his mother's hand and looked up anxiously into Jessie's face. He saw tears trickle down her cheeks as she recalled the kindly young man, little more than a boy himself, who had come skimming down the ropes with her precious child clinging to his back. Alexander Beaton, his glance following that of her son, came across to her side to offer his support.

'You should not have left your bed so soon,' he remonstrated. She felt Alexander's firm grip on her arm, and relaxed a little. 'I had to come,' she replied. 'I had to say thank you.'

For an instant she had thought she might faint.

'Come along, my dear, it is time to go in,' he murmured. She leaned heavily on him as he steered her away to her berth.

With the entire ship's compliment assembled, the Captain delivered his news about the shortage of water.

'I have had the doctor draw up a scheme for rationing what water we have left. There will no longer be free access to a barrel kept on deck. Every passenger and crew member will receive an allocation of one quart of water per day for drinking and cooking purposes. Under no circumstances will fresh water be used for any other reason, not for washing, not even for cleaning one's teeth. From now on only sea water will be freely available. All supplies of fresh water will be kept under lock and key.'

Julian Frawley had blanched as the captain spoke. It did not require a genius to understand the importance now of his emergency supply of water of which one barrel had already been partially emptied by Miss Nellie Parker. As the captain spoke Julian avoided the girl's gaze and when she approached him after the company had dispersed he pleaded important duties and sped away before she could challenge him on the question of the water.

Nellie was not so foolish as to underestimate the importance of what she had done at the instigation of the midshipman. She realised now that in tampering with the emergency supply they had committed a crime which might have serious consequences should the fresh water run out while they were in mid ocean. She pondered the idea of confessing at once in case the half empty barrel should form a vital part of the doctor's rationing calculations. Fearing punishment, not least the censure of friends she had made during the voyage, she decided to remain silent. Julian Frawley was responsible for what had happened. Let him take the blame when the deed was discovered.

Guiltily, she made her way to the hospital hoping to mitigate her crime by offering to help the doctor in the sick bay.

*

The main supply of water lasted them until they reached the Indian Ocean. Here tropical storms provided the only real excitement. The days were long, sultry and so hot that it was impossible to stay on deck for any length of time. Down below in the steerage cabins it was too close even to breath. Torrential rain fell for a while each afternoon and the Captain had rigged awnings in which to catch and save what fresh water he could. Barrels contaminated by the leak into the hold had been emptied and cleaned of salt and were now stacked on deck to be ready for the slightest downpour. After a week, only two of the barrels had been filled in this manner and it would soon be necessary to break out the emergency store in the chain locker.

'Do you think the captain will put in to one of the islands in the Southern Ocean?' Jessie asked.

They had found a shady spot way up in the bows of the ship where the gentle motion of the ship could be felt to full effect. Despite a huge spread of canvas, the light breeze was scarcely sufficient to keep the ship under way. They had covered no more than eighty to a hundred miles a day for the past three days.

'I am sure he would if he could,' Alexander replied, 'but in these latitudes there are none charted. We are now well south of the equator and heading into the Antarctic currents. It will soon be getting colder and no doubt the winds will increase. Then we shall fly along, just mark my words.'

Alexander had spent many hours in the chart room under instruction from Mr Wallace. He was now very familiar with the area south of the Indian Continent and those waters through which they must pass to reach the southernmost part of New Zealand. Their most convenient point of contact with Australia would have been Van Diemen's Land but to put in to Hobart would be to court disaster at the tail end of the season of cyclones. It was a period of ferocious winds which gathered to the north of the continent of Australia and sped along its eastern seaboard whipping up the ocean into mountainous waves which no vessel the size of the Albatross, was ever designed to withstand.

'Will New Zealand be hot like this or cold?' she asked. 'They say the country is mountainous just like the Highlands of Scotland and yet it is warm as the tropics.'

'Reports which we were given before we sailed, were somewhat exaggerated I fear. Mr Wallace affirms the winters are as cold and wet as any in Argyll.'

'What a good thing it is that we shall have the summer in which to build our homes and get settled,' she pondered. 'I shall plant a garden and grow vegetables. Old Archie the pump man, do you remember him? He gave me a packet of seeds to be grown, cabbages and carrots, peas and beans. If the climate is as good as they say we shall not want for fresh vegetables.'

She turned for his approbation only to find that Alexander had been called away by the captain's steward and was deep in conversation. He had not heard a word she had said.

'How many did you say?'

What the steward had whispered to Alexander had filled him with alarm. A few cases of diarrhoea were inevitable in tropical heat and with food beginning to deteriorate after the long voyage but this sounded more extreme. With that single case of cholera still fresh in his memory he hurried down into the steerage quarters with the steward's list of ten names in his hand.

It was even worse than he feared. The ten patients were of various ages from elderly men and women to a child of two years. Some lay quietly in their beds, grey faced and dull eyed. Others cried out in their agony and threw themselves about in their narrow bunks so much as to require physical restraints.

'When did this begin?' Alexander asked of one of the women who was already collecting soiled linen from her own family and making for the laundry.

'About three o'clock this morning,' she replied. My husband was the first, he woke moaning and couldn't make his way to the heads. I was up and about trying to clean up the mess when little Annie Clairemont woke up in a cold sweat and vomited. It's been going on since then with never a moment's peace.'

'Why was I not called?' demanded the doctor.

'The officer of the watch presumed it was the usual malady caused by rotten food and said you should be allowed to rest. Then it all quietened down. The sick ones went to sleep and we all decided to snatch a few hours but at daybreak it started again, worse than before. That was when we decided we must send for you'

She looked worried now, realising that perhaps they should have called him earlier. The trouble was that these people were unused to calling out a doctor every time some-one had a stomach upset. They were used to treating themselves and indeed they did not have money to waste on doctor's bills, even at sea.

Alexander examined those afflicted by the disease one by one. The symptoms mirrored those of Lady Wimborne in every detail. Had both instances occurred simultaneously he would undoubtedly have identified the same source in every case. How could it be that the disease should lie dormant for weeks and then break out suddenly in so many individuals at once?

He sent someone to fetch Toby, his assistant, and also Jessie Dundas. There was no doubt in his mind that he was dealing with a severe outbreak of cholera and it was time to put their carefully laid plans into effect.

Mr Wallace appeared as if by magic.

'What can I do to help,' he demanded. 'The captain has instructed me to stand by to carry out your orders.'

'I cannot believe that anyone is doing otherwise but I must reiterate my instructions to drink only boiled water. People must eat only properly cooked food. Nothing is to be ingested that has not first been heated to a high degree. All these sick people must be moved out of here. The lazaret is too small. We must convert the single women's cabin into a hospital. All the bedding should be given an extra airing but any linen used by the patients is to be soaked in lysol and boiled separately from that of the other passengers. With only salt water it is going to be difficult to keep everything scrupulously clean but we will have to do our best.'

'I don't hold with all this washing,' mumbled one elderly woman, used to sewing herself into her flannel underwear for the winter. Early in the voyage she had been requested to remove her underwear to wash it and had been threatened with dire consequences if she did not. 'Never 'ad no nasty diseases like this when I was at 'ome, I didn't,' she informed Alexander with a self- satisfied expression.

Deaths began to occur on the third day and by the following Sunday three women, one of them the governess Alice Montgomery, four men and half a dozen small children were ready to be sewn into their canvas shrouds.

Among the children was the wee daughter of the Mackie family. It seemed that while Alexander had managed to save their son, he could do nothing for their daughter. Mackie himself constructed her tiny coffin in the carpenter's workshop. He painted it white and the kindly carpenter even found some small brass fittings to make a casket fit for a princess.

The burial services became shorter as the list of casualties lengthened and when it was children's bodies which were cast over the side only the immediate families were on deck to hear the reverend Bantrie deliver his special prayer for dead children. Those other parents who could afford to, also had the carpenter make their coffins. The rest had to be satisfied to have their little ones sewn into canvas and weighted with crude lead weights. The stricken families watched each pathetic little bundle topple over the side, roll a few times in the surging waves and disappear. Mackie's masterpiece of joinery however and two other similar wooden caskets, carried too little weight to sink at once. Each returned to the surface almost as soon as it was cast overboard. With the ship scarcely making any way at all, the wretched parents were obliged to watch for hour upon hour while the little coffins bobbed up and down in the waves, carried along in the same current which propelled the ship. Among them the white casket stood out, still clearly visible even when the sun went down. Those watching could only pray that the sea would get up during the night so that they would not be obliged to continue their vigil on the following day. When the parents had retired worn out by their grief, Captain McCallum had a boat lowered and the ship's carpenter was rowed out to collect each of the floating coffins. He drilled holes in their bottoms and reverently lowered them back into the sea, one by one. In a few minutes all had sunk to the bottom.

'Tell the carpenter that there will be no more coffins made on this voyage.' McCallum's face was grim as he gave the order. Wallace, visibly moved by the whole sad incident, hurried away to deliver his message and assist in returning the boat to its davits.

Once cholera had been diagnosed, the patients isolated and the passengers and crew trained in the correct procedures for handling the situation, there was nothing Alexander could do but hope that the disease would run its course and die out.

Jessie Dundas, now fully recovered from her terrible experience at sea, worked tirelessly beside Alexander, directing a team of women in nursing the sick and ensuring that isolation of those afflicted was as complete as possible in such a closely confined community. Toby undertook the supervision of the laundry and directed daily scrubbing out of all the sleeping cabins and proper airing of bedding. Whatever the cause of the pestilence, all three were determined to see the end of it.

After a week of tireless effort, Alexander reported to the captain that there were no new cases and that several of the less seriously affected patients were on the mend.

'What is the water situation, Mr Wallace?' the captain demanded.

'In the past two days we have managed to fill a further three barrels with rain water,' the mate reported. 'I shall use what water we are able to catch while it is available. It is much more convenient to distribute rations from the main hold than the chain locker. When the time comes to use the emergency supply again, I propose to remove it to the main hold a barrel at a time.'

'There is no doubt that the rain water we catch is preferable to that taken on board at the start of the voyage,' Alexander added. 'I had no idea that water could become so foul smelling, standing in barrels for two or three months.'

'When you have been at sea as long as I, you learn to put up with almost anything,' laughed McCallum.

'It is such a relief to be able to drink water that has not been boiled for once,' Wallace added, innocently.

Alexander turned on him almost viciously. 'What do you mean… not boiled? I ordered all water to be boiled until further notice.'

'I thought there would be no harm if the rain water was drunk without boiling. After what had come out of the one or two emergency barrels we broached, the fresh rainwater was such a marvellous relief. The women asked if it would be all right to drink it untreated and I said yes.'

'You had no right to do that, not until I have tracked down the cause of the contamination!' Alexander knew that he was being unreasonable. There was surely no harm in drinking water which had fallen out of the sky. What disease could possibly lurk there?

Captain McCallum, anxious to calm the atmosphere between these two men whose anger was more the result of extreme weariness than any other disagreement, suggested calmly that Wallace's action seemed to have had no dire effects.

'I understand that the number of new cases has reduced dramatically since we began collecting the rainwater,' he observed.

Shame-faced, Alexander nodded in agreement.

'It's true, ' he said. Then to Wallace, more calmly and smiling, 'nevertheless I consider it essential that we continue to boil everything until the disease is quite eradicated.'

'Of course,' Wallace said, 'It was remiss of me to suggest otherwise.' He grinned at Alexander and the two men shook hands.

The rainwater lasted a further two days, during which time there were no new cases reported. The ship had by this time moved out of the tropical belt into the great Southern Ocean. The seas became mountainous, the wind increased in strength and while to everyone's relief, the Albatross began to make real progress at last covering perhaps two hundred miles in a single day, the problems were by no means over. Without the regular downpour of tropical rain each evening, the water barrels in the main hold were quickly used up and on the day when Alexander was able to report to the captain that all the remaining patients would undoubtedly be recovered by the time they reached Otago, Mr Wallace called for two barrels to be transferred from the chain locker to the main hold.

Judith Bantrie in her seventh month of pregnancy, had maintained good health throughout the emergency on board. James had insisted that she keep clear of the patients, refusing to allow her to assist Jessie Dundas with the nursing. The fact that the Bantries had their own cabin had ensured that contact, even with those who were in the early stages of cholera and showing no symptoms, was avoided.

The Bantries had observed Alexander's rules most scrupulously and not a drop of drinking water was consumed in the cabin which had not been boiled.

One afternoon in March when the roaring gales had ceased for once and the sea was relatively calm, Judith took the air on deck with some of the ladies from the single women's cabin. With the number of convalescents down to only three, Alexander had agreed to the women returning to their own quarters thereby vacating that section of the main steerage cabin to which they had been assigned for the duration of the epidemic. For most this was a blessed relief, but there were amongst the ladies those who had enjoyed the closer proximity of male members of both the crew and passengers, out of the watchful eye of their matron. Nellie Parker was one such. She had made several friends amongst the crew and those unattached young men who would be leaving the ship in Otago. Determined to appear at her best the moment she set foot on shore, she was today busily adjusting a gown passed on to her by Lady Wimborne only days before her death. Until now the girl had not had the heart to carry out the alteration but now, with the prospect of arriving in New Zealand within a week or two at the most, she felt she must do all in her power to improve her wardrobe. A neat and attractive appearance would ensure her a good position when the time came for her to seek employment. She worked busily over her sewing only half heartedly joining in the conversation taking place around her.

'Until now I have been happy to accept a cup of tea, drunk even without milk,' Judith Bantrie was saying. 'But just lately the very thought of tea, let alone the taste has made me nauseous. Unfortunately, it is the only thing to drink and also abide by the doctor's rules. The water, even when boiled, is so distasteful.'

'A little lemon juice can make all the difference,' observed Mary McBride. She put down her knitting and made her way down to the single women's quarters where she poured a little of her own water supply into a cup, added some juice from a lemon squeezed only that morning and hurried on deck.

'It's from my allocation of this morning she explained. It's still quite fresh and relatively cool. Judith sipped at the drink and wrinkled up her nose just a little for there was a curious smell about the potion she had been offered. Nevertheless, she swallowed it down so as not to appear ungrateful for her friend's offering.

'I always think that the rain water is so much sweeter than what we brought with us,' said Mary with a satisfied smile, 'and the best thing is there's no need to boil it.'

'Oh, that is not so,' intervened Jessie Dundas, 'Dr Beaton insists that all the water must be boiled no matter from what source.'

The other women exchanged glances and smiled benevolently. Everyone knew that Jessie obeyed Dr Beaton's words for one reason and one reason only. She simply adored him!

Ellie looked up momentarily, wearing a puzzled frown. Only last evening she had overheard Mr Wallace ordering more barrels to be brought up from the chain locker. That wasn't rain water and it should have been boiled. Suppose Mary had neglected to boil water from the chain locker? There was no point in causing alarm when her fears might be unfounded. She did however speak up in defence of Jessie.

'The doctor has done well to curb the worst ravages of the disease, 'she said. 'Perhaps we owe it to him to humour him in this. I think that all the water should be boiled just as he says.'

The others looked at her with surprise. Usually Nellie was the last person to be swayed by rules of any kind.

Mary McBain was sufficiently impressed by the argument to go right away and put her little kettle on the galley stove to boil, smiling sweetly at the cook as she did so for passengers were usually given set times at which they might brew up and this was not one of them.

Judith began to feel unwell two days later. Thinking her condition was due to her pregnancy she said nothing when diarrhoea took hold. Only when she had vomited twice and had finally fainted away in James' arms, was the doctor called. By then her fever was raging and she was already severely dehydrated.

'Why did you leave it so long?' Alex demanded angrily. 'Surely you are sufficiently conversant the symptoms by now.'

James looked at him aghast.

'You don't mean to say that it is the cholera again,' he cried in alarm. 'I thought you had eradicated it.'

'I had hoped we had it under control,' said Alexander, exasperated. 'Without knowing the source of the disease it is impossible to say that it is eradicated. Quite clearly the pestilence lurks somewhere on board the ship and your wife has managed to unearth it yet again.'

Judith's pregnancy made her the more vulnerable to the ravages of the disease. In the circumstances, there was little hope of saving the baby and Alexander was certain that Judith's chances of survival would be the greater if he removed the foetus as soon as possible. With a heavy heart he put his proposal to James.

The minister stared at him, uncomprehending. 'How do you know the baby is dead?' he demanded.

'I don't,' Alexander admitted. There had been the flutter of a foetal heartbeat the last time he had examined Judith, but now there was nothing to indicate the baby was alive. It was not however, unusual to miss the beating of the foetal heart using the primitive stethoscopes of the day and no physician would be justified in making so definite an assumption on observation alone.

'Suppose the child is not dead. You would be committing murder to abort it now.' That the doctor could even contemplate deliberately destroying his child was beyond belief.

'I would consider myself a poor physician if I did not do everything in my power to save your wife, James.'

'But not at the expense of the child?' Despairingly James turned to his wife hoping for her agreement. Judith was now unconscious, grey-faced against the stark whiteness of her pillows. What would be her response to Alexander's suggestion? She would never sanction the baby's murder of that he was certain.

'I must have time to pray.' Torn between his love for Judith and the denial of every Christian principle, he pushed past the doctor and retreated to the stern of the vessel where he might commune in solitude with his Maker.

Alexander continued to apply the remedies perfected after so much experience with the disease, sponge baths, cold compresses, a mixture of drugs which had proved most efficacious, including laudanum to dull the pain. Aware that the drug alone would put paid to any chances which the infant might have of survival, he felt no compunction. Judith's life was of greater importance than that of a child almost certainly doomed from the outset.

He turned expectantly as James Bantrie re-entered the cabin.

'Well?' he demanded, impatient to be about his business.

'I cannot allow it,' said James firmly. 'I have prayed and prayed and I can find no excuse in my heart for the deliberate destruction of my child's life. Let matters take their course.'

He glanced up at Alexander's stricken countenance and misunderstanding the anxiety he saw there, he added, 'Whatever the outcome, I shall not blame you my friend. This is between myself and the Lord, Jesus Christ.'

'But your wife man, what of Judith?'

'If the Lord wills it, she will survive.'

He crumpled up and collapsed into a chair. Slowly he began to pray aloud, quietly at first but them getting louder and more insistent.

'Do you not understand, James? 'Alexander's tone had softened. 'The child has no chance at all and Judith's life is balanced on a knife edge. If you will let me remove the foetus it may give her some small chance of survival. Think of your family. How will they regard a father who deliberately allows their mother to die?'

Alexander's pleading however seemed only to strengthen the minister's determination.

'You must allow me to be the judge in this, my friend. I know that you believe you are speaking from the best of motives, but my conscience will not allow it. Do what you will to make Judith comfortable but I cannot permit you to murder my child.'

In the stark, cold hours, shortly before dawn, Judith Bantrie died in her husband's arms. Alexander immediately performed a Caesarean operation in the faint hope of saving the child. The infant, a boy, lived for an hour. Blue from lack of oxygen and gasping for air, he too passed away.

Alexander, at a loss to understand his friend's decision, walked away from the scene leaving Jessie Dundas to comfort the grieving husband as best she could.

*

Alexander did not find any credence in the old wives' tales which attempted to account for cholera in the cities. Suspicion that the condition was due to dampness or foul air, hardly applied at sea. Despite the close atmosphere, particularly in the cabins below decks, the sleeping spaces had been aired whenever possible and bedding hung on the deck to allow the breeze to cleanse it of all ills.

'Had I not sought out a suitable water supply for myself,' he suggested to the First Mate, 'I would have been the very first to suspect our drinking water as being the source of contamination. Mr Wallace, has there been any change in the water distribution since rationing began?' Alexander demanded. 'Did anything specific happen a few days prior to the outbreak of cholera on the second occasion?' He still believed that Lady Wimborne had come on board carrying the disease. He had no reason to connect her illness with that of the other passengers.

Wallace shook his head. 'Other than the location for collecting the daily ration, nothing changed,' the mate replied.

Alexander looked up sharply.

'Why, what changed there?' he asked.

'We had been using up what little uncontaminated water was left after the affair off Tristan da Cuna,' Wallace explained. 'That kept us going for some time but after a few weeks we were obliged to broach the first of the emergency barrels stored in the chain locker and for a while we distributed water from there until we were able to replenish the main supply with rainwater. I had a couple of the barrels moved from the chain locker. That was three days ago.'

Wallace looked to Midshipman Frawley for confirmation of the dates. During their discussion, the young midshipman had paled quite noticeably. He now looked as though he was about to collapse. Alexander caught him before he did so and sat him in a chair. He loosened his collar and felt for a pulse.

'What is it man, are you ill?" he demanded, fearing Mr Frawley was to become his next victim.

Frawley shook his head and mumbled something which Alexander was obliged to have him repeat.

'It's not my fault,' the boy protested. 'The men refused to go all the way out beyond Dumbarton. They were quite mutinous at the time, it being their last night on shore, d'you see Sir? They threatened to desert if I didn't let them do it.'

'Do what?' Alexander demanded, exasperated by the fellow's hesitancy.

'Take the water from a spring nearer to the centre of the city It was somewhere north of Maryhill.'

Frawley crumpled under the steady, accusing gaze of his superiors. 'I didn't recognise the place in the dark,' he whimpered.

Wallace prepared himself to issue a tirade against the stupidity of the young midshipman but he stopped himself when he saw the tears streaming down the boy's cheeks. If anyone was to blame it was he. He had placed a boy in command of the water provisioning party. He had sent a child to do a man's job. How could a fifteen-year-old boy be expected to stand up to a bunch of determined older men bent upon their own pleasure? This was not the Royal Navy. Men did not respect the discipline of junior officers once they were on dry land.

The tears shed by Julian Frawley were part remorse and part relief. The lad had suspected much earlier that the water from Maryhill might be the culprit and even had he not realised the truth himself, Lachy Stuart had not been slow to point out the possibility. He and Dougie Watts never let an opportunity pass to remind the midshipman of his involvement in their escapade. They had made sure they were always in Mr Frawley's watch and had enjoyed a relatively easy passage under his command. It had meant them crewing the longboat when they were fighting for their lives off Tristan, but then there had been nothing else for it. They had, even then, exercised their power by insisting the boat return to the ship at the earliest opportunity. Julian had suffered nightmares wondering when it would be discovered that he had deliberately left Mrs Dundas behind.

Alexander took no interest in apportioning blame for the tragedy which had occurred because of the boy's carelessness. He was too busy working out the significance of Frawley's confession.

He recalled something he had read soon after they had sailed from Clydebank. Of course, it was the report of an outbreak of cholera in the northern part of the city. That was it! Frawley had taken water from a polluted supply.

Alexander thought back over what Mr Wallace had just told him. They had broached the first chain locker barrel three weeks ago. Shortly afterwards, cholera had broken out.

'Well, at least we now know the source of the contagion,' he said turning back to Wallace. He was surprised to find the midshipman had left them.

'What happened to the boy?' he asked.

'I dismissed him with a reprimand. This business has been an important lesson to him. He won't allow the men to walk all over him again!' Wallace had considered reporting the midshipman's misdemeanour to the captain but what was the point. No recriminations would bring back to life those who had died. A court of enquiry would only add to the grief of the families. It would be better to let things be.

'Are you saying that our entire water supply is undrinkable?' Wallace demanded of the doctor.

The voyage had two further weeks to run. They were probably four hundred miles from the shores of the Australian continent and there was no knowing where, on the shores of that arid land mass, they were likely to find water. To make for Hobart was to court further disaster.

Alexander continued to think aloud.

'Boiling the water, foul as it is, renders it harmless. How Judith Bantrie came to be so foolish as to take it untreated we shall probably never know. From now on we must be certain that nothing is taken straight from the barrel no matter what the water source is believed to be. The galley crew must be responsible for boiling every mouthful of water consumed on the ship.'

'We are running short of fuel.' Wallace announced gloomily. 'All this boiling of the drinking water and the vast quantities of washing that have gone on, have reduced our fuel stocks to almost nothing.'

'There must be something which may be burned in the stoves,' Alexander insisted. 'Surely even the sacrifice of a few bunks and tables at this stage of the voyage is not too much to expect if we are to avoid further outbreaks of cholera?'

'I'll inform the Captain,' Wallace got up and pulled on his storm jacket.

'One good piece of news is that we have now encountered a favourable current and a following wind. It will probably be rough, but we should make good progress from now on!'

Chapter Eleven

While the *Albatross* skirted the south eastern shores of the Australian continent and negotiated the notorious Hobart Strait, her passengers experienced day after day of gale-force winds and angry seas. With fuel for the galley fires running low the young unmarried men volunteered to sacrifice their personal comfort for the benefit of the entire ship's company. During those last weeks of the voyage the bachelor's cabin was stripped of its furniture so that everyone might have one hot meal a day.

Alexander now conducted a strict control over the handling of the drinking water. Mercifully there were no further cases of cholera even though for days at a time, below decks was awash with filth. As each mountainous wave crashed down onto the main deck, sea water came pouring through poorly fitting hatches and burst open cabin doors to flood everything below decks.

Many of the passengers, overcome by sea sickness, were confined to their bunks. Human excreta and vomit combined with sea water to make a filthy midden through which all must paddle until there came a lull in the storm long enough to allow Tobias Leny and his band of willing helpers to mop up. In the main steerage cabin bedding was constantly damp. During the worst of the storms few on board escaped the ravages of sea sickness, while those who could get about were bruised and battered from colliding with all manner of obstacles as the ship lurched and plunged. Alexander was kept busy tending the injured and making the sick as comfortable as possible. As compensation for all this distress the passengers again knit together in comradeship and mutual self help.

Jessie Dundas managed to keep to her feet when those about her appeared completely helpless. She worked tirelessly to keep some semblance of order in the single women's cabin. The ladies unaffected by the ship's motion, made room for the children entertaining them to keep them from disturbing their sick parents. They conducted school and supervised the children's playtime activities.

Among these stalwarts was Nellie Parker who during the voyage, had discovered a natural aptitude for entertaining the children with her own little stories which she told with great expression and illustrated with charming drawings. Although her education had been scanty, she wrote a neat hand and read accurately if somewhat haltingly. With so many of the professional teachers and governesses laid low, she was frequently called upon to help. As the days passed she gained in confidence and began to wonder if she might find employment as a governess. What if she were to approach the sponsors of the late Alice Montogomery who would be looking forward to the arrival of someone to take care of their children?

She approached Jessie with the idea.

Jessie had felt sorry for the girl when her mistress died. After all, she had set out on this journey not of her own choice but because of her employer's appointment in Wellington. Unaware of what the voyage held in store for them, the Wimbornes had made no provision for their servant's future. Without the money for her fare home, Nellie must fend for herself in circumstances where employment as a lady's maid was almost certainly unobtainable.

'Will you not do better to continue on to Wellington, as Sir Tristram intended?' Jessie asked.

'I would rather stay amongst the friends I have made on board ship,' Nellie told her. 'If I go to Wellington I shall be alone among strangers.'

'Then I shall be happy to support your application for a post as governess,' Jessie told her, kindly. 'I am sure you will do as well as any of the women I have met on board. You need to work hard to stay one step ahead of your pupils but in certain respects Nellie, you are very talented. If you struggle a little with your reading, you make up for it in your drawing and painting and I have seen you dancing. That is a subject much thought of by mothers who appoint a governess for their children. What about arithmetic? Are you able to calculate sums of money and so forth?'

'Oh yes, Mrs Dundas,' Nellie assured her. 'That was one thing my father insisted upon my being able to do. He was a great one for the horse racing you see, but he was also a heavy drinker. It was my duty to keep an eye on his investments, as he called it. Once he had had a pint or two of ale he became so drunk he could never remember which bookie he had laid on with, let alone the size of the stake!'

Jessie wondered what those good people awaiting Alice Montgomery's arrival in New Edinburgh would say to a governess whose knowledge of arithmetic stemmed from frequenting the race track.

'I think perhaps you would be wise to be rather reserved when questioned about you own education,' she suggested diplomatically. 'If you are sufficiently confident at your first interview your employers will assume that you are adept in the basics and a collection of your charming little sketches will demonstrate your artistic ability. We will compose a letter of application together, which you may copy out carefully in a fair hand.'

'Then you don't think it would be too presumptuous of me to suggest that I might take Miss Montgomery's place?'

'Not at all,' Jessie assured her. 'In fact, I would be happy to recommend you myself. Better still, I will ask the doctor to write a letter of recommendation.'

'Will you help me with my reading while we remain on board?' the girl pleaded. 'Oh, how I wish I had thought of this before. There have been so many wasted weeks when I might have been improving myself!'

'I will do what I can for you, of course.' Jessie had already thought of a way to help Nellie while, at the same time performing a particularly distressing task which the captain had thrust upon her.

'In fact,' she said excitedly, 'I have already decided what must be done. Apart from a few personal items which are to be returned to her relatives in Scotland, Miss Montgomery has left a trunk full of school books and teaching materials which the captain has asked me to dispose of where they will do some good. I am sure that Alice would have been only too pleased to see them used in exactly the way she herself intended.'

*

Summoned on deck by the shouts of 'Land ho!' from the lookouts, the passengers caught their first glimpse of their new homeland in the early dawn of the seventh day of May in the year, 1848.

Approaching the South Island of New Zealand from the southwest, their first sighting was of Stewart Island, the third and smallest of the three main islands. The coastline was low lying with large sandy bays and marshy inlets separated by brush- covered headlands. Porpoises played around the ship as she drew closer to the shore, clouds of sea birds rose from the waves at her approach and seals and other sea mammals such as many aboard had never encountered, thronged the beaches.

The ship's next tack took them out of sight of land for some hours and it was nearly dark before they encountered the more forbidding coastline of the South Island. Here steep headlands fell away to small grassy coves with sandy beaches. The rugged cliffs were more reminiscent of the coastline of Argyll than had been the flat plains of Stewart Island. There was a stir, an air of expectancy with tense and mounting excitement amongst the passengers.

Here too the beaches were crowded with wild life. There were several kinds of seals and thousands upon thousands of strange flightless birds which walked upright and looking like small gentlemen dressed for dinner. The sky was filled with seabirds which flocked around the ship, wheeling and diving in ever increasing numbers as she tacked close in to the shore. As she veered away to avoid the jutting headlands, those on board could recognise auks and guillemots, skuas and divers, reminding the Highlanders of the wild cliffs of their homeland.

While the passengers marvelled at the profusion of living creatures surrounding them, from over the horizon to the north, flying some twenty foot above the sea, dipping and soaring upon air currents created by the waves themselves, flew a single enormous bird. From a distance its plumage appeared uniformly dark, but as it came nearer not only could those on deck appreciate the bird's truly gigantic size, but they could also see that the head and underbelly were brilliant white in sharp contrast with the darker feathers on the back.

While passengers and crew alike stood transfixed following its graceful flight, the huge bird was joined by others of its kind which flew together in a graceful aerial ballet, swooping and diving between the masts. At each pass they displayed every feature of their magnificent plumage. How they missed the rigging by a hair's breadth was a wonder. Once clear of the ship they resumed their acrobatic demonstration to the delighted cries of all on board. It was almost as though the newcomers had recognised a sister in the *Albatross* and had come to welcome her home.

'What birds are they?' Tommy Dundas demanded of Catherine, his eyes wide with wonder. Julian Frawley had joined them on fore deck.

'It is the Royal Albatross,' he explained, 'the legendary seaman's friend. He will sometimes escort a single vessel from the time she appears in the Great Southern Ocean until she crosses the tropic of Capricorn on her journey northwards. The albatross is never seen to rest. A solitary bird will circumnavigate the globe continuously until the time comes for it to return home to breed.'

Catherine suspected that Julian Frawley was indulging in one of his tall tales and was determined to challenge him. 'If they pick up a ship south of the tropic of Capricorn as you suggest how have we seen no albatross until now?'

'They do not like a calm sea without wind,' Frawley told her. 'If you remember, it was still calm and hot even when we were far south of the Indian continent. The Albatross requires a strong breeze and a stormy sea to perfect his flying.'

'Since the weather changed there have been such storms that we have not been allowed on deck to see the birds even if they were there,' said Charlie, in defence of his friend.

'When we reach Otago Harbour,' Julian told Catherine, 'You will see the headland where the albatross breed. The whole cliff is white with the thousands of birds gathered there.'

'But they are so large!' cried the boy as another of the great birds dived across the bows. 'With its wings spread that one must be almost as big as me!'

'Bigger,' said Frawley. 'Some are as much as ten foot across from wing tip to wing tip.'

In their carefree display the magnificent creatures had filled Catherine with a kind of envy. Inexplicably she felt a pricking behind her eyes and quickly brushed away a tear. The wild creatures represented a degree of freedom she could never now experience. How she wished that she might cast off the burden of responsibility which had come to rest so heavily on her shoulders during the voyage. How she longed to be free of all cares, just like the Albatross!

Seeing her tear- stained cheeks and mistaking the reason for her distress, Julian placed a comforting arm around her shoulder and was surprised when she surrendered to his warm embrace. Since Julian Frawley had confessed to his part in the cholera tragedy he had studiously avoided Nellie Parker and concentrated instead upon bringing comfort to the bereaved Bantrie family. He had deliberately sought every opportunity to ease Catherine's burden in caring for her distraught father and attending to the needs of her little brother. In the absence of the sibling rivalry and adolescent infatuation which had so coloured their earlier encounters, a casual acquaintance between the pair had grown into a comfortable companionship. At the same time Julian had found in his dealings with young Charles, bereft both of his mother's love and his father's attention, an opportunity to make some small atonement for his stupidity and carelessness over the water supplies.

Perversely, the midshipman would have preferred a severe physical punishment to the verbal rebuke he had received from the mate. He knew that he deserved dismissal or at the very least demotion. Corporal punishment, a lick of the Cat or confinement in irons would in the eyes of the crew at least have made a martyr of him. He could have borne the discomfort stoically, recovered and gone about his business. This way, obliged as he was to watch how the bereaved families were attempting to mend their lives, he was faced with his misdeeds every day and what he saw filled him with remorse. Most importantly he could not forgive himself for what he had done to the Bantrie family.

Since Judith's death, James Bantrie had become a recluse, communing constantly with his God and speaking to his fellow passengers only during the formal services which he conducted at daily prayers and twice on Sundays. Even Catherine, always a great admirer of her father's calling, was becoming suspicious that what she had believed to be the words of God were being subverted to her father's purpose, by his own disturbed imagination. When one of the young female passengers was caught in a compromising situation with a member of the crew, setting aside all thought of compassion James had called her a harlot in public and made her stand on a stool in front of the entire congregation at the Sunday services. When Charlie was discovered playing an innocent game of cards with Philip Mackie his father thrashed him with his leather belt and forbade any further liaison with the blacksmith's boy.

Catherine was not the only one to be concerned at the change in the minister's demeanour. Jessie Dundas too had noticed that James had developed a fanaticism which excluded all humanitarian considerations. His admonitions for the slightest wrong-doing or the simplest mistake became more and more harsh as the days went on, the minister's children bearing the brunt of this change in his personality.

Jessie discussed the problem with Alexander who made light of her worries.

'It is James's manner of dealing with his grief,' he told her. 'Once we land in New Zealand there will be so much to think about, finding a place to settle, building a house, establishing his parish, he will soon recover his old spirits and return to the benign character we all recognise. Just you mark my words.'

Jessie was not so sure. She spent long hours talking to Catherine, trying to make her understand how her father must blame himself for her mother's death.

'Had Mr Bantrie not placed you all in the situation which brought you to Orchy in the first place and had he not embarked upon this particular adventure your mother might still be alive.'

'But we all encouraged him in this,' protested Catherine loyally. 'Mother never blamed him for sticking to his principles and leaving his comfortable living at Kilmory.'

'Nevertheless, he blames himself. When he utters the harsh words which upset you so he is really punishing himself.'

Catherine tried to understand, but it was asking too much of one who had been forced to take on the burden of responsibility far too soon.

Jessie could empathise with her for had she not herself been obliged to take on the care of an ailing father at an early age? Suddenly she found that she was committing herself in a way which she had never even considered before this moment.

'You have your own life to live my dear,' she said, 'It is time for you to leave your father's care to others.' Catherine looked at her wide-eyed, not believing that there was anyone in the whole world who could help her.

'But who?' she demanded, quietly.

Jessie continued gently, 'There is something which I should have told you a long time ago. When we thought that the ship might founder and I volunteered to join the boat's crew, I asked your mother to take care of Tommy if I should not return and I know she would have done so, gladly. Unhappily it was she who was the one to go and not me. I know that she would expect me to care for both you and Charles as she would have cared for my Tommy. Be assured my dear that I shall never leave you to shoulder the burden of your father's grief alone.'

Catherine put her arms around Jessie's neck, buried her head in the widow's shoulder and wept with relief.

*

As the ship approached journey's end, the captain informed Alexander no passengers would be allowed to leave the ship until the Port authorities had assured themselves that everyone was fit and free from communicable disease.

'You have no idea how vulnerable the Maori are to conditions we regard as mere inconvenience,' McCallum explained. 'They have been known to die of influenza. Measles was brought in by one emigrant family arriving in the North Island and a whole tribe was wiped out!'

'Well, we appear to be free of cholera,' said Alexander. 'The Mackie boy would pass muster under any scrutiny my medical colleagues care to apply and I am not aware of either measles or any form of pox on board. I cannot believe that we shall be denied entry.'

'I sincerely trust that you are right,' said McCallum. 'The thought of our passengers remaining on board a moment longer than is absolutely necessary frankly appals me!'

'Have you found them so difficult to contend with?'

'No, not at all. In the circumstances, they have been an exemplary group but do you not notice how with their destination almost in sight even the most malleable and co-operative of folk are beginning to find things to criticise? Once they begin exchanging experiences with others who arrived on earlier ships there will be complaints about the way the voyage compares with what happened before. No allowance is made for the hazy glow of reminiscence. If our people are held long on board, for whatever reason it will be put down to my incompetence and the Company will seize upon what is said to reduce the salary due to myself and my crew.'

'I fear you are speaking from bitter experience,' Alexander observed. 'Does your diagnosis of the situation include me?'

The Company owed Dr Beaton almost double the amount he had been promised at the outset. He had kept the crew free of illness and fit for work despite a pestilence which might have destroyed them all. There had been deaths of course but many more had been averted by the care and vigilance applied by himself and his little team of workers. Tobias Leny and Jessie Dundas deserved praise for their tireless devotion to duty. Alexander was determined to see that they were properly rewarded for their efforts.

No matter by what underhand means Tobias had wangled his passage, Alexander had him to thank for much of his own success with keeping the passengers contented. The man was practical and able to see straight to the heart of a problem. His solutions, although somewhat unorthodox, usually worked. His experience as a janitor had proved invaluable when it came to clearing up after the violent storms at sea. He had invented hanging stoves which could be swung from the beams of the lower deck to dry out the soaking wet bedding and had suggested the spreading of hot sand, heated on the galley stove, to dry the decking in the cabins. To amuse the passengers he had invented innumerable games which occupied both children and the adults on board. A game of deck billiards had had the sternest of gentlemen grappling with his grip on the quoits to achieve that little extra finesse which would win a valuable point. On the hottest days, he had organised a paddling pool for the children by trapping the water used to sluice down the decks. When wild creatures showed themselves, Toby was the one to organise a competition shoot. Dolphin and porpoise were easy prey providing targets large enough for the poorest shot to hit, but there was real skill required in bringing down a Cape pigeon or one of Mother Carey's chickens. What a cheer had gone up when a shark was killed and all the other sharks from miles around homed in upon the kill. It had been a spectacle for all aboard to enjoy. All that is except Catherine Bantrie and one or two of the more sensitive ladies.

On the final morning of the voyage when the two men stood at the door of the dispensary admiring the wide entrance to Otago Bay and marvelling at the numbers of albatross gathered on the cliffs of Taiaroa Head, Alexander broached the subject of Leny's future employment.

'I shall find some means of making a living Doctor, have no fear,' Leny assured him.

'I don't doubt it, Toby,' Alexander laughed. 'I was thinking however that you could be very useful to me especially in the early days. I shall have to establish a medical practice very soon if I am to make enough money to keep myself and my wife and stepson. I had hoped you would stay on as my partner for a while at least, while we set up premises and perhaps establish a smallholding of some kind.'

'Do I take it then that Mrs Dundas has agreed to become Mrs Beaton, Sir?' Toby asked, delighted by the news.

'That is certainly my intention Toby, although I have yet to persuade the lady that she will be doing the right thing by marrying me.'

'I don't see how she could refuse you, Sir, if I may be so bold.'

'We shall see, Toby. Whatever her decision, I shall need assistance so what do you say? Will you be my partner?'

'Delighted, Sir, always assuming I may carry on some small enterprise of my own, should the opportunity arise.'

'Naturally! This is the land of opportunity Tobias. Everyone with ideas will find some outlet for them I'm sure.'

'Then it's a bargain, Sir!' exclaimed the little man.

'And Tobias,' Alexander paused, wishing to put his words in a manner which would be taken as kindly as he intended, 'Once we leave the ship we shall as I said, be partners and I hope, friends. Will you address me as Alexander or Alex if you please but never again as Sir.'

'Delighted S...' he grinned, 'Alexander!' They shook hands on the matter.

*

Once past the protective headlands at the entrance to the harbour the vista opened to a vast expanse of open water skirted on either shore by high hills, wooded slopes and open scrub lands. Close at hand, on the starboard quarter, a low-lying spit of sand forced the vessel to take a tack to the south. The air was so still that the ship's shadow, cast ahead of her by the low-lying early morning sun, formed a perfect replica on the unruffled surface of the water. The boats were lowered and the crew bent to the oars to tow the Albatross home, just as they had hauled her away from the rocks in the South Atlantic Ocean.

They passed a Maori village on the southern shore and as they did so, canoes were launched to come out and meet the *Albatross*. Some of the passengers, fearful that the natives intended to attack, reached for their sporting guns, but Captain McCallum raised his megaphone ordering that all arms should be put aside.

'The natives are friendly. They are coming out to greet us and to help with the towing,' he shouted.

A pilot had come aboard soon after they passed the headland, a grizzled Scotsman who had been among the first of the whaling fraternity to visit these shores. The man was familiar with every sand bar and every deep channel in that vast harbour. Under his orders the helmsman steered the *Albatross* into a path which veered in a northerly direction to where a secondary inlet of deep water allowed her to find an anchorage close by the shore.

'What do you call this place?' enquired the captain surprised to find a deep-water anchorage so far inside the harbour. On an earlier voyage, he had been obliged to anchor in the roads and, finding no suitable place to land other than the Maori village they had recently passed, he had turned his ship about and continued northwards to Wellington in the North Island.

'It's a native village called Koputai,' the pilot told him. 'Recently it has been renamed Port Chalmers, after a famous preacher so I believe.'

'Who has settled here?' asked McCallum, intrigued that so early in the history of the place people had chosen to settle here rather than choose the protection of the main settlement.

'Those who are particularly concerned with shipping,' was the reply. 'There is a chandlery and a provisioning store and, a short way along the shore to the west, a wood yard. The very first settlers came here from Nelson and chose this as the site for their operation. They are the McKays, Janet and Alexander who run the hotel. When you think of it, it makes sense to have such facilities available here,' McCallum observed to Alexander. 'This appears to be where the ships are most easily serviced. It will be a long time before vessels of this size will be able to reach the inner harbour, if ever. Also, there's good farming land on the northern shore of the inlet and as well as the timber yard, there is a source of stone for quarrying.'

Captain McCallum could only marvel at the advances that had been made in the two years since he had last sailed into the bay of Otago. His first impression had been there was no chance of a successful settlement of any size.

'This is a very small village,' Catherine observed as she stood with Jessie and Charles viewing with some dismay the tiny group of huts and houses scattered along either side of a single street. 'Is this New Edinburgh?' she demanded of Alexander Beaton, who had come to stand beside them at the rail.

'No, this is just a convenient anchorage. New Edinburgh is around this headland and a little further to the south and west.

The pilot, whose task was finished now that the ship was riding at anchor, had joined the gathering of passengers on the main deck to await the boat to take him ashore. Anxious for any news from home, he had been conversing with the blacksmith, Mackie, when he overheard Alexander's explanation and ventured to update him.

'The settlement was recently renamed, Dun Eideann which is the old name for Edinburgh, but you'll find that the true Gaelic has already been corrupted,' he laughed. 'Only this morning I saw the name of the settlement written down as Dunedin.'

'Now that's a name that really does roll readily off the tongue,' said Alexander. 'Let us hope that Dunedin is what it will remain!'

The pilot addressed Alexander directly. 'Mr Mackie here tells me you are the ship's surgeon.'

'Yes, I am he. Dr Alexander Beaton, at your service.'

'Archibald Blackstaff,' the pilot introduced himself. The two men shook hands.

'I have a message for a Mr James Bantrie,' Blackstaff told him, 'a reverend gentleman I believe.'

'Mr Bantrie is below, preparing for disembarkation.' Alexander did not care to say that James had been praying in his cabin ever since the ship had docked.

'Dr Burns, the leader of our settlement, is most anxious to make his acquaintance, Doctor. Would you be so kind as to tell Mr Bantrie that a boat will be dispatched to carry him to the Manse at high tide this evening. Mr Burns has arranged for his party to be ferried ashore at the head of the harbour, tomorrow morning. I have no doubt,' he added hastily, 'that there will be room on the boat for you and your effects, should you wish to avail yourself of the convenience.'

'Thank you, but I am obliged to remain on board until all the passengers are declared fit to disembark,' said Alexander. 'I shall however convey your message to Mr Bantrie, without delay.'

They shook hands again. The pilot glanced upwards to where captain McCallum was watching from the bridge. He touched his cap before nimbly climbing down the Jacob's ladder into his waiting boat.

*

In the days which followed, there was much activity aboard the *Albatross*. One after another, whole families and individual passengers alike, disembarked for the new colony. Some were eager to get started on the business of making a new life for themselves while others appeared reluctant to leave the confines of the ship they knew for the unknown challenges presented by the wilderness out there beyond the hills surrounding the bay.

Alexander remained on board until all his duties as ship's surgeon had been completed. He and Toby were in the dispensary where Alexander was sorting out what supplies should be left for the return voyage and which he could carry ashore with him. On the advice of the New Zealand Company's secretary, he had brought with him supplies of those medicines and equipment of which there was a shortage in the colony. These had remained in the hold throughout the voyage. He had also carried in the hospital certain items which only a competent physician could use. There was no point in leaving these on board for the return journey which would be made without a ship's surgeon. He calculated the value of this equipment and made the captain an offer to purchase it.

'The chances of your getting the money owed to you for the work you have done whilst on board, are slim, Alexander,' Captain McCallum told him. 'Take the property in lieu of payment. I will square it off with the powers that be.'

The arrangement suited Alexander very well. Since their arrival, he had very soon come to realise that money was less useful than material items in a place so remote from all sources of supplies. Local men, coming on board to help unload the cargo, would have bought the shirt off his back had he let them. With the captain's blessing, he stripped the dispensary of all but the barest necessities and began to shift the packing cases on deck ready for his departure.

In the midst of all this turmoil, James Bantrie appeared.

The minister seemed well rested after two nights in port and Alexander wondered if some of the man's difficulties of late could be attributed to lack of sleep during the heavy weather at sea. James had shaved and put on clean clothing and now appeared nearly as good humoured as he had been at the commencement of the voyage. Incongruously, to go ashore he wore a tall hat and carried his Malacca cane with the silver handle.

'We are off now, Doctor, he said approaching Alexander with hand outstretched. 'I thought I should say goodbye before we leave.'

Alexander looked at him, astounded.

'But we shall be seeing one another again within hours,' he said. 'I requested the land agent to see that our allotted sections in the town should be side by side.'

'Ah, yes,' James seemed hesitant as he continued, 'Perhaps I should have mentioned it before. The fact is, Beaton, I was as you know, obliged to pay a visit to Dr Burns, the leader of the Dunedin settlement yesterday. He has persuaded me to undertake the establishment of a new settlement in the hinterland, some few miles to the west of here where there is a goodly population of natives whom he wishes to bring into the Christian fold.'

'And you propose to leave right away, before establishing your claim to property here in Dunedin?'

'There is no time to waste when souls need to be saved.' He appeared astonishingly cheerful and full of purpose. 'We shall remain in Dunedin only so long as it takes me to find a suitable wagon and horses to carry our belongings.'

'But how will you manage, alone, with only the children to assist you?'

'I have no doubt that Mrs Dundas will prove to be as competent a pioneer as she has been a nurse and stalwart companion during the voyage.'

'Mrs Dundas is coming with you?' In his frustration, Alexander shouted out the question. What could Jessie be thinking of? Why had she said nothing of this to him? How could she contemplate disappearing into the wilderness with a widower and two children? What of *her* reputation, she who had been so concerned for his own? So rapidly did these thoughts come tumbling through his brain that he nearly missed the minister's final, crushing blow.

'For propriety's sake, Mrs Dundas had agreed to become my wife.'

Unable to speak to the man, Alexander pushed past him emerging on deck at the very moment when Jessie was about to tap on the door of the dispensary and admit herself.

'Oh, Alex, I…,' she stopped, realising by his expression that he had already been told of her intentions.

'I am so sorry,' she said. 'I had hoped to be the one to tell you. You must forgive James's clumsiness. He is not aware that there has been any attachment between us.'

'Has been! Has been!' What are you talking about, has been? Have I not asked you to be my wife? Do we not have an understanding?' Whether anger, frustration or disappointment was the cause the doctor's eyes filled with tears.

Embarrassed at what she saw in his face, Jessie lowered her eyes unable to bear his pain.

'I never promised to marry you,' she reminded him gently. 'James has great need of me and the children too. This motherless family has a much stronger call upon my services than you can possibly imagine. I am sorry Alexander. I know you are disappointed but there will be others, far more suitable women than I, who will be only too willing to become the wife of a surgeon, a man of standing in the community. James and I will be far away from here. Somewhere where there will be no Scottish eyes to accuse us of any impropriety.'

'But you do not love him!'

Alexander's final thrust fell upon ears closed to all but duty, promises to a lost friend and obligation to a pair of children she had vowed to protect. She reached up to him and kissed him lightly on the cheek. He in turn sank the fingers of both hands in her lustrous chestnut locks, disturbing the neat coiffeur and dislodging her cheeky little bonnet. Drawing her upturned face towards him he kissed her firmly on the lips.

'Don't do this Jessie,' he pleaded. 'Please don't do it.'

'I must. Goodbye Alexander,' she murmured. 'When you come ashore we shall already be gone.' Then, hoping to mitigate the blow, 'Perhaps later, when we are all settled in our various locations, you will come and visit us.'

He knew that tone. Jessie had made up her mind and nothing would deter her now. He turned away quite unable to speak.

When he looked back to where she had stood she was gone. Absently, Alex watched as James Bantrie handed his daughter onto the companion ladder but then, unable to resist the temptation to snatch one last glimpse of Jessie he moved across the deck and leaned over the bulwarks. He saw young Charlie perched upon a pile of luggage stacked in the bows of the vessel. The boy looked up at that moment and their eyes met. His face lit up when he saw the doctor peering down at them and he waved excitedly. Automatically Alexander raised his hand in response. Tommy Dundas, the child Alexander had already begun to look upon as his own son, clung tightly to Catherine's skirts where they sat side by side on one of the thwarts. Behind them, the minister himself watched calmly as the men prepared to cast off. At James side, motionless and apparently divorced from the activity taking place around her sat Jessie Dundas, staring into the future with empty eyes.

Chapter Twelve

The settlers arriving on the *Albatross* had many advantages over their predecessors the first of whom had sailed into Otago Harbour towards the end of March, nearly two months before. Their ship the *John Wycliffe* having anchored in the roads, they had been ferried ashore by the ship's boats but they had been landed in a swamp at the head of the harbour. Men had waded through brackish water and soft mud carrying their wives and children on their backs.

To their dismay, those first arrivals had found no neat streets of homes, shops and workshops as displayed in the artist's impressions shown to them before sailing. Instead they were confronted by acres of dense scrub where the surveyor's pegs and lines of the previous year had all but been obscured by the prolific re-growth of vegetation.

One of their first tasks had been to construct a suitable jetty to allow folk to step ashore without getting their feet wet. It was upon this structure, built of the trunks of native trees with the piles sunk deep in estuarine mud that Alexander Beaton set foot on shore after four and a half months at sea.

The jetty ran out perhaps one hundred yards from the shore and as his baggage and packing cases piled up on the boards, Alexander left Toby to keep an eye on their possessions while he went off in search of some form of transport. The jetty eventually gave way to metalled road. To either side of this a few clapboard houses and one rather more substantial building gave evidence of the work which had already been accomplished. Both road and houses soon gave out however and he found himself on a deeply rutted track between flimsy fences marking the boundaries of the various plots. Makeshift shelters had been erected consisting of tents and buildings of rough-hewn timber with fern leaf roofs. There were even a few more substantial dwellings made from timber frames in-filled with dried mud bricks. Alongside each ramshackle house an open fire or in just a few cases, an iron kitchen range, belched smoke. The smells of cooking reminded the doctor that he had eaten nothing since seven o'clock and it was now past noon.

As he cast about for someone to give him directions, it began to rain. At once, from inside one of the tents a man appeared and opened his black umbrella. It might well have seen service in some Edinburgh or Glasgow street. He held it above his wife's head as she prepared their midday meal over an open fire.

Alex approached them over hummocky ground which had been roughly stripped of vegetation and upon which he could make out the newly laid foundations of a more substantial dwelling.

'Good day to you, Sir,' he called approaching warily for the rain had already turned the scoured surface into a quagmire. 'I wonder if you could direct me to a carrier, someone with a vehicle which will transport my possessions to my plot?'

'Best come inside,' suggested the man, still holding the umbrella over his wife as she scurried into the tent with their dinner.

'I don't wish to intrude,' Alexander protested, feeling foolish in these extraordinary circumstances.

'Not at all, not at all. You'll be off the *Albatross,* I don't doubt.'

Alexander had been right about one thing the voice was clearly Glaswegian.

'I have seen the land agent and received the location of my plot, but no one suggested what I might do with my belongings while I find some form of accommodation.' Alexander told him.

'Did they no' tell you down at the wharf? You can get canvas there to make a tent like this.' He looked about him, proudly. 'Or you can get a bed at the hotel always assuming they have room and you have the money. With so many newcomers they can afford to raise their prices. Of course, you might get a berth in the barracks for the time being.'

Alexander was beginning to think he would have done better to stay aboard the ship until he had made his arrangements. Oh well, it was done now. He thanked the couple for their assistance and refusing their generous offer of a share in their frugal meal, he set off back in the direction by which he had come.

Where the road ran out onto the jetty he met Toby advancing towards him and looking particularly pleased with himself.

'Where have you been?' he demanded. 'I was just about to send out a search party.'

Not a little annoyed at having to confess his failure to find them a place to stay or even a wagon to convey their belongings, Alexander told him briefly what the man had said.

'Oh, you don't want to worry yourself on that score Alexander.' Toby was irritatingly cheerful. 'I've already got us fixed up at the hotel and our luggage is all under cover over there on the wharf.' Toby indicated a long low shed which although he had it noticed earlier, Alexander, seeking the kind of carrier's yard to which he was accustomed, had quite ignored.

'How did you move all those bags and packing cases?' he demanded.

'Barrows. I paid the boatmen and a couple of lads down by the shore to push them.' Alexander knew now beyond doubt that he had made the right decision in inviting Toby to become his partner. Gratefully he followed the little man to the one substantial construction in the entire street. Advancing before him, Toby opened the swing doors and led the doctor through into the public bar of the Wharf Hotel.

*

Angus Fergusson had come out to the South Island several years previously as a junior member of the original surveying party headed by Frederick Tuckett the Chief Surveyor of the New Zealand Company. When his principals returned to Scotland, Fergusson was left behind in the provisional capacity of land agent, his task to carry on with the building of the settlement's infrastructure and to allocate plots to the settlers on their arrival.

After two years of uncertainty in which the New Zealand Company failed to raise sufficient funds to carry out any building operations, a steady flow of settlers began to arrive, principally from Scotland. Never doubting that the development would take place eventually, Fergusson had gone ahead with pegging out the territory and designating the areas allocated for roads and public facilities. With no funds and insufficient skilled labour to carry on with the public works, he could occupy his time in constructing a house for himself and the family he had left behind in Scotland. He chose a fine site on one of the higher pieces of ground surrounding the bay and built a bungalow of local stone having four substantial rooms together with a kitchen and bath house at the rear. Following Maori tradition, he thatched his house with the bull-rushes which crowded the swampy shores of the bay. It was the finest and indeed at the time, the only permanent dwelling in the township.

Fergusson's wife and family had joined him the previous March, arriving on board the *John Wickliffe* as fellow passengers of Dr Thomas Burns, the settlement's designated leader. His wife Margaret was horrified to discover that during the four years they had been apart her husband had achieved so little. A few acres of scrub had been cleared and a checkerboard of plots was laid out but there were no public buildings, few permanent houses and no school.

Despairing of her children's education, she had sent immediately to her parents asking them to appoint a governess and agreeing to sponsor a Miss Alice Montgomery of Dundee.

The *Albatross* had been at anchor in Port Chalmers for two days when Margaret Fergusson, impatiently awaiting word of her new governess, was summoned to her door by a loud knocking. She opened it to find not the expected Alice Montgomery, but an officer from the *Albatross* who saluted her smartly and handed her a bundle of letters. Refusing her invitation to step inside and take some refreshment, the young man hurried on his way leaving her to sort through the various packages. Tucking those from her own family into her pocket for later consumption, she opened one addressed to herself and bearing the crest of the New Zealand Company. The letter was from the captain of the *Albatross*.

Dear Mrs Fergusson,

It is with the utmost regret that I must inform you of the tragic death of Miss Alice Montgomery from Cholera, during the voyage from Scotland. Miss Montgomery was given dignified burial at sea, the service being conducted by the ship's chaplain, the rev. James Bantrie. She is greatly mourned by all who came to know her during her time aboard the Albatross.

I am, dear madam, your obedient servant,
Walter T McCallum, Master.

In her disappointment and frustration, Margaret crumpled up the letter and threw it across the floor. What was she to do now? For months she had struggled alone to organise the household and keep the children occupied. The new emigrants had set up a school house down by the shore but it was a very mixed bunch of children that went to it; a most unsuitable environment in which to place the children of one of the town's most important families.

Angrily she turned over the remaining envelopes on the desk in front of her. There were a number addressed to her husband which she set aside and two addressed to them both, which she decided to open.

S V Albatross
May 18th 1847

To Mr and Mrs Fergusson
Maryhill House
Dear Sir and Madam,

Captain McCallum will have apprised you of the sad circumstances of the death of Miss Alice Montgomery. As her physician at the time of her death, I can assure you that everything was done to make her comfortable during her last hours.

Among those who were with her at the end was a young woman whom Miss Montgomery had befriended. Her employers, with whom she was travelling, having both perished during the voyage, Miss Eleanor Parker finds herself far from home without any form of support. She is an intelligent young woman of good health with many excellent features. I have myself observed her as she worked with the children of other passengers in our improvised school aboard ship and have been most impressed by her manner. May I recommend her to you as one entirely suitable to take the place of the late Miss Montgomery within your household.

I am your obedient servant,
Alexander Beaton MB.ChB.

Margaret Fergusson's mood changed as she reread Alexander's letter of recommendation. In an instant, her total dejection had turned to hope and expectation. She picked up the last of the letters which was addressed in a clear round hand reminiscent of her eldest child. It was writing such as might have been found in any schoolroom.

Dear Sir and Madam,

I am eighteen years of age, of clean habits and well spoken. My last employment was in the household of Sir Tristram and Lady Wimborne with whom I was travelling when they tragically met their deaths.

On board the Albatross, I met the late Miss Alice Montgomery and was made aware of her engagement to you. After her death, I tried to take her place spending much of my time teaching and entertaining children of all ages from four to sixteen years. Although I am not an experienced governess, I can offer all the basic subjects and in addition drawing and dancing. I respectfully ask to be considered for the vacant post of governess in your household.

I may be reached at any time at the Wharf Hotel.

Your obedient servant,

Eleanor J Parker.

It was not the most accomplished of letters but it was properly spelt and the handwriting was clear and neat. In any case, what alternative did they have but to give the girl a trial?

Margaret called out to the eldest of her four children.

'Anna, I have to go out for a while. Make sure your brothers do not get into any mischief while I am gone. Oh, and see that the wee one get's his mid-morning nap on time today. He is so grouchy if he does not get enough sleep.'

It would not do for the new governess to be confronted by a miserable four-year-old on her first day!

*

The Wharf Hotel stood beside the shore and close to the landing stage. It was a two-storey tree fern and clapboard construction, boasting both short and long-stay accommodation in a number of smaller rooms as well as two dormitories each sleeping up to ten individuals.

Tobias Leny, with his usual capacity for striking a good bargain, had negotiated a one month tenancy of one of the single rooms on the ground floor and a second, on the floor above. This he had accomplished despite the heavy demand for temporary accommodation by pointing out to the landlord that by establishing his consulting room within the hotel, the doctor would be bringing additional custom into the bar as it provided a very convenient waiting room!

Having seen for himself the primitive conditions in which many of the settlers were living, Alexander was relieved and delighted with Toby's arrangements. Here was a relatively comfortable lodging as well as a ready- made office in which to set up his practice.

'I hope this will do for you and your good lady Alexander,' Toby said, as he led the doctor into a small square room on the first floor of the building. 'You may perhaps choose to use this as a consulting room and the one above as your living accommodation?'

'Where do you propose to sleep, Toby?'

'Oh, I can find a bunk in the men's dormitory, or I'll put up a cot in the consulting room, here.'

'We are partners now,' Alex reminded him. 'I should take it as an insult if you refused to share with me while we are obliged to remain here.'

'Naturally, I had assumed that you and your wife…' Toby hesitated.

'No.' Alexander offered no further explanation why Jessie would not be joining them.

Toby, mystified but nevertheless secretly relieved not to have to bunk in the rather less than agreeable sheds which housed the dormitories, readily agreed to the doctor's suggestion. Having inspected the rooms the two men made their way to the one public area in the house which was the dining room and public bar. Here they ordered food and a glass of ale.

'I never realised it would be quite so cold,' Alexander shivered as he crouched over his glass, glad to be inside out of the wind and rain.

'There were many on board ship had not realised that the seasons were turned about in this hemisphere,' Toby observed. 'When they asked back in Scotland what the weather was like in December they were pleased to be told that temperatures might reach seventy degrees. What they didn't realise was that they could fall to forty and below in June!'

Toby's finding them decent accommodation had lifted Alexander's spirits for a time but his comment on the weather immediately caused him to turn his thoughts to the little party making its way inland at this very minute towards the higher ground where snow already lay on the tallest peaks.

What was Jessie thinking of at this moment, he wondered. Was she uncomfortably wet and cold? He could not bear to think of her making her first home in a tent like those people he had met earlier in the day. James had spoken of a marriage but if they were leaving immediately they might not have had time to make the bond. Should he not try to follow her? There might yet be time, another opportunity perhaps to persuade her to change her mind.

When she agreed to accompany James, Jessie could not have known just how difficult conditions would be. Now she had seen for herself how extreme they were and how desperate her situation, surely she would want to reconsider her decision. How could she contemplate so primitive a life in the bush with an unbalanced man and his two children?

Alexander was by now quite convinced that James Bantrie was unhinged. He wondered what might be the effect that such a person would have upon a tribe of Aboriginals, many of whom already believed that the white man had been sent from the devil. He feared for the lives of all of them but most of all he feared for his beloved Jessie.

While Toby went off to arrange for their baggage to be taken to the rooms he had hired, Alexander approached the landlord.

'I wonder if you have news of some friends of mine who came ashore two days back. The party consisted of the reverend James Bantrie, a Mrs Dundas and three children.'

Fergus Harding thought for a moment. 'There have been so many strangers in and out of here the last few days, it's hard to say. A reverend gentleman and his family you say? Come to think of it there was a small party of that nature. They waited here for a wagon as I recall. Just a moment, I'll ask the wife. Bess! Bess!'

A stout woman, who might have been any age between twenty and forty years, emerged from the kitchen rapidly removing the greasy white overall she had been wearing. Her face glowed from a morning spent over a hot stove, the perspiration standing out on her forehead in tiny glistening beads. As she joined her husband behind the bar she mopped her face with the screwed-up pinafore and ran her fingers through her tousled hair to give it some small semblance of order.

'Bess, do you remember those youngsters you were asked to keep an eye on the other day while the reverend and his lady went off to find Dr Burns? This gentleman was enquiring what became of his friends.'

The landlady immediately picked up on the story.

'Mr and Mrs Bantrie?' she confirmed. 'They spent the night here after their wedding and set off yesterday morning, just before sunrise.'

All Alexander's hopes were dashed. Too late! It seemed he was destined to be always too late in all things!

'Did they travel alone?' he demanded, anxious for Jessie's safety.

'Dr Burns came down to see them off, 'Bess told him. 'He brought with him a Maori guide.'

'Did they say where they were making for?' he asked, despairing now of ever setting eyes on Jessie again.

'Mapourika, it's about forty miles from here as the crow flies but there are rivers to ford and rough country to be traversed. It would take a wagon party with women and children three or four days at least. There's no proper track and no shelter along the way. It's not a journey I'd care to make myself at this time of the year.'

A small group of men was seated around a table in one corner, playing draughts. They had paused in their play to listen to the exchange.

'I've been up there to Mapourika,' one of them claimed. 'There's nothing but a Maori village, a few huts on the river bank. I can't think of any reason for a white man in his senses to want to go there.'

'Missionaries go anywhere where there are souls to be saved,' observed Bess, herself a devout Christian. When she had agreed to marry Fergus Harding he had promised her a temperance hotel.

In a few short weeks however it had become plain to them both that the men needed a supply of alcohol and considering it better to provide this under well supervised arrangements rather than leave them to visit the fearful go-downs of the Maori women, Bess had reluctantly agreed to import wine and whisky and set up her own brew house. She did not forgo her strict religious principals entirely however. Woe betide any man who took a drop too much. Swearing, cussing and fighting were forbidden and any transgression resulted in immediate exclusion from the bar. Even the most belligerent of men feared and respected the buxom landlady of the Wharf Hotel.

'Pity any man who tries to make Christians out o' they heathens,' observed one old fellow, by his dress and manner a long serving seaman. 'I was up near Wellington a few years back when the Maori attacked the white settlers. I talked to some of them as found the bodies. Gruesome it was by all accounts. I can't tell you the terrible sights they saw.'

Alexander was concerned enough for Jessie's safety without listening to these unpleasant reminiscences. Attempting to distance himself from the discussion he turned his attention to the remaining figure in the room.

Apparently oblivious to the general conversation going on around her, seated in the deepest of shadows the woman sat alone drinking tea. On the floor beside her were stacked a trunk, a large valise and a smaller carpet bag. It was clear that she was waiting for someone to appear for at every new arrival she looked up hopefully, watched the newcomer until he settled himself with a drink and then lowered her head dejectedly.

There was something about this solitary figure which Alexander recognised. Toby would know who she was but he had not yet returned.

Suddenly the street door swung open to admit a woman of quite extraordinarily statuesque beauty wearing incongruously fashionable attire. Her soaking wet cloak was made of the finest woollen material and her inappropriate straw hat was quite overburdened with multi- coloured silk flowers. The neat doe-skin shoes which reached up over her dainty ankles were thick with mud while the umbrella, which she opened and shut several times spraying all about her, was more suited to warding off a Parisian sun than a Dunedin downpour.

She advanced to the bar, spoke in a sotto voice to the bartender and then glanced across at the young woman in the corner.

'Miss Parker?' she enquired in a commanding tone which caused every head in the room to turn with interest towards the figure in the corner.

As the younger woman rose and moved into the light, Alexander recognised her as Nellie, the Wimborne's maid. Although he scarcely knew the young woman, Jessie had persuaded him to write her a letter of recommendation. If he had had any doubts about a lady's maid posing as a governess it was too late now to withdraw his support. Jessie had assured him the girl was capable and entirely worthy of his recommendation.

At the time he would have done anything Jessie asked of him. Now however his confidence in her ability to judge character had been severely shattered. In any case, had she not promised to act as mentor to this girl? How was she going to do that he wondered bitterly, living forty miles up-country in the wilderness?

Alexander watched as the two women shook hands and the newcomer accepted an invitation to sit down. Then, realising that he was staring rather rudely, he turned away to welcome Toby's return.

Margaret Fergusson listened to Ellie's tale of what had happened to Alice Montgomery and the Wimbornes in genuine consternation. 'What a terrible journey you have had to be sure,' she said. 'Thank goodness nothing so disturbing occurred aboard the *John Wickliffe*! You should seek compensation from the shipping company for such inconvenience.'

'I will be frank with you, Miss Parker,' the woman continued, 'Had you been a veritable Gorgon, I would have accepted your application this morning. It is not easy to keep an eye on four unruly children and carry on with the household work particularly when every simple task is made so complex by the lack of amenities here. It is not made any less onerous by the thought that one has been used to having servants about the place.' The pause was deliberately intended to impress but Nellie, terrified out of her wits by her own audacity in requesting this interview, was too stunned to appreciate the significance of what was being said.

'I do hope you are not going to be one of those governesses who balk at performing a few simple household tasks. If you can be a little flexible in what you consider the duties of a governess to be I feel we shall get along very well.'

Had she got the job? That was all Ellie wanted to know. Was she to have a roof over her head and three square meals a day?

'Thank you, ma'am,' was all she could think of in reply. 'I shall do my best to give satisfaction.'

'Very well then, let us agree upon a one year trial period at a salary of twenty pounds a year and all found? If things do not work out between us that will give me sufficient time to send to Scotland for a replacement.'

'Oh, thank you ma'am,' Nellie cried out so loudly that once again all heads turned in their direction.

'You had better arrange with the landlord to have your boxes carried to the house,' Margaret Fergusson suggested. 'He will give you directions. I shall expect to see you at three o'clock precisely.'

She stood up, gathered her damp coat about her and looking neither to right or left, made for the door. There she paused for an instant to look up at the sky. Not liking what she saw there she opened the impractical umbrella with a flourish and stepped out into the roadway.

Nellie, thrilled with the outcome of the interview, rushed across to where Alexander and Toby were seated.

'I recognised you the moment you came in,' she said, sitting down without invitation. She reached out and grasped Alexander's hand. 'Thank you, thank you, Doctor. Thank you so much. Because of you and Mrs Dundas I have been taken on as governess to Mrs Fergusson's children.' She looked around hoping to be able to give her good news to Jessie in person.

'Where is she?' she demanded, surprised not to find them together.

'Mrs Dundas is accompanying the Rev. Bantrie and his children up-country to settle amongst the Maori.' Alexander's blunt explanation startled Ellie. She blanched as her momentary elation disappeared in an instant.

Tobias regarded Alexander curiously. He had watched Jessie Dundas leaving the ship with the reverend Bantrie but, assuming by so doing she was merely observing some form of etiquette prior to her marriage to the doctor, he had waited for Alexander to tell him what was planned. So, this was why Alexander had invited Toby to share his room. Toby had discreetly left it to the doctor to tell him when his new bride would be joining them but now it seemed there was to be no wedding and Alexander was to remain a bachelor.

Nellie was not so reserved in her reaction to the news of Jessie's departure.

'Oh no, she cannot have agreed to go off into the wilderness with the preacher and his children. Whatever can she be thinking of?'

'What indeed!' Alexander thought. His answer was less explosive.

'I understand that the minister has been assigned to a new parish in the bush. Naturally his children must travel with him. Mrs Dundas has gone along to take care of them all.'

'Such a noble lady,' Nellie sighed, 'I shall miss her.' She stood up and made her way to the bar where she made her arrangements with the landlord. Soon she was on her way, perched beside the driver in a crudely constructed two-wheeled cart which was pulled by a single mule. Toby, handing her baggage up into the cart, wished her good fortune in her new position.

'Take care of the doctor,' she whispered to him. 'Poor man, he seems so sad.'

'Yes indeed,' Toby murmured. He turned away thoughtfully. So the widow had gone off with the minister. Now there was a pretty kettle of fish and no mistake!

Chapter Thirteen

The Bantries had been travelling for two days through course bush and dense woodland. Thankfully the rain had eased soon after they set out and bright sunlight had taken the place of the damp mists as they moved away from the coast. The wind soon dried their sodden clothing but there was little warmth from the winter sunshine and they were quickly chilled to the marrow.

The bullock cart which James had hired in Dunedin was piled high with all they had brought with them to begin their new life. Alongside tools and building materials was packed a modicum of furniture brought with them from Scotland, the most outstanding piece being Judith's harmonium which they had recovered from the furniture store in Inverness before embarking for New Zealand. With a great deal of heart searching James had decided to leave it behind in Dunedin because of its weight but Jessie, sensing that the instrument meant as much to Catherine as it did to her father, insisted that it go along. How many times on that long trek was she to regret her decision as they forced their six sturdy beasts up stony paths and struggled to forge rivers in full spate after the winter rains? How glad she was nevertheless when they arrived at their destination with the instrument intact.

The wagon had rumbled easily enough across the scrubland on the outskirts of town but very soon they left behind the well-beaten tracks and began to make their way through more dense undergrowth. At this point their driver had been obliged to ask them to step down.

Chilled as they were, in the beginning the little party was only too pleased to walk, the children running on ahead delighting in every unfamiliar flower and bush, seeking out hidden rivulets and chasing the little wood hens, small flightless birds which peered curiously at them from the undergrowth then boldly dashed out at them, in defence of their territory. Their stunted wings which were mere tufts of brown feathers were unable to lift the little creatures more than an inch or two above the ground as they scuttled to and fro.

When from time to time, the going became a little firmer one or other of the party would take a short ride, but for the most part everyone save their Maori driver, Tuki, walked.

After months aboard the *Albatross,* where normal exercise had been limited by the confines of the ship, by the end of the second day they were all exhausted. At Jessie's request, they had stopped early to make camp for the night.

Tuki had chosen well. Their camp site was a small clearing at the base of an overhanging cliff where the surrounding vegetation provided natural walls and a roof of sorts, to keep off both rain and wind. While the driver attended to the horses, Jessie began to unpack the cooking utensils while Catherine and the boys gathered firewood. Amid this frenzied activity, James sat apart on the trunk of a fallen tree and consulted his prayer book. Catherine watched her stepmother returning from the stream struggling with a pail of water, while her father for the second night running excluded himself entirely from their activities. Incensed by his idleness she decided it was time to put things to rights. She stood before James, hands on hips and gave him the full force of her pent-up fury.

'It was you who made the decision to bring us out here Pa, instead of staying in town with our friends. When you accepted Mr Burn's request, did you think for one moment what it would be like to come into the wilderness alone with no one to help us but a Maori who can barely speak our language?'

James looked up from his reading, startled. Her voice was so like Judith's that for a moment he had believed it to be the ghost of his late wife speaking to him.

'When we are about the Lord's work we must resign ourselves to his protection and mercy,' he replied.

'I don't see your Lord gathering any firewood or carrying water from the stream,' his daughter observed dryly.' We have walked many miles today and we are all equally tired and hungry yet you have seen fit to pray while the rest of us do what is necessary to make us comfortable for the night.'

On hearing this exchange, Jessie set down her heavy pail and straightened her back. Then, crossing to where Catherine stood haranguing her father, she pulled her away.

'You must not speak to your father, so, Catherine. Apologise at once.'

'No, I will not!' cried Catherine.

'Say you are sorry or go without your supper. The choice is yours.'

'But that's not fair,' Catherine was weeping now. 'He does nothing to help and I have to go without my supper!'

'Just say you are sorry,' said Jessie, mildly.

'I am sorry Papa.' Catherine moved away, not waiting for James to reply.

Relying upon Jessie to take charge of the situation, James returned to his prayers.

As she walked away with Jessie at her heels Catherine continued to mutter a protest.

'Your father has his own priorities, child, just as you have yours. I am sure he will help us when he has the time.'

'How can you allow him to get away with it!' demanded Catherine suddenly. 'Is this what you married him for, to be his slave?'

'I have an obligation to see that you are properly cared for,' Jessie told her. 'It would have been unthinkable for me to have come away with you like this not married to James.'

'But you don't, you cannot love him!'

'Not all marriages are romantic attachments my dear,' her stepmother explained gently. 'Sometimes marriage is a matter of convenience. Your father and I are good friends. I am sure that we shall come to love one another eventually.'

Catherine, whose idea of marriage was born largely of the flimsy novelettes provided by the farm girls and maidservants she had met aboard ship, was horrified by Jessie's words. If she had indeed married James for the sake of his children it made his treatment of her even more shocking. Her father seemed to regard Jessie as a servant rather than a wife.

Although he showed no sign of having heard Jessie admonish Catherine for her attack James could not ignore his daughter's criticism. He lay awake for a long time and when he dozed at last it was a troubled sleep peppered with dreams. In them Judith had figured largely, admonishing him as always but somehow supporting Catherine's summary of the situation.

When they struck camp the following morning, to everyone's surprise James raked out the ashes making sure there was no risk of a bush fire. James it was who gathered the cooking pots and took them to the stream to scour them. Catherine, seeing his solemn face as he carried out these chores was filled with remorse and wished she had never spoken.

On the third morning, they left the coastal plain surrounding Otago Harbour and began the steady climb into the surrounding foothills. Here the scrub gave way to dense forests described by Tuki as Pukatea, stately trees with massive buttresses supporting the huge branches and dense foliage which formed an impenetrable canopy overhead. Their branches soared upwards like the vaulted ceiling of a cathedral. Ferns as tall as houses occupied the next layer of growth while on the floor of the forest, tangled roots, low growing ferns, mosses and lycopodiums covered the ground. Here and there an ancient tree had died and fallen giving a pool of bright light when the sun shone. Here, from the bed of tangled undergrowth, delicate saplings had sprung up, their dark green foliage in sharp contrast to the lighter green of the feathery ferns. The smooth slender tendrils of aerial plants waved aimlessly in the still air, hanging like serpents from the boughs and in places reaching down to the soil where they had taken root. The untidy mass of dead and decaying branches rotting on the forest floor was here and there, decorated with clematis vines which grew upwards from the ground, tumbling luxuriantly over any obstacle in their path. Some had rooted in the forks of trees and these grew downwards to form a curtain of light green leaves and star-like creamy and snow-white flowers. Here in the dark recesses of the forest there were no seasons.

Jessie had struck up an instant rapport with the sturdily built Maori warrior, Tuki. From him she learned the names of the trees and those birds which were unfamiliar to her. Stunned at first by his strange appearance she had been relieved to find she could converse with him, if not fluently at least sufficiently well to make herself understood.

Tuki was a solidly built young man and although nearly as tall as Alexander Beaton, his upper body was long while his legs were short and sturdy. She guessed he must be around twenty years of age. Over what amounted to little more than a loin cloth woven from flax, he wore a long cape of feathers, mostly sea bird skins by the look of them. His almost total nakedness was covered by an intricate pattern of the most extraordinary tattoos, their design comprising neat parallel lines and circles of dots which stood out blue against his coffee coloured skin. His tightly curled black hair was close cropped and heavy black eyebrows overhung his wide set eyes. There were laughter lines about his mouth and the deep brown eyes were warm and friendly. If he was typical of his people, then the Maori must be an intelligent race. From his explanations of the countryside through which they passed, it was clear that the Maori's was a culture rooted in the distant past, drawing for its symbolism upon the landscape and the creatures in the world of nature.

When Tuki named plants and geographical features, Jessie was thrilled to learn the translation of the Moari names; Ao-rere, flying cloud; Pukearuhe, ferny hill; Wai-rarappa, glittering water. Although the tribes of the South Island had come only recently to know and be known by European settlers, they had seen no threat to their future in the presence of the small numbers of white men who visited their shores. At first these had been largely whalers and seamen of all kinds. The men of the New Zealand Company with whom they had negotiated sales of land, had also come in small numbers. They had been for the most part reasonable people, respectful of the Maori traditions and anxious to learn about the country and its potential. They appeared to take no interest in conquering or in any way subjugating the Maori people.

For some years Maori and white man had lived amicably side by side learning something of each other's ways while retaining their own identity. Virile young white men, thousands of miles from home sought female companionship amongst the Maori and many mixed marriages had already taken place.

While it was true that the latest shiploads of immigrants, with their strictly Calvanistic principles, might frown upon the close relationships which had been drawn between the two races, they could not deny that it was better to mix freely with the native population than to be constantly at war. Treaties drawn up to acquire land for settlement had so far been respected. There was no repeat of the terrible land wars which had so dominated the early settlement of the North Island. By the time Dr Burns arrived on the *John Wickliffe* in the spring of 1847, many Maori had learned sufficient English to communicate with the newcomers and like Tuki, had found employment in and around the new settlement of Dunedin.

This morning they had come to some relatively smooth open ground and Jessie had managed to persuade the Maori to allow Charles to handle the wagon. While the two lads sat up behind the bullocks, she strode alongside the guide, soaking up all he had to tell her.

'Tuki, this village… pa… where you are taking us…'

'Yes madam?' No matter how she tried to get him to call her Mrs Bantrie or even simply, Jessie, she could not.

'Do you know it well?'

'Yes madam, it is my own village. My father is the head man.'

'How will they receive us? Are they ready to become Christians?'

'It is hard to say madam. The tribal law is very strong.'

'You know that my husband is a preacher; that his mission is to convert the Maori to his own religion?'

'Oh yes, madam.'

'How will they receive him?'

'I do not know madam. My father must be persuaded. If he agrees, all will follow him.'

It was as Jessie feared. These were not people who would take easily to new ways. They would have to be wooed. James' recent bouts of fanaticism would not be appropriate in such circumstances. How was she going to persuade him that he would achieve so much more by a gentle approach?

'Will you be able to influence your father's thoughts in the matter?' she asked, choosing her words carefully so as not to offend.

'That is why the Reverend Burns chose me to come with you, madam.'

'Then you are already a Christian yourself, Tuki?'

'No madam, I must have my father's permission also.'

'But you would like to be?'

'I think so, madam. I shall listen to what is said within the Pa and then I shall decide.'

'You don't think my husband is in any danger do you, Tuki?'

'No madam. The Maori's taste for boiled white missionary has been greatly exaggerated.'

She could tell by the twinkle in his eyes that he was laughing at her. She smiled and moved back in the line to see how James was faring.

Chapter Fourteen

Until Alexander's arrival, medical care had been provided by the occasional visiting ship's surgeon. Settlers arriving by the first ships had for the most part been selected for their fitness and baring accidents, of which there were certainly plenty, there had been little need for a doctor. Many of the settlers came from those areas of Scotland and Ireland where doctors had been a luxury and where home nursing was a part of every young bride's repertoire. There were women sufficiently experienced to deal with the occasional birth and an old seafarer amongst them had learned to cope with simple fractures and abrasions. Patent medicines were high on the list of imports from home and when all else failed some had ventured so far as to consult the local Maori healers.

The news that a qualified doctor was in town spread fast amongst the families but people were slow to consult Alexander. He was however, greeted with open arms by the town's dignitaries. Civic leaders such as Dr Burns and William Cargill, the spiritual and secular leaders of the colony who had arrived aboard the *John Wickliffe,* were among the first to make his acquaintance. With his tall, robust figure and handsome highland features, he was soon popular amongst the younger ladies of the settlement. What he needed most and did not seem to be getting, was paying patients. For the time being he turned his attention to the building of premises of his own.

Together with Tobias Leny and a pair of Maori whom his partner had managed to employ as labourers, Alexander laid out the foundations of his surgery and living accommodation on the quarter acre plot which he had been allocated on Cumberland Avenue. The four men collected stone for the foundations from the surrounding countryside but they had great difficulty obtaining the necessary timber. For this they would have to hire a bullock cart and drive out as far as the woodlands which covered the surrounding hills. Apart from his acknowledged ineptitude for lumbering Alexander was anxious not to stray too far from the settlement at a time when patients might require his attendance.

In hopes of rectifying this problem, Alexander borrowed a dinghy belonging to the hotel and sailed himself across to Port Chalmers, where once again he consulted Captain McCallum about the money he was owed.

'I have found temporary accommodation in the hotel,' he explained, 'but with nothing but promises with which to pay my dues. I have started work on constructing my own place but have no money for materials. As I understand it, the Company owes me some thirty pounds and in addition there is the money collected from passengers for medical care while on board. By my reckoning, that should be a further twelve pounds ten shillings.'

'I do assure you, Alexander, that I did my utmost to collect what was owing from the passengers before they disembarked.' Captain McCallum was genuinely concerned for the doctor's plight. 'Many of those treated for cholera were sponsored passengers and consequently unable to pay. It was unfortunate that your two wealthiest clients died. Their property is under lock and key and must remain so until the lawyers come aboard to take it off my hands when the ship docks in Wellington. That is when your bill for their treatment will be presented for settlement with additional charges from the Company. Even then you will see nothing of your money until Sir Tristram's will has received probate.

'Just tell me how much you can pay me now.' Alexander was in no mood for procrastination.

Embarrassed at the paucity of the amount, the Captain counted out seven pounds five shillings and four pence and pushed it across the desk. 'That is all there is from the passengers,' he explained. 'Your wages as ship's surgeon will be paid to you when the next vessel arrives from Scotland. The Company's agent will be on board and it is he who has charge of all wages to be paid to members of the crew. As you will remember, we have already offset money owing to you from treatment of crew members with the equipment taken from the dispensary and there was the advance you received before sailing.'

With that, Alexander had to be satisfied. He gathered up the coins and placed them in his waistcoat pocket. 'Perhaps you will give me a letter of credit for the remainder so that I may at least reassure the landlord of the Wharf Hotel about my prospects?'

'I can do that, certainly,' replied McCallum, relieved that the matter of Alexander's money had been properly aired at last. He had not been looking forward to this confrontation.

'I don't hold you responsible for this mess, Walter' Alexander assured him. 'I would prefer to regard you as a friend.' He leaned across and shook the captain's hand. 'I hope you will look me up whenever your travels bring you back to these parts.'

'Of course, I'm just sorry that things have worked out so awkwardly for you,' said McCallum. 'I do believe I may be able to help you in another way. You said you needed materials for building?'

'Timber is the worst thing,' Alexander explained. 'Toby and I are no lumberjacks and I had hoped to be able to pay someone else to do the logging for me.'

'There I can help you,' McCallum told him. 'I have to strip out the passenger accommodation to make room for a cargo of wool to be taken on board further up the coast. If you can find some men to help with dismantling the bunks, you may take all the timber you want. Its good Scots pine, ideal for building.'

Seeing a solution to his most pressing problem, Alexander's depression lifted in an instant. He jumped up, delighted. 'That would be ideal,' he said. 'I'll get Toby out here right away.' He paused. 'There'll be a charge I suppose?'

'It's second hand timber so I cannot ask a great deal. If your own men remove it, shall we say five pounds?'

Alexander reached into his pocket to extract the necessary sovereigns but McCallum grinned as he added, 'to be deducted from what we owe you.'

As the winter months started to take their toll, lung complaints such as colds and influenza began to appear amongst the settlers, both new and existing. Those who had escaped such problems previously blamed the new-comers for the epidemic, whilst others accused the rats which left the ships as they arrived in port and quickly established themselves in and around the human dwellings.

The weather never deteriorated to the extent which some had predicted. The Europeans although discomforted, quickly recovered from their ills but in the Maori village near Otago Heads influenza had reached epidemic proportions and was causing the death of many of the native population.

When news of this was conveyed to Toby and the doctor by their Maori worker, Hongi, Alexander, knowing full well that his attendance upon these people would do nothing whatever to swell the empty coffers nevertheless saw it as his duty to try and help them. Leaving Toby to oversee the erection of a timber framework to their new building, he set out on foot for the village of Otakou.

Taking Hongi with him as interpreter, Alexander approached the huge, intricately carved gateway to the pa, the Maori village. His natural trepidation was quickly overcome by his acute interest in everything he saw about him and by a sincere desire to help. After a few days of working alongside their two native labourers, Alexander had summed up the Maori as a capable but indolent race having extraordinary skills in some ways but ultimately lazy. He did not condemn them for this however. From the beginning, he had studied their state of health and was inclined to the theory that their problem lay in a lack of physical stamina. This he attributed to inherent, chronic disease.

Alexander had spent time during the voyage reading everything he could lay hands on referring to the Maoris and their way of life. He had formed the belief that their indolence might be due to the presence of the Europeans, particularly the early whalers and sealers who had first arrived in the country towards the end of the previous century. These were often men of dubious character with low moral standards. Undoubtedly it was they who had transmitted their foul venereal diseases, first to the women whom they took for wives and then to their children.

Alex was determined to study the problem formally and during this first visit to a Maori kaika, he began to make careful records which he might use later in formulating and substantiating his theories.

The village with its population of some one hundred Maori and a handful of white residents stood on high ground commanding a fine view of the harbour. The huts, built of wattle daubed with mud and roofed in fern leaves, were surrounded by a double stockade, the fencing for which was built of woven branches reminiscent of the birch-tree hurdles so familiar on Scottish farms. Between the inner and outer ring of fencing was a shallow ditch in which sharpened sticks were placed, points upwards and close together. On these, potential invaders would become impaled and were thus effectively dissuaded from attempting to climb the inner stockade.

The huts were ranged around a central open space to one side of which stood a larger building, again heavily decorated in carved wood, which Hongi described as the long house, a kind of meeting hall. Today it was deserted, the residents being confined to their huts by sickness.

Hongi led him to some of the larger and more permanently constructed of the houses where he found not only Maori women and children but also some of their European husbands, of several nationalities and many of advanced years. Within the huts the children sat about nearly naked despite the winter weather. Their eyes and noses were streaming and they were sneezing and coughing but otherwise behaving normally. By the same token, the Europeans he met showed every sign of having colds and chills by were for the most part, up and about carrying on with their lives as usual.

Here and there a small child lay languidly in a corner, coughing occasionally, wheezing and gasping for breath. Some Maori adults, struck down by the disease, seemed to be in a very bad way indeed. Feverish, choked with phlegm, their throats raw with coughing, they lay still. The symptoms were entirely what Alexander would expect of a severe dose of influenza and yet these Maori appeared close to death.

How Alexander wished Jessie was here with him now. With her help he might have brought some semblance of order to the situation. As it was, he would do his best for these people on his own.

In one of the houses they entered they came upon a particularly handsome young Maori woman administering to the sick using some evil smelling potion which she had apparently brewed herself. Whatever it was, it seemed to have little effect in reducing the coughing, although Alexander was forced to admit that the patients in this house seemed rather less distressed by fever and several were sleeping peacefully. He was also surprised to find that despite working amongst the sick for some time, the girl herself seemed to have resisted the disease.

'This is a great healer brought here by the white man,' Hongi told the girl, and to Alexander he explained.

'This is my sister, Teri. Our father sent her here with my brother and I to keep house for us while we work amongst the Pakeha. At home Teri is medicine woman. She knows the healing plants; makes sick people good.'

Alexander examined the potions Teri was administering with suspicion, inclined to regard anything not appearing in the British Pharmacopoeia as a witch's brew. He greeted her politely however, and asked how she had come by the medicine.

'I make with these,' she replied gathering up a handful of leaves. 'This is Matuka.' She showed him the small prickly tipped leaves which she was crushing into a hollowed-out stone with a pestle shaped from an animal bone. 'I put Totara leaves,' she grabbed a handful from the heap beside her, 'and cook them. Good for fever.' She pounded the dried leaves together until they formed a fine powder and poured boiling water over them to make an infusion.

Alexander although sceptical, determined to take time in the future to find out more about the plants she was using. For the present however there were sick people to be treated and it was clear from the sounds of mourning from other huts and the obvious preparations taking place on the far side of the compound, that Teri had not been totally successful in her administrations.

He brought out from his medical bag bottles containing standard treatments for fever, congestion, headache, gave measured amounts of each to the patients she had not yet tended and turned to Hongi.

'We shall soon see whose medicine is the strongest,' he declared rather smugly and then indicated that perhaps they should move on elsewhere.

Rather to his surprise, Teri followed them to the next hut. Here she made no attempt to treat the sick herself but indicated that she wished to see what Alexander was doing. She watched carefully as he measured out suitable doses and took note of the names he gave to each of the medicines.

'This is a mixture of peppermint oil, creosote and cod liver oil, he told her. It relieves the symptoms of the disease. For fever, I have a tincture made of Peruvian bark.' He allowed her to sniff each bottle as he poured out the substances, 'and for the headache, this juice from the poppy seed which we call opium.'

She was clearly anxious to learn from him, distinguishing between the substances and repeating the amounts he gave to each patient. They came to a child of perhaps three or four years.

'For little children you give less?' she enquired.

Impressed that she should have recognised the need to vary the dosage for children, he remarked, 'Children have so much less body weight than adults, they require less medicine.'

She smiled at him with sparkling eyes and he was struck by their doe-like quality, the deep brown irises being greatly enhanced by the contrasting whiteness of their surrounds.

Assuming she understood the substance of what he said although she might not know every word, he continued. 'Because a little medicine can do good it does not mean that to give more is to do better. Sometimes if you give too much you may poison the patient.'

She nodded, watching his lips as he spoke as though memorising every word.

Outside the stockade, they came upon a cluster of huts, shabbier and poorer dwellings than those within the main village. Both Teri and Hongi tried to dissuade Alexander from visiting these hovels, explaining that they belonged to newly arrived Maori who, attracted by stories of a living to be gained in the settlement of the white man, had moved from inland to the sea shore.

'Are they sick too?'Alex demanded.

'They are not like us,' she told him hurriedly. 'They know nothing of the white man's ways.'

Nevertheless, Alexander insisted on visiting the sick. If there was a particular source of infection he felt obliged to root it out.

The contrast in living styles was dramatic. Whilst the European men had taught their wives to keep the home clean and tidy, no such niceties were evident here. The whalers had introduced cooking methods which encouraged the use of fresh fish and meat and newly harvested vegetables. The Maori way was to leave game to hang until the meat was rotten and to soak maize in the stream until it was a smelly mush whose odour did not improve on cooking. There was no thought of removing waste food from the floor of the dwelling hut, meat bones were simply thrown down for the kuri, the semi wild Maori dogs, of which there were an inordinate number. It was clear also that there was no thought of sanitation. The occupants urinated and defecated where they lived. The stench on entering one of these hovels was one which Alexander was to remember to his dying day!

Entire families, victims of the epidemic, lay unattended on their crude beds of fern leaves. Naked children cried from hunger and neglect and old people struggled to fetch water and keep a fire going.

While the Maori brother and sister hovered in the doorway Alexander entered the first hut. He looked around for somewhere to stand his medical bag but seeing no clean surface anywhere he called Hongi inside to hold it. He began measuring out his doses to alleviate fever and congestion and for good measure an emetic of Jalap to clear the system of bad humours.

Teri, overcoming her distaste for the conditions, followed them inside and shared the work of administering to the patients until all had been treated.

As they left the hovel Alex turned to Hongi.

'Can you get someone to make up a vegetable broth with good barley or maize to thicken it? These people are starving. They will never recover from the disease if they are not properly fed.'

Hongi hesitated. Would the people inside the stockade agree to provide for these vagrants? He would have objected had he not already learned that Alexander expected his orders to be obeyed. Reluctantly he went off to see what could be done. To Teri, Alexander remarked, 'Perhaps some of the village women might try to clean the huts and show these people a better way to live?' Teri made no indication that she had even understood him let alone that she might accede to his suggestion.

As Alex and Teri moved from hut to hut, the sorry case of these people became more and more apparent. They found one woman trying to give birth while a group of little children looked on. She was weak from fever and starvation and had no strength for her ordeal. Alex shoed away the onlookers, did what he could to relieve her influenza symptoms and stayed with her until the child was delivered, stillborn. She appeared to have no regret that the infant had not survived. Clearly such stillbirths were common and accepted as normal.

His visit to the Maori village had convinced Alexander of two things.

Teri's response to his instruction had shown him that she, at least, was intelligent, quick to learn and ready to accept new ideas. He had also seen that there was a great deal to do in teaching the native population how to improve their own lifestyle to arm them against the pestilences which would inevitably be brought in by the Europeans. He had heard no mention of any disease transmitted from Maori to the white man and concluded that the European's generally better health and more comfortable living conditions had much to do with this. His experience in the Maori village made Alexander even more concerned for Jessie's welfare. He never ceased to think about her, wondering how the minister's party had fared on the journey through the wilderness. What had been the response of those Maori they had encountered? Was the minister's little party still alive?

As the chill winter weather continued the Europeans, unused to living in their hurriedly erected crude huts or under canvas, succumbed to many of the common ailments associated with the cold and dampness. Rheumatism was rife and those already prone to arthritis were badly affected by the conditions. In addition, nearly everyone had feverish colds. There were other diseases which Alexander could only suppose to have been carried ashore by the emigrants themselves. The worst of these developed amongst the school children towards the end of August in that first year, when Diphtheria spread like wildfire amongst those children who daily gathered in the primitive schoolroom-cum-church which had been constructed by the earliest settlers.

Twenty or more children crowded into one small room which was heated by a central iron stove. There being no materials available for glazing, daylight had been provided by windows which were covered in calico. The cold winter winds could be excluded only by using close boarded shutters and the children huddled together around the stove for warmth. In such an ill-ventilated atmosphere, disease might be expected to flourish.

Now at last, the townsfolk were to know the value of the doctor they had previously ignored. Alexander suddenly found himself in constant demand. He had no means of curing diphtheria. All he could do was treat the symptoms of the disease and allow it to take its course. There were occasions when drastic measures were required. It was here that his surgical skills were called into play and to his dismay the first of these cases involved his old friends, the Mackie family. In the early hours of an August morning he was roused from his bed by the landlord of the Wharf Hotel.

'Wake up, doctor,' Harding shook him roughly by the shoulder, none too pleased to have been awakened himself. 'There's a lad downstairs asking for you.'

Pulling on his clothes, unshaven and tousle headed, the doctor descended to the surgery on the floor below to find young Philip Mackie anxiously awaiting him.

'It's ma wee brother, doctor. He's had a gie sore throat for a couple o' days and now he canna' catch his breath at a'.'

'Where are you living, Philip?'

Alexander knew that the blacksmith had bought land in town for a stable and smithy but they had also discussed the most suitable site for housing Philip, to ensure that the pthysis did not reoccur.

'It's away up on the brae, Doctor,' the boy told him. 'I have brought along an extra horse for you to ride. It'll no take long and it's a fine night.'

They trotted through the empty streets and then began a slow steady climb out of the town towards the west. The sharp frosty air left little breath for talking as they rode along but enough was said to convince Alexander that the blacksmith had made great strides in setting up his business and housing his family.

'Your brother attends the school, no doubt?' Alexander asked. He had seen several cases of diphtheria, mostly of a mild nature, in the past few days.

'Aye.'

'And what about you, are you still studying?'

'My father bought a few sheep and goats and a couple of breeding mares. We have good grazing land up on the brae and it's my job to take care of the stock,' he announced proudly.

'Breeding mares eh?' Alexander was intrigued. Mackie must be setting up his own livery stables. The man was enterprising enough, there was no denying it. Open air work was exactly what Philip required and his father had solved the problem by initiating what would undoubtedly prove to be a lucrative enterprise.

'Come the spring we intend to get more horses brought down from Canterbury,' the boy told him proudly. 'Would you believe that until now no one has thought of providing riding horses for hire?'

Following the boy as skilfully, he negotiated the steepest part of the climb, Alexander marvelled at the change in him. The past months of exercise, good food and fresh air had worked wonders. It was impossible to see in him now the weedy little specimen who had been dragged from his hiding place in the lifeboat on that first day aboard ship.

The Mackie's shack stood on the crest of a low hill, sheltered from the west winds by a belt of cabbage trees and white pine and enjoying a fine view across the harbour towards the Heads. As they approached, they could see an oil lamp standing in every window to light the way for the travellers. At the veranda steps Alexander dismounted and handed the reins to the boy.

'Leave her to me, Doctor,' Philip said confidently, 'I'll give her a good rub down so she'll be ready for your return.' He disappeared into the shadows leaving Alexander to enter the house alone.

Mrs Mackie opened the door to him with a sad smile. Her worried frown told him that it was a bad as he feared. The Mackie's would never have sent for him in the dead of night if the matter were not urgent. Silently she led him through to a small bedroom in which cots had been provided for their three remaining children. Only one of these was occupied however.

'I thought it best to bed Bessie down in the kitchen,' she explained and Alexander nodded in agreement, thankful that she had had that much common sense.

The little boy's colour gave Alexander the greatest cause for concern. His pale face was tinged with blue, a sure sign that the child was lacking air. The dullness in his eyes and his abnormally low temperature were indications that the disease was in an advanced stage. His breathing produced a rasping sound which was accompanied by a soft groan at every expulsion. Alexander prised open the child's mouth to expose a throat coated in the white filaments which were the most dangerous phenomenon of the disease. The trachea was all but closed over and the boy was slowly choking to death.

'I shall have to cut into his windpipe,' Alexander told Mrs Mackie, gently. 'There is nothing else for it. The filaments are preventing him from taking in sufficient air.'

The mother cried out in dismay and hid her face in her husband's chest as Alexander took a sharp scalpel, made a neat V-shaped incision low down in the throat and inserted a small glass tube which he carefully fixed in place with firm bandaging. They heard a sharp inrush of air as the child's lungs attempted to expand and the woman, fearing it was the expected death rattle, raised her eyes to the doctor trying to read something in his expression.

Mackie who, unlike his wife, had watched the doctor's every move, saw the change in his child almost at once and as the breathing noises steadied and became quieter, he pressed his wife's shoulder, turning her and encouraging her to look towards their son.

'It's a miracle!' she cried as the tears streamed down her face.

Alexander was not so easily satisfied however. He rummaged in his bag until, finally, bringing out a small bottle of sulphurous acid and a swab with which to coat the child's larynx. The boy struggled so much that the doctor had to call upon Mackie to hold his head while he administered the treatment.

'Mrs Mackie,' he said gently, all the time keeping an eye on his patient's reactions, 'Will you get a kettle boiling on the stove. We have to rig up a steam tent.' To Mackie he said, 'Do you have a spirit stove of any kind, to keep the kettle boiling?'

The blacksmith hurried out leaving Alexander to attempt to irrigate the child's nasal passages with carbolic acid solution. When they had rigged up the tent over the patient's bed and sited the steam kettle so that it could not be overturned, he showed Mrs Mackie how to make up a poultice to place around the boy's throat. 'Change this as soon as it cools,' he instructed, 'every half hour at least. You must keep the tube clear by blowing through it from time to time.' He demonstrated how this should be done.

The boy, warmed by the steamy tent and breathing more comfortably, had fallen asleep. Alexander lowered the curtain around his head and began to pack away his instruments.

'You'd like a wash doctor?' the blacksmith offered and Alexander followed him gratefully into the kitchen where a bowl of hot water, soap and towels had been laid out.

‘I don’t know the reason for it, but our old doctor in Glasgow always used to wash his hands after seeing a patient,’ the smith observed.

‘It’s a wise precaution,’ said Alexander. ‘My professor always told us, cleanliness might not do any good for a patient but sure as anything it can do no harm!’

While Mrs Mackie plied him with hot sweet tea and freshly baked bread with cheese, Alexander took in his surroundings with undisguised admiration. The room was crudely furnished, only a few bits and pieces having been brought from home, but to make up for this, colourful fabrics had been used to cover the seats of benches and stools and lacy curtains framed the properly glazed windows. The walls of the mainly wattle and daub shack were lined with matting woven from toetoe grass such as he had seen in the Maori dwellings. On some of these hung carefully framed pictures, several of them sketches of places he recognised in the vicinity.

‘Young Philip has been busy at his drawing, I see,’ he remarked, recalling the boy’s drawings aboard ship.

‘Aye, he takes his pencils and sketch book with him to the pasture,’ the boy’s mother told him, proudly. ‘Scarcely a day goes by when he does not come home with something to show us.’

‘Some of these drawings are very fine,’ said Alexander. ‘Maybe he could learn to make engravings. There is a press being set up in town. A newspaper is to be started. You should perhaps see if the boy cannot be employed in some way.’

‘Och, there is work enough for him here at present,’ said Mackie. ‘The fresh air is what he needs, not some stuffy newspaper office.’

‘Nevertheless,’ Alexander insisted, ‘such talent should not go to waste. There is little enough of it hereabouts.’

Philip himself had appeared at the door. ‘The mare’s ready when you are doctor,’ he announced, giving no indication that he had heard what had been said about him. As Alexander pulled on his long travelling cloak and tied a woollen scarf tightly over his ears against the frosty night, Mrs Mackie asked how long it would be before they could expect to see signs of recovery in the sick boy.

‘If he gets a good rest tonight and the tube is kept clear of matter so that his breathing is easy, he should do very well,’ Alex assured her. I will leave you a solution of carbolic acid to swab his throat and tincture of iodine to coat the skin, but be careful not to dislodge the tube. At this stage, it is difficult to estimate how soon we can remove it. I shall come back tomorrow evening to see how things are.'

'If you will leave the mare at my stable when you get back, Doctor, my man will attend to her,' Mackie told him. 'Just go in at any time and take a mount, whenever you need one.'

'That's very handsome of you, Mackie,' Alexander was genuinely pleased. Since the onset of the diphtheria epidemic, he had found it difficult to get around quickly enough on foot.

'Thank you for coming, Doctor Beaton.' Mrs Mackie handed him his hat. Although close to exhaustion she looked happier now.

'Try to get some rest, both of you,' Alex instructed, 'and keep a sharp eye on the other children. Philip would not stand up to a bout of fever the like of that.'

Out in the yard, holding the horse's head, Philip Mackie awaited the doctor.

'What you said about my drawings,' he began hesitantly.

'Yes?' Alexander was impatient to be on his way now.

'Did you mean it? Do you think I am good enough to draw for a newspaper?'

'I see no reason why you should not try,' said Alexander.

'Then will you take these?' the boy pleaded. 'Show them to the man who is to start the newspaper?' He thrust a sheaf of papers at the doctor who scarcely looked at them before replying.

'I thought you enjoyed your life out here, looking after the stock. Alexander, fearing his intervention might cause a rift between father and son, was already regretting his suggestion.

'I do, and will be happy to work here while my Pa has need of me but I canna' be a herdsman all my life. I want to paint and draw. 'T is something I have to do.'

Alexander took the sheaf of papers and folded them carefully into his coat pocket.

'I'll see what I can do,' he said and sticking his heels into the mare's belly he urged her forward into the dawn of a new day.

Chapter Fifteen

Towards the end of May, the Rev. James Bantrie's party came at last to the outskirts of the Maori pa at Mapourika. At the suggestion of their guide, Hongi, they refrained from approaching the village after sundown deciding to remain for one further night in the bush.

They had negotiated dense forest, dry scrubland, high stony pastures and low lying swamps through which they must wade, waste- high in water. Manhandling the heavily laden cart through mud was particularly difficult for the glutinous material seemed determined to swallow everything and everyone attempting to pass through it. Had it not been for the six tough oxen James had hired from Dunedin, they could never have negotiated the unmade track. As it was, they had been obliged on more than one occasion partially to unload the great dray carrying their worldly possessions and make two trips across particularly difficult ground with the lightened vehicle.

Catherine's unexpected outburst had served to shake her father into some realisation of what was required of him in these extraordinary circumstances. The instinct to survive had finally replaced his obsession with prayer and self recrimination. The journey continued to demand exhausting physical labour from them all and James, obliged to participate in the team effort which was required to overcome every daunting step of the way, had slept better than he had in many months. When he awoke on the final morning of their journey he stretched, breathed deeply of the clear mountain air and darted into a glade of trees which screened a deep pool fed by a fine waterfall. It was a glorious spot which they had discovered on their arrival the previous evening.

Stripping off his clothes, he dived into the dark waters of the pool and touched the sandy bottom before breaking surface. With the pressure changes popping his ear drums he did not at first hear the tinkling laughter as he emerged from the pool, shaking off water like an exuberant hound. Only when he turned around and looked up, did he realise that he was not alone. To his embarrassment, he found that the white sandy beach on the far side of the water was occupied by a group of Maori maidens who were gazing in admiration at his glistening white, naked body and chattering loudly amongst themselves, pointing and waving in his direction.

In an instant the girls had thrown off the scanty garments which they wore wrapped loosely about the lower part of their bodies and stood poised to dive into the pool so recently vacated by the white stranger.

Overcome by the grace and elegance of their movement through the water, James stood transfixed, his embarrassment at his own nakedness forgotten in the sheer delight of watching these beautiful water nymphs. Two of them approached him, quite unabashed, emerging from the water to take him by the hand. Laughing, they urged him forward until he was forced to dive into the pool or be pushed. Now they were all around him jostling, splashing, diving beneath him, whirling about him and shouting with laughter. At first bewildered, he soon began to enjoy the experience. They laughed and splashed beside him like infants taking a bath.

Unable to resist temptation, James joined in their merriment and it was to the sound of his deeper, masculine chuckles and occasional shouts of glee, that Jessie emerged from the bushes intent upon enjoying a quick bath before the others awoke. When she realised the pool was already occupied she drew back hurriedly but then, filled with curiosity she turned and stared in amazement. Unbelievably it was James who was at the centre of the games. Far from being shocked, she felt an overwhelming sense of relief. Her husband was at last showing signs of being human. She removed herself from the scene as quietly as she had come.

Having thrown all inhibitions to the wind, James was enjoying himself for the very first time since Judith's death. Jessie, praying that this might be that moment of catharsis for which she had so longed, determined to keep her observations to herself. She returned to the camp and lay down as though she had never stirred and that was how James found her when he returned a short while later, glowing from the combined effect of the icy waters and his unexpected encounter with the village maidens.

At Tuki's suggestion they entered the pa at Mapourika at midday, when the village elders were gathered in the long house. While he went in to announce their arrival, their Maori guide left the pakeha standing somewhat awkwardly beside their cart, in the middle of the open space.

On all sides they could see villagers gathering to inspect the new arrivals. At first it was only the Maori children who had the courage to approach the strangers. Attracted by the white boys, some urchins ran forward and pulled at their strange clothes and touched their white skins to see if the colour came off on their fingers. When it did not, they stepped back shouting to each other in amazement.

Tommy and Charles had been given strict instructions by James to make no approaches to the natives until it was clear that these would be welcome. His words did not however prevent them from smiling and it was this which encouraged the Maori children to gather around. Soon there was loud laughter at the Scottish boys' attempts at conversation for all along the trail they had pestered Tuki, demanding to know key words of the Maori language in preparation for just such an encounter as this.

When the adults saw that these strangers posed no threat to their children, they too came forward to poke at Catherine and feel her dark silky ringlets. They pulled at the ribbon of Jessie's poke bonnet and when she pulled it free they marvelled at her chestnut brown hair which fell in dishevelled fashion about her shoulders. They admired her parasol passing it from one to another of the women and prancing about with it. When one little girl darted away into the bushes and returned carrying a wide fern leaf held above her head in a parody of Jessie's actions with the umbrella, everyone laughed.

A group of younger women stood a little apart, giggling amongst themselves and holding their hands in front of their faces as though to hide their identities. From time to time they glanced in James' direction, exchanged further conversation and laughed aloud. At this, Jessie could not resist the temptation to remark upon their behaviour.

'You appear to have struck a chord with the ladies, James,' she said and was pleased to see that although he wore what Judith used to call his 'minister on parade' expression, he actually blushed a little.

The headman and his elders received the newcomers with due ceremony. Ngakete Taiaroa and his tribe claimed ownership of the vast territories to the west and north of Otago Harbour and had been quick to realise the wisdom of striking up a friendly relationship with the white men from across the ocean. Ngakete had heard tales of the slaughter which had taken place in the North Island and was determined that his people should live in peace with the newcomers to their mutual benefit. He had negotiated at first with the surveyors and land agents and had been happy to receive an envoy of the headman of the new settlement on Otago Harbour. That this new envoy appeared to represent the white man's God did not discomfort him in any way. Did the Maori not commune with their own Gods in similar fashion? When Dr Burns had suggested that the people of Taiaroa might wish to ally themselves to this same God, he was more reticent but agreed to allow a missionary to come among them and promised not to interfere with him or his party.

Momentarily blinded by the sudden change in lighting levels as he entered the windowless long house, James Bantrie bowed his head. It was a gesture which evidently met with approval, for the head man motioned to him to come forward and squat upon a mat placed facing the village elders.

With Hongi acting as interpreter, the conversation ranged over the health of her Majesty Queen Victoria, her husband and children, her ministers and people, and finally the wife and family of Minister Bantrie. This topic was followed by others concerning the nature of the next harvest by comparison with the last; the quality of fish now being caught in Otago Harbour and the numbers of Albatross breeding on the Heads. James had been advised to allow all this talk to be got through before getting down to the crux of their discussion but he was beginning to feel extremely frustrated by the time that Ngakete himself raised the subject of land upon which to build a church.

'I must have a meeting house for those who would worship my God,' explained James. 'I shall also need to build a hut in which to house my family.'

The old man nodded thoughtfully, said something sharply to one of his acolytes and indicated that James should follow the man out into the compound. He was led across the open square to where, a short distance from the main village, there was an area of flat plain which formed the bank of a wide meandering river. In one loop of the meander a grassy knoll rose steadily to a height of some thirty feet above this plain, falling away steeply to the river on the far side.

It was an ideal site for James' church. The Maori councillor indicated that the ground all around would be his to build on as he chose and James was quick to identify the ideal spot to place his house, a little below the summit with a fine view westwards towards the mountains.

They returned to where the rest of his party were being entertained by the villagers to an al fresco meal on the steps of the long house and although Jessie eyed some of the dishes somewhat warily, the children, whose appetites were never satisfied, were tucking in without any inhibitions. There were dishes of extraordinary fruits and vegetables and, laid out upon broad green leaves, fish, fowl and meats of unknown origin which the children held in their fingers and ate off the bone.

'So far so good, 'James whispered to Jessie as he sat down to join them. 'We have the best site in the village for a church. Now all we shall need is some help to build it.'

*

'Gyp! Gyp! ' Charlie called. The dog came obediently at his call and the stone which he had carried in his mouth since they had left the village he dropped at the boy's feet. Charlie bent to pick it up, drew back his arm and cast it far out into the swirling waters above the waterfall. Without a moment's hesitation, the dog leapt into the stream and swam strongly to the spot where the stone had disappeared. He re-emerged without his stone, dived again a once, twice and finally swam to shore. Having failed to locate his quarry he had returned with a satisfactory alternative.

Gyp had been a gift to the boys from Ngakete on the day that James had declared the church building complete and had invited the head man to join them in a little ceremony of dedication. Gyp, with his bright eyes and intelligent, sharply pricked ears and long silky coat, resembled the almost wild Kuri dogs which inhabited all Maori villages. This one however, had been bred from ancestors who had attached themselves to man so long ago that they had allowed themselves to become thoroughly domesticated. Some cross breeding with the white man's working dogs had produced an interesting mongrel. Instead of the squashed pug-like face of the Kuri, Gyp's nose was sharply pointed like a collie and he was sooty black in colour, hence his name, Gypsy, which had quickly become shortened to Gyp.

The dog bounded up the bank, paused and shook himself, soaking the minister in his enthusiasm. He dropped the stone he was carrying and licked Jessie's hand affectionately. They both knew his love centred on the freshly baked bread and rich smelling pork meat which she had brought along for their picnic. Seeing that his mistress was not yet ready to distribute her bounty he snuffled about in the long grass, retrieved his stone and presented it to Charlie for another throw. The boy bent to lift it and tossed it high, away into the bushes alongside the path.

Jessie threw herself down on a bed of ferns and grasses and breathed deeply of the clear mountain air. All around them leaf buds were bursting heralding the spring. The scent of sap rising in the tall white pine trees was overpowering. The Kamahi bush and the darker tones of Totara contrasted with the lighter southern Rata, its leaves long, narrow spears, its branches sturdy and flexible as a willow, reminding Jessie of home. The vivid greens of the Matai set off the paler leaves of the white Hebe, the Koromiko bush.

Unlike the flower-strewn meadows of the Scottish lowlands ground cover was almost entirely fern. Every variety of fronds and every shade of green covered the ground around her making a carpet richly patterned and sweet smelling. Jessie had seen the village women using plants to dye the cloth which they wove from a flax-like plant which grew on the marshy flood plains of the lower reaches of the river. She suspected also that certain herbs had medicinal value, but had found no one to tell her which of them were healing plants. It seemed that the village's medicine woman had left the village some time before and there was no one left who practised the art. Contemplating this and the many other challenges which their new life posed, she drifted into sleep.

While the village men had been building a home and a church, under James Bantrie's supervision, the boys had been free to explore the lower reaches of the river where the currents were sluggish and safe enough in dry weather. No strangers to handling boats, the two youngsters quickly learned to paddle the small canoes used by the village children and had become adept at the art of fishing for the muddy tasting river fish upon which the tribe depended for its food.

Today, free at last for the first time since their arrival at Mapourika, James had agreed to accompany the boys on a trip into the high country and not to be left out of any adventure, Jessie and Catherine had insisted upon coming along. All morning the cheerful little party had followed the course of the stream into the hills to where in its upper reaches, the river became a fast flowing, narrow waterway, cutting deeply into hard volcanic rock. It fell over steep cliffs in spectacular waterfalls and gushed through narrow gorges in a flurry of white water.

The boys pleaded to be allowed to make a raft to ride the rapids as the village boys did but James, aware of Jessie's anxiety at the suggestion, insisted they wait until they were strong enough to handle the long oar needed to steer these heavy craft.

'The force of the water is too powerful for the uninitiated to handle,' he told them. 'Continue to practise on the quieter waters at the village and we will see about white water rafting when I am convinced that you know what you are doing.'

Disappointed, they turned to other pursuits. Each found a suitable stick and casting it into the stream set off to follow the course, each claiming to have the faster vessel. They raced down stream in their efforts to keep sight of their makeshift boats while Gyp yelped in delight and would have plunged into the water to retrieve the sticks had not Charlie taken a firm grip on his collar.

At last Tommy's stick became lodged between two boulders in mid stream. Yelling with frustration, he ran down onto a tiny boulder- strewn beach at a spot where the bank had given way and using a line of natural stepping stones, he tried to retrieve it. Crouching close to the water, he reached far out, lost his balance and fell into the swirling waters.

As the younger boy was carried away by the swiftly moving current, his cries were lost in the roar of the huge waterfall beside which they had climbed earlier in their walk. Charles reacted quickly. He charged down towards the deep pool which had formed above the waterfall, pulled a long straight branch out of the brush and held it out across the water as Tommy was swept down towards him. Tommy made a grab for the stick and caught hold but his weight, increased by the force of the water, would have been too much for his stepbrother had not the dog leapt into the water and grabbing Tommy's trousers in his firm young jaws, swum strongly against the flow, allowing Charlie to pull back on the stick. At last he could grasp Tommy's hand and with super human effort, he pulled him from the water. The younger boy lay panting on the shore so wet and exhausted that he did not even complain when Gyp scrambled out onto the rocks and proceeded to shake himself all over them both.

After a while the two boys sat up and examined one another in dismay. Tommy was soaking wet while Charlie was covered in mud from his efforts to pull his stepbrother from the stream. Tommy stripped off his shirt and trousers and wringing them out carefully, he spread the garments on the rocks to dry out. Then he lay down to bask in the warm sunshine.

Charlie soon gave up trying to remove traces of his exertions. The mud would brush off when it was dry. He sat beside Tommy, idly sorting through the pebbles. They were all rounded by the action of the stream. Many of them contained white quartz while some carried fragments of the greenstone so valued by the Maoris as ornaments.

Watching Charlie and suspecting it was time for another game, the dog searched the undergrowth for the stone which he had dropped when he dived into the river. Soon he came trotting back to place it at his master's feet. He wriggled backwards, ears cocked, nose on his front paws, tail wagging, and barked sharply.

'All right old chap. Hang on a minute.' Charlie scrambled to his feet and picked up the dog's sharper-edged, stone. He was about to throw it when he realised that it weighed substantially more than others of a similar size. Turning it in the sunlight, he saw a glint of yellow and examined it more closely.

On the slate island of Orchy, the young Charlie had learned to recognise Fool's Gold, the iron pyrites which occurred as shiny yellow cubic crystals in the slate but the yellow fragments contained in Gyp's stone were quite unlike the pyrites. He turned the stone over and over in his hand as his excitement grew. Someone aboard ship had spoken of the possibility of finding gold. There had been some men determined to explore hundreds of miles of bush for this very purpose. Saying nothing to Tommy, he slipped the stone into his pocket as he poked the other boy with his toe.

'Come on,' he said. 'Mother will be waiting.'

'My clothes aren't dry," moaned Tommy, anticipating his mother's wrath.

'Och, they'll do,' exclaimed Charlie. 'You can't be expected to keep clean on a picnic.'

*

While James smoked his pipe, and read his copy of the New Testament which he carried at all times, Jessie kindled a fire and set a kettle over it to boil. She spread their meal out on the level summit of a little headland which faced down river. From this vantage point she could still see the village in the distance.

The new church, brilliant in its fresh whitewash, stood high above a grassy plain with the river curving around its base. How proudly it perched on the summit of the knoll just as James had envisaged it on that first day.

When Ngakete had suggested that the village men should build a house for the pakeha, James had been truly thankful. He had little skill in his own hands and the women were not strong enough to help him to cut the fibrous timber of the tree ferns. The house, constructed of vertical tree trunks, was clad in woven flax and lined with matting made from toetoe grass. The roof was thatched with rushes from the marshy plain down-stream of the village. It was a substantial building with separate living accommodation and sleeping rooms. A wide veranda gave access by a single door to a large central room with very small windows. In the early days when the winter winds still howled around the house at night, they were glad to be able to block up the ventilation holes and keep out the draft. When the days grew warmer, they would be able to sit out on the veranda to eat their meals and enjoy the quiet of the evening.

The church had been a rather different proposition. James wanted the building to be more like a conventional church such as one might find anywhere in Scotland. The building was timber framed and clad in planks of white pine.

James drew out a rectangular shape of suitable proportions, on the ground and indicated how the foundations should be dug out. There was nothing he could teach the Maori about the construction of a timber building with a thatched roof, but the windows, tall rectangles with a simple pointed arch, were a concept they did not recognise. Using bricks made from mud mixed with straw and baked hard, he had formed the window arches himself.

The great double doors presented an opportunity for the Maori to show their skills as carvers in wood. This was, however, the cause of a deal of soul searching on James's part. His Calvinistic upbringing had taught him to deplore the use of decoration of any kind within a church. He recognised, however that if he wanted to win over these people to the true church, he must bend a little and allow them to decorate the woodwork in their own way. He was also going to have to let them decorate the furniture within.

The Maori would have chosen their own traditional designs for the work, incorporating the plants, animals and natural phenomena which they themselves worshipped, but James persuaded them to use instead designs acceptable to Christians. He drew out in the sand different kinds of cross, Celtic and St Andrew's crosses as well as the simple cross of Calvary. In addition he sketched a fish, an angel and a lily flower, regarding these as suitable symbols of Christianity. The men seemed willing to comply with his wishes relishing the opportunity to try out these new designs. The finished effect was a compromise between the Maori tradition and church symbolism which was most pleasing to the eye and much admired by all who viewed it.

On the exterior front, a huge wooden cross had been hauled up to the apex of the gable-end. Jessie strained now to make it out.

'The cross should have been left in the natural colour of the timber,' she sighed. It had been Hongi who insisted upon painting it a dull green, paint which he had acquired on his most recent visit to the settlement. James, reluctant to disappoint him, had allowed him to go ahead but viewing the church from a distance, he had to agree with Jessie. It would have been better left unpainted and polished to bring out the deep rich tones of the natural wood.

'One can't have everything just so, my dear,' he said. 'Hongi is one satisfied gentleman and that is worth a hundred perfect crosses.'

She looked across at him, wondering what had brought about such a change of attitude in her husband. Could Catherine's outburst have been responsible for turning him away from his continuous self deprecation? Whatever the cause, the change was to be applauded.

Although the Bantrie's marriage had never been consummated, the relationship between husband and wife was now one of companionable comradeship. She could only hope for absolute fulfilment to follow later.

'What can have happened to those boys,' Jessie asked, suddenly aware that time was passing and they had heard nothing of the generally noisy pair for more than an hour.

'Catherine,' she called out to the girl who was sitting quietly a little apart, listening to the birds and watching for fish in the stream. 'Go along the river bank and see if you can spot Charlie and Tom.'

Catherine had scarcely reached the edge of the clearing when Gyp bounded up to her and placed a stick at her feet. He stood back, eagerly anticipating her throw. As she bent to retrieve it the boys burst into the clearing.

Surprised by the mildness of scolding he received for the state of his clothing, Tommy sat down and began to devour the meal Jessie had laid out. Charlie ate slowly and thoughtfully, turning the stone in his pocket and wondering whether he should show it to his father. He was almost certain that the pebble contained gold but he did not want to make a fool of himself. He decided to broach the subject in a round- about fashion.

'Tuki says that a white man came by here some time ago carrying a yellow stone about which he was very excited,' said Charlie. 'Tuki said he had often seen stones like that and thought nothing of them. The people around here look only for the green stone which they make into necklaces and brooches. What do you think it could be; this yellow stone, Papa? Do you think it could be gold?'

'Now you should know better than that,' laughed James, 'a boy who has lived amongst the slate workers of Argyll and learned to recognise Fool's gold when he was a baby!'

'It doesn't look like pyrites,' declared Charlie, producing the pebble from his pocket.

Everyone had a look at the stone.

'It might be real gold, mightn't it?' suggested Catherine, seriously. 'There was a man aboard ship who was determined to seek it out if there was any to be found.'

'I know nothing of the rocks and would not recognise the metal if I were to see it. Suffice it to say, it will not be in the shape of a gold coin. It will not be shiny and I don't suppose we would recognise it even if we did see any.' James dismissed the notion that the stone the boy had found contained precious metal.

Catherine on the other hand was not so sure that her brother was wrong. She studied the rock very carefully when magnified by her father's reading glasses and was as sure as Charlie that the mineral was not iron pyrites. In the privacy of their shared sleeping quarters she and Charlie discussed what should be done.

'We will send it to Ian in Cornwall,' she decided. 'I will write a letter saying how we found it and ask him to verify that it is gold.'

'Don't we have to lay claim to the area where we found it before someone else comes along and does the same?' Charlie had listened to the tales aboard ship and had some notion of the excesses of men desperate in their search for gold.

'We should,' Catherine agreed, 'but father will not make such a move until he is convinced that we are right. It is best we have Ian's confirmation. Meanwhile, say nothing to anyone. Not to anyone at all Least of all, Tommy. You know how he prattles on to any stranger he comes across.'

'It will take three or four months for a parcel to reach Ian and a similar time before we can receive his reply,' Charlie protested.

'We don't even know exactly where the stone came from,' Catherine pointed out. 'Gyp could have picked it up from anywhere. What we must do meanwhile, is to search the rocky outcrops for a similar type of stone so that if we are right, we shall be able to go straight to the spot and lay claim to it.'

She found a small wooden box which had once contained a piece of her mother's jewellery and lined it with soft cotton in which Gyp's stone could nestle. She wrote a letter to her brother explaining how they had come by the stone and requesting that he have it assayed. With many endearments and the oft' repeated request that her brother come soon to join them, she ended her letter:

The country hereabouts is beginning to open up at last. Even today a family has arrived in the village destined for the hill country to the west, where they intend to farm sheep. It was good to meet folks newly arrived from home. Only six months ago we too were newcomers. Now we feel like old hands at the business of settlement and were able to give them much wise council most of which they will no doubt ignore!

Papa is much improved of late. Working amongst the Maori villagers has given him a new zest for life but he still treats Jessie as a servant. I doubt if he will ever come to regard her as a proper wife. I do not think he quite understands how much of a sacrifice she has made coming out into the bush with us. She would surely have made a better life for herself in town. Charlie and I will ever be grateful to her for accompanying us however. Charlie misses our mother as any little boy would. Jessie and I try to make it up to him but you can imagine how deeply we all feel her loss. You really must join us as quickly as possible. There are infinite ways in which you with your special knowledge of Geology could make a living out here!

How we all pray that you will be able to tell us we have found gold. Come home soon for whether it is a humble fern hut or a glittering mansion, where your family is will always be your home.

Your loving sister, Catherine.

Chapter Sixteen

The Mackie child recovered within days of Alexander's operation to relieve his breathing and after a further two weeks the doctor felt justified in declaring that he was out of the wood. During the epidemic Alexander had been too busy to follow progress in the building of the surgery so when at last he was able to stop by his plot, he found the thatching of the roof was nearly complete. Toby, whose woodworking skills had improved immensely since their first halting attempts to construct the timber framework of the building, was putting the finishing touches to a pair of doors.

'They look grand, Toby,' Alexander remarked, genuinely impressed.

'The doors are all well and good,' came the despondent reply. How we are to fix them is another matter entirely.'

'How do you mean?'

'Well, it's a question of hinges and latches. Ironwork costs money, Doctor, a commodity which despite this epidemic is still lamentably non-existent.'

'Thankfully, the diphtheria epidemic is now on the wane but most patients have a way to go yet to full recovery. I can hardly start sending out bills when the treatment is not completed.'

'There's nothing for it then. I shall have to devise something in leather for hinges and wooden fastenings for the time being. The windows will, of course, have to remain fixed until we can afford hinges and stays.'

'I leave it to you, Toby. Just do the best you can.'

Alexander was about to take his leave when he noticed William Mackie leaning over the hitching post at the front of the plot and gazing intently at the newly constructed building.

'Good morning William,' called Alexander. 'Won't you come a little closer if you wish to inspect our handiwork?'

Mackie laughed and sauntered forward to join Alexander on the wide veranda.

'It's a fair-sized building you have here Doctor,' he commented. Scrutinising the craftsmanship carefully, he found little to criticise.

'It must serve as both a surgery and living accommodation,' Alexander explained. 'That is why there are additional rooms, a waiting area, consultation room and dispensary. Here at the rear, we have a good sized living area, kitchen and two bedrooms and,' he paused on the threshold of the final small room, a bathroom.'

Mackie was very impressed. 'Will you be looking for piped water and a waste pipe?' he wondered. Thomas Crapper's water closets had become all the rage before they had left Glasgow but only the newest and most prestigious buildings could be fitted with the intricacies of plumbing required for the innovation.

'Do you know anyone who might be able to manufacture and install such a device,' asked Alexander, intrigued to see if his friend would take up the challenge.

'I might be persuaded to undertake the work myself,' said Mackie, thoughtfully. If the doctor's installation worked it would be a fine advertisement for further work of the kind.

'If you can make it, I will find the money to pay for it,' said Alexander, recklessly. No doubt by the time Mackie got around to the task, his money problems would all have been solved.

'How many doors and windows?' it was a rhetorical question for before Alexander could respond, Mackie had the answer for himself. Without explaining his interest, the blacksmith suddenly found pressing things to do elsewhere and excused himself. Alexander watched until his friend was out of sight then turned at the sound of a galloping horse approaching from the north-west.

The mounted figure was soon recognised as Hongi's brother, Tuki, whom James Bantrie had engaged to accompany his party into the wilderness.

The Maori leaned out of his saddle to hand a package to his younger brother. He was out of breath from riding so hard and made it clear that he had urgent messages to deliver elsewhere and must be on his way.

Anxious for any news of Jessie, Alexander called after the departing figure. 'The reverend Bantrie and his family – are they well?' The fellow was riding away from him but even from the rear it seemed to Alexander that he had shaken his head. With a terrible foreboding, the doctor glanced down at the package which Hongi had thrust into his hands. He recognised her neat handwriting at once and tore open the packet. There were several envelopes enclosed addressed to people back home. A single folded sheet was addressed to himself.

Mapourika July sixteenth, 1848

My Dear Alexander

By the time you receive this I fear it may already be too late for you to do anything, but nevertheless I believe we must do all that is possible to avert the disaster which is threatening the villagers here.

Some two weeks ago a settler family passed through on their way west. Not content to stay in or around Dunedin, they have purchased a run directly from the village Chieftain here, spending several days during the negotiations. At the time we very much enjoyed the company of white folks speaking proper English instead of pigeon, but towards the end of their stay one of the children, a small girl, fell ill and since she showed all the symptoms of an ordinary cold, fever, sore throat, dry cough, I gave the mother some ipecac, creosote and olive oil and suggested they get on their way, knowing how quickly the Maori succumb to such conditions. To my dismay, two days later the father rode into the village having left his family in the bush. He described the little girl's worsened condition and I feared that I recognised the symptoms of Diphtheria. Whether she contracted it on board ship or in Dunedin, in passing through, I do not know. I went at once to the campsite to see what I could do but by that time the child was choking and she died in my arms only two hours after my arrival.

The settler's children had played with the Maori youngsters and also with Tommy and Charles. I watch my own boys every day for signs of the scourge but so far, they have remained well. I cannot say the same for the village children however. Today I spotted my first definite case but others are showing the early symptoms and I am powerless to help them. It is not only the children who are affected. I fear that adults too will suffer greatly from the disease. I am attempting to carry out similar isolation procedures to those we used aboard ship, but you cannot, I think, imagine the conditions in which these people live. Cleanliness is not a word to be found in their language. Please come and help us or at least send me the necessary medicines and instructions that I may deal with it before we have an epidemic.

The family have taken this opportunity to write home. Would you be kind enough to put these letters on the first packet leaving for Scotland?

Yours in haste,

Jessica Bantrie

The sight of her name written thus formally, made the hairs on the back of his neck tingle. He felt a lump forming in his throat and hurriedly brushed a hand across his misted eyes.

'What is it, news of the Minister?' Toby asked cheerfully, then seeing Alexander's doleful expression he asked more soberly. 'Is all well with Mrs Bantrie?'

'Diphtheria has reached their village already. She asks for help with the Maori children.'

'Not her own boy or the Bantries?' Toby demanded anxiously. He had grown inordinately fond of Catherine Bantrie and her brother and particularly of little Tommy Dundas.

'Not as far as I know. Not yet at any rate.' Alexander could not bear to think of any of them going through what he had seen these past weeks amongst the children of the settlement.

'Toby, I must go to her,' Alexander declared. 'The women here have a good idea what to do now and in any case, the worst of the epidemic is over.'

'You can rely on me to keep things going here while you are away,' Toby assured him. 'What can I do to help you on your way?'

'For a start, you might deliver these letters to the barquentine standing in to Port Chalmers. She sails for Wellington on the morning tide. Meanwhile I shall go to Dr Burns and tell him about the trouble at Mapourika. He may be able to give me a guide, perhaps the Maori who called here earlier.'

'Hongi's brother you mean? His name is Tuki.'

'That's the fellow. If Dr Burns can spare him and Mackie can find me a decent mount, it shouldn't take us too long to get there. I'll be back as soon as I can.'

*

Jessie's simple medical supplies were no match for Diphtheria. Once she had recognised the disease for what it was, she knew there was nothing she could do to stop the scourge from taking its toll other than by sending to Dunedin for help.

The farming family whose daughter had so lately died in her arms had stoically laid their infant to rest where a shower of acacia branches could tumble over the grave, their prolific swathes of tiny white flowers brightening the dark green foliage to resemble a magical waterfall. Once satisfied that they had done all they could for their little one, the settlers went on their way leaving behind a legacy which was to devastate the Maori village as nothing had done before.

On her return to Mapourika, Jessie had found that what she had dreaded most of all had already begun. Village children, showing early symptoms of the dread disease, were playing listlessly alongside the healthier, more robust Europeans and although she quickly separated her boys from the tribe, it was to be three anxiety ridden weeks before she could satisfy herself that James and Tommy were safe from infection. All she could do for the village children was isolate them from their siblings, treat their symptoms of fever and sore throat with what remedies she had and feed them a nourishing gruel and broth which she made with her own hands. A few survived but the majority succumbed to the white filamentous growths which slowly and painfully choked them to death. Then the only recourse left to her was the blissful oblivion provided by opium which while no kind of a cure, at least eased their passage into the next life.

Having delivered Jessie's message to Alexander Beaton, and before returning to Mapourika with the doctor, Hongi had made his way to the Maori village at the Otago Heads where he passed on to his sister their father's request for her to return home.

Thus it was that within hours of Alexander's arrival at Mapourika,

Teri, the Maori medicine woman he had met previously at Otago Heads, appeared in the village administering her herbal remedies to those children whose parents would have no truck with the white man's medicine. While Alexander, with Jessie at his side, moved amongst the little thatched huts perfecting his operation with scalpel and tube, Teri administered analgesic drugs without a name which sent her patients peacefully to sleep never to open their eyes again.

It was inevitable that the two should meet at last.

Alexander entered one dimly lit hut to find the Maori girl kneeling beside a pallet on the floor. On the primitive bed, a tiny form lay curled in a foetal position. All was silence save for the occasional painful rattle of a sharp dry cough. In her hand Teri held a small cup made of some seed case which Alexander did not recognise. From time to time she attempted to coax a little of the liquid it contained down the child's throat.

'What's that?' he demanded, unreasonably angry, Jessie thought. There was sufficient work here for all three of them and the disease presented no less a challenge to Alexander's medical skill than to the girl's. The children were dying no matter what the doctor tried. Even the last resort of tracheotomy could not succeed if the wound suppurated, for blood poisoning was as sure a killer as choking in undernourished infants lacking any natural stamina.

Teri, unable to give him an explanation for what she used, thrust a few small, heart shaped leaves into his hands.

'Matipo', she told him and laid her head on her hands, imitating sleep.

'It is an analgesic,' Jessica interpreted, sniffing at the contents of the cup. 'It's like a kind of tea. It seems to be effective in taking away the pain and inducing sleep.'

As much annoyed by Jessie's championing of the girl as by the use of the potion itself, Alexander removed the cup roughly from Teri's grasp and threw it out of the door.

'I'll have no voodoo medicine practised in my presence,' he declared pompously and crouched down to look more closely at the patient. He felt the thready pulse. He lifted one eyelid and then the other, seeing all too plainly the yellow colouring which indicated the child's liver was already hopelessly affected by the disease. To perform a tracheotomy in the circumstances was merely to prolong suffering before the inevitable death. Somewhat sheepishly he removed a phial of tincture of opium from his bag and poured a measure into a medicine glass.

Jessie watched him accusingly. He was only doing what Teri had attempted to do moments before, and they both knew it.

The truth was that Alexander's behaviour was nothing to do either with Teri's medicine or with any exceptional concern for his patient. He had set out on this errand of mercy convinced that Jessie, regretting her hasty rejection of his love, was using this emergency to renew their association. Since his arrival however he had been forced to accept that he had made a mistake. Far from seeking his help as some excuse to see him, Jessie had called upon his expertise with no thought at all as to how their reunion might affect either of them.

Much to Alexander's surprise, James had greeted him in as friendly and cheerful a manner as he had ever used in the past. The Bantries showed every appearance of being a well-suited couple with a happy family ranged about them. Catherine was fast developing into a fine young lady and the boys seemed completely at ease in their new surroundings. Their apparent contentment merely served to fuel his feelings of rejection.

While the epidemic raged amongst children and adults alike taking a severe toll of the Maori population, there was little time for further displays of antagonism between Alexander and the chief's daughter. Towards the end of the fourth week of the doctor's stay in the village, a day came when there were no new cases of Diphtheria reported. Jessie's insistence upon isolation in the early stages, the application of simple methods of hygiene and greater attention to cleanliness in the handling of food and drink amongst the natives, combined to eradicate the disease as suddenly as it had appeared.

When the last patient was out of the wood and due attention had been given to rituals for the dead, the chief ordered a great feast of celebration that the evil had been dismissed. James Bantrie seized upon the opportunity to make it a double celebration inviting the village people to a ceremony in the church on the hill. He and Catherine worked on the selection of tuneful hymns which would appeal to the natural musicality of the people. He created a sermon in pigeon English which they would understand and had the church decked with leaves and flowers in the Maori way. The service, more of an entertainment than the solemn ritual of the Free Church of Scotland, would most certainly have been frowned upon by Dr Burns and his worthy parishioners. Jessie on the harmonium led Catherine and the boys in the singing with the voluble if tuneless assistance of Alexander Beaton. As he listened to the deep throated Maoris struggling to get their tongues around the strange language of the hymns, James recalled with some amusement the surly Robert Shaw, that disagreeable, insensitive creature who had engineered his downfall. What would *he* have made of this attempt to bring the word of the true God to the heathen? He was surprised what satisfaction it gave him to watch the obvious pleasure on the faces of his parishioners. In Scotland, the last thing one would have expected to see in the congregation was any expression of enjoyment!

The feast, spread on the ground with broad leaves for dishes, was a mighty accumulation of sea fishes, barracuta and hapuka, a kind of groper fish, meat which appeared to be wild pig and fruits of the forest. The staple was a potato-like vegetable consisting of small round white tubers with a blueish vein running throughout, very sweet and pleasant to the European palate. The fish was clearly fresh caught but Jessie, having witnessed how any meat was hung from the rafters of the huts until rotten, warned Alexander against it.

The Maori produced liquor made from fermented potato which served as an alcoholic beverage but there was also a kind of tea brewed from the bitter leaves of the Manuka tree. Alexander was fascinated by all these products and found himself questioning Teri concerning the origins of each dish as it was presented. While he was loath to accept that she knew anything at all about medicine he was happy to try the beverages and dishes of the Maori people. Alex found himself respecting her superior knowledge concerning the products of her native land. Even this new awareness of her attributes was insufficient preparation however, for the proposition which the chief put before him as the celebrations reached their climax.

The village maidens performed a swaying, somewhat suggestive dance which was accompanied by singing in soft seductive tones. James, suspecting this of being a mating ritual, turned somewhat apologetically to Jessie and engaged her in quiet conversation to distract her attention from the indelicacy of the performance. The dance was followed immediately by a fearsome demonstration of a war dance given by young men with crudely decorated faces and magnificent plumed headdresses. Despite the friendliness of the proceedings so far, this caused Jessie great alarm and quite terrified Catherine and the boys.

Through his son, Hongi, who acted all the while as interpreter, Ngakebe Taiaroa indicated that in recognition of his services in ridding the village of the evil sickness, he wished to offer the doctor the greatest gift at his disposal. Thinking this might be some bauble made of the greenstone so prized by the Maori and used as currency between the tribes Alexander smiled politely and awaited the presentation with mild interest.

Ngakebe Taiaroa leaned across his guest and summoned his daughter Teri to his side. Then, in a ceremonial manner and with great dignity, he placed the girl's hand in Alexander's.

The bewildered doctor turned to Hongi for an explanation.

'The Chief wishes you to take my sister as your wife, Doctor.'

Unable to think of any way in which to respond to this extraordinary suggestion, Alexander turned to James Bantrie for help.

'What on earth can I do, James?' he demanded, not daring to look to Jessie for her reaction.

The minister appeared quite unfazed by the proposition.

'It is very clear that you are being given a singular honour,' James replied. 'It is equally clear that you are in no position to refuse. Who knows what damage would be done to relations between the Maori and the settlement should you cause the chief any offence.'

Although he could not fail to notice that smug grin on his friend's face which indicated his amusement at the doctor's predicament, Alexander was forced to admit that there was truth in what James said. He turned to Jessie for some support but she was looking stolidly ahead showing no sign of her own feelings in the matter.

Alexander now turned back to Chief Ngakebe and forcing a smile to replace his fleeting look of dismay, lifted the joined hands of Teri and himself, indicating how happy he was to accept the gift.

Teri could not have failed to see and interpret correctly, the exchange between the white men. Nevertheless, she sat quietly, her face expressionless and only when Alexander thanked the chief through his interpreter and turned to give her a smile, did she make any sign of awareness of the proceedings. Even then, while her lips showed pleasure her eyes told a different story. She had not failed to notice Alexander's anxious expression, the despairing glance cast in Jessie's direction and his final expression of resignation. It was not for her to make objection to her father's decision however. With a swift and graceful movement, she placed herself in a kneeling position before her future husband and kissed his dusty feet in what could only be described as a gesture of supplication.

The union of the doctor and his Maori medicine woman was celebrated both in the church, in the Christian manner, and before the village elders, following the custom of the tribe. A week later, Alexander returned to Dunedin with his bride anticipating the objections of the prudish Scottish community and fearful of what this strange relationship would do to his so recently established and still fragile medical practice. What had hurt him most of all however, was the apparent joy expressed by Jessie at the union and her genuine good wishes to himself and to Teri for a long and happy relationship blessed with many healthy children!

Chapter Seventeen

During the months which followed, Jessie and James worked tirelessly amongst the Maori while at the same time laying out for themselves a good sized vegetable plot where they grew all manner of plants both of the native varieties and those imported from home by their fellow passengers.

James would have preferred to think that the Maoris came to the church to hear for themselves about the true God and all his works but he suspected as Jessie never ceased to remind him, that they came for the singing and for the afternoon teas which she and Catherine prepared so assiduously whenever there was cause for celebration.

On these occasions, Catherine took out the old story books with their woodcut illustrations and read to the Maori. Originally the intention had been to entertain the children while her stepmother talked to the women, but the adults were as keen to listen to the stories as the children and it was not unusual to find one or two of the men lounging on the veranda just outside the door, hoping to overhear something of what was being said within.

When news got about that the Bantries had made a decent home for themselves amongst the Maori many of their shipboard acquaintances came out to see them or called in on their way to seek new pastures further inland. Mapourika became a staging post for such expeditions and soon other white men succeeded in acquiring land from Ngakebe Taiaroa.

While Catherine awaited anxiously the analysis of the stone she had sent to her brother, she became increasingly concerned that one of these newcomers might acquire the very area which harboured the gold mother load. She and the boys spent the long summer days in a search for likely rock outcrops but not knowing what they were looking for, their hunt proved fruitless. The only individual to get real satisfaction from their expeditions into the bush was Gyp who grasped at every opportunity to accompany his young mistress and masters up country.

James Bantrie, convinced that the mineral they had found was nothing other than Fool's gold, had counselled against drawing Ian's attention to the matter and only Jessie knew the contents of the mysterious package the children had sent home. When an old prospector who had cut his teeth in the gold fields of South Africa, arrived in Otago and came to Mapourika carrying his primitive equipment on his back, James Bantrie was quick to dismiss the idea that the region might yield any workable amounts of gold. The man stayed in the district for some while but finding nothing to give him encouragement and hearing of a lucky strike somewhere out in the western Australian desert, he embarked upon the next boat leaving for Adelaide.

When Ian's long-awaited letter eventually arrived, it gave little encouragement to the young prospectors.

> *I have shown your rock fragment to my professor in the school of mines, he wrote to his sister. The specimen yielded only a tiny fraction of an ounce of gold and it is his opinion that the nature of the bonding of minerals is such that it would be uneconomical to extract the gold even if the mother lode were to be discovered. He has advised me against foregoing the remaining years of my apprenticeship in what might prove a fruitless expedition. I have therefore decided to remain at Delabole and finish my training. I understand your remarks about Charlie needing his elder brother but I also hear from our stepmother that Papa is much improved and that the boy is well and happy. While I have every intention of coming to join you as soon as I can, it would be best for me to come properly prepared to make a decent living and that requires that I remain here to complete my studies. No doubt you will think me selfish, but maybe one day you will understand and appreciate my position in this.*

Catherine's disappointment was profound and although she took her brother's word for it that any gold there might be was not worth discovering, she still harboured the wish to purchase the ground where Gyp had uncovered his stone. James, mellowed by his pleasant surroundings and amiable flock, was inclined to indulge her whim and the following year, as a present for her fifteenth birthday, he purchased from Ngakebe a two mile wide run which occupied both sides of the stream for a distance of one mile above the waterfall where Tommy had so nearly met his end. It was a strange gift for a girl but Catherine was delighted to receive the grant of land from the old chief and vowed that even if no gold was found, she would one day build a house there for herself. If she had any romantic notion that she might live there with her husband and family, she kept it to herself. She had no illusions regarding her prospects of marriage. Few single men came by this way and those that did were largely penniless itinerates wandering from homestead to homestead in search of what work they could find.

With Jessie's encouragement, Catherine concentrated upon teaching the Maori children and with them her two younger brothers and the increasing numbers of white children who had come to live in the area.

By the onset of winter in the year 1851 Charlie, fast approaching his twelfth birthday, had absorbed most of what Jessie and Catherine had to teach him. James had attempted to give him instruction in Latin and Greek but it was clear that if he was to succeed in one of the professions he needed tutors with skills greater than those provided by the family.

James Bantrie travelled on horseback to Dunedin to consult with Dr Burns and with his old friend, Alexander Beaton. At the end of a week the boy's future had been settled to the satisfaction of everyone except Charlie himself.

*

In the years following the diphtheria epidemic at Mapourika, Alexander's marriage to the Maori princess had flourished despite his initial misgivings. Teri's upbringing had taught her to expect nothing other than a life of devoted service to the husband chosen for her by her father. There had been few inhibitions amongst the Mapourika women who had tutored her early life so that at puberty she already knew all that was expected of her in the marriage bed and exactly how to give satisfaction as a sexual partner.

Alexander had settled easily into this comfortable new life, soon coming to take it for granted that his every whim would be instantly satisfied. Teri was quick to learn. Even those functions of a European household which were completely alien to her such as the use of porcelain plates and tea cups and silver table ware, were very soon absorbed into her daily routines. She adjusted surprisingly easily to those aspects of their life together which were outside her former experience. Most Maori women understood the need to sweep their houses clean, but Teri had not found it necessary to wash bed linen and furnishings or to polish cutlery. Even so, Alexander had very soon found himself able to trust his wife with the scrupulous cleaning demanded in his surgery.

Despite the absence of romance in their marriage, Alexander found his sexual needs attended to with the same enthusiasm and precision as all other aspects of their relationship. Teri was a strong young woman whose health was never in doubt. The improved diet which she enjoyed under Alexander's roof turned her from a skinny maiden into a buxom woman within the space of a few months. By the time their second son was born Teri had developed the fulsome features of all well-nourished women of her race and although at home in Scotland Alexander might have considered her too overweight to be healthy, her ample proportions did not seem out of place in a Dunedin society which was steadily absorbing Maori citizens alongside the immigrant Europeans.

Nor was the union frowned upon by the settlement's leaders. Dr Burns had welcomed Alexander's bride, giving her all the courtesies of visiting royalty which her father's exalted position demanded. Where Dr Burns led, everyone of any position, followed. Soon Teri was being invited to visit the drawing rooms of many of Dunedin's dignitaries and had become a familiar figure at the soirées and concerts so dear to the hearts of the middle-class Scotswomen of the town. It was on one of these occasions that Teri first encountered Nellie Parker.

The scarcity of suitable females in the settlement available to take on the job of children's nanny or governess, meant that the ladies of the town, shopkeeper's wives and those of the town's professional men including Mrs Burns herself, were usually obliged to take their infant offspring along with them to social gatherings. When a meeting was held at the

Fergusson house, it fell to Margaret Fergusson's governess, Nellie Parker, to supervise the crèche while the mothers enjoyed themselves. Teri's first born, Malcolm, was already three years old and Teri was seven months pregnant with her second child. Malcolm Beaton was a sturdy boy with a quick intelligence. His mother's olive skin formed a striking contrast to his tightly curled light brown hair which was delicately touched by his father's auburn tints. He had walked before he was a year old and at three years could already communicate well in both Maori and English, giving the impression of a much older child. It was this misconception which was the cause of friction on a certain afternoon in the late summer of the year 1852.

The ladies had scarce got out their knitting and embroidery and had sunk their teeth into satisfyingly chunky slabs of Margaret Fergusson's delicious shortbread when there was a loud screech and a great deal of cattawalling from the playroom. With tight-lipped apologies to her friends, Margaret reached the hallway in time to see several terrified little girls hurtling towards the garden door pursued by a fearsome monster, none the less terrible for his small stature. He was almost naked and covered from head to foot in colourful lines and squiggles.

Two older boys stood, laughing, at the playroom door while Nellie Parker brought up the rear uttering a series of oaths which her mistress would certainly never have expected from a governess.

'Miss Parker, what may I ask is going on?' demanded the surveyor's wife.

'It's the boys Ma'am,' Nellie attempted to explain.

'Boys? Which boys?'

'Our... your boys, Ma'am.' Nellie was confused and justifiably so.

She had been attending to the little girls, showing them how to cut out paper dolls and make dresses for them by colouring in the designs she herself had prepared earlier. Everything had been quiet. Alan and Keith Fergusson had taken the smaller boys away to their bedroom where she supposed they were indulging in some harmless activity. At last, hearing no sound coming from that quarter, she wondered if things were not perhaps too peaceful and went to look for the missing children. When she found the children's bedroom empty she began searching every room in the house, calling out as she went.

At her approach, the older boys had melted away, leaving little Malcolm Beaton standing alone in the middle of the adult Fergusson's bedroom.

Using their mother's cosmetics, now spilled untidily over the fine white lace mats covering her polished dressing table, the Fergusson boys had been drawing designs on the smaller child's nearly naked body. The drawings were crude imitations of Maori patterns and in truth with his dark colouring and smouldering brown eyes, Malcolm had been made to look very like a miniature warrior prepared for performing the haka.

Finding himself suddenly alone in the governess's presence, the terrified child let out a yell and, darting around her skirts, fled across the passage and into the playroom. Here the little girls, who were clustered around the doorway to see what was going on, were parted by what appeared to be a charging demon and flew out into the garden screaming and calling for their mothers. Equally frightened by all the commotion his weird appearance had caused, Malcolm cried out for his mother and on spotting her amongst the mass of enraged matrons, tore towards them and threw himself sobbing loudly, into her arms. The mascara with which his nose and cheeks had been so painstakingly freckled only moments before mixed with his tears and flowed in smudgy rivulets down either cheek and into his wide-open mouth.

In an instant Margaret Fergusson grabbed Teri by the arm and shook her savagely.

'How dare you bring that little heathen into this company to pollute good Christian children. I don't care what Dr Burns says, there is no place for your sort in our midst. Please leave my house at once and take your monstrous little brat with you!'

The other ladies had mixed reactions to the incident. Some like Margaret thought the half Maori child should not have been there in the first place. Others were inclined to be less damning. White children were just as capable of such mischief.

On seeing him for the first time that afternoon, Ellie Parker had taken immediately to the dark eyed piccaninny, as she called him, and had at once remarked upon his polite manners and friendly disposition. Knowing her own charges as well as she did, she was not so quick to allocate blame. Nor was she about to stand by and see little Malcolm's mother verbally abused by Mrs Fergusson. Nellie had witnessed the behaviour of real aristocracy and knew that whatever else Margaret Fergusson might be, she was no lady of breeding.

'Forgive me Madam,' she began, politely enough. 'I think you are too hasty in casting blame. Little Malcolm could not have coloured his body by himself. I believe that the older boys had a hand in this.'

'It was not my boys who frightened the little girls,' Mrs Fergusson protested venomously.

'No Madam, that was because they were too cowardly to stay and face me when I caught them at their tricks.'

'Are you calling my children cowards?' demanded her employer.

'Yes Madam, I am. They are sneaky, nasty little cowards.'

'How dare you Miss!' Mrs Fergusson was screeching now at the top of her voice. 'You will leave my employ immediately!'

'Pay me what is owing to me and I shall go most willingly.' Nellie stood her ground, secure in the knowledge that she had all the witnesses she could want to this senseless argument and totally unfair dismissal. Rather like the children however, the ladies were hastily excusing themselves on every side and quietly melting away.

'Go... now!' shouted her employer, in a most unladylike manner which quite shocked the remaining guests. 'As to your wages, you must speak to my husband about that. I want you out of my house before sundown.'

Nellie turned on her heel and made straightaway for the tiny wooden shack attached to the back veranda where she slept.

Treated as something between a servant and a member of the family, Nellie had enjoyed none of the advantages of either condition. It was not considered suitable for her to eat with the Maori servants but neither was she invited to join the Fergussons at their meals. She ate alone or if there were guests and the boys excluded from the dinner table, with the children. Nellie's duties as a governess had never been clearly defined. Obviously, she expected to spend her time tutoring the children, attempting to improve their manners and overseeing their play, but she sometimes doubted that Alice Montgomery whose position she had taken, would have been prepared to wash clothes, help with the spring cleaning and even cook for the family when occasion demanded.

While the house servants enjoyed well defined holidays, Ellie's infrequent moments of freedom depended upon the activities of her young charges and their parents. Above all, Ellie had in all this time enjoyed nothing but the briefest contact with the outside world and was sadly lacking in her exchanges with adults other than her employers and their Maori servants.

She had at first been content to accept this somewhat isolated existence in return for a roof over her head and three square meals a day. Every free moment of her time was spent in improving herself through reading. When the children were off hand for a whole day, which was very seldom, she would wander out into the hills with sketch book and water colours and paint the scenes which unfolded before her. Recently however she had begun to feel her isolation more keenly. This altercation could bring about a welcome change in her circumstances.

Having finished packing her meagre wardrobe, a task which did not take long, she tore from the walls the numerous colourful sketches she had made and rolled them into a tube which she stuffed hurriedly into her valise. Her collection of books weighed heavily. Still angry, she piled them into her trunk and struggled to drag it out onto the veranda, wondering as she did so how she could possibly manage to carry it all the way into town.

She need not have worried. Out in the yard she found Teko, the Fergusson's yard boy, carefully backing a somewhat scraggy pony between the shafts of the Fergusson's wagon. When Nellie appeared Teko finished harnessing the horse and lifted her heavy trunk on board the dray as easily as though it were a bag of feathers. He came back for the carpet bag and was about to give her a hand up when she asked,

'Who ordered the cart?'

'Master said I was to hitch up and take you into town, Missie,' the boy replied, two rows of shining white teeth exposed by a broad grin.

'Mr Fergusson has come home?' she asked in surprise. If her employer was already present, she might as well collect her wages before she left.

'Wait here Teko, I shall not be long,' she said, and slipped back inside the house making straight for Mr Fergusson's study.

'Come in my dear,' the town's surveyor addressed her most cordially. 'I am sorry to hear that you are leaving us. My wife tells me it is by agreement?'

She stared at him in disbelief. Did he not know the truth of the situation? Had her mistress not confessed to her outburst of ill temper and her unreasonable behaviour towards her Maori guest?

'We had a disagreement, Sir. It is best if I go.'

She did not feel it was her place to describe the incident. No doubt he would hear the details from one or other of his cronies before the day was out.

'There is the matter of wages, however,' she continued. 'The mistress said I should ask you for what is owed.'

He opened a draw in his desk and took out a notebook in which he kept careful account of the household expenses. Under her own name she saw several entries and to one side a neat row of figures.

'You were engaged at a salary of thirty pounds per year,' he said as though speaking to himself. 'It is six months one week and five days since you last received payment, which means that I owe you fifteen pounds and thirty pence. Is that correct?'

Too agitated to make the fractional calculation in her head, she nodded in agreement anyway. Suddenly all the force of her anger had dissipated and realisation of her situation had set in with a jolt. Here she was at the age of twenty-three, with a couple of bags of cast-off clothing, a few second hand books and fifteen pounds odd, in her pocket. She was without any prospect of employment and had nowhere to lay her head for the night. When the story of her dismissal got around town, with the inevitable lurid embellishments added by eye witnesses, she was unlikely to find further employment as a governess and would therefore have to find alternative work and her own accommodation. She could take a room at the hotel of course, but fifteen pounds would not go far if she spent her money that way.

She accepted the sovereigns he counted into her hand and was mortified to find her eyes had filled with tears of self pity.

'Oh, come now, Miss,' he cautioned abruptly, 'You will soon find another place. I am very surprised you are unable to satisfy my wife. I thought you were doing a splendid job. Our girl has grown into a fine young woman under your tutelage. The boys are quite troublesome I know, but nevertheless you have taught them well. However, it is for Mrs Fergusson to decide about the household staff. I am sure you understand.'

He studied her tear stained face silently, his eyes begging her forgiveness for treating her so shabbily after four years of loyal service.

She understood his position only too well. There was no question who wore the trousers in this household. She knew Fergusson to be a man of simple needs who indulged in few pleasures. Provided his meals were on time, his clothes kept in good order and peace reigned, he was content to allow his wife to rule the roost. The prospect of friction between two spirited women under one roof would be more than he could stand.

'In lieu of notice I shall add a further two guineas,' he said impulsively and thrust the additional coins into her hands just as his wife entered enraged that the hussy was still on the premises and had dared to approach her husband without her knowledge.

'What, still here, Miss,' she cried indignantly. Then, to her husband, 'Quite contrary to my instruction, I find Teko in the yard with the cart loaded with this woman's luggage. How is this?'

'I ordered the cart my dear. You would not wish our neighbours to think us so uncivil as to dismiss Miss Parker without providing means of transport to her next abode.'

The barb struck home. Mrs Fergusson was always very anxious for the good opinion of her neighbours. It was enough that some of them had taken the girl's part that afternoon. With a toss of her head, she turned on her heel and left Nellie without a word of farewell or any acknowledgement of the years she had spent in her service.

The kindly surveyor shook Ellie by the hand.

'If work is hard to find, do not hesitate to approach me again, Miss Parker but,' with a quick glance in the direction of his departing wife, 'if you should wish to see me, perhaps it had best be at my office in town.'

She took his hand, made a deep curtsy and hurried outside before she gave way entirely to her emotions.

The dray overtook the doctor's wife and son before they reached the hotel. Dismissed unceremoniously from the Fergusson house, Teri had left on foot, disinclined to wait for her husband's chaise to collect her. It was a hot afternoon and the Maori woman, heavy with child, her weary little son dragging at her heels, was near the end of her tether.

Nellie called the wagon to a halt.

'May I give you a lift along the way, Mrs Beaton?' she called.

Gratefully, Teri lifted little Malcolm into the back of the wagon and climbed up beside Nellie and her driver.

'It was kind of you to stop,' she said in her careful English. 'I was near to fainting away.'

Ellie patted her hand reassuringly and turned to Keto.

'You must know the doctor's residence, Keto, you have been there many times.' The Maori boy smiled, nodded encouragingly to Teri Beaton and clicked the horses into a trot.

'It has been a bad day for you Miss Parker, Teri said. 'I am so sorry you have lost your employment for defending my little boy.'

'It was time I had a change anyway,' Nellie dismissed her apology lightly. 'Those Fergusson boys are devils. I am quite sure your little fellow would never have got into such a prank without their encouragement.'

'He still does not know what he did wrong,' said Teri. 'Often at home he paints his face and puts on a feather headdress, one which his uncle made for him for play. Being a warrior is a game played by all small Maori boys.'

'And if those silly girls had had any sense at all they would have known the boys were only having fun. After all, what harm could a three-foot unarmed warrior have done them even had he been in earnest?'

Both women began laughing at the notion and when Ellie told Teko what it was all about, he too joined in with his deep belly laughs. In this suddenly lightened mood the little party drew up before the doctor's residence on Cumberland Avenue. Ellie jumped down to assist her passenger while Teko lifted little Malcolm out of the back of the wagon.

'Where will you go now?' asked Teri. 'Do you have a place to stay?'

Ellie hesitated before replying. Not wanting to distress Mrs Beaton further, she made light of her predicament.

'Not immediately,' she answered. 'I shall have to find somewhere temporarily until I can gain other employment.'

'Then you must stay here,' decided Teri, with typical Maori hospitality. 'It is our fault that you are homeless.'

'What would the doctor say?'

Nellie could not imagine Alexander Beaton welcoming an ex lady's maid, an unemployed governess, into his household.

'Stay for one night at least,' suggested Teri. 'Then we can think of something better for tomorrow!'

Nellie, who believed she understood Dr Beaton's position rather better than his Maori wife, was torn between upsetting his standing in the community and saving as much of her hard-earned money as possible. Reluctantly, she agreed. After all, it would only be for one night.

She followed Teri into the house, entering by the back way, the front being reserved for Alexander's patients. A wide veranda gave access to a back hall, a large kitchen and a charming living room which Alexander had furnished with locally made pieces for the most part. The multi-coloured rush matting which was hung against the polished pinewood panelling was of Maori design, made no doubt by Teri herself or members of her family. Covering the comfortable sofa and armchairs arranged before a wide stone fireplace, was a woollen fabric in a bright tartan pattern, no doubt imported from Scotland. The solid dining table and wooden dining chairs were intricately carved, Maori fashion, while shelf brackets, door handles, latches and window stays, were all in elaborate wrought ironwork.

'What a lovely room,' Nellie cried admiringly, feeling at once the welcoming atmosphere which had been created by the doctor and his wife. How she would love to have a home like this.

Keto stood uncertainly in the doorway carrying on his shoulders Ellie's heavy trunk.

'Where to put, Missie?' he enquired.

Teri turned to her visitor.

'Will you share Malcolm's room, just for the night?' she asked. 'The doctor's partner, Mr Leny, is in the guest bedroom. You know him?'

'From the *Albatross*? Yes, of course! They still share a house then?' Nellie asked, remembering the cheerful little man who always had a solution to everyone's problems aboard ship.

'Oh no!' Teri laughed. 'Mr Leny has his own place now, on the Taieri river not far from my family's village of Mapourika. He has many wagons and some fine bullocks and horses for… transport?' She had some difficulty with the unfamiliar word. 'Sorry, I sometimes forget proper words.'

'Your English is excellent,' Nellie commented admiringly. 'I wish I could speak Maori even half so well. I can speak only a few words of your language which I picked up from the house servants at the Fergusson's.'

'I could teach you,' said Teri, enthusiastically. It was a great joy for her to have another woman with whom she could talk so freely. Alexander's work often took him away for days at a time and she was left with only little Malcolm for company. There was always the apprentice, Charlie, of course but he usually accompanied the doctor on his rounds.

Realising suddenly that she was neglecting her duties as a hostess, Teri struggled to her feet saying, 'I must make tea.'

The effort, after the excitement of the afternoon, was rather too much for her condition and she sat down again, suddenly. Ellie feared that she was about to pass out. Malcolm, coming back into the room with Teko following behind carrying Ellie's carpet bag, ran to her side.

'Mummy faint. I fetch smelly bottle.' He disappeared into his parent's bedroom, returning almost at once carrying a small bottle of smelling salts which he held beneath his mother's nose until with a little splutter and a flickering of the eyelashes, Teri regained consciousness.

'It is the baby," she apologised.

'Wee Malcolm is quite the little doctor,' commented Ellie, most impressed by what she had seen.

'Oh yes, he is a good boy,' said his mother with a little smile, 'most of the time.' She rested her head wearily on the back of the chair and it was Nellie who got to her feet.

'If Malcolm will show me where, I will make us all a nice cup of tea,' she said.

She had included Teko in the invitation but the Maori boy declined. 'Mistress be annoyed if I stay any longer,' he explained. 'I go now Missie. Good luck!' He held out a hand to Nellie but on impulse, she took him by the shoulders and rubbed noses affectionately in the Maori fashion. Startled at first, the boy glowed with pleasure and immediately returned the compliment.

'Goodbye Teko, and thank you,' breathed Nellie, bidding farewell to her past life in this one final gesture.

When Alexander Beaton returned home from his afternoon's round of visits, he was surprised to find his wife already at home and came in ready to remonstrate with her for not waiting for him at the Fergusson house.

'You know Teri, I have told you before that you must not walk so far in this heat. It is not good for you or the baby!' He paused on seeing that his wife had a visitor.

'Why, upon my soul, if it isn't Miss Parker, from off the Albatross' He stepped further into the room to take her hand. He had been surprised not to have come across Ellie Parker on his infrequent visits to the Fergusson household and had often wondered if she had indeed been employed there at all. Mrs Fergusson being such an overbearing female, he had assumed that when her offspring were unwell she must automatically take charge.

'Miss Parker has lost her position because of your naughty son,' said Teri, weakly. 'She kindly gave me a ride home.'

'You didn't have to walk? That's something anyway. I would have had words with Fergusson had he allowed you to come home on foot all that distance.' He turned to Ellie. 'What's this about being dismissed, Miss Parker? How does Malcolm fit into the story?'

He glanced down at his grubby little son and ruffled his curly locks affectionately. 'What have you been up to old chap?'

The boy, quite fearless of his father's disapproval, grabbed a handful of trouser leg and stuck a grubby little thumb into his mouth.

'It is rather a complicated story,' said Ellie. 'Malcolm was encouraged to be naughty by the Fergusson children, but Mrs Fergusson would have none of it. She accused your boy of being a little savage and was very rude to Mrs Beaton so I let her have a piece of my mind!'

Alexander could quite imagine it.

'If she was rude to my wife, she will apologise for it,' he said, mildly. 'But to dismiss you for sticking up for the boy, that is unpardonable. Do you wish me to try and have you reinstated?'

'I don't think it would do any good,' Nellie told him,' and anyway, I do not wish to work there in future. She is an impossible employer. I should only lose my temper on some other occasion.'

'The Fergusson's carry a great deal of weight in the town. It may not be easy to find another position.' Alexander did not wish to be too pessimistic but he had a good idea how the remaining townspeople would view the matter. It had been a very public dismissal by all accounts.

At this moment, a little moan from Teri drew the doctor's attention away from Ellie's problems. He went to his wife asking anxiously, 'Are you well, Teri?'

His wife moaned gently and leaned forward rubbing her back.

'I don't know,' she said. 'Ever since this affair at the Fergusson's I have been feeling the baby might be coming.'

'Oh, no! We don't want it arriving too soon.'

Alexander was forced to smile when she said, 'even you can't do anything to stop it if it has made up its mind.'

'No, my dear, as you say. Let's get you into the bedroom and I will try to find out what is happening.'

He led his wife away and Nellie, collecting the cups from their tea, asked Malcolm to carry a plate of sweetmeats out into the scullery for her. There she handed him a cloth and said, 'Do you wipe the dishes for your Mummy sometimes?'

Wide-eyed, he shook his head, solemnly.

She washed a cup, took the cloth from him and wiped it.

'See, it is very simple.' She placed the cup carefully on the tray and repeated what she had done a second time. Taking the third cup, she washed it and handed it to him with the cloth. He made a passable attempt at wiping it.

The pair were so engrossed in their simple task that they did not see Alexander standing in the doorway, until he spoke.

'The baby is going to be born prematurely. Might I ask you to keep an eye on Malcolm for a while. I am going to be rather busy.'

'That's not good, is it? For it to come too soon, I mean.' Nellie could see he was worried.

'There could be complications.'

'Don't worry about the boy. Malcolm and I will get on just fine. Is there anything else I can be doing?'

'Just keep that very large kettle on the boil for me. Otherwise there is nothing I can think of.'

'Have you eaten today?' she asked him, knowing he would not think of such a thing for himself.

'No, but don't worry about me. Malcolm will be looking for his supper about six o'clock.'

'I will do something for you both. Your wife said I might have a bed for the night. Perhaps it would be best if I stayed with Malcolm in his room, as she suggested?'

'Oh? Yes… please do. Make yourself comfortable.'

Distracted, he moved off into his surgery to gather what instruments he might need, giving no further thought either to his son or their guest.

*

The baby was born in the early hours of the morning.

Malcolm Beaton slept through the entire event, waking next morning to discover that at some time in the night the stork had arrived with a baby brother in its beak and deposited it in his mother's lap, a place hitherto reserved for himself, alone. While he quite liked the little thing and quickly made a pet of it, he was rather disturbed at the amount of time his mother gave to it. Had it not been for Nellie Parker who entertained him and helped him take care of his mother and the baby, he might have been just a little jealous.

It had been a difficult birth, taking more out of Teri than on the previous occasion. Since it was so premature, the baby was small and there had been breathing difficulties at first. Had it not been for Nellie's presence at his side throughout that long night, Alexander might well have been forced to choose between the failing infant and his wife, who had lost a great deal of blood during the birth. As it was, Ellie gave every moment of her attention to the baby, rubbing his back gently as Alex had shown her, keeping the steam kettle on the boil in the little tent he rigged up to assist the child's breathing and feeding him with eye droppers filled with sugar water until he was strong enough to suckle at his mother's breast.

Alexander meanwhile was faced with the problem of staunching Teri's fearful haemorrhage. At his wits end, with Teri clearly slipping away under his hands, he heard her whisper, 'In my little chest, Alexander, Pohatu.

Her little chest was a constant source of disagreement for it was here that Teri stored her potions made from the wild plants of the fields and forests. Normally Alexander poured scorn upon her claims for their efficacy but so desperate was he now that he must try everything available to him. He went to the cupboard where her dresses hung and removed a small, delicately carved wooden chest. He placed it on the bed so that she could show him for herself what she wanted.

Feebly, she lifted her hand and indicated a small glass phial.

'Pohatu.'

'What do I do with it?' he asked.

She indicated that she must drink from the bottle. He held it to her lips and she swallowed a small portion of the fluid.

What would his father say, Alexander wondered, to see his son using Maori magic to cure a haemorrhage? He held the bottle for a moment to see if more were needed.

Feebly, she smiled at him and murmured, 'a little is good. Too much is poison.'

Silently, he returned the phial to the chest and closed the lid. As the night wore on and Alexander witnessed for himself Teri's miraculous improvement, he began to wonder if he might have been too ready to dismiss her other remedies. The sap of the wild turnip seemed a strange potion to have such a potent effect.

By daybreak, both utterly exhausted, Nellie and Alexander were at last able to relax before the fire which Nellie had somehow found time to rekindle during that long night. As they sat silently over steaming cups of tea, Alexander said suddenly.

'It was like fate, you being dismissed yesterday and turning up here just when you were needed most.'

Ellie did not choose to remind him that had there been no upset at the Fergusson's, Teri might not have gone into labour. She felt somehow responsible for everything and would never have forgiven herself had things turned out badly for the Beatons and their baby.

'Since you are presently without home or occupation,' Alex continued, 'I wonder, would you consider staying on here for a while until Teri is on her feet again? I can't pay you much, not anything in fact. The practice doesn't run to servant's wages I'm afraid, but you may have the run of the house, your board and accommodation. Live here as a friend.' Seeing her hesitate, he jumped in before she could refuse him.

'You would have your own room of course. Tobias Leny will be off on his travels this week, vacating the annexe which he used to occupy before he set up on his own. It's a nice little suite of rooms. I think you'll like it.'

Why should she refuse? This was exactly what she needed. She would have time to look around and see where and how she might make a living for herself without squandering all her savings.

'I would like that very much,' she replied.

Chapter Eighteen

'Malcolm! Malcolm! It is time to get ready for Mrs Mackie's!'

Teri walked out onto the veranda, her baby bouncing on her hip. She eased little Toby into a more comfortable position and made for the tall tree fern in the corner of the yard, searching the dense fronds for a sign of a small bare foot. She spotted her elder son and caught hold of his leg with one hand.

'Come down from there at once,' she cried. 'You must get washed. We shall be late!'

'Nellie said I needn't go,' wailed the boy as, with an unrelenting tug, his mother dislodged him from his perch and forced him down to ground level.

'It is not for Nellie to say,' replied his mother, sharply, 'I decide where you go and who you play with. Your Papa would be very cross if he knew you had ignored Mrs Mackie's invitation.'

'I don't like Joe Mackie. He's a big bully and he's stupid!' shouted Malcolm crossly. 'He can't even read yet!'

The blacksmith's youngest child, born exactly one year after the *Albatross* dropped anchor in the harbour at Port Chalmers, was older than Malcolm by only ten months. He was a giant of a child by comparison with the doctor's son. His broad shoulders and overly-long arms which in adult life would equip him admirably for his father's trade, gave the lad the appearance of a small gorilla. What he lacked in mental agility was compensated for by his phenomenal strength, a strength which would one day carry him into the world of championship caber tossing and all- in wrestling. It was understandable that Malcolm should find him somewhat overwhelming as a playmate.

From Teri's viewpoint, the Mackies were good friends of her husband

and to turn down any invitation to visit the blacksmith's homestead on the brae, was quite unthinkable. Mrs Mackie had been very kind to the doctor's young bride during the early months of her marriage. She had taught the Maori girl to cook in the traditional Scottish way, had revealed all the secrets of the white man's domestic arrangements and shown her how to knit and sew. She had helped her to dress herself in the European fashion and, when the time came, to prepare a suitable layette for her babies.

'We are going to visit the Mackies this afternoon and that is that!' she declared, forcefully.

Angry tears formed in Malcolm's eyes. He spotted Nellie Parker as she turned into the yard from the street, her shopping basket on her arm.

'Nellie, Nellie,' he cried , 'You promised I should not have to play with that awful Joe Mackie again. She says I must!'

He threw himself into Nellie's arms, causing her to loosten her grip on the basket. Eggs and potatoes flew in all directions and Nellie was obliged to disentangle herself from the boy's wiry limbs before she could stoop to retrieve them. Teri rushed forward to save the eggs but failing to do so, she turned on Nellie.

'Oh, how careless of you,' she shouted angrily. 'You would not waste money so readily if it were your own husband's hard won earnings you were spending!'

'You saw what happened,' Nellie replied curtly. 'It was an accident.'

Turning to the distraught child she said, 'Now then, Malcolm, what is your trouble?'

The boy sobbed out his story.

'I hate Joe Mackie he always plays such rough games. I am always the enemy and I get put in the dungeon and flogged and tied up… and things.' He wept. 'You promised I shouldn't have to go there again!'

'Your Mama wants you to go, so go you will,' said Nellie firmly. 'Perhaps Philip will allow you to go with him to see the mob. You know you like to do that.'

'And take the dogs? I love the dogs. Mamma, why can't I have a dog?'

'You know your father will not have a dog around the house, because of the patients,' said Nellie.

'There is nothing wrong with a dog,' Teri intervened. 'Always we have dogs at home. I shall ask your father if you may have a dog for Christmas.'

Satisfied that he had broken down the arguments of both protagonists, the little boy departed in triumph for the bathroom where he made the slightest improvement to his appearance before declaring himself ready to go to the Mackie's for Sunday luncheon.

Nellie Parker's presence in the Beaton household, intended to last one night, had extended to a stay of more than a year. Following the birth of the doctor's second son, Tobias. Teri, greatly weakened by her ordeal, took a long time to recover. For many months Nellie had kept house, cooked, tended the garden in which essential vegetables and herbs were planted and acted as teacher and surrogate mother to Malcolm.

Teri, left to concentrate on rearing her sickly second child, returned only slowly to a normal life. The bond which had been forged between herself and her first-born, broken by the arrival of his demanding sibling, seemed impossible to repair. Malcolm had grown accustomed to running to Nellie for comfort whenever things went wrong. He had learned to abide by her rules and as his mother regained her command over the household, any alterations she made in the routines which had been laid down by Nellie Parker, were deeply resented.

While the two women tried their utmost to work in harmony, Malcolm managed to create a wedge between them which slowly gnawed away at their friendship. They began to draw lines of demarcation around their self- allocated responsibilities and avoided contact with each other as much as possible.

If Alexander Beaton was aware of the friction developing in his household, he made no comment. His maxim had always been to let sleeping dogs lie. If the establishment ran smoothly and efficiently there was no reason to upset things. While Teri remained unfit to take the full weight of responsibility for a doctor's household upon her own shoulders, Nellie, who possessed certain attributes quite lacking in his Maori wife, made a most effective major domo.

Nellie could communicate well with the patients, taking messages and accurately delivering his instructions in his absence. Teri sometimes became confused with the language when relaying Alexander's orders and found it difficult to get white patients to accept the doctor's instructions from her lips. Nellie alone, was sensitive to those small signals in dealing with patients, which enabled her to distinguish between the true emergency and the panic of an inexperienced wife and mother and she was adept at smoothing the ruffled feathers of those dignitaries of the town who felt themselves slighted when the doctor considered that the needs of lesser mortals should take priority above their own.

The truth was that Alexander was entirely satisfied with his ménage a trois and saw no reason to alter things in any way. For the two women however, this morning's altercation was to prove the last straw. It was time for Nellie to move on.

*

One of the great pleasures for Nellie when visiting with the Mackies was her contact with young Philip Mackie whose drawing and painting had come on by leaps and bounds since he had been given a few commissions to produce line drawings and woodcuts illustrating articles in *The Witness,* Otago's main newspaper. Long hours spent alone in the hills, sometimes sleeping out under the stars for days on end, gave him every opportunity to record details of the plant and animal life around him and impressions of the huge landscapes confronting him on every side. These too were beginning to find a market in the homes of the province's wealthier residents. It could not be long now before the boy was making a full-time career of his talents.

Nellie studied Philip's most recent efforts with care.

'The colours are vibrant,' she suggested, 'perhaps a little too garish for the average taste. Still, it's up to you whether you paint for your own satisfaction or to sell your work for a living. The pictures which end up in art galleries after a painter is dead are not necessarily the ones which paid his rent!'

She studied the landscapes with a keen eye. Her years in the Wimborne's household had exposed her to fine paintings of every kind. When she had once expressed an interest in art, Sir Tristram himself had been at pains to inform her about the artists and their works displayed so liberally in his various establishments. A chance encounter with a portrait artist engaged to paint Sir Tristram and his spouse, had encouraged her to try her hand at drawing, herself. From this man, she had learnt a little about light and shade and the perspective which she found to be lacking in Philip's larger works.

'This is all too flat,' she decided, critically as she studied a watercolour sketch of the blacksmith's forge down in the town. 'Take this side of the building, for instance. You may know that there are so many posts and windows along it but when you look at the building from the front, you do not see half of them. Nor are they evenly spaced as you have shown them.'

With a few deft strokes, she transformed the flat, almost child- like drawing into a three dimensional representation of the building.

Philip gasped in delight.

'How did you know just what the angle of that roof should be?' he demanded, immediately absorbed by her demonstration.

She spoke at length about vanishing points and drew little sketches on the side of the paper to illustrate her lecture. Suddenly she stopped; appalled that she had been working over his painting.

'Oh, it's nothing,' said the boy, thrilled by all she had shown him. 'I would tear it up right away were I not so keen to keep your little sketches. I can't tell you how often I have tried unsuccessfully to make my drawings more real. Thank you, thank you!'

To her surprise and somewhat to her dismay, he grabbed her hand and kissed it. I shall treasure this piece of paper, always,' he told her.

Nellie envied Philip the opportunities presented to him during the past years, chances which had been denied to her, first because of her employment as a governess and then by her decision to take care of the doctor and his family until Teri was back on her feet. Even so, through the good offices of her last employer, Angus Fergusson, who true to his word had done all in his power to help her, she had managed to sell one or two of her landscapes under the assumed name of Isla McLean. It gave both the surveyor and Nellie herself, some considerable satisfaction to know that the magnificent picture of the sun setting behind the western hills of Otago which was so admired by visitors to the Fergusson homestead, had been painted by none other than that despised and vilified Miss Nellie Parker, Mrs Fergusson's ex-governess. It amused Nellie to know that Mr Fergusson had spent no less than fifteen guineas on this gift for his wife; fifteen guineas which had gone to swell her meagre savings and were about to set her on the road to independence.

*

'I wondered if perhaps you could spare a piece of ground on the edge of your run for a modest house and a wee bit of garden.'

On the pretext of wishing to see what progress had been made with the farm, Nellie had managed to persuade William Mackie to take a little stroll with her following the luncheon party.

'I would not want more than just enough ground to grow a few vegetables, with a place to sit out when the weather is fine.'

William considered her request kindly. He had always liked the young woman whom fate had treated so cruelly by taking away her livelihood before she had ever set foot on New Zealand soil. Undaunted, she had carved a niche for herself in society and despite setbacks, was now able to discuss terms for buying a place of her own. He admired such enterprise and was happy to help her now.

'I could sell you an acre of pasture down in the hollow beyond the home run,' he said, pointing along the valley in the direction in which they were walking. 'There's a stream running alongside, which would provide your water and it's within reasonable distance of the main track into town.'

'That sounds ideal,' she agreed but she knew that it would cost a considerable amount to have a house built, even if she were to help with the work herself. His answer to her next question was all important.

'How much would you charge for the one acre?' she asked.

'I'm inclined to give it to you,' he replied but then, seeing the expression of doubt which flashed across her brow, he added hastily, 'however in matters of land, it is best to make one's transactions legally binding. Forty shillings an acre was what we paid in the first place, but that was an average price which included a prime quarter acre plot in Dunedin and a ten-acre section on the outskirts of town. Shall we say one pound per acre of pasture land and if you will help Alice in the dairy two hours a day until the work is complete, I and my boys will build a fine shack for you to live in.'

'That's a very generous offer.'

Nellie, overwhelmed by his kindness, was at a loss to show her true appreciation. 'I will be happy to work for Mrs Mackie, of course, as many hours as she wants. As to the materials for building, I have sufficient saved for the essentials and can make my own mud bricks if you think their use appropriate.'

'Tell me what you want in your house and I will draw up a plan. Then we can see what materials we can find to hand and what must be purchased.'

They had wandered well away from the house for their business talk. Down in the valley, beside the stream which was to form the boundary of Nellie's newly acquired property they heard the sound of children's voices mixed with the uncertain, somewhat deeper tones of an adolescent.

Billy Mackie was now fully recovered from the diphtheria which had laid him low four years earlier. He had grown into a fine lad who had taken to his apprenticeship in the smithy as to the manner born, occupying the post which his older, less physically robust brother, Philip, had left unfilled. This afternoon, with the two youngsters in tow, he was engaged in constructing a dam to create a pool in which the cockabullas, a trout-like river fish, might gather for easy netting. Occupied as they were in this enthralling enterprise, the two younger boys worked together contentedly under Billy's instruction. Malcolm Beaton was relieved to find that Joe Mackie had chosen to use his phenomenal strength for the work in hand rather than for tormenting his younger guest. As the work progressed, Malcolm was pleased to be able to contribute a little knowledge of his own.

The construction consisted of a row of large stones set across the stream to form an underwater barrier. Against this, Billy had constructed a wattle fence but still the water was only partially prevented from passing.

'We need a second hurdle,' said Malcolm confidently, 'and between the two, we should put rubble. That is the way the Romans worked. To make it a secure barrier, the outer leaves should be of stone but the wattle fences will serve as well for now.'

Billy considered the plan, saw it was good and immediately set about constructing a second hurdle.

'You two collect as many small sharp stones as you can,' he ordered. 'Round stones will leave too many gaps for the water to flow through.'

Malcolm and Joe soon had a huge pile of stones gathered ready to infill between the hurdles when they were completed. The barrier was now almost too effective for very quickly the pool rose to a height which threatened to engulf the surrounding land, encouraging the river to carve a new course for itself.

'What we need is a sluice to control the flow,' Malcolm suggested.

The other boys looked at him with puzzled expressions.

'What's a sluice?' demanded Joe.

'A shutter that can be lifted up and down to let some of the water out if you want.'

'But we've just done all this work to keep the water back!' protested the younger Mackie. With a friendly, if over enthusiastic shove, he tripped Malcolm into the pool.

'The kid's right,' said Billy as he stretched out a hand and hauled Malcolm from the water. 'We have to control the flow so that the pool doesn't overflow the banks. Come on Malc' show us what you have in mind.'

He handed Malcolm a pointed stick and indicated the sandy patch on which they were standing. Malcolm knelt in his soggy breeches and drew out a crude sketch of a simple sluice gate.

'We can position it to one side of the dam and make a platform from which to stand and operate it,' he suggested.

Joe looked scornful still, but Billy nodded, seeing in his mind's eye how the thing could work.

'I'll have to make it down in the workshop,' he decided at last. 'It won't be done before next Sunday.'

'We'll need to leave a passage for the water meanwhile,' warned Malcolm. 'Otherwise the barrier will be carried away by the force of water building up.'

*

Once Nellie had made up her mind to leave the Beatons, the atmosphere between the two women improved. Teri helped Nellie to draw up lists of household requirements, cooking pots, plates, cups, cutlery, in which the Maori girl now considered herself something of an authority, together with bedding and other furnishings. Nellie had come to New Zealand expecting such items to be all found. It was an exciting time for her, building up a stock of household supplies for the very first time.

On the day of Nellie's departure to take up temporary residence in a tent close to the foundations of her new house, Teri insisted upon rising before dawn to help her load the hired bullock cart with her personal possessions. When all was ready, a little shamefacedly, Teri put out her hand. 'Thank you,' she said, shyly.

Nellie stepped closer and enfolded the other woman in her arms. 'Don't think I haven't understood how you felt, you being so weak and me taking over your household. I want you to know that I never meant to replace you in Malcolm's eyes.'

'We could not have managed without you this past year,' Teri assured her. 'I know I have not been an easy person to live with.'

Nellie made to protest but the doctor's wife shook her head. From a corner of the veranda she withdrew a roll of matting. 'I have made a mat for your new house,' she said. 'It is tradition.'

They rolled it out across the veranda. Woven from fine toetoe grasses and elaborately patterned in bright colours using the natural dyes gathered in the countryside, it was a work of art.

'I shall treasure this always,' Nellie told her, re-rolling the mat and handing it up to the driver. She climbed up alongside him.

'I wish you would wait until Alexander comes back,' Teri implored. 'He was called out late for a confinement. He should be back very soon.'

'I have hired the cart by the hour,' Nellie explained. 'I can't afford to keep it any longer than absolutely necessary. Goodbye Teri, you must come and visit me as soon as the house is built. Bring the children!'

As the cart pulled away, there was a shout from around the corner of the house and Malcolm tore into view. He chased the cart along the street calling for her to stop. When the driver at last drew the wagon to a halt and the little boy caught up with them, he was gasping for breath and tears were streaming down his face.

'Where are you going?' he demanded.

'You know where I am going,' she replied patiently. Although she had explained carefully, her need to find a home of her own, they had argued frequently about her departure. Malcolm had refused to accept that talk of her going was anything other than a threat to keep him in order. Now he could see that she had meant every word, he was full of remorse.

'It's my fault you are deserting us,' he cried out. 'Please don't go. I will be good, I promise.'

Nellie climbed down from the cart and held the child to her bosom.

'Malcolm,' she said gently, cradling him in her arms, 'my going has nothing to do with you. It is simply that it is the time for me to move on. You will find as you grow older that life is made up of episodes such as this. While they are happening, it seems that things must stay the same way for ever, but always a time comes for change and when it arrives, it is best to make a clean break. It is not as though we shall never see one another again. You will come and visit me often but for the time being, you must help you mother take care of little Toby, and not be a trial to her. Promise me?'

Solemnly the boy nodded his head.

'Say goodbye to the doctor for me.'

She remounted the wagon and bade the driver move off.

*

Tobias Leny had shared the doctor's house on Cumberland Avenue until the diphtheria epidemic took his partner away into the bush only to return some weeks later, with his Maori bride. Even after that, there had been room enough in the building for him to remain for so long as he wished, but understanding the newlywed's need for privacy he determined to find separate accommodation for himself as soon as possible.

Alexander, wishing to see his partner properly settled in a situation which would make him entirely independent, determined to find a way to help his friend.

Of the three sections of land allocated to the doctor by the New Zealand Company as part of his payment for services during the voyage out, only the quarter acre plot in the town centre had so far been developed to any degree.

The fifty-acre grazing run outside town alongside the track to Mapourika, Alexander wished to retain. Later, he hoped to build a country house there for his family but for the present he was content to graze a few sheep and cattle on the coarse pasture, employing a pair of Maori lads from Teri's village to keep an eye on the beasts.

The third allocation made to Alexander was ten acres of land in the suburbs for which he had no plans at present. This property he transferred to Toby for a peppercorn rent, on the understanding that it would revert to the doctor's family on Toby's departure from the district or in the event of his death.

On his rented plot of land Tobias wasted no time in getting to work. To the puzzlement of his neighbours, he first built a long shed with a cookhouse at one end and an ablution block a little way off, close by the stream which ran through the property. Inside this building, against the walls he constructed a series of bunks like those used on board the emigrant ships. Down the centre of the hut he installed a long refectory table and stools sufficient to seat twenty men. The barrack-like building caused his mates in the bar of the Wharf Hotel much amusement. They accused him of starting some new religious sect or low class whore house and even suggested he planned to raise a private army. Despite all their taunting and teasing, Toby kept mum. He was not about to divulge his splendid idea to anyone until he had matters all signed and sealed.

Before putting his plan into action, he completed his constructions by building for his own use a small shack consisting of two rooms and a bathroom, with a wide veranda out front and a cookhouse at the rear.

When all was ready, Toby vacated his accommodation in the doctor's house, moved his belongings into the shack and made an appointment to see Captain Cargill and the Reverend Thomas Burns at the town's civic offices.

The two men kept Leny waiting in an antechamber for some minutes while they discussed the proceedings of the council meeting of the previous evening.

The growing developments in the settlement meant that there was an increasing need for labourers to quarry stone, dig drains, clear the undergrowth and lay down properly metalled roadways for easier access into the interior. The settlers themselves, many of them having been professional and business people in the Old Country, found this kind of work hard and while they were willing enough to labour at building shelters for themselves and their livestock, they were less inclined to engage in public works for the good of all. Once a church and gaol had been completed, other similar public enterprises hung fire for a very long time.

'What we need is the kind of labourers used in the American sugar plantations,' one of the councillors had suggested.

'If not slaves, then we must get people who will work for little or nothing. We can't afford a huge wage bill!' added another.

'What's wrong with using the Maori, or people from the islands off the north coast?'

'The Polynesians should be a source of labour,' Captain Cargill had intervened at this point, 'but they would require a deal of training and it is not in their nature to do heavy labouring work. In my experience of travelling to the Eastern countries, the Indians and Malays are hard working people and their economy is such that you could probably afford the wages they will demand.'

'That's all very well,' said William Mackie, now one of the town's leading businessmen, 'but who is to go abroad to recruit such workers? It will cost money for their passage by sea and who is to house them when they arrive?'

On this practical note of caution the meeting had ended, but after a long night when neither Thomas Burns nor Captain Cargill had slept for thinking about it, the two men were no nearer finding a solution to the problem.

Considering that they had exhausted all possible avenues, 'Best see what this fellow Leny, wants,' said Cargill. 'Do you know him?'

'Only through the doctor, they have some kind of partnership arrangement so far as I can see. Odd combination of interests I suppose, but adversity makes strange bedfellows of us all!'

Cargill raised his eyebrows at this innocent remark of the reverend. He knew the doctor had recently married a Maori girl so presumably there was nothing unwholesome about the pair.

'Mr Leny, do come in and join us.' Cargill held the door wide to allow Leny to enter before him.

The Civic Hall was simply constructed of timber framing with the usual corrugated iron roofing much favoured for larger buildings. Nevertheless, the committee room had been equipped lavishly with solid mahogany furniture, brought from home. The floor of polished pine, was partly covered by a fine Persian carpet whose rich jewel-like colours gave the room a warm and comfortable appearance. But for the small windows and the matchboard lining to the walls, the room might have been located in any sizeable town in Scotland.

'Now then Mr Leny, what can we do for you?' Cargill demanded.

'It is more a question of what I can do for you, Sir.' Toby replied. He sat back comfortably in the chair they had provided and glanced at the two men over the top of his spectacles.

'The greatest problem facing the province at this moment is lack of labour, is that not so?' Toby's glance darted from one face to the other.

Startled that this stranger should have hit immediately upon the very matter which had been exercising the Council for so long, Cargill wondered if someone had leaked the subject of last evening's discussion. This man's planning was longer term than that however, as they were very soon to realise.

'I can solve the problem for you,' said Leny decisively, 'but it will take a small investment on the part of the citizens of Dunedin, to do so.'

Cargill leaned forward eagerly. 'If you have any suggestions, Man, let us have them. We'll talk about the cost, later.'

'Chinamen,' said Tobias.

'I beg your pardon?' The enquiry was from Thomas Burns.

'They are great workers' Toby continued as though there had been no interruption, 'I've seen them for myself, working in the docks of Glasgow and London. They have strong family ties and will travel anywhere in the world to make money which they can send home to their people.'

'I'm sure that what you say is true,' said Cargill, 'but saying is one thing, getting them here to work for us is quite another.'

'That is where I can help,' said Tobias confidently. 'I am prepared to sail to China, recruit your workers and bring them back. Mind you, this will cost money. There will be passage money for the men, some small retaining fee on their signing a contract for, say three years, and once arrived, they must be fed and housed, equipped and transported around the province as and when they are required. In due course the enterprise will pay for itself. Men can be hired out to individuals by the hour or they can be employed directly by the town council from the communal fund. The money earned in hiring fees will go towards maintaining the Chinese and will pay their wages. In due course, it should be possible to recover the original stake which you will be lending me to get the project started!'

'Hold hard,' protested Cargill. 'I don't wish to suggest that you are anything other than an entirely honest man Mr Leny, but we cannot put substantial funds belonging to the people of the province, into the hands of a stranger. What guarantee do we have that you will not simply take the stake money and run?'

'My own investment in the enterprise is your guarantee, gentlemen,' Toby insisted. 'At my own expense, I have already constructed substantial accommodation to house these Oriental labourers.'

'You were taking a considerable risk, Mr Leny. Suppose we were to turn down your request for investment?'

'Then I would look elsewhere for finance,' said Toby confidently. 'Any long-sighted businessman must see the value of my plan. The colony cannot progress without manpower. Every individual in the land will at one time or another need to hire labour. What more sure-fire enterprise could there be than this? I have come to you first, because I wish to benefit the settlers themselves rather than some obscure outsider who would soon be coining money at the province's expense.'

While William Cargill was clearly interested in Toby's proposal, Thomas Burns seemed hesitant in giving his consent to the plan.

'Slavery is against the law, Mr Leny,' he pointed out. 'I want no stain upon our settlement in that respect. These recruits must come willingly, for fair payment, their rights protected by a contract of employment for a fixed period. There is to be no suggestion either of a Press Gang or of slave labour in this country!'

Tobias Leny looked genuinely shocked at the reverend's suggestion.

'It is my intention to have the transactions made legal and above board, Sir,' he replied, with an injured expression.

Cargill, fearing that Leny's offer might be withdrawn, quickly intervened.

'I have no doubt that Mr Leny's intentions are entirely honourable, Thomas. Since our investment will be the major share, we will have control over what is done.'

Toby's response to this was guarded.

'May I suggest that if your committee is willing to join me in this enterprise, we have lawyers draw up an agreement assessing the total investment of both parties and their subsequent shares in the business?'

Confident that Leny's investment would be less than their own, the two representatives of the provincial committee were happy to agree. The three men shook hands on the matter and Tobias Leny departed in search of the best lawyer in town. He was determined to retain the greater share in the enterprise even if he had to go personally to every small businessman in the district for support.

Chapter Nineteen

Within a few months, Tobias Leny returned from China with his first contingent of labourers. In accordance with his plan he had set up an agency in Shanghai which recruited Chinese labourers for a set period of three years and guaranteed a small retaining fee to be paid to the families left behind in China.

In return for their services, the men were to receive free board and lodging and a daily wage to be agreed dependant upon the nature of the work required. Their passage money to and from New Zealand would be paid by Leny's company, the Otago Employment Agency.

In addition to his group of vigorous, powerful young workers, Toby had brought along a husband and wife team to oversee the accommodation block and cook for the men. After a brief period of acclimatisation, he had all twenty five of his employees scattered amongst the outlying farmsteads, at the timber mill in the forest on the edge of town and in the stone quarries which were continuously under pressure to provide materials for building roads, bridges and an increasing number of more prestigious offices and dwelling houses.

A second contingent arrived unescorted, a few weeks later and subsequently a steady flow of immigrant workers from China took up the tasks considered too heavy or too onerous for their European counterparts.

Wisely Tobias had insisted upon retaining a controlling interest in this enterprise. While the committees of the council urged caution, he went ahead with building a second accommodation block, thereby increasing his own stake in the company and his share of the profits. Soon he was making money for his independent investors while the town council, obliged to pay for the labour it used for public works, also took its share of the profits. Toby built a third accommodation block and increased each new intake by fifty percent.

Wei Lun and his wife ran the hostel efficiently and to the apparent satisfaction of its inmates. In matters of routine, Tobias left them to get on with the job, he himself becoming more and more involved in the actual exercises for which he had initially imported the labour. He invested his gains in schemes concerning roads, ferries and coastal transport bringing in the first of the steamers to ply up and down the eastern seaboard, linking the major towns of the South Island with the seat of government in Wellington. Tobias Leny was fast becoming a figure of influence in the Province.

Like his employer, Wei Lun was quick to seize upon any situation which would turn a profit. Soon he had persuaded Toby to recruit a couple of additional women to help his wife with the hostel, leaving him to pursue his own schemes.

As settlers moved further and further inland, carving their livelihood from the unknown wilderness, Wei Lun recognised the need to keep them supplied with those commodities for which substitutes could not be found in the bush. He persuaded Tobias to invest in a travelling shop. This was a closed- in cart fitted out with shelving and cupboards suitable for carrying everything from a packet of sewing needles to a can of fuel oil. His wagon, colourfully decorated with red and yellow dragons and pulled by a pair of mules, became a familiar sight on the less frequented roads of the province. His regular appearances were the cause of great celebration at those outlying homesteads where neighbours lived as much as forty miles apart and news was hard to come by.

Not only did Wei Lun carry goods for sale, he brought with him packages from home, deliveries from ships or from the larger stores in town. Occasionally he would give a lift to a traveller along the road. For these services, he charged a small amount, nothing extortionate but sufficient, together with the small profit he made on every item of stock he sold, to begin to amass a substantial balance at the Bank of Otago.

His other increasingly profitable enterprise concerned the immigrant workers, themselves. The Chinese being inveterate gamblers, large sums of hard-earned cash were soon being won and lost at dice and card games in the work camps and the hostel, at local wrestling matches and at the horse races which had become a popular pastime in settlements throughout Otago. Every pay day saw its winners and its losers; those whose wives were expecting a regular supply of cash and would be wanting know, if it did not materialise, why. It was when they found themselves in a temporary predicament of this nature, that the men turned to Wei Lun for help.

For every small loan made, he charged ten percent interest. Two shillings in the pound does not amount to much until the debt, being left unpaid and the interest being at compound rates, a few shillings becomes many pounds and the amount owing becomes a burden never to be lifted.

To all appearances, Wei Lun remained the simple peasant who had arrived from China with nothing but the clothes he stood up in and a jar containing the ashes of his most revered ancestor. There was little about this wrinkled, slightly built and rather bent little figure to suggest that he would some day become one of the richest men in town.

*

The tall young man, broad shouldered, with the confident swing and steady gait of one accustomed to life in the open, climbed the brae with ease and stopped for a moment on the level track to look back upon the route he had been following, all morning.

From this vantage point he could see the whole town of Dunedin laid out before him. The main streets, although not yet metalled, were bordered by substantial buildings. Each quarter acre plot had been fenced and developed for housing or for one of the many thriving enterprises which had developed as the population grew and its demands increased. There was still much to do before it could begin to resemble the architect's completed plans but there was constant activity and an air of purpose about the place. Dunedin was certainly a town on the move.

They had suggested to him on the ship that he should enquire in town for a local carrier who might be setting out in the right direction as the chances of his picking up a lift along the road were very slim. If he travelled light however, he should cover the distance on foot in no more than a day or two.

He had left the major part of his luggage at the hotel to be called for later. Only his immediate requirements had been packed into the canvas sack which he carried on his back. He had only a change of clothing, a loaf of bread, brought with him from the ship and the tools of his trade which were a small pick hammer, a powerful lens and a wooden box containing an assortment of chemicals.

Over to the left of the harbour where a narrow inlet was shielded from the main settlement by a sharply contoured hill, he could see a flurry of activity aboard the vessel from which he had so recently departed. Clearly the *Nelson* was already preparing for sea. With a wave of farewell he turned and started down the further slope.

It was then he caught sight of a little house tucked down in the valley, sheltered by a spinney of trees looking for all the world like the willows and birches of home. After the searing heat of the African bush, the tranquil scene appeared so familiar that for a moment he imagined himself to be in Argyll. Only the tall cabbage trees, the extraordinary tree ferns and the little flightless birds, which scurried out of his path as he advanced towards the house, reminded him that he was in yet another alien land.

From above the trees a plume of white smoke rose steadily in the still air. Someone must be at home. Hoping he might be able to purchase a midday meal and perhaps a few additional provisions for his journey, he heaved his bulging haversack higher on his shoulders and sauntered along the path which led downwards from the road.

Nellie Parker wiped her brush clean on the turpentine- soaked rag at her waist and stepped back from her easel to regard her work with a critical eye. Lifting her hands in front of her face to form a frame around her view across the valley, she checked what she could see against her own representation on the canvas. Should she bring that group of bushes forward to make a little interest in an otherwise featureless foreground she pondered? With deft strokes, she made the changes. Now the foreground appeared to leap out of the picture while the hills behind faded satisfactorily into the distance.

The set of cow bells she kept hanging on the porch in place of a door knocker began to ring tentatively at first, the gentle sounds creating music in harmony with her peaceful surroundings. Then, as though the caller having tested the effect had found it wanting, they were struck more loudly, urgently. With an unladylike expression of annoyance at the disturbance, Nellie went to see who was calling.

She showed little surprise in finding a stranger at her door for the time had long gone when she could claim to know every face in Dunedin. Each ship arriving in the harbour brought with it families emigrating from the old country and single men who, for the most part, were intent upon discovering the gold which everyone believed to exist but which had so far proved to be so elusive.

Despite his heavy workman's boots, his coarse tweed breeches and rough flannel shirt, her visitor did not appear to be one of the usual run of prospectors. His voice, although certainly Scottish, possessed the more refined accents of the professional men she knew, not the broader, common speech of William Mackie and his friends.

'Good morning, Ma'am,' he doffed his cap politely, 'I wonder if you could oblige me with a bite to eat and perhaps a cup of tea? I'm afraid I wandered out along the road ill prepared, hoping to find a farm or perhaps a store where I might purchase some provisions.'

'Did they not tell you in town, there is no settlement along this road for another twenty miles?'

She could not disguise her astonishment that anyone should travel abroad so unprepared to fend for himself.

'I never went in to Dunedin,' he explained. 'Having been put ashore at Port Chalmers, I asked at once for the road to Mapourika. I was assured that it would be possible to acquire provisions along the way.'

'Tea, I will happily provide,' she told him. 'It is time I stopped working anyway. As for provisions to take along the road with you, Mrs Mackie at the farm may be able to help. I will just put on the kettle and if you would care to refresh yourself with a dip in the pool,' she indicated the stream which had been dammed to provide a substantial pond, 'I will send to the farm to see what can be done.'

'Oh, please, that is asking too much. Can I not call at the farm myself?'

'It will take you far out of your way.'

She picked up a little stick and rattled the cow bells. Their melodious summons echoed across the valley to where, on a higher piece of ground, Philip Mackie and his dog were cutting out new season's lambs for market.

Normally Nellie would not have interrupted his work, but William

Mackie had insisted that she should feel free to call Philip to her aid should she receive unwanted visitors. It was not that she feared the newcomer, but it was near enough time for the boy's midday meal and it was a natural precaution to take to let the stranger know that she was not entirely alone.

On hearing her summons, Philip closed the temporary pen in which he had trapped the stock already singled out and leaving the dog to keep watch, he picked up his satchel and set off down the slope at a steady trot. He was within a hundred yards of the house before he caught sight of an unfamiliar figure splashing in the pool. By the time he came up with him the stranger was out of the water and shaking himself dry.

'That's a pleasant change from the salt water douches aboard ship, the fellow said, using his discarded shirt as a towel to rub at his fair, curly hair.

'The name's Bantrie, Ian Bantrie,' he called and seeing Philip's distrustful scowl, 'the lady of the house has invited me to luncheon. I do hope you don't mind.'

'Would you be related to the minister?' Nellie asked, overhearing his introduction as she returned to the veranda.

'The reverend James Bantrie is my father Ma'am,' Ian informed her. 'Do you know him?'

'We travelled with him and his family, aboard the *Albatross*.' said Philip.

'When we landed, they went straight to Mapourika. I haven't seen them in years,' Nellie told him.

'I meet Charlie Bantrie from time to time, when he comes out to the farm' said Philip, 'but the Reverend seldom comes into town.'

Nellie ushered the two men inside, poured tea from a large brown pot and gave each of them a platter of cheese and ham. Ian, who had been on the road since early morning, ate ravenously. Generously, Nellie plied him with more of her delicious home baked bread and offered pickles.

'Do you think your mother would supply Mr Bantrie with cheese and eggs and perhaps a bag of tea to take along with him?' Nellie asked Philip. She smiled across at Ian as she spoke. 'We can't allow a newcomer to our country to venture into the bush without food to sustain him.'

Philip glanced quickly from one to the other of his companions and sensed something which raised in him an anger he could not explain.

'I have the sheep to attend to,' he complained.

'Oh, look here. I don't want to be a trouble to anyone,' Ian protested.

'It's really no trouble,' said Nellie smoothly. 'Philip would have been going over to the farm on an errand for me, anyway,' she added pointedly.

Philip scowled and would have made some further excuse not to leave her alone with the fellow had they not at that moment, heard the sound of a horse and cart on the road and the familiar call of the travelling salesman.

'Why, what a stroke of good fortune,' exclaimed Nellie. 'It's Wei Lun. He will be able to sell you what you need, Mr Bantrie. He may even give you a ride for part of the way.'

She ran outside, leaving the two young men glaring at one another across the table.

'You'll be the mining engineer Miss Catherine was forever boasting about,' Philip said, still rather surly. Even though it would not after all be necessary for him to go to the farm, the resentment was still there. 'By the way she spoke I thought you would have been here long before this.'

'I have been in the gold fields in the Rand,' Ian explained.

'They say there is a fortune to be made in South Africa,' said Philip, wishing with all his heart that Ian Bantrie had remained where he was. He had seen the way Nellie looked at the newcomer and he did not like it.

'If that is the case, I was not one of those chosen for the honour,' Ian laughed, but his laughter had a hollow ring. 'It is a hard way to make a living and those who get rich are rarely the ones who do the work. Those who supply the miners, handle the claims and provide the entertainment, these are the people who reap most of the benefits of a gold field.'

'You would not recommend that I should go there?' Philip asked. He had wondered often of late if it would not be the way to make a fortune quickly, so that he might concentrate for the rest of his life on his drawings. It was hard to combine being an artist with tending his father's stock but in his present circumstances he saw no way of ever gaining his independence.

'Why not try your hand at prospecting right here?' asked Ian. 'There were plenty of people on board ship, convinced that gold is to be found in Otago.'

'I have lived here for seven years and I've seen many a prospector pass along the road to the north and west but I have yet to meet a millionaire coming in the opposite direction.'

They both laughed and the tension between them lifted. Philip related some of the adventures he had had with Ian's young brother Charles, aboard ship, 'When,' Philip insisted, 'I was just a youngster.'

Ian regarded the younger man with some amusement. At first glance he appeared to be no more than sixteen or seventeen years and to hear him speaking so sagely of his youth seemed quite incongruous. Philip had celebrated his twenty first birthday at the turn of year but despite having recovered completely from the tuberculosis which had blighted his childhood, his complexion remained pale and his physique was slight. He had an ethereal quality about him. He might be a poet perhaps or a musician. Anything less like a prospector it would be difficult to find.

'I had thought of going to the gold fields just to record the scenes there for the newspapers. I'm an artist you see. I sometimes have my work published in the Otago Press.'

That Ian Bantrie could envisage.

'How did you learn to draw out here in the wilderness?' he asked, intrigued.

'I have always been able to use a pencil,' said Philip, 'but it was Miss Parker who taught me to draw properly whilst we were on the ship. She is a fine artist. Her pictures hang in many of the better houses in the province.'

'Miss Parker?'

'Eleanor Parker, your hostess.'

So, that was her name. In all the to-ing and froing she had not found time to introduce herself. So, she was an artist. How Ian would have liked to see examples of her work. His gaze took in the various ornaments and decorations which made this cosy little house into a home belonging exclusively to the charming lady who had treated him so kindly.

'Did she paint that?' he asked, indicating a picture hanging above the mantelshelf. It was a scene depicting a farm yard with cattle, sheep and hens so lifelike he thought they might fly off the wall at any moment.

Philip nodded. 'It's not her best work,' he assured Ian, 'but how I would love to be able to paint so well.'

Ian, whose ability with a pencil stopped short at geometric and technical drawings could not but agree. Her brushwork was exquisite and her colours clear and vibrant. He studied the painting and noting the signature, questioned Philip again.

'Isla McLean is her professional name. She does not exhibit as Nellie Parker. The Scottish name appeals more to the local people and preserves her anonymity.'

At that moment, Nellie returned carrying an assortment of pots and packages. These she dumped unceremoniously on the kitchen table and said, 'You'd best hurry, Mr Bantrie. Wei Lun will take you as far as the fork to Patearoa which is well on your way. He carries stocks of tea, sugar, and bacon so you will not go hungry.'

Ian rose to go then hesitated.

'What do I owe you for the meal, Miss Parker?'

'Nothing,' she replied, surprised that he had used her name which she had purposely concealed. 'It would be a sorry place if one could not offer hospitality to a friend.'

Pleased that she should regard him thus, he was nevertheless embarrassed by her generosity.

'I asked for food and drink, fully expecting to pay,' he insisted. 'It is not as though I had come by invitation.'

'Nevertheless,' she ushered him out of the door. 'I have no doubt Mrs Bantrie would offer me the same.'

'I shall tell her we met.'

He caught her regarding him quizzically. There was a spark of something there. What was it, amusement perhaps? Was she simply making fun of him? There was interest certainly and warmth; some feeling maybe, with which she reciprocated his own overpowering emotions.

Taking her hand gently, he bade her farewell and with a cheerful wave to Philip who had watched these last moments with growing dismay, he went out into the noonday sunshine to meet the Chinese carrier.

They had been travelling for an hour or more, the older man quizzing Ian concerning those items a gold prospector might require once he had staked his claim. The Chinese had clearly decided to be in the forefront of those supplying the prospector's camps. Rounding a corner,, they came upon two fellow travellers contemplating a billycan which was already bubbling away over a fire. One of the men got to his feet and waved the travelling shop to a halt.

'Good day,' said the Chinese in his sing song voice. 'Is there something I can do for you gentlemen?'

'Indeed, there is,' said he who had stopped the cart. 'We need sugar, tea, bacon, wheat flour for dampers…' he continued to reel of the list of items so rapidly that Ian wondered if the men had been waiting here for the shop to appear. As Wei Lun shuffled around in the back of the wagon, Ian got down to stretch his legs and approached the second man who had remained to tend the fire.

'Going far?' he asked.

'Into the mountains, 'the other replied, indicating a vaguely westerly direction.

'Prospecting?'

The other nodded. 'And you?'

'I'm just hitching a ride along the road towards Mapourika. My folks live there.'

'I thought I might stop in Mapourika myself and explore the countryside around,' said the man. 'They tell me there is an excellent accommodation house in the township.'

'I'm afraid I know no more of it than my sister has told me in her letters. Until recently it was a Maori village, nothing more. I believe it is quite a sizeable place now.'

Suddenly they heard raised voices from inside the cart and thinking his friend Wei Lun might be in trouble, Ian strode across to see what was going on.

'Twelve shillings for a few measly groceries, that's extortion, nothing less!' The stranger shouted at the old man.

'But Sir, all goods must be purchased in town where prices are set by the city council. My mules must be fed and my cart kept in good order. I must add a little extra to my prices to pay for this.'

The disagreeable fellow would have none of it. Throwing down a handful of coins in the dust he gathered up his purchases and carried them across to the fire. 'There's ten shillings and sixpence there,' he called over his shoulder. 'Take it or leave it!'

The Chinese bent to retrieve the money and Ian Bantrie went to his aid. Together they collected the scattered coins which amounted to ten and sixpence as the man had said. Ian crossed to the roadside fire.

'You owe the shopkeeper one shilling and sixpence,' he said, quietly. 'Pay up like a good fellow or hand back items to the amount owing.'

'What's it to do with you?' demanded the other belligerently.

'I like to see justice done,' said Ian. 'This man has a living to make just like the rest of us. Pay what he asks.'

'Or?' demanded the other measuring up to the young Scot. He was a good three inches taller than Ian and although not of the younger man's broad stature, held himself as one who might know how to use his fists.

'Or this!' said Ian. With surprising strength, he caught the fellow by his shirt front and lifted him onto his toes before landing a solid punch to the jaw. Taken completely by surprise, the man staggered back, caught his heel on the edge of a flat rock and sat down hard in the roadway. As he struggled to regain his feet, Ian stood over him, hand outstretched. 'One and sixpence, I believe that was the amount.'

Still sitting, reluctantly the fellow reached into his trouser pocket and held out a handful of coins. Ian counted out the exact amount, handing back the remainder.

'There now, that didn't hurt a bit, did it?' He grinned as the fellow rubbed at his tender jaw. If looks could kill, Ian Bantrie would have been struck dead at that moment.

With a cheerful wave to the more amenable of the two travellers who had never moved away from the fire in all this time, Ian climbed up beside Wei Lun and handed him the additional money.

'You are a good man,' said the Chinese. 'You are Wei Lun's flend.' He whipped up the mules and the cart clattered on along the road. When Ian looked back he saw the two men were again crouched over their fire. Sensing Ian's gaze was still upon him his adversary lifted his closed fist and shook it in his direction. He may have made a friend of the Chinese, but he appeared to have acquired a troublesome enemy in the process.

After another hour or two, the road ahead forked. At the junction, Wei Lun reigned in the beasts and the cart came to a stop.

'You get down here,' he said. 'Mapourika is that way.' He pointed along the second track which was less well defined than that which they had been following. 'Maybe another cart will come along plitty quick. If not, three maybe four hours walk before Mapourika.'

Wei Lun got down from the cart and went into the back from where he emerged a few moments later with a bundle wrapped up in a towel. 'You camp before sundown,' he said. 'Here enough tucker for your dinner I think.'

Ian reached into his pocket. 'How much do I owe you?' he enquired.

'For the lide, thlee shilling. For the food, nothing. I will not charge my flend!'

Try as he might Ian could not get the Chinese to take more than was asked. With a further word of thanks, he stepped down from the cart and pulled his haversack after him. Opening the flap, he thrust the Chinaman's package inside and drew the sack across his shoulders.

'I visit Mapourika later,' called Wei Lun. 'We meet again!'

*

'Katy! Katy!' Tommy Dundas pushed through a group of Maori children who were jostling one another, laughing and shouting, enjoying their freedom now school was over for the day. Ignoring the calls of the lads from the European settlement beyond the village, he sped frantically along the river path and stumbled up the steep steps formed in the bank alongside the waterfall.

'Oh Tommy,' Catherine said, reprovingly, as he dropped down beside her. 'How often must I remind you to call me Miss Bantrie when my pupils are in earshot?'

'But you're my SISTER!' Tommy exclaimed impatiently. 'Everyone knows that. People would think it odd if I did not call you by your Christian name.'

'Step- sister,' she corrected him riffling his curly red hair in a way she knew irritated him.

'Anyway, what brings you tearing up here on such a hot afternoon?'

'These have just come by the mail,' he said, pulling a handful of letters from the canvas bag he carried over one shoulder. 'This one has a government stamp and is addressed to the minister, so Mr McMoran asked me to bring it straight up to the school.'

Before going inside to hand the important looking envelope over to James he dug once again into his satchel. 'Oh yes, these two are for you!' Thrusting the envelopes at her, he disappeared inside.

'At last!' she cried with delight, examining the larger of the two packages he gave her. She turned it over to read the heavily embossed legend, ***Royal College of Preceptors,*** together with an impressive coat of arms, both of which decorated the stuck down flap. Carefully she tore it open, extracting the stiff, parchment-like certificate contained within.

This is to certify that ***Catherine Mary Bantrie*** *has satisfied the examiners with distinction in English Composition; English Literature; Latin& Greek Languages. She is qualified to teach in public schools within any country of the British Empire.*

She scanned the page rapidly, overcome by the enormity of her success. Of her English, she had had high hopes, but distinctions in Latin and Greek – that was much better than she had hoped for.

A cursory glance told her that the second letter was from her brother, Ian. Much as she had looked forward to hearing from him, his letter must wait for the moment. Stuffing her brother's communication into the pocket of her pinafore, she took the veranda steps two at a time and burst into the schoolroom.

'It's come at last, Pa,' she exclaimed, placing the impressive document in front of her father.

James looked up from the letter he himself had been reading. She was dismayed to see that his face was white as a sheet. Without a word, he thrust the document at her, stood up and went to the door of the schoolroom. She watched him stand and stare up towards the distant mountains. Then she turned to his letter, the words dancing before her eyes as she began to read.

From the office of the Superintendent, Otago Province
To the Rev. James Bantrie
Mapourika Settlement

Dear Mr Bantrie,

I am pleased to report that during his last visit to Scotland, the agent for the Otago District was successful in recruiting one Edward Archibald Moodie to teach in one of our public schools. Your school, having been always without a registered schoolmaster, would seem to be in greatest need of this long-awaited addition to our list of qualified teachers.

Mr Moodie comes well recommended and will arrive at Port Chalmers aboard the SV Nelson within the next two weeks. I know you will make him welcome and help him to overcome the exigencies of his first days in our country.

I am, Sir, your most respected and obedient servant,

Wilbur J Armitage, for the Superintendent

When the Bantries arrived in Mapourika seven years earlier, it quickly became a tiny Christian outpost in the wilderness. Its half dozen white residents shared the fruits of forest and river with their Maori neighbours. Now it was a flourishing township with its own shop, post office and bank. Along either bank of the river, homesteads had sprung up. The fertile alluvial plain had been ploughed for the sowing of crops and the wooded hillsides, cleared for grazing. A well marked track now linked the new township with the rest of the province and above the waterfall stood a school and schoolmaster's house, the gift of the people of Dunedin to the new township of Mapourika. In the absence of any properly qualified person, James and his daughter kept school for the Maori children and the offspring of the white settlers.

Anxious to make her position in the school legitimate, Catherine had spent three years studying for her licence to teach by means of a postal course.

She re-read the Superintendent's letter, too stunned to take in the full enormity of the message it contained. Surely it must be possible to reverse the position? It was such a cruel stroke of Fate that on the very day she found herself to be qualified to make a formal application, the post of teacher at Mapourika should be filled by a complete stranger. She wondered how the Maori children would fare at the hands of a newcomer straight from a Scottish school, one who was unfamiliar with the language and accustomed to keeping discipline with the taws beneath his desk. She shuddered at the thought.

Something similar must have been going through James's mind for he turned to his daughter at last and said, 'Maybe the country will not suit him, my dear. Not everyone is content to live so far from all the excitement and entertainment to be had in town.'

'What if we were to send news of my qualification to the Education Secretary right away, Papa? Might there yet be a chance of forestalling his arrival?'

James showed her the envelope which had contained his letter from the Superintendent. The date stamp indicated that it had already been a week on the road from Dunedin to Mapourika.

Following his lead, Catherine examined her own correspondence. Across one corner of the envelope which had contained her certificate from the College of Preceptors there was a faint blue inscription, carelessly marked, indicating that it had been carried aboard the sailing ship, *Nelson*. If the ship had already anchored in Port Chalmers, Mr Moodie's arrival must be imminent.

Sadly, she went to her father and put her arms around him. Why was it, she wondered, that whenever they were at their happiest, things always seemed to go wrong.

'Anyway, I have my certificate,' she murmured.

James, who had sunk into one of his old black moods, suddenly revived his spirits. He took up the certificate which in his despair he had carelessly set aside, and read its contents with growing satisfaction.

'Indeed, you have!' he exclaimed. 'And what a certificate – distinctions in three subjects!' Generously, he claimed no part in her success even though two of the distinctions were gained in subjects of his own teaching. She had been such an excellent pupil.

'It will not be long before you are offered a post,' he assured her. But for Catherine that was not enough. It was this school where she wanted to teach and it was here, in Mapourika that she wanted to live.

Together, they gathered up books and writing materials abandoned by the children in their eagerness to get away from the schoolroom and it was nearly dusk when James finally closed the door behind him and joined his daughter outside the newly completed schoolmaster's house.

Catherine had secretly looked forward to the day when she moved out of her parent's house and came to live here on her own. Deeply disappointed, she turned away and joined her father at the top of the steps.

'Mr Moodie will need some furniture,' she observed, remembering her own plans to have her chairs and table specially constructed from local pine and imported mahogany.

'We'll see what can be found amongst the settlers. They may be able to provide sufficient to give him a start,' James replied.

The main street linked the general stores and post office with the manse which perched on the slope below the church. As they approached they saw that a large, ox-drawn wagon had pulled up outside the bank and was rapidly disgorging several passengers and their luggage. With sinking heart Catherine approached the group, supposing that Mr Moodie must surely be amongst them.

Suddenly, a single figure broke from the ranks of the newcomers and came bounding towards them.

'Father! Katy!'

Ian Bantrie gathered his sister in his arms and swung her around as though she were a rag doll. He set her on her feet and turned to greet his father.

'By God, Sir, you are looking well!' he cried.

'We were not expecting you, my boy!'

James, overcome with emotion at seeing his eldest son after so long, was at a loss for words and found himself resorting to petulant criticism.

'Did you not receive my letter? I had hoped to warn you in advance by sending word ahead from Port Chalmers. The ship dropped anchor a week ago.'

Shame-faced, Catherine withdrew the letter she had, earlier, stuffed into her pocket.

'Is this it?' she asked. 'It arrived by the post this afternoon and I was saving it to read to the others, after supper.'

'No matter,' said James, recovering his composure. 'You are here now.' Uncharacteristically demonstrative, he hugged his boy to him. Gently disengaging from his father's embrace, Ian looked about him eagerly, seeking out the remainder of the family.

'Where are Charlie… and Mrs Dundas?' he asked. Then, noticing the flash of annoyance in his father's expression, he corrected himself. 'I'm sorry… my step-mother. It is hard to imagine her as Mrs Bantrie.'

‘Then call me Jessie. At your age, you can hardly be expected to start calling me mother.’

Seeing the commotion in the street from her front porch, Jessie had come to find out what was going on and had witnessed the family reunion from afar.

‘It is good to see you again Jessie.’

He made to shake her by the hand but she drew him to her and kissed him full on the mouth.

‘You may be too old to call me mother but that does not prevent my greeting you as a son.’ She laughed.

‘Is that all your luggage?’ James asked, indicating the single haversack.

‘I left the remainder at the hotel in Port Chalmers,’ Ian told him. ‘I was in too much of a hurry to get here to come weighed down by a cabin trunk.’

‘I must go and have words with the carter,’ said James. ‘We are expecting another visitor.’ He wandered off still slightly dazed by his son’s sudden appearance.

Ian again asked after his brother.

‘Charlie is in Dunedin, living with Dr Beaton and apprenticed to become a physician,’ Catherine explained. I mentioned it in my last letter.’

‘It must have crossed the ocean while I was en route. Had I known Charlie was in town, I would have called on the doctor while I was there,’ said Ian. ‘I was so keen to get here to be with you all that I could think of nothing else. You have no idea how the time dragged while we were in the harbour sorting out the legalities before they would allow us to land.’

‘The Superintendent of the Colony is determined to keep out the riff-raff,’ Jessie explained. ‘Only bona fide settlers with substantial funds or those joining already established families, may stay permanently. With so much talk of a gold rush on the horizon it is certain there will be many undesirables attracted to the province.’

‘Until now we have managed to remain free from criminal elements,’ Catherine added. ‘For the most part the Dunedin gaol remains empty except for the occasional fight between drunkards after a football match on a Saturday and at celebrations of course, such as Hogmanay!’

‘Those I was travelling with were questioned very thoroughly,’ Ian confirmed. ‘Even men of means were given only three months in which to establish some legitimate business or become otherwise self supporting.'

While Ian went off to collect his baggage, Catherine stared curiously at the two remaining travellers. One figure had woken in her a memory still fresh, despite the lapse of years. Suddenly he turned in her direction and their eyes met. Catherine gave a startled cry of recognition for his roughly cut civilian clothes did nothing to disguise those well remembered features.

'Mr Frawley!' she cried out, 'Look Jessie, you remember. It's Julian Frawley from the *Albatross*!'

'Why, Miss Bantrie. This is a pleasant surprise and no mistake.' The young man stepped forward and doffed his hat to Jessie. 'Mrs Dundas, Ma'am, what a pleasure to see you again.'

'Mrs Bantrie now,' she corrected him. 'What might you be doing here, Mr Frawley,' she enquired. 'It's a long way from the open sea.'

'Seeking my fortune,' he said smiling. 'I was paid off at the end of my last voyage and having been told of a possible strike up country from here, I intend to spend a month or so prospecting for gold before joining another ship for the homeward voyage.'

'You must dine with us this evening.' Catherine was eager for any excuse to renew their acquaintance.

'My friend and I have spent a great deal of time in each other's company since leaving the ship. His journey ends here while I shall be moving on in a day or two. In the circumstances, I feel I must continue to give him my companionship until the time for my departure.'

'Your friend will be welcome at our table,' Jessie said but Julian shook his head. 'I fear he will decline also. But thank you Mrs Bantrie all the same. Perhaps on my return journey I may call in a pay my respects.'

Disappointed that she had been denied the opportunity to show him how much pleasure this unexpected encounter had given her, Catherine watched Julian as he rejoined his companion and disappeared into the guest house.

At that moment, James returned with the information that the remaining member of the party was none other than Mr Moodie, and that he had promised the new school teacher he would spend the following day installing him in the schoolhouse.

'I asked him to join us for supper but he declined. A rather gruff and unsociable creature in all respects I am sorry to say.'

He looked apologetically at Catherine, noting the flash of anger in her eyes. It was bad enough to be displaced by a decent sort of fellow but for her to lose her cherished school to such an unpleasant person was one insult piled upon another. 'I dare say he is an excellent teacher.' James added lamely, hoping to sooth his daughter's ruffled feather

'I suppose I must call on one or two of the church elders,' the minister grumbled, almost to himself. 'We shall have to find a few bits of furniture from somewhere for the school house.'

Watching James as he shuffled off, Ian was made acutely aware how greatly his father had aged since he had seen him last.

'Did you have a chance to get to know Mr Frawley?' Catherine enquired of her brother. 'We hoped he might join us for supper but he seemed most reluctant.'

'I met with Frawley and his friend on the road, yesterday,' Ian explained. 'There was an unpleasant incident which resulted in my having to hit this other fellow. Then, this morning, while I was walking along the track just a few miles from here, I was overtaken by the carrier's cart. Imagine my discomfort when I discovered that these two had been picked up further back along the road and that I must share a ride with my adversary of yesterday. Mr Frawley is quite correct in suggesting that his travelling companion would not be welcome in my father's house.'

'I don't see why that should prevent Mr Frawley from coming, alone,' Catherine protested.

'I am sure Mr Frawley knows best, 'Jessie told her, firmly. 'And it would be just as well if you did not mention your fight with this man in front of your father, Ian. He might not be as understanding as I.'

Ian grinned while, unconsciously, he rubbed the knuckles of his right hand, still sore from their contact with Moodie's chin.

Chapter Twenty

Nicholas Moodie, footsore and dirty after several days on the road, was not ready to seek out those responsible for the school until he had resumed his normal degree of cleanliness and felt fully rested. Julian Frawley, who had turned down a pleasant evening with the Bantr to keep him company, found his companion argumentative, discourteous to the warden of the hostel and quite insulting about both the food and standard of accommodation. Frawley was obliged on more than one occasion, to apologise for his companion's behaviour and at last became so exasperated with him, that he left Moodie to his own devices and sought out Ian Bantrie and his charming sister instead.

On the following morning, recovered from his exertions and with his laundry washed and ironed to his complete satisfaction, Nicholas Moodie at last ventured out into the settlement seeking directions to the house of the minister and Chairman of the School Board.

Following directions given him by the warden of the hostel, he walked through the settlement towards the church, coming upon the manse in a well protected hollow, halfway up the hill. He paused at a neat little picket fence to take in his surroundings.

The minister's residence was a low building with a thatched roof of magnificent proportions. The low eaves provided shade to the wide veranda which surrounded it on all sides. Pieces of serviceable furniture manufactured from local timber, were arranged here, giving the place a comfortable air of carefree family life. He wondered at the ability of any woman to create such a peaceful haven here in the wilderness.

He heard Jessie singing before he saw on her. She rounded the corner of the house carrying a large laundry basket and set it down unaware that she was observed. Her movements as she bent down to lift some garment and then stretched up to attach it to a line slung between two spindly trees, mesmerized him. It was a long time since any woman had so excited him.

She was tall and dark, well into her middle years but none the less good to look at. Nicholas Moodie was not a difficult man to please when it came to female company; an aspect of his character which had led him astray in the past. When it came to moral judgements however, the Otago Peninsular was hardly Aberdeen or Edinburgh. Who was there here to administer justice?

Thinking himself in luck and anticipating the exchange of a few pleasantries with this enchanting being who was clearly a servant of some kind, he opened the gate and strode across the green turf in front of the house.

'Good day!' He called, startling Jessie so much that she dropped the sheet she was holding in the dust.

'Oh, no!' she exclaimed in annoyance and bent to retrieve it.

Hurrying forward the stranger grabbed one corner of the fallen sheet as she took hold of the other and together they folded the expanse of white cloth, coming closer at each doubling of the material. He did not relinquish his hold until he was nose to nose with her. She saw the gleam of saliva on his bottom lip, vivid pink against the dark bush of whiskers and found it difficult to disguise her revulsion. Then, at last he let go.

Not a word had been spoken. She turned her back to pin the sheet to the line and found him at her elbow, holding out a wooden peg.

'Do you have some business with the minister?' she asked rather coldly, holding out her hand for the peg and finding it difficult to escape his steadfast gaze.

'I have to report to the Chairman of the School Board, a Mr Bantrie.'

Why, this must be the new schoolmaster. Surely this was a person to be trusted. Embarrassed that her initial response to him may have seemed overly cautious, Jessie tried to make amends by holding out her hand and shaking his warmly.

'You will be Mr Moodie, our new schoolmaster,' she said. 'My husband has been expecting you to call.'

She still had an uneasy feeling about the way the fellow looked at her. Ian had made some mention of a small dispute on the road concerning this man, something to do with Wei Lun, he had said. The Chinese travelling salesman was her good friend and she did not like to hear of anyone attempting to swindle him. If Mr Moodie was to live and work amongst them however, she must try to make him welcome if only for James's sake.

'Is he here then?' Moodie seemed almost disappointed.

'My husband will be in shortly. Won't you sit out on the veranda and have a cool drink? Maybe you would care to join us for luncheon?'

He had been about to address her as the serving woman he had taken her to be. Embarrassed by thought of the gaff he had so nearly committed, he took a seat in one of the cane chairs and continued to watch Jessie as she moved gracefully around him. At last she disappeared inside the house only to reappear some moments later carrying a tray with a jug and glasses.

There was something about this woman; the way she moved, the manner in which she held the tray and poured the cool lemonade into tall glasses. Something in her had stirred an ancient memory. Thinking no more of it at the time, he engaged in conversation about the school children, the nature of the countryside here about and the possibility of finding gold, further west. Soon the sound of footsteps approaching up the steep path from the town, interrupted their conversation and the minister appeared. James was sweating profusely in the noonday heat. He mopped his brow with a large white handkerchief and strode up the veranda steps to be introduced to his visitor. The formalities were necessarily brief for James had an important message to deliver.

'There is sickness in the village my dear. There was a Maori wedding feast yesterday and it seems that some of the food was tainted. I told them I would send you down to them to see what you can do.'

'I'm so sorry Mr Moodie,' Jessie said, getting to her feet once again, 'It seems my luncheon invitation must be withdrawn. Another day perhaps?'

'I rarely eat luncheon, Madam,' he pronounced grandly, 'Please, don't let me keep you from your mission of mercy.'

She hurried away to gather what few remedies she could lay her hands on before collecting her bonnet and making her departure.

It was the indication that she was somehow involved in healing the sick of the parish which finally triggered the recollection which had eluded Moodie from the moment he had set eyes upon Jessie Bantrie. Now, as he watched her hurrying along the path towards the Maori village, he remembered where he had seen her before.

Jessie was perplexed both by the sudden appearance of the sickness which had struck down so many of their Maori neighbours and its severity. Before seeking out the cause however, she must first relieve the symptoms. Without the emetics and purgatives which Alexander would almost certainly have prescribed, she was forced to have recourse to the remedies which Teri Beaton had described to her.

As a purge, she had selected the leaves of the hebe plant, Koromiko. Bruised, crushed and boiled in water until all the juices had been extracted, these leaves yielded a fluid as effective as anything Alexander could recommend. Tataramoa roots, the bark of which had been boiled to produce an infusion, helped to cure the diarrhoea while a drink made from the leaves of the sow thistle, Puha, Puwha, aided in the relief of biliousness.

Even those Maori most seriously affected by food poisoning, made a quick recovery and after twenty-four hours only a few very elderly folk and young children continued to display symptoms. With careful nursing and by feeding vegetable broth made from her own recipe, Jessie managed to save the lives of all but two of her patients. Both were so old they had been close to death even before the feast.

In one sense, she believed these two were better off dying in this manner rather than face the lingering death by starvation inflicted upon the old and useless by the younger members of the tribe. No matter what Christian teaching James tried to inculcate into their culture, he had been unable to break the Maori tradition of leaving the elderly to die of starvation once they could no longer contribute to the life of the community.

When she was satisfied she had done all she could for her patients, Jessie began to make enquiries around the village about what had been eaten at the feast. As always there had been fruits and vegetables, all of which seemed harmless enough. The meat eaten, wild boar and weka, the little wood hen, had been caught and eaten within a reasonable period. Surprisingly, there had also been a large quantity of fish.

In the height of summer, lack of rainfall meant that the water level was low and normally at this season the fish would be concentrated many miles inland in the upper reaches of the river. Jessie wondered where the men could have gone to catch enough to make a feast for the entire village.

'Water gone,' explained one of the lads whom she questioned. 'Fish gather in pools… easy catch.'

'Show me,' she demanded, with an uneasy feeling that she knew what they would find.

The village boys led her to a part of the river a mile or so below the church where she seldom went. At this point the stream began to meander slowly through flat water meadows bordered by extensive reed beds. Near its mouth it spread out into a shallow delta before reaching the ocean. Today the mud of the river bed was exposed in many places, leaving behind small pools some only a few inches in depth. Here fish had been stranded in their hundreds. Many of them, already dead, floated belly up on the surface while beneath the bloated corpses was a writhing mass of the silvery bodies of those still living.

'You gathered fish from here and the women cooked them?' she asked.

The boys nodded.

'Don't you know that it is bad to eat fish which have died like this?' she asked, incredulous. Maybe something other than a lack of water had caused the fish to die; disease perhaps, or poison. Whatever it was had killed the fish would surely make men sick also. She sent the boys into the stream to collect a few of the tainted fish. When they returned, each boy carried a pair of fine looking kokpura which they placed on the grass at her feet before turning back for more.

'No, no,' she called, 'these will do. I want to look at them more closely. That is all.'

Seeming to misunderstand her, however, the boys again plunged into the muddy stream bed but when they returned with further fish, she threw the corpses back with warning gestures.

'This fish is bad,' she shook her finger at them menacingly, 'no good to eat! Make people sick!'

Reluctantly, her young guides returned to her side and retrieving the miserable catch they had made, followed her back along the path, into town.

*

The fish lay side by side on the marble topped table Jesse used for preparing their meals. Each had been slit open at the belly and the gut levered out gently to be displayed along its length. Jessie smelt the flesh but found nothing unusual. The contents of the gut seemed normal enough but the flesh was certainly discoloured. The muscle which in cooking should break down into solid white flakes, seemed already mushy and unstructured. Immediately beneath the skin the flesh was almost black. Gingerly she touched the discoloured muscle and brought her fingers to her lips. The taste was sharp, almost metallic. With his knowledge of chemicals, Ian would undoubtedly be able to throw some light on the matter. She gathered the mutilated corpses together, wrapped them in broad green leaves and laid them in the coolest part of the larder with wet cloths draped over them to keep them cool.

*

Nicholas Moodie was a fastidious man, neat in his appearance and particular about cleanliness in all things. Jessie saw how he paused at the entrance to her living room and studied the seating, deciding for himself which chair would do least damage to his tight stove pipe trousers. She noted also, with some resentment, how he surreptitiously ran a finger over the surface of her polished table and examined it for dust before lowering his starched cuffs onto it and how he examined each item of cutlery for stains and food particles, before using it. She wondered how such a person might have managed aboard ship for she had never met anyone less adapted to the uncertainties of life as a pioneer.

''I trust you find the school house to your liking?' Jessie asked.

'I am sure that it is the best the parish can manage under the circumstances,' Moodie replied, ungraciously. 'Hardly the standard one would normally be accustomed to, of course.'

'Oh, of course,' repeated Catherine, with uncharacteristic sarcasm. She would dearly have liked to correct his grammar but refrained for fear of embarrassing her stepmother.

A week had passed since the arrival of the carrier's cart and his three passengers. Once Moodie had been established in his new schoolhouse, Julian Frawley had considered all obligations to his travelling companion to have been fulfilled and prepared to depart for the mountains to the west. Catherine, pleased to see a good rapport developing between her brother and Julian, was not surprised to find that the two had agreed to go prospecting, together.

'My interest is more in locating building materials than in finding gold,' Ian insisted.

'Good,' said Julian, laughing. 'Does that mean that when we do find gold, you'll leave it all for me?'

With much good humour and many helpful suggestions from James who, after seven years in the place considered himself an expert in all aspects of the terrain, the two had set off into uncharted territory taking with them a couple of young Maori boys from the village to act as porters and guides.

With Julian and Ian safely out of the way, Jessie had felt it was time to invite the new schoolmaster to dinner. While she appreciated Catherine's quite natural aversion to Moodie and had listened to James's derogatory remarks about his attitude to Maori and the white settlers alike, she was still curious to renew her own brief acquaintance. She had issued her invitation at church on Sunday and Moodie had condescended to accept.

As he passed his guest a platter of meat and a dish of potatoes James asked, 'How was your voyage?'

'Unspeakable!' Moodie replied. 'I was obliged to keep to my cabin for the entire time and had my meals cooked privately and brought to me there. As for washing and such arrangements…' he shuddered before continuing, 'I do not know how I endured for so long!'

He prodded the meat and recognising it to be mutton, accepted the plate without comment. The potatoes were however a different matter. Eyeing the small rounded tubers suspiciously, he made note of the blue veins running through the white flesh and with an ill- concealed gesture of distaste set the dish aside. A plate of green vegetables unlike any he had seen before was equally spurned. The cockbulla fish which Tommy had caught as a special treat sufficiently resembled trout for the man to have consumed an entire fish before discovering his error.

'Does this country offer nothing in the way of that good food which the Lord provides for his Christian children?' he asked. Then, realising his remark might be interpreted as a slur upon the cooking prowess of his hostess he had the grace to observe, 'I am sure you do your best Madam but, none-the-less, I find it extraordinary that white people should be expected to eat the food of the natives!'

'How do you imagine we can live here without eating what grows in the country?' James demanded.

'There seemed to be no difficulty in obtaining suitable food aboard ship,' the man complained. 'No one asked me to live entirely upon seaweed and sharks.'

'You cannot expect all the food for a nation, even in its infancy, to be imported from abroad!' said Catherine indignantly. 'We have to follow the lead given us by the Maori.'

'If you will take my advice, Mr Moodie,' James added, 'you will not speak in too derisory a fashion of *natives*. The Maori are a proud people, steeped in their own traditions. Their customs indicate a wisdom and understanding of nature which is quite as advanced as our own. What is more, they adapt readily to *our* ways while we are slow to learn from *them*. I have no doubt that future generations of Maori will live and work alongside their white brothers and, saving only their appearance, you will be unable to tell the difference between them.'

'But it is a well known fact that blacks have no greater level of intelligence than that dog of yours, Reverend!' Moodie was adamant. No words of James were going to persuade him. 'Nevertheless, I shall do my best with what pupils I have. Black or white, I have no doubt that all children respond readily enough to a firm hand and an occasional cut with the taws.'

Catherine shuddered. She knew the taws to be a disciplinary tool much favoured by Scottish schoolteachers, but nevertheless she could not condone its use. Like a miniature cat 'o nine tails, it was a short stick to one end of which, strips of leather were bound into a multi- thronged lash. When used in anger, this vicious weapon could cut deep wheals into the flesh. Children rarely misbehaved in the presence of any master who carried one.

'The Maori children are learning to speak English,' she told him, 'but it is a slow process. They respond best to patience and understanding.'

'In my classroom, Miss Bantrie, the children will work at my pace and do as they are told!'

Having thus dealt with Catharine's advice to his own satisfaction, Moodie turned his attention to the fruit filled pudding Jessie set before him. She neglected to tell him that her so-called redcurrants had been gathered from the forest and the fat for the dumpling was rendered down from a wild boar caught by the Maori.

Catherine studied their guest with a growing suspicion that the man was not all he seemed.

'Had you taught school for long, before deciding to emigrate,' she asked now, disarmingly casual.

'Ever since I graduated at Aberdeen University,' said the other. 'My degree was in the Classics. My choice was between the Church and Teaching but I found it expedient to take up teaching.'

Expedient did not seem to be an appropriate word for the vocation which Catherine loved with all her heart.

'And where was that may I ask?' she demanded.

'My uncle, His Grace the Earl of Stirling, is a patron of the Tailors and Merchant's School in Edinburgh. He was pleased to recommend me for a position.'

This reference to his previous situation seemed to create in Moodie a tangible growth in stature. As he spoke of his patron, he puffed himself up like a turkey cock. He was not to know that the very mention of his uncle's name was enough to cause James Bantrie to bristle with indignation. The Earl of Stirling was that same member of the Scottish aristocracy who, through another of his relatives, had contributed largely to James's own downfall.

'With such an influential patron,' the minister observed dryly, 'One wonders why anyone would want to give up a comfortable billet to emigrate to New Zealand!'

Moodie paled, his slim talon-like fingers fidgeting with the tableware as he composed his response.

'There was a misunderstanding... a disagreement between myself and the headmaster of the school. I was obliged to leave.'

Catherine, like a terrier with a trapped rat, delved deeper.

'They must pay well at the Tailor's and Merchant's School if you were able to accumulate sufficient funds to travel first class aboard ship,' she observed.

The fellow casually dismissed Catherine's remark which, in Jessie's opinion, had been more than a little impertinent.

'My patron was most accommodating' he replied disdainfully, using his napkin to pat away the food particles attaching to his generous whiskers.

'Mrs Bantrie, Ma'am,' their visitor rose to take his leave, 'I thank you for your hospitality but feel that I must go away to my bed before dropping off to sleep at your table. I am looking forward to meeting my pupils for the first time, in the morning.'

'I thought perhaps my daughter should come along in the morning to introduce you to the pupils,' James suggested. 'I know she would be happy to assist in any way she can. She is of course a qualified teacher, herself.' He allowed this last piece of information settle upon a stony silence.

Although this pronouncement had clearly taken him off guard, Moodie said nothing. Finally, he commented, 'I was given to understand there was no person suitably qualified to teach in the settlement.'

'Catherine received word last week, that she has been awarded the College of Preceptor's diploma with distinction,' James informed him, proudly. 'Too late to forestall your own appointment of course, but nevertheless she would be happy to help out should you require it.'

'I shall manage well enough, on my own,' Moodie replied imperiously. 'Best if I make my own assessment of how things are, don't you know? Discover for myself all that needs to be put to rights!'

Catherine, who could think of nothing in her former management of the school that needed 'putting to rights,' fumed inwardly, but held her tongue.

Moodie bowed slightly to Jessie and took his leave, his departure being accompanied by a stunned silence which Catherine was the first to break.

'The insufferable prig!'

'Well,' said James. 'I do rather wonder what the immigrant children will make of him; not to mention the Maori!'

Catherine now relieved of her duties as schoolmistress, found herself at a loose end. With Ian and Julian gone, life seemed empty and devoid of purpose. How she wished she had had the courage to ask to accompany them on their expedition. She had been prevented by the thought that Moodie might have need of her assistance in the classroom. Although the new schoolmaster had made it clear that he would brook no interference from others, she was convinced that before long he would be forced to ask for her help. For the sake of the children she wanted to be available when he did so.

*

Charlie Bantrie stretched out in the warm sunshine and focused his telescope upon the ship which lay at anchor across the bay. She was a three-masted barquentine much the same size as the *Albatross* but, built along the more slender lines of the new American clipper ships, she was probably faster. The bosun had told him that she had taken only three months and fifteen days to make the passage from Southampton.

He picked out the tiny figures of the crew working over the masts and stays and wondered if there were any there that he had met ashore. Fergus Harding had had a big party of seamen in the hotel bar a few nights before and Alexander Beaton and his apprentice had been up until all hours attending to their cuts and bruises after the inevitable fighting which had ensued.

To his great joy, Charlie had been dispatched the following morning to Port Chalmers, to deliver the doctor's bill for his services to the crew. While he waited on board for the Captain's response, he had been shown all over the *Nelson* and had had a long talk with the bosun.

He focused now on the poop deck and felt sure he had the figure of the captain in his sights. If only he had had the presence of mind to ask him, while he had the opportunity.

Charlie had no wish to disappoint either Alexander Beaton or his own father, but the truth was that he found his work in the surgery unpleasant and although he had never admitted it to the doctor, the sight of blood made him sick. As for the studying, no matter how hard he tried, he could not get his tongue around the Latin terms and failed dismally when he tried to memorise the names of muscles and bones. He was just not cut out to be a doctor and the sooner the adults understood that, the happier he would be. Even young Malcolm Beaton, eight years his junior, had more understanding of the medical vocabulary than him.

A chance remark by the landlord of the Wharf Hotel, one morning when the doctor was attending Mrs Harding, had first woken in Charlie the yearning to quit the doctor's practice and run away to sea.

'How do you like Dunedin?' Fergus had asked the boy. 'Rather different from Glasgow, don't you think?'

'I don't know Glasgow well,' replied the boy. 'I was living on a little island off the Argyllshire coast, before we came away. It was not so very different from this.'

'I lived in the Gorbals until I was ten years old,' Fergus told him. 'My parents were killed in a fire. The tenement where we lived burned to the ground.'

Charlie stared at him in horror. He could not imagine what it would be like to lose both parents in an instant. His recollections of his mother's death were still fresh in his memory and his heart immediately went out to the young Fergus, ten years old and not a soul in the world to take care of him.

'What did you do?' he asked, wide eyed.

'They were going to put me in an orphanage,' Fergus replied. 'I didn't like the idea of that, so I ran away to sea. The ship became my home and the crew, my family.'

'Didn't the captain mind that you had run away?'

'He never asked questions. There was a place for a boy in the crew and he took me on.'

It all sounded so simple. Fergus had only been ten. Charlie was twelve, going on thirteen and old enough, surely, to make up his own mind.

'Why did you leave the sea?'

'Everyone has to eventually. I'd sailed these waters several times on whalers; came ashore on one occasion and saw the opportunity for starting a business. Then it was just a case of raising the money. I solved that by marrying a woman with a bit put by and we set up this hotel together, Mrs Harding and me. I've never regretted it.'

Reverently, he lifted a telescope down from the shelf and showed it to the boy.

'This was given to me by the master of my first ship. I sailed in her for more than seven years.'

Charlie held the instrument with great care as he examined it in every detail. Aboard the *Albatross* Mr Frawley had sometimes allowed him to peer through his glass but this was a much finer instrument with engraving on the exposed brass fittings and a black Morocco leather covering as a hand-hold.

'You may borrow it when you want,' said the landlord. 'Use it to watch the vessels sailing to and fro. You can learn a lot about ships from just doing that. Help yourself, any time you want.'

From then on, whenever he had a free afternoon, Charlie would collect the spyglass and climb to one of the high points around the harbour. As the months passed, an ever-increasing number of vessels of all kinds entered the bay and as Fergus had suggested, Charlie soon became familiar with the characteristics of the different types.

In his dreams, Charlie relived the marvellous days he had spent aboard the *Albatross*. When he should have been concentrating upon exercises set him by the doctor, his mind wandered into the realms of fantasy where, as the captain of his own vessel, he plied uncharted seas or fought off marauding pirates.

Thoughtfully, Charlie replaced the telescope in his pocket and made his way back into town. With his mind made up he saw no reason to wait any longer. The *Nelson* was making ready to sail on the evening tide and there was not a minute to lose.

When he reached the surgery in Cumberland Avenue he went straight to his little annexe room at the rear of the building and pulled from beneath a loose floorboard, a small tin box. Knowing full well the exact amount which the box contained, nevertheless he counted it again. Here was the golden guinea his father had given him the day he had deposited him on the surgery steps and ridden off alone along the road to Mapourika. This crown had been given to him only that morning by Mr Harding, in payment for working in his cellar every Saturday evening for the past month. The remainder of the money, amounting to twelve shillings and sixpence, was in smaller coins, sixpences, three pennies and even the occasional halfpenny. These latter had been saved from money the doctor gave him for making special deliveries of medicines to his patients and from tips given him by the grateful recipients. One pound eighteen shillings and sixpence was little enough to start out on his new life, but it would have to do.

He bundled his clothes into a small haversack, pausing for a moment over the books which had been given to him by his sister. He must not lumber himself with too much weight for it would be a long walk around the shore to Port Chalmers. He discarded her copy of Robinson Crusoe in favour of the almanac given to him by Fergus Harding and then, at the last minute, thrust a thin volume of poetry in between his spare flannel shirt and his Sunday breeches.

He must leave some message for his family. Just because he was defying his father, there was no reason to leave them in any doubt as to what had happened to him. For an instant, he envisaged his sister's stricken face when she heard that he was gone and his resolve began to waiver.

From out in the street he heard the Beaton's chaise drawing away from the curb, the delighted shouts of the doctor's two little boys could be clearly distinguished. The family would be away all evening. The ship should have sailed before they realised he was gone.

A note left here at the surgery would probably not be opened until morning but what if they returned early. Suppose the doctor were called upon to attend a patient? Were they to realise too soon his intentions, they might signal the ship and prevent it leaving harbour with him on board. He sat down to write to his father. It was only as he struggled over the correct phraseology and tried extra hard with his spelling, the solution occurred to him.

My Dearest Papa,

I have tried very hard to be a dutiful son and to become a physician as you wanted, but I have not the brains to remember all those long words and know that it is hopeless for me to go on trying. Since our voyage aboard the Albatross I have only ever wanted to be a sailor so that is what I have decided to do. When you read this, I shall already be on the high seas.

Suddenly he thought of Gyp's sharp black muzzle, the dog's bright, appealing expression and soft, silky head and a single tear ran down his cheek and dropped onto the paper, mingling with the ink. The letters smudged a little but it was too late now to re-write the whole thing. He allowed the ink to dry, folded the paper once; twice; and sealed it with the wax which had been a present from Catherine on his last birthday. He wrote his father's name on the outside, scribbled a few words of explanation to Alexander Beaton and folded his father's letter inside that of the doctor. Slipping the package into his pocket together with Fergus Harding's telescope, he slung the satchel over his shoulder and crept out into the fading light.

As Charlie approached the hotel, the swing door was thrust open and a dark figure disappeared into the gathering gloom. Even in that brief glimps he recognised some faces he knew. Cautiously he pushed open the door and slipped inside, not wishing to attract the attention of any of the regulars. Fortunately, there was quite a crowd, making it possible for him to slide right up to the bar without being recognised. There were men here whom he had met aboard the *Nelson*, enjoying their last evening ashore no doubt. They must, after all, be leaving on the morning tide. That meant he had more time than he had thought in which to reach the ship but it also meant that there was a greater chance of discovery before she sailed.

He recalled his original plan to leave his note at the surgery, and experienced a momentary rush of blood to the head. The doctor might well have read it before the *Nelson* set sail. With an enormous feeling of relief, he climbed onto a stool and leaned across the bar.

'Thanks for the loan of the telescope,' he said, as Fergus Harding approached. He handed over the instrument and watched his friend tuck it into its accustomed place above the bar.

'You're out late, 'Fergus remarked. He noted the haversack Charlie was carrying, but said nothing.

'The doctor's family are all away for the evening. I thought I might take the opportunity to have a word with some of the seamen from the *Nelson*. I hear she's sailing very soon.'

'High tide is at two bells of the first watch. The ship will be gone before dawn.' The landlord pulled a measure of mild ale and set it down before the boy. 'Here, wet your whistle with that.'

'Thanks Fergus,' Charlie swallowed a long cool draught. The excitement had made his throat dry and he had eaten and drunk nothing since noon. Cautiously, he scanned the faces of those gathered at the bar. If he could find someone he knew, he might even get a lift aboard the *Nelson's* jolly boat which he had noticed tied up alongside the wharf. He spotted the bosun at the far end of the bar and taking up his half- empty glass he forced his way through the throng.

'Evening, Bos'n,' he addressed the man as he had heard the crew speak to him.

'Oh aye, the doctor's wee laddie,' was the bosun's response.

'Not anymore,' said Charlie, trying to sound convincing.' I'm signing on with you, as ship's boy.'

The bosun seemed surprised. Only that morning the captain had told him one of the youngsters was leaving the ship and that they would be seeking a new hand, but he had not imagined the place would be filled until they reached Wellington or Aukland, on their homeward leg.

'You'll be rowing across the harbour with us, then,' he said, raising a hand for silence as Charlie downed the remainder of his beer. 'You must have another to celebrate joining the ship.' He set up Charlie's glass for a refill and called out to his men, 'How about it lads? This here's our newest recruit!' There was a loud inebriated cheer and several more pints were sunk without trace.

The bosun's remarks had centred attention upon Charlie just when he would have preferred to lay low but the only person to show any surprise at the announcement was Fergus Harding. As he drew more beer for the crewmen to toast their latest recruit, he looked oddly at Charlie but it was only as the noise began to return to its former level that he leaned across the bar and spoke to the boy.

'What's this, young'n?' he demanded. 'Skipping off without your people knowing, is it?'

'It's the only way, Mr Harding. They'll never let me go otherwise.'

The old man nodded. Who was he to stand in the way of this young romantic? Had he not once done the very same thing himself? The boy would learn soon enough what a tough life it was. Sure as hell he was not going to listen to an old sea dog now. The lad was the right stuff to make a sailor sure enough, so good luck to him. Reaching up he retrieved the telescope and began to polish it upon his sleeve. He gazed at it for one last time before handing it to Charlie.

'Best take it,' he said, as the boy began to protest. 'It will be more use to you than sitting up there on the shelf.'

Too moved even to thank his friend properly, Charlie slipped the instrument back into his jacket pocket. It was then that his fingers encountered the letter he had written. He withdrew it and placed it on the bar.

'Might I ask you to deliver this to the doctor, after the ship has sailed?' he asked.

Harding nodded, for he was too choked with emotion to make any comment. Then, taking up the packet he slipped it into his pocket.

*

Captain Collins was obliged to grasp at a convenient stay as he stood at the head of the companionway and watched the shipping agent descend to the dock. He had imbibed rather more brandies than he might normally have allowed himself on this last evening. With an enormous effort he straightened up as the Jolly Boat tied up alongside.

'Crew on board and ready to make sail, Sir!'

'Thank you Bos'n.'

Captain Collins returned the salute.

'That includes the recruit, Sir. We brought him across with us.'

The captain, befuddled and ready for his bed, nodded as though he understood.

'Carry on, Mr Mate,' he called to his number one, and stood aside while his most efficient officers made preparations for sailing.

Charlie's shipmates showed him where to sling his hammock and bade him turn in. The deck of a vessel making ready to put to sea in the dark was no place for a raw recruit. It was to be several days before the captain realised he had a stow-away on board by which time Charlie had mastered sufficient tasks to make himself useful. With holds filled with cargo for the North Island and a tight schedule to maintain, there was no turning back to put the lad ashore.

Ignoring any consideration of reprisals from a doting family deprived of its youngest son, Captain Collins signed on Charlie Bantrie as ship's boy.

Chapter Twenty-One

Alexander's first instinct on reading Charlie Bantrie's letter was to attack his wife.

'He must have spoken to you,' he exclaimed, 'He would never have gone off like this without first discussing it with someone!'

'He say nothing of leaving,' she assured him. 'He speak all the time of ships he see in the harbour. He knew all their names, where they were from and where going but he never say he go away.'

'Was going,' irritably, Alexander corrected her automatically. The doctor had from the very start of Tommy's apprenticeship, envied his wife's comfortable relationship with Jessie's stepson.

The lad's unexpected disappearance seemed to affect Teri more than him. She missed his cheerful presence about the place and his mastery of the Maori language had meant that there was always one person in the household with whom she could converse in her own tongue. The boy had made a much-needed buffer between herself and her husband.

Alexander's growing discontent with his medical practice had made him morose and uncommunicative at home. Those who could afford his services demanded the patent medicines and pampering of the hypochondriac while those whose need for medical care was genuine, chose to doctor themselves, rather than employ him. His skills as a surgeon were called into play most often on the building sites, in the logging camps and the stone quarries where crushed bodies and broken bones were frequent occurrences. Such accidents usually occurred at a distance and necessitated a long journey with protracted absence from home.

Teri had begun to see less and less of her husband. His children were growing up hardly knowing their father and despite the plethora of literature which his parents sent him from home, Alexander never had sufficient time to keep abreast of developments in the medical world. He had tried to set aside time to write his paper on the treatment of phthisis which he had carried out on board ship. He had watched Philip Mackie grow from a sickly youth into a fine strong young fellow with the prospect of a long and vigorous life ahead of him. The material was there for an excellent report on the efficacy of the sea voyage as a means of combating the disease. If only he could get around to putting it down on paper.

Alexander was convinced had Jessie been beside him through these early years in the settlement, everything would have been different. He blamed James Bantrie for blighting his life and Jessie for deserting him in favour of Judith's children.

Charlie's departure had landed the final blow to Alexander Beaton's self esteem. He had failed to hold the interest of Jessie's stepson in that very profession which had from his childhood, been his own all-consuming passion. His work should have been sufficient inspiration for any young man to follow.

She would surely blame him. Charlie was as dear to her as her own child. Judith, on her death bed, had begged her to look after the boy and Jessie had vowed to protect him. How could she ever forgive him for not seeing the signs of Charlie's discontent; for not preventing his departure?

Alexander turned over Charlie's note which he had addressed to his father. He might take the easy way out of course, and simply dispatch the letter by the next carrier going out in the direction of Mapourika. For a long time he gazed out of his study window, watching the movements in the harbour and wishing Harding had brought him the letter before the ship had sailed. At last he made up his mind. He would, himself, break the news of Charlie's departure to James and Jessie. He drew on his coat and strode into the kitchen.

'I must take this letter to Mapourika,' he told Teri. 'It would be cowardly to just send it on by the carrier. I'll leave instructions for that new fellow in Caversham to cover for me.' After years of being the only medical man in the district, Alexander had recently been joined by a colleague, one Dr David Gambol from London.

Teri watched his departure with tears in her eyes. He had not even paused to say goodbye. So anxious had he been to run to Jessie Bantrie, he had even forgotten to take his medical bag.

*

Alexander became more and more agitated as he neared his journey's end. Towards evening on the second day he reined in his horse at the summit of the ridge and stared down at the growing settlement of Mapourika. The long ride and an overnight rest under the stars had helped to clear his mind somewhat but he could not throw off the growing conviction that this most recent failure on his part was to be the cause of his final separation from Jessie.

Mapourika main street was deserted as he entered it from the south and walked his horse slowly past the stores and houses, many of which had been newly erected since his last visit. Fully prepared to be ordered from the premises the instant he had conveyed his message he hitched his horse to the post and opened the gate. As he entered the garden, Jessie herself came out onto the veranda to breath in the fresh evening air.

'Alexander!' she waved excitedly on seeing him. "

She hugged him in that sisterly manner of hers which put him firmly in the position of family friend and destroyed any lingering hope that she might yet regard him as something more.

He held her at arms length for a moment, savouring the scent of her freshly washed hair and admiring those elegantly chiselled features which had first stirred his heart a decade before. Her smile was as warm and welcoming as ever and her pleasure at his unexpected appearance entirely genuine.

'Such news, Alexander,' she cried excitedly. 'Ian has arrived at last! He has been in the African gold fields for a while, that is why we have heard so little from him. Now he has come home perhaps he will find our fortune for us and we shall all live like kings!'

He knew she was joking. Nothing about Jessie Bantrie suggested for one moment that she was not entirely satisfied with her life as it was at present. Any hope that she might still harbour romantic leanings toward himself was dispelled in that instant. Here was a truly contented woman and he was about to shatter that happiness.

'A nice little gold mine would just suit me, too,' he said, affected by her excitement, despite his own distress. 'How is everyone? 'Keeping happy and healthy?'

'Last week we had a really bad outbreak of food poisoning amongst the Maori. Unfortunately, I had to throw out the fish I believed to be the cause of the problem.' She went on to give him a detailed explanation of what she had found when she examined the fish.

Welcoming any excuse to avoid the real purpose of his visit, Alexander addressed her problem enthusiastically. 'It sounds like some kind of chemical poisoning,' he decided when she had completed her description. 'Disease in fish is usually attributed to lice or worms but you say that these were free from both. The condition of the flesh suggests acid degeneration but the blackening is something I can't explain.'

All this while, they had remained on the veranda. As Jessie turned to invite him to enter the house Alexander remembered his horse. 'Is there a stable where I may leave the mare?'

Jessie called Tommy out from the rear of the building where he had been chopping wood for the fire.

'Show Dr Beaton where to put his horse and help him to bed her down, ' she told him.

'Good day, doctor.' The boy greeted Alexander politely, gathering the mare's reins as he spoke. Then, looking about him expectantly, he asked, 'Is Charlie not with you?'

Guiltily, Alexander shook his head, wondering if Jessie had heard the question. When he turned back to her he saw she had already disappeared inside the house. With a sigh of relief, he followed Tommy, catching up with him as he was about to lead the mare into a well constructed stable at the rear of the property.

Tommy studied the doctor thoughtfully.

'Charlie's gone, hasn't he?'

'You knew he was planning to leave?' Alexander asked, surprised.

'He's spoken of little else since he first went down to Dunedin as your apprentice.' Tommy answered. 'The only reason he agreed to go with you was because he would be close to the harbour and could talk to the seamen. He was waiting until he was old enough to sign on with one of the clipper ships.'

'He never wanted to become a doctor?'

'No. He tried of course, if only to please my mother. He knew she would never willingly allow him go to sea. Judith had feared it too much you see, after Ian nearly drowned. When Mrs Bantrie was dying, my mother promised she would never let Charlie go to sea.'

Alexander had no reason to doubt the truth of what Tommy said. If Charlie had been so set on becoming a sailor, then neither Teri nor he himself could be blamed for the lad's disappearance.

'Well, now that he has gone, perhaps you will tell the minister and your mother, what you have told me,' the doctor urged. 'But allow me to give them Charlie's letter before you do.'

Giving his mount a hearty slap on the rump, he set to with the curry comb while Tommy went off to fetch water from the well.

'Mercury or lead I would think; some heavy metal anyway,' Alexander suggested. He had listened carefully to Jessie's description of the contaminated fish and thought he could throw light on the problem.

'But why should anything of the kind occur in the water when it has never caused problems before?' Jessie demanded.

'It may be that the contamination in the water is normally in quantities too small to be troublesome,' Alexander suggested. 'The fish could accumulate quite large quantities of the poison before it killed them. By eating the flesh in which these accumulations have occurred however, the Maori must have ingested a concentration of the poison which was enough to make them sick.'

'But that does not explain why we have only just noticed this effect. Something has changed recently.' Jessie was still not satisfied that the phenomenon was natural.

'The water level in the river has fallen so that the fish have become trapped in small pools in the river bed. It's possible that as the water evaporated from these pools, the concentration of salts increased. That would explain the unusual quantities of poison but it does not explain the presence of poisonous substances in the first place. That is generally associated with concentrations of minerals in the bedrock through which the water passes.'

'What kind of rock?' Jessie asked.

'Volcanic rock such as granite, containing metals like zinc, lead, iron, mercury even gold! I remember an old quarryman back home, telling me that the epidiorite schists which associate with the slate on Seileachan, contain a similar suite of minerals. On Seileachan, there was too little gold to make its extraction worth-while but…'

'Here it could be a different story!'

It would be difficult to say who was the more excited by the possibilities, Tommy for whom the thought of unlimited adventure loomed large, or Alexander who saw in the situation a means of softening the impact of his own bad news. There followed some excited chatter between all three of them containing a deal of wild speculation and many exaggerated claims of what could result if Alexander's supposition proved to be correct.

When James and Catherine arrived, Jessie insisted upon relating Alexander's solution of the mystery thereby delaying further the purpose of his visit.

'We already know that there is gold in this area,' Catherine declared with conviction. She looked a little shame-faced when she saw James' surprised expression. 'I sent Ian that rock sample,' she confessed. 'He was advised that there was gold but that it was too difficult to extract to be of commercial value.'

It was too late now for recriminations so James overlooked his daughter's confession.

'It may be that there are more viable deposits nearby where we found that first sample,' he suggested. 'We must not lose sight however of the possibility that all we shall find is proof of what we already know.'

Alexander was not so easily put off. 'It may be worth investigating the alluvial drift from this river,' he suggested. 'Has anyone gone into the high country?' he asked.

'Ian has gone west already,' Jessie told him.

'There have been several prospectors passing through bound for the foothills, but so far as I know none of them has filed a claim.'

Dismissing the subject abruptly James turned to their guest. 'It is always good to see you Alexander, but I do hope that your presence here does not mean that you have a patient. Have you come to see anyone in particular?'

Unable to delay the inevitable any further, Alexander at last withdrew the letter which had been burning a hole in his pocket for so long.

'It was not a patient I came to see, James. It was you. I have with me a letter from Charlie.'

As he withdrew the white package, dog-eared now from much handling, Jessie's hand went to her mouth. It was as though she knew already what the letter contained. She clutched a chair for support as James, having observed Alexander's wooden expression, began to tear open his son's letter. For what seemed an interminable age he studied its contents in silence and then began to read aloud.

> *.... Please do not try to have me stopped. I shall try my best to become a good seaman and one day I promise I shall return as captain aboard my own ship. Tell Catherine I love her and thank Mrs Dundas for taking care of me all these years. She will understand that even now I do not call her mother for no one could ever replace my dearest Mama. Take good care of Gyp. I have missed him so much since I have been here. Tell Tommy he may have my catapult and my fishing rod. He will make a much better doctor than me.*
>
> *Your loving son,*
>
> *Charles Patrick Bantrie.*

Without comment, James folded the letter very deliberately, and slipped it into his pocket. Turning to the doctor he said, 'Thank you, Alexander. I believe I know what it must have cost you to come here with these tidings.' Solemnly, he shook Alexander by the hand and excused himself. 'Forgive me. I must be alone for a while.'

They watched in silence as James took the path to the church, his overly long grey hair blowing in a sudden breeze from off the salt marshes. The same breeze brought with it the salty tang of the ocean, instantly conjuring a vision of the child whom Jessie had come to love as her own son.

Tommy was the first to speak.

'I might have had something to do with this,' he confessed.

'You?' Catherine, her eyes blinded by tears, looked at her young step-brother in surprise.

'Yes. On board the *Albatross*, I was the one who pestered Mr Frawley for his tales of adventure and daring. I just enjoyed the stories but Charlie took it all far too seriously.'

Catherine, seeing his distress, ran to him and quite unselfconsciously held him in her arms.

'You were only children whiling away the time,' she said. 'Suppose Charlie had decided to be a highwayman. Should I have blamed myself for reading to him about Dick Turpin?'

Alexander watched the shadow of a smile pass across Jessie's chalk white face and began to hope.

Catherine recalled her brother Ian's burning ambition to go to sea. He had given up the idea when it had so nearly ended in tragedy. Her younger brother must have a lot of spunk to go, regardless of his father's feelings in the matter.

Alexander went across to Jessie and placed a hand gently over hers. So tight was her hold on the chair back that he was obliged to prize her fingers away from the wood before he could persuade her to sit.

'I'm so sorry, Jessie. I had no idea what he was planning.'

When, finally, she turned on him, it was as a female tiger protecting her young.

'I trusted you.' She spat the words out at him. 'I left him in your care. Surely between you, you must have seen what he intended. You could have stopped him!'

She turned on her heel and entered the bedroom she shared with James, slamming the door behind her. Left speechless by Jessie's unprecedented display of rage, Catherine and Tommy could only stare after her.

Like a wounded dog, Alexander hung his head and retreated from the scene. In a daze, he made his way around the house to the stable and saddled the mare. It was too late to get far along the road before nightfall but he must leave this place now. He could not bear to see that look on her face… ever again!

Chapter Twenty-Two

The village children were not as pleased as their parents appeared to be about the appointment of a new school teacher from Scotland. Mr Moodie came with fine references and the settlers felt honoured to have an ex-pupil from Fettes school, no less, to oversee the education of their little ones. While Mr Moodie appeared affable enough when confronted by any parent concerned for an individual child's progress, his demeanour changed dramatically once alone with his class in the schoolroom.

The classroom was no longer suffused by the gentle murmur of excited young voices carrying out some fascinating task set them by Miss Catherine. Mr Moodie's class worked in complete silence except when learning some fact or quotation by rote at which time the rafters rang with the monotonous chanting of childish voices. The pupils, used to spending a life in the open, learning from the world about them, now found themselves incarcerated for six hours a day in an airless classroom, door closed and windows too high to see out. They spent most of their time committing tedious passages to memory and working out impossible sums in their heads. Any failure to provide a correct answer met with a slap around the ears at the very least. At worst the dreaded taws appeared, familiar only to those children old enough to have attended school before leaving for New Zealand. Its cruel leather thongs left great red wheals upon hands, thighs, arms – wherever the master chose to inflict them.

While the settler's children struggled or succeeded in their lessons according to their innate ability, the Maori were doubly confused not only by the nature of the lessons but also by the language used by their tormentor. Miss Catherine had made a point of interchanging Maori and English words in order to give both races in her classroom a smattering of the other's language. Moodie, resenting the presence of the Maori children in school at all, at best ignored them and at worst inflicted severe punishment upon those who did not respond favourably to his teaching.

On the day when Alexander Beaton arrived in the village with his devastating news for James and Jessie, the afternoon had proved to be one of the hottest in a long period of drought. Inside the schoolroom, all was silence save for the flies which buzzed around sweaty brows and the voice of Mr Moodie reading from a book of translations from Homer. As the master's monotonous tones droned on, little heads began to nod in the stifling atmosphere.

Matilda Brown, concerned for her little Maori playmate, nudged the boy beside her as his eyes began to close. The master's steely eye fell at that moment upon the luckless Tiko.

Tiko was not a stupid child by any means. He knew all the creatures of the forest and could name the trees. What was more, he had learned from his older sister which of the plants were poisonous and which could heal. As the son of the village chieftain he was held in some awe by the other Maori children and even the settler's could be swayed by him when there was mischief afoot. He was not however a willing student in the classroom. Moodie had quickly recognised Tiko as a source of rebellion and as such, one to be observed closely and firmly suppressed whenever necessary. Seeing the boy apparently feigning sleep the master smacked him around the ears.

'Pay attention, you little savage!' he shouted. 'In which country will you find the city of Carthage?'

Tiko stared at the teacher a look of puzzlement on his face.

'Come along Man, Carthage. If you had been paying attention you would know the answer!' A second heavier blow landed on the back of the boy's head.

Swiftly coming to the defence of her friend, Matilda picked up a steel rule which lay on the desk before her and attacked the school master with all the strength she could muster. A thin red line appeared on his cheek where the metal had landed and a trickle of blood slowly traversed the line of his jaw until it seeped finally into his stiffly-starched collar.

Startled by the sudden attack, for a moment Moodie said nothing. He fingered the wound and, on withdrawing his hand, gazed dumbfounded at the blood on his fingers.

In the next instant, he had grabbed Matilda by the scruff of the neck and dragged her to the front of the class. Reaching for the taws, kept always to hand upon his desk, he beat her about the head and shoulders until she fell to her knees crying for mercy. He did not stop. With the child now conveniently prone, he flayed her across thighs and buttocks continuing the beating until he was forced to stop for want of breath. In the lull the girl crawled under the desk seeking safety and when the master failed to pursue her further, she scrambled to her feet and ran for the door and freedom.

Within the classroom not a sound could be heard. Even the flies had stopped their buzzing.

Moodie took a deep breath and returned to the book he had been reading to the children, picking up the text mid-sentence where he had left off. On dismissing the class at the end of the lesson he made just one reference to what had occurred earlier.

'There will be no discussion about what happened here today.' So saying, he picked up the taws and flicked it once in the direction of the first row of little faces. There was no mistaking the threat in his action.

*

A little wood hen scurried about in the litter of the forest floor, using its stunted wings for balance as it hopped from fallen tree to mossy bank. The girl woke suddenly, startled by a flurry of feathers. Realising that he was not alone the bird gave a startled squawk and dived for cover in the flimsy ferns growing around the foot of a giant Rimu tree.

Matilda sat up painfully, her limbs stiff and sore from the beating Moodie had given her. For a few moments she lay still, wondering what she was doing here beneath the trees and not in the comfortable truckle bed she shared with her sister. Then it began to come back to her; her own sudden rage at the treatment the schoolmaster had meted out to her friend Tiko. She remembered grabbing the steel rule and laying about him. Attempting to stretch her legs, she was racked once again with pain. After a while however the pain began to recede and she managed to focus more clearly upon her situation.

A gap in the canopy overhead told her that it was daylight, although the sun was still quite low in the sky. It was still early morning. Habit told her it was time to get moving. If she hurried, she might still get to school before the bell. Then she remembered the wicked instrument of torture the teacher had produced from inside his coat and knew she could not go back. Nor could she return home for her father, always impatient with her slow wittedness, would beat her again and lock her in the dank little cellar where her mother kept meat and the produce from the dairy. There was nothing for it but to go deeper into the forest. She knew she had nothing to fear from the wild creatures, the flightless birds and the feral cats and dogs. Unlike human kind, they would make her welcome and do her no harm. She scrambled to her feet and began to limp towards a poorly defined track through the undergrowth. Travelling slowly at first, for she found that every movement of her bruised and battered body produced some further agony, as time passed she felt her tough little limbs begin to recover. Soon she picked up the pace and was soon jogging through the trees, luxuriating in her new-found freedom.

The ground began to slope upwards and the forest trees to close in upon her. Now she was obliged to take a short stick to beat at the dense foliage which blocked her path. Here the going was slow, the climb strained her injured muscles and the pains returned. Hunger and thirst alone kept her moving forwards in hopes of finding something, anything to eat.

She watched the birds pecking at red fruits on one of the bushes and thought they would do her no harm. Plucking a few of the berries, she sucked at the soft outer part and spat out the seed. There was little in them to sustain her but the action of eating made her feel better. The berries made her thirsty so that when at last, she came upon a stream, she crouched down to suck up the fresh spring water like a young fawn. Having drunk her fill, she washed her face and hands, filled her pinafore pocket with more of the fruit and went on her way. She was aware her parents would be out hunting for her by now. Throughout the morning, she struggled to put distance between herself and Mapourika. She kept her eye on the position of the sun, knowing that when it was overhead it would be noon. As the golden orb slid down over her right shoulder she realised that by veering to the left she would be making for Dunedin where they had lived for some months before moving up to Mapourika.

In Dunedin, she had friends who would take her in and give her food. From time to time, she bit into another of the fruits and whenever she came to a stream, she drank the cool, refreshing water.

The path she had followed for much of the morning petered out and she found herself having to force her way through dense curtains of clematis which climbed the trees on every side, only to cascade downwards, their white star-like flowers brightening the otherwise dark, dank forest. It was impossible to see ahead and underfoot the carpet of delicately feathered ferns hid from view sharp boulders and those deep gullies, which everywhere lurked in the shadows, ready to trip her or twist her ankles.

Having climbed several steep sided hills and scrambled down into the narrow valleys between, she began to experience a different kind of pain. It seized her gut, causing her to double over and fall into a moss-lined pit beneath the roots of a giant tree. She was unable to get up. From time to time she moaned and drew her knees up to her chest. She wanted to be sick but could only manage an unproductive retching which did nothing to relieve her agony. After a while she felt the need to open her bowels but the effort of squatting only increased the pain and she soon lay down again, exhausted. Weakness overcame her. As she lay back on her bed of leaves and mosses, she could feel her own pulse beating in her head and there was a singing in her ears. She stared up into the canopy above her head and the trees seemed to whirl about her in a kaleidoscope of colour. The last thing she remembered was a little wood hen gazing down at her from a fallen trunk, his head cocked on one side and a puzzled expression in his beady eye.

*

Even though Alexander had anticipated Jessie's reaction to the news of Charlie's departure, her tirade against him had both shocked him and wounded him to the core. Charlie's letter had made it plain that the doctor was not in any way responsible for his departure and still Jessie blamed him. Was this simply a feeling of guilt on her part? Was it that, by not keeping her promise to the dying woman, she believed she had let Judith down? How could she accuse Alexander of driving the boy away to sea? Surely Jessie must realise neither he nor she herself could be held responsible for the lad's departure. Charlie was no longer a child so why should he not make his own decisions concerning his future? Perhaps that was the problem. Maybe Jessie found it hard to accept that Charlie was no longer a child.

Alexander consoled himself with the expectation that Jessie would soon see how unreasonable she was being and apologise. He could not believe that she would allow this one negligence on his part, to come between them permanently. Thus, swinging continuously between hope and dire despair, he turned his horse for home.

He had travelled only a few miles out of Mapourika when darkness fell. Pulling off the main track, he found a grassy bank beside a shallow stream where he could make his camp for the night. The provisions Teri had packed for him had been intended for the outward journey only and there was very little left. Nevertheless, he was able to boil water in the billie-can and make tea. He spread stale bread with a little butter left in the bottom of the jar and finished the cheese.

For a long while he lay under the stars, trying to sleep. Ideas churned incessantly in his head, denying him the rest he so badly needed. He tormented himself with thoughts of what could have been done to avoid the rift between himself and Jessie, a division which now seemed irreversible. Without hope of ever realising the dreams which he had nurtured for so long, there seemed to be no point at all in his continued existence. Here he was, half a world away from the life which he had mapped out for himself, in a situation which could do nothing for his professional reputation and which offered little in the way of future happiness. Teri was a good housewife. He could not deny her that, but he had been able to give her nothing more than his respect and protection. His heart had remained firmly with Jessie Dundas. He had never accepted the fact of her marriage to James Bantrie.

He loved his sons of course, but with so much of his time occupied by his own interests, he had spent precious little of it with them. They had grown up regarding him as protector and provider maybe but not as friend or mentor. When any problem arose in their young lives, it was to their mother that Malcolm and Tobias went for comfort and solutions. He had given more attention to Judith Bantrie's children than to his own only because, in taking an interest in Charlie and Catherine as well as Tommy Dundas, he had gained access to Jessie herself.

At long last he fell into a troubled sleep in which he relived that final parting in his dreams. Now however, Jessie seemed to tower over him, rage twisting her mouth into grotesque shapes as her angry, soundless words poured over him like a blast of hot air from the very fires of hell. He found himself running as though through treacle, so reluctant were his legs to move under him. He was trying to catch up with a tall ship as she slipped out between the Heads at Otago Harbour. On her poop deck, his hands clasped firmly behind his back and his dark hair blowing in the breeze, Charlie Bantrie stared out to sea. Heedless of Alexander's shouts, the boy fixed his gaze on the far horizon, never turning his head to see who was calling after him.

*

The sun was high in the heavens when the mare, startled by a wild boar crashing through the thicket at the edge of the clearing, gave a terrified whinny, disturbing the doctor's dreams and bringing him instantly awake.

'All right girl, nothing to be afraid of.'

The doctor untied his horse and led her to the stream to drink before feeding her the last of the oats in his saddle bag. There was nothing but a little flour and salt remaining of his own stores. He lit a fire and mixed flour and water in a pan to make dampers, the traveller's drop scones. He left the dough to bake on an iron plate over the red -hot fire and fetched water in the billie-can. The water had scarcely begun to boil when the mare lifted her head again, pricked her ears and turned towards the bushes at the side of the track.

It was a moment before Alexander too heard the sound which had attracted her attention, a low moaning, undoubtedly human. Following the direction given by the horse, he advanced cautiously into the thicket and came upon the child almost at once. She lay in a tight little ball, her arms clasped about her abdomen. It was clear to Alexander that she had been laying here for some time in her own vomit. It was a miracle she had not choked.

He lifted her away from the mess, straightened her tense little limbs and examined her for vital signs. Her breathing was shallow and her pulse rapid. She was feverish and when in response to his gentle questioning she spoke, it was with the meaningless babble of delirium. He examined her body, discovering the terrible bruises and lacerations inflicted by the schoolmaster and swore under his breath. The child's bare feet were torn and blistered from her long walk through the forest. It was a wonder that she lived at all!

His greatest concern for the moment however, was to find the cause of her sickness for she had undoubtedly been poisoned by something. He had not long to search. In the pocket of her soiled and torn pinafore he found reddish yellow berries from the Karaka tree. The fruit pulp was an important food source to the Maori he knew, but he was also aware that the poisonous seeds must be boiled for some hours and washed in a flowing stream before they could be safely eaten.

It had been some hours since the body's natural aversion processes had acted to expel the poison. The fact that she was still alive suggested that all trace of the poison had already been removed. Now that he was sure he knew the cause of her sickness, Alexander could concentrate upon the child's wounds. Cursing himself for having neglected to carry his medical bag, he cast about for suitable alternatives with which to treat her injuries.

The bright yellow, pea-like flowers of the Kowhai tree caught his attention. He knew that Teri stripped the bark of this species and boiled it in water to produce a substance she claimed to be quite as effective as Peruvian bark for reducing pain. Casting aside those prejudices which had caused so much friction between them in the past, Alexander tore strips of bark from the younger branches and placed them in the already boiling water. When the fluid was cool enough to drink, he pored a little of it into his own tin mug and raised the girl, supporting her head in the crook of his arm. She groaned and opened her eyes, staring up at him fearful and bewildered.

'Here, little one, drink this. It will make you feel better.'

She gazed into his light grey eyes and seeing there only compassion and kindness, she was no longer afraid. Her throat was parched and sore from so much retching and she drank down the bitter tasting liquid in great gulps. Then, fearing a resurgence of pain from her wounded shoulders she laid face down, her head resting on the doctor's folded coat.

Alexander, lacking any kind of cloth or salve to place upon her open wounds, gathered mosses from amongst the tree bowls and washed clumps of the spongy green plants in the stream before placing them green- side- down upon her wounded thighs and shoulders. The cool moss and the stringent potion he had brewed caused her to slip once more into sleep.

Surprised at how clearly he remembered Teri's instructions, to which he had paid little enough attention at the time, Alexander now sought out a Kahikatea, the white pine of the South Island. While the child slept, he gathered leaves from the tree, bruised them and set a pan of water to boil them. Tearing Matilda's soiled pinafore into strips for bandages he took hands full of the sodden leaves and packed them around the little legs and arms which had been so severely bruised and lacerated. Her clothes were filthy. Instead of replacing them immediately, he wrapped her in his blanket and took the garments to the stream where he washed them and hung them to dry on the surrounding bushes. Only then did he settle down to rest.

For several hours, Alexander kept watch over the child while she slept. When she woke, her fever had dropped and she spoke quite normally although her voice was weak. Alexander made tea and persuaded the child to sip the hot sweet liquid.

'Who are you?' she asked.

Her eyes darted from his face to the mare and then to her clothes hanging out to dry. Realisation dawned. She peeped beneath the blanket and saw that she was, as she had feared, completely naked. In her prudish upbringing, Matilda had been indoctrinated with the notion that nakedness was sinful. Never in her life had she taken a bath without wearing a cotton shift. As Alexander bent over her to feel her pulse, she screamed out and cringed away from him.

'It's all right, don't be afraid. I am a doctor. I shall not harm you.'

Seemingly convinced by the mild tone of his voice, she allowed him to examine her pulse and her eyes, still bloodshot from the retching, but she held the blanket tightly across her chest and refused to release her grip when he attempted to examine her further.

Her eyes never left him as he gathered her dry clothing from the bush. Respecting her modesty, he turned away momentarily while, slowly and painfully, she pulled on drawers and petticoat over her stiffened limbs.

'I had to use the pinafore for bandages,' he explained, smiling. 'It was in shreds and hardly worth bothering with.'

'Ma will be that cross with me,' she cried, weakness and weariness causing tears to well in her eyes.

'Your mother will be so pleased to see you safe and well, she will not worry about any old pinafore,' he assured her. 'Could you eat something?' he asked, taking up one of the dampers he had made. It had gone cold and the crust had hardened into a leathery consistency but it was all he had to offer her.

She took it gratefully, swallowing the tough dough down with mouthfuls of hot sweet tea.

Hungry as he was himself, Alexander spread the remaining damper and handed it to her. This time she savoured the bread and took her time over it. When she had finished, she gave a satisfied little sigh, finished off the tea in her cup and smiled at him.

'Thanks,' she said, 'I missed me supper last night.'

'My name is Alexander Beaton,' he told her. 'What is yours?'

'Tilda.'

'Where do you live Tilda?' he asked her gently. He did not want to alarm her by suggesting he take her back, not until he knew what she was running from.

'At the top of the main street, near the Maori village.'

'And the name of your village?

'Mapourika of course!'

Why, if she had been on the road all night, had he not come across her before?

'Which way did you come?' he asked, mystified.

'Over the hills.' She pointed to the steep rise behind them. Because of the inaccessibility of the range of hills, the road had taken a tortuous route along the bottom of the valley, making the journey many miles longer than the direct line which Matilda had taken. Alexander wondered how it was possible that the child had managed to negotiate such dense forest.

'How did you know the right way to take?' he asked her.

'I didn't,' she said, 'I just made sure that the sun was behind me, all afternoon.'

It was a miracle that she had not wandered off to the right and been lost forever.

'Why did you run away?' he asked her.

' 'e beat me and I ran. I can't go back!'

Tears filled her eyes as she realised, perhaps for the first time, the enormity of what she had done.

'Me father'll kill me,' she told him.

'Your father beat you?'

'No, but he will, when he finds out what I did!'

'Who beat you, Tilda?'

'Teacher.'

'Your teacher at Mapourika beat you?' Alexander could not believe his ears. Catherine Bantrie was the mildest, sweetest creature. Dumb animal or child, she would never lay a hand on either.

'Miss Catherine never did such a thing,' he said, angrily.

'Not her. She wouldn't hurt a fly would Miss Catherine. No, it was him what come last week, that Mr Moodie. He's the new teacher.'

'Not for long, if I have anything to do with it,' Alexander said, fiercely. 'Now Tilda, I don't want you to be afraid, but I have to take you back to your parents.'

She was about to protest, but he insisted. 'Your father shall not beat you and neither will the schoolmaster do so again. Trust me. Now then, we will just get you seated comfortably on the mare, and its back to Mapourika.

With some difficulty, he hoisted her onto the folded blanket in front of his saddle and climbed up behind her. Turning the mare in the direction from which he had come the previous evening, he set off at a slow walk so as not to give the child as little pain as possible.

*

It was late afternoon when Alexander, the little girl asleep in his arms, pulled his horse up outside the store and called for assistance.

‘I found a child wandering in the hills,’ he announced. ‘She says her name is ‘Matilda Brown. Has she been reported missing from here?’

‘Indeed, she has, Doctor,’ replied the storekeeper. ‘The entire village was out half the night. The mother is distraught and even the Maoris have given up the hunt, fearing she must be dead already.

‘Show me the way to the house,’ said Alexander, ‘and be so good as to let people know that she is found.’

‘Of course, Doctor. That’s where the Browns live, up there.’ The fellow pointed to a filthy shack at the end of the lane running alongside the Maori village.

‘On second thoughts, I shall take her to the manse,’ Alexander decided. ‘The child needs careful nursing and I believe Mrs Bantrie is the one to do it.’ The appearance of Matilda’s home filled him with apprehension. It did not bode well for a good recovery from her wounds.

‘Right you are, Doctor. I’ll cut along and tell Mrs Brown the good news while you get on up to the manse. Just leave it to me.’

As Alexander approached the manse for the second time in twenty-four hours, Tommy emerged from the rear and seeing the doctor still mounted on his horse with the missing girl in his arms, he ran inside to fetch Jessie.

She had known it was Alexander the moment she heard his horse’s hooves on the roadway. At Tommy’s summons, she was already halfway to the door. Jessie was ready to apologise there and then for her behaviour on the previous day. She had watched Alexander’s sudden departure with dismay knowing herself to be in the wrong, yet unable to prevent herself from venting her anger upon her dear friend. She was only too well aware that her wrath should have been directed at herself and her husband. James had made no attempt to consult Charlie as to what he wanted to do in life. He had planned the boy’s apprenticeship before even mentioning his arrangement with Alexander Beaton. Jessie, for her part, had made no attempt to interfere. She accepted that as Charlie was not her son, his future should be a matter for the boy and his father, alone. She had allowed matters to take their course and this was the result. Alexander Beaton had played no greater part in Charlie’s going than any of them.

Last evening, she had tried to write to him but had torn up one sheet of precious notepaper after another, deciding at last that to send a written apology was to take the coward's way out. She had almost decided to go herself to Dunedin to tell the doctor how sorry she was when she heard Tommy's call from the yard and knew that Alexander had returned of his own accord.

The moment she saw the child he was carrying, Jessie flew to Alexander's aid, lifting Matilda down from the saddle and supporting her until he could dismount and pick her up in his arms.

'Oh, the poor wee thing,' she cried in dismay when she saw the bandages and the bruised limbs. 'Wherever did you find her?'

'She took a straight path across the mountains and intercepted me on the road to Dunedin, this morning.' Alexander's tone was that of the professional physician, intent upon his patient's welfare. This was not the moment for any expression of personal feelings.

'She must have walked for miles,' said Jessie and then, noticing the bruises above the bandages, 'What happened to her legs? Did she have a fall?'

'Has nothing been said about the reason for her departure?' he demanded.

'Only that she was to be punished by the schoolmaster and ran away instead.'

'And who told you that? The man himself, no doubt!'

'Well, yes. It was Mr Moodie who reported Tilda as being missing from afternoon school,' she said, somewhat taken aback by his abrupt manner.

'Did the children not say anything?'

'Well, no,' Jessie admitted. 'James did question them but they seem strangely reluctant to talk about what happened. One little Maori boy said something about Matilda hitting the teacher but Mr Moodie denied it and nobody really believed the boy. The other children have refused to confirm or deny anything.'

'No doubt he will have threatened them with some dire retribution, should they talk,' Alexander muttered.

'You seem to be making the man out to be some kind of a monster,' she said, half joking.

But Alexander was not amused.

'Only a maniac or a sadist would inflict this on a child.'

He laid Matilda down in the cool bedroom to which Jessie directed him. As the doctor stripped off the girl's rags to reveal her tortured little body, Jessie cried out in disbelief.

'All the way along the road, I have been considering what is to be done,' he told her. 'This vile creature must not be allowed anywhere near the children. He must be dismissed immediately from his post and arrested for assault.'

'I suppose as Chairman of the School Board, James is in a position to relieve Mr Moodie of his position,' she suggested, 'but as to an arrest, the Sheriff is in Dunedin as you well know.'

'Then James must make a citizen's arrest or I will do so myself!' The doctor was quite adamant.

He cast a glance at the little waif still sleeping where he had laid her. 'Let her sleep while she can. She ate fruit which poisoned her and she is still very weak. When she wakes, barley water would be best and maybe a little thin broth. When she is stronger, I would be grateful if you will attend to her bruises and replace the bandages.'

'Of course, Alexander, you know you can rely on me.'

She ached to tell him how sorry she was for all that had been said yesterday but she could see that his mind was fixed upon the child and the fate of her tormentor.

'You will find James with the child's mother. She has been out of her mind with worry. As you will have realised, Matilda is not the brightest of children. Her mother was convinced she had lost herself in the forest or fallen to her death from the rocks.

'I think you do Matilda an injustice,' Alexander told her, bluntly. 'She managed to steer a direct line from here across the hills to the main road. Had she not eaten poisonous fruit and made herself sick, she would have found her own way into town. Without doubt, someone would have picked her up along the way. You should not be so quick to assume, Jessie. Things are not always what they seem.'

She took the rebuke in silence knowing it to be well deserved.

He checked his little patient once more, as though he were reluctant to leave her. Then with a curt nod to Jessie he set off for the shack where Matilda lived.

*

'Lacerations to the shoulders and lower trunk, two ribs broken, a severe contusion above the left ear...'

As Alexander dictated the extent of Matilda's wounds, James Bantrie wrote them down carefully in his notebook. The Sheriff had been sent for but in the four days or more it would take him to receive and respond to their summons, signs of the beating would have begun to disappear. A written affidavit would be required to be produced in court when Moodie was brought to trial. The doctor finished his report and signed and dated what Bantrie had written down. James and the storekeeper added their names as witnesses so that no one would be able to dispute the extent of the girl's injuries.

'Now, I think the next thing is to close the school and confine Mr Moodie to his house until the Sheriff arrives,' said Alexander.

'Should we not keep the children occupied?' asked the storekeeper. 'Perhaps Miss Catherine...?'

'I think it important that we cannot be accused of implanting ideas of what occurred in the children's minds,' said Alexander. 'Moodie's lawyers might well suggest that Catherine had swayed their testimony against the teacher. If she is given no such opportunity she will not be under any suspicion.'

'You are determined to have the man pay heavily for this momentary loss of temper, aren't you Alexander? There are those who would say that the master was within his rights to chastise the child. The taws is an accepted weapon in the classrooms back home.'

James, always one to avoid conflict whenever possible, was not sure that Alexander was justified in taking such a strong line against Moodie.

'I have listened to Matilda's account of what happened,' said Alexander. 'The teacher had already assaulted one of the Maori children when Matilda attempted to stop him by grabbing his ruler. It was in defence of her little friend that she picked it up and hit out at the man. Moodie then turned upon her with the taws and beat her to the ground. He continued to beat her almost into unconsciousness; scarcely an act of schoolmasterly chastisement, nor does it suggest a momentary loss of temper. Indeed, it is nothing less than brutal savagery.

Defeated by the doctor's argument, James Bantrie sighed deeply and took up his hat and walking cane. 'Very well, we will gather together the remaining members of the School Board and challenge the man.'

Alexander was gratified to find that among the members of the board were two solidly built farmers and the keeper of the hotel, a man renowned for his ability to control the rowdiest mob of a Saturday evening. With the support of these others, James and he should have no difficulty in dealing with the schoolmaster.

The members of the Board, not wishing to warn Moodie prematurely of their presence, approached the schoolhouse quietly and allowed the minister to precede them up the shallow flight of steps and across the veranda. At the door he paused for a moment, then without knocking, he went in with the others close behind him.

A deathly hush hung over the classroom except for one lone, childish voice. 'Let us now praise famous men and our fathers that begat us, for their work continueth... er... continueth...'

Seeing the figure of the minister silhouetted in the doorway, the boy who had been stammering his way through his verses, stopped in mid sentence, his mouth agape.

Moodie, unaware that a visitor had joined them, strode up to the child's desk and brought his heavy wooden ruler down sharply within an inch of the boy's fingers. The child flinched and any last vestige of the elusive passage disappeared from his recall.

'Well, is that all? What is the next?' Using the flat of his hand, Moodie cuffed the lad cruelly around the ear. 'Repeat from the beginning. Now!' The teacher barked.

The remaining children hung their heads and studiously scrutinised the wood grain in their desk lids. No one wished to catch the teacher's eye for he or she would surely be the next to undergo the torment.

'Good morning.' James spoke quietly but in that silent atmosphere he felt himself to be shouting.

Moodie turned, angry at the disturbance. 'What?'

His exclamation died on his lips when he saw, standing behind the minister, a group of villagers, all of whom must have witnessed the previous few moments.

'Mr Moodie, as Chairman of the School Board it is in my power to dismiss your class and close your school at a moment's notice. I do this, now.'

James turned to the children who were staring, wide eyed, from the newcomers to their teacher and back to the minister as he addressed them.

'You are to leave your desks just as they are and return to your homes. Please inform your parents that there will be a meeting in the church at six o'clock this evening when matters concerning the running of the school will be discussed. Go quietly now. Everything will be made plain at this evening's meeting.'

The children stood up and filed out in orderly fashion. Not until they were outside in the open air did the noise of their excited chatter begin. Alexander closed the door after them while the minister proceeded with his business.

'You will be relieved to hear Mr Moodie that the missing child, Matilda Brown, has been found and once she has recovered from her ordeal, will be returned to her parents.'

Moodie gasped with surprise and then gave an unconvincing expression of his relief. 'What on earth could the silly child have been thinking of,' he asked, blandly, 'running off like that and scaring us all half to death. She might have lost her way and never been found.'

'She ran away,' said Alexander, 'because she had been so severely beaten that she dared not return either to her own home or to this school.'

'Beaten?' Who does she say beat her?' Moodie's attempt to appear innocent met with little reaction from any of the men present. 'The children will tell you how she ran off when I threatened to give her a stroke of the taws; on her hands, of course. I assure you gentlemen I never touched her.'

Seeing no understanding or response of any kind in the faces surrounding him he continued talking. Despite his protestations of innocence, perspiration poured from his brow.

'Of course, Matilda is not quite right in the head you know. You shouldn't believe a word she tells you. She is forever making up stories I attribute the habit to her close fraternisation with the Maoris.'

His endless stream of words tailed off at last. In the silence which followed, James Bantrie, speaking with all the authority of his cloth, read out a statement he had prepared.

'Nicholas Moodie, in the presence of these witnesses, I arrest you for the brutal beating of an innocent child while she was under your care and protection. You will be confined in your own quarters until such time as the Sheriff from Dunedin arrives to take you into custody. Should you attempt to leave, my colleagues here will hunt you down and place you under lock and key. Is that understood?'

'But this is outrageous!' Moodie protested.

'No. A while back I was of a mind to give you the benefit of the doubt,' James said. 'What I have seen with my own eyes in the past few moments, convinces me that Matilda Brown is correct in her interpretation of events and that you, Sir, are quite unfitted to be put in charge of the young. Whatever the outcome of any court hearing you will never again be welcomed here, either as schoolmaster or in any other capacity.'

Still protesting his innocence, the schoolmaster was led away to his residence and pushed inside without ceremony. Although the door was not locked on him, the men agreed amongst themselves to keep a constant watch on the house and the first of Moodie's guards took up his position in the old rocking chair on the veranda.

'I never liked the fellow,' James explained to Alexander as they made their way through the village and up the hill towards the manse, 'but you see, I was aware that my dislike was at least in part, fired by Catherine's disappointment at not being appointed to the position herself. I suppose I over-compensated for Moodie's failings, for that very reason. There have been rumours of his severe discipline ever since he started. I was however, conscious of the fact that when she was in charge, Catherine might have been accused of being overly soft with the children.'

'One wonders how this creature came to be on the teacher's register for the Province,' observed Alexander. 'I was given to understand that such appointments were made only on the highest recommendations.'

'He taught at the Tailor's Merchant's School in Edinburgh before emigrating,' James assured him, 'and his sponsor was none other than the Earl of Stirling, himself.'

'One wonders why anyone with such auspicious backing would choose to emigrate to New Zealand?' said Alexander.

'I have been asking that question, myself,' said James. 'I am of a mind to write to an old friend of mine who seems to have his ear close to the ground in matters clerical and academical. Maybe he can throw some light on the mystery. If there is to be a court case brought against our Mr Moodie, the more evidence to support our claims, the better.'

Alexander marvelled at the strength of purpose gained by the minister in these past few years. When he had first known him, he was a man floating on a dark ocean with only his wife to keep his head above the water. This new James Bantrie was a different fellow altogether. It was as though he had gained in stature by taking upon himself the mantle of patriarch in this remote settlement, a community which he had helped to carve out of the wilderness with his own hands. His confidence had returned and with it his self respect. For the first time in their long association, Alexander felt that he actually liked James Bantrie.

'By the way, Beaton,' James seemed a trifle ill at ease now that they were nearing the manse. 'I'm afraid that Jessie let off steam in rather an unnecessary manner yesterday. We were both shocked at Charlie's departure, of course, but there was no cause for her to vent her rage upon you. I know she regrets her outburst but I'll leave her to make amends. Be charitable. I would not want to think that a boy's youthful indiscretion could mar our long-standing friendship.'

The cloak of despair which had fallen upon Alexander's shoulders from the moment he had read Charlie's letter fell away in an instant. She regretted her outburst. She did not blame him for Charlie's departure. Putting behind him the endless days and sleepless nights which had bedevilled him, Alexander Beaton strode over the threshold well in advance of his host. Jessie came forward to meet him and without exchanging a single word, they came into each other's arms. Before Jessie was aware of James's eyes upon them, she had kissed Alexander full on the mouth.

'Matilda is so much better,' she announced, confused by the spontaneity of her own action. 'I wanted you to be the first to know.'

'Oh yes of course, Matilda.' Alexander also seemed confused but in a moment, he had regained control. 'Has she taken anything to eat?'

At once he was the professional, advancing to his patient's bedside and taking up her hand to feel for a pulse.

Jessie followed him.

'She had a little broth as you suggested, and then went back to sleep. I have changed her dressings and there does not seem to be any sign of suppuration.'

It was a relief to know that the wounds had not putrefied. After this length of time it was unlikely that they would do so. Teri would be pleased to hear how well her mossy dressings had performed! He examined the bruised legs and arms and turned Matilda's head so that the discolouration above her ear was exposed.

'He might have killed her with that blow, alone,' he said angrily as he replaced the covers and turned towards Jessie.

'I'm sorry,' she said, 'about Charlie. I was wrong to say the things I did.'

He saw that she had deliberately closed the door after them so that James could no longer observe them. He crushed her in his arms in one wild exalted movement. Lips and tongues met before she pulled back.

'I feared I might have driven you away, maybe forever,' she told him, breathlessly. 'I could not bear that.'

'But I am scarcely ever here, as it is,' he said, her taste still on his lips, the scent of her hair in his nostrils.

'You have always been here in spirit; always, when I needed you most. If I had lost you, I could not have borne it.'

'Oh Jessie, what a mess we have made of things.'

She pushed him away.

'How can you say that?' she demanded, fiercely. 'We came out here to make a new life for ourselves. If Fate has decreed that that life shall be with partners other than we might have chosen for ourselves, then so be it. You have a thriving medical practice, a fine house, a good wife and two healthy children. I have the satisfaction of knowing that I have kept faith with a friend who supported me in my darkest hours. I have cared for her family and helped to lift James out of his depression into a man of purpose and vision. Between us, Alexander Beaton, we have made an important contribution to the well being of our new nation. Do not suggest for one minute that we have made a mess of things!

He studied her face, flushed with the passion of her outburst, her limpid brown eyes gleaming from beneath darkly curling lashes and saw that she was smiling. He bent to brush her lips once again, tenderly, a butterfly's touch.

'Friends?' he asked.

'Friends,' she agreed.

'I'm thirsty,' said Matilda Brown from the nest of pillows in which she lay. Jessie fussed with barley water and a squeeze of lemon while Alexander opened the door softly and went out to join James on the veranda.

'Everything all right?' he enquired.

'Fine, everything's absolutely fine,' Alexander replied.

Chapter Twenty-Three

For more than two weeks, Ian and Julian Frawley had tramped over mountains and through the steep sided gullies which separated one range of hills from the next. They had traversed wide open plains covered by wild flax and tough spindly grasses which tore at their legs and hampered their progress. They had fought their way through dense brush and dark forest always keeping within the sound of the river. Gyp kept ahead of the party, running three miles to every one of the men and thus it was that he was the first to come across the abandoned prospector's camp.

The dog paused in his rambling, standing stock still at the edge of a clearing. He could smell the dead embers of a camp fire and a second, tantalisingly sweet odour of rotting meat. His muzzle went up and his ears lay back against the sides of his smooth black head. Thus he remained until Ian caught up with him a few moments later.

'What is it old fellow?' he demanded, scratching the dog between his ears and laughing at his determined stare. 'Found a bitch have you? I shouldn't think so, not out here.'

He allowed his eyes to follow the direction of the dog's gaze and saw the miner's camp. He let out a low whistle and indicated that his approaching companions should proceed with caution.

Several roughly constructed huts and a makeshift tent occupied one bank of the stream which at this point meandered across a broad plain. Beyond this, to the west, a ridge of dark volcanic rock rose steeply from the valley floor. At the foot of the cliff where the river tumbled into a natural rock basin, the stream had been crudely dammed to hold back water to form a reservoir. This certainly seemed to be associated with the mining process. Below the dam the water level was low and the river flowed only sluggishly.

Ian crouched down in the bushes beside the dog.

'Easy Gyp, Good dog.'

He laid a steadying arm across the animal's quivering body.

'Quiet now', he said as Julian and Keto, their Maori guide, joined him. 'let's see if there's anyone at home before we go blundering in there.'

'Let me go,' Teko volunteered. 'If there is anyone there, I will signal with my machete, so.' He raised the broad bladed knife in line with his shoulder.

'If there are men sleeping there you must creep away without disturbing them, Teko,' Ian cautioned. 'Gold can make murderers of the mildest of men. We do not want a blood bath on our hands.'

They watched the Maori slip in and out of sight, using tree trunks and flowering bushes to shield him from view. Soon they lost sight of him altogether until he emerged upon an area of flat land which was devoid of any cover. Across this open ground the Maori ran swiftly towards the camp, shielded now by the shadows cast by the makeshift dwellings. They watched him enter first one then another of the structures, emerging each time to give the watchers on the hill a reassuring wave. In the last tent he took so long that Ian and Julian had already picked up their muskets ready to cover his escape, when he emerged waving his broad knife from side to side to indicate that all was well. By the time the remainder of the party arrived, Teko had already kindled some life from the dying fire and had set a billie- can to boil. Ian, curious to know what had kept the Maori so long in the largest tent, made straight for it.

'Don't go in there, Mr Ian, Sir. Bad spirits in there.'

Despite both the Maori's warning and the foul smell which emanated from within, Ian lifted the flap. Inside the tent on a makeshift canvas bed, lay the corpse of a white man in his forties or early fifties perhaps. After several days of summer temperatures, the flesh had turned grey but it was clear that the man had been well bronzed by working in the wind and sun and had been well used to rough living. There was no evidence of foul play and nothing to suggest that the cause of his death was anything other than natural. The man had been panning for gold in the river bed. This was evidenced by the equipment scattered all around the camp site. That he had not been alone was indicated by the additional sleeping quarters and the large quantity of stores. There was no way he could have carried everything out here by himself.

Where were his companions?

Teko threw light on the mystery when he explained to his white companions, how the Maori treated the dying.

'This white man had Maori servants.' Teko showed them utensils and tools which could only have been the property of his own people. 'Maori afraid of death spirits,' he explained. 'When white man sick and likely to die, Maori shut him up in his place and leave him without food or water. He die quick and easy that way. 'That's a matter of opinion,' Julian muttered, under his breath, 'but at least it explains how the old boy comes to be left abandoned here.'

Ian, having extracted a shovel from his pack, walked back to the foot of the ridge they had just descended and began marking out a suitable sized rectangle. The alluvial soil made for easy digging and in no time at all a grave had been prepared for the unknown prospector. Wrapping the rotting corpse in a blanket, Ian and Julian carried it to the site and lowered it into the grave. Then, taking up his bible, Ian read a few verses over the stranger before they shovelled back the sandy loam.

There had been nothing in the man's clothing to indicate who he was or where he came from. There was not even a certificate claiming the right to prospect for gold at this spot and they could only assume that the man had simply been trying his luck at panning and had not yet registered a claim. There was nothing to show that he had found any gold, but his companions would almost certainly have carried his hoard away with them. Maybe there would be something in his tent to identify him.

Ian took two flat pieces of wood to make a cross and crudely inscribed the words:

UNKNOWN PROSPECTOR
December 18th 1855

During the interment, Teko had stayed well away from the site of operation leaving the white men to dispose of their dead in their own way. While they were otherwise occupied, the Maori pulled the prospector's tent to the ground, bundled it up into a heap with whatever other contents remained inside and set light to it. He did not know what his companions had intended for the man's possessions but he was determined that everything the man had should follow the stranger into the next world. He had no wish to encounter the spirit of the white man wandering back in search of his belongings.

By the time Julian and Ian realised what the Maori had done it was too late to save anything from the fire. When the embers were cool enough they kicked about in them, searching for anything which might lead to his identification but all that remained were charred fragments of the wood and few unrecognisable pieces of black metal. Nothing remained to show that the poor fellow had ever lived at all.

The afternoon sun had dropped to a point where it hovered just above the western range of hills when Ian noticed a flash of light in the opposite bank. The water level had by this time, fallen so low that a layer of muddy deposits previously completely covered by water, was now exposed. It was from within this blackened band that the flash had come. He studied the exposure carefully and soon spotted a second momentary flash. Jumping down into the bed of the stream he forced his way through the shallows to the opposite bank and peered intently at the band of soft rock.

'Teko, fetch me a trenching tool and the pan,' he yelled excitedly. Gyp, thinking this was another game, leapt into the stream with him and had to be shooed away as Ian began to hack at the sandy bank knocking lumps of material into the great metal pan.

Ian poured water over the material he had dug out and began swirling the pan, pouring off water, adding more and swirling again. When all the light-weight material had been washed out and discarded what remained in the bottom of the shallow dish was a few minute flecks of yellow gold.

The dead prospector had been working at the right spot, sure enough, but the water level had dropped too late for him to have known it. From the condition of the bank it was clear that the lode- bearing alluvium had been exposed to the light and air for only few hours.

All three men continued to pan for the next hour and when it became too dark to see to work, they retired to the campfire and pooled their findings. Ian took out a small set of brass scales and weighed their hoard. It was a little under two ounces. In the short time since they had started panning they had unearthed gold worth in the region of five pounds sterling. It wasn't a fortune, but it promised well for the future. For long into the night they sat over the campfire planning their next steps.

Chapter Twenty-Four

'Panning is all very well,' declared Ian when they had been working the exposure for some days, 'but the most effective way to get out the gold, would be to use water under pressure. That may have been the purpose of the dam that's already here. Unfortunately, that construction is totally inadequate. If we are to continue to work this exposure once the rainy season begins, we shall need to divert the stream. That will require building stone and heavy timbers. A suitable dam must then be built to hold back a sufficient quantity of water for the pressure we need.'

'Won't that be expensive?'

Julian's initial intention had been to spend a few weeks of shore leave prospecting before joining another ship.. He had had no thoughts of any major investment.

'Yes, it will,' Ian agreed. 'My father may be able to stump up a certain amount and perhaps Dr Beaton might be approached, but we shall probably have to float a few shares on the stock exchange to raise sufficient capital to get started.'

'That surely means a trip into Dunedin?' Julian suggested. He would quite like to see a little of the bright lights after the past few weeks spent in the wilderness.

'It does, but we can't both go,' Ian declared. 'Someone has to stay here and guard the site and since I'm the one who knows what is needed I suggest that you and Teko hold the fort here, while I go and register the claim and have a proper assay made. Then I'll set about raising the necessary capital before I come back to relieve you.'

Julian was obliged to agree with the logic of this argument. Together with Teko, they drew up and signed an agreement of co-ownership of the claim and each wrote out a will, leaving his share to the others. In uncertain circumstances such as these, it was wise to cover all eventualities. Ian set out the following morning to retrace their route to Mapourika.

*

Catherine closed the schoolroom door and made her way over to the master's house. Although she knew it to be empty still she opened the door cautiously, anxious to see what Nicholas Moodie had made of the little house which she had designed for her own occupation. A full week had passed since the sheriff, arriving in great haste had taken the schoolmaster into custody and returned with him to Dunedin to await trial. Although the School Board had agreed that Catherine should resume her duties as village schoolmistress it had been decided that the school house should remain untenanted until Moodie's fate had been decided.

On the pretext that she should remove any food stuffs or clothing which might go mouldy or be subjected to attack by insects, Catherine had obtained the key from her father. Full of curiosity, she stepped inside the little house.

The furniture, much of which had been supplied by the villagers, made it a homely enough place but she could see how it could be made more comfortable and longed for the time when she would be able to place pretty chintz curtains at the windows and sew cushions for the hardwood chairs. Until the trial, however, she could make no preparations to take over the house. She had made the mistake of taking her tenancy for granted once before. This time she would wait until she was officially appointed to the teaching post before making any move.

Having assured herself that there was nothing left inside to go rotten, she closed the front door and made her way towards the steps beside the waterfall. A shout from behind made her glance up in time to glimpse a familiar figure amongst the scrubby bushes at the edge of the forest. She hurried back along the path to greet her brother, looking hopefully beyond his shoulder expecting to find Julian Frawley following along behind. Seeing no one, she asked anxiously, 'Where are the others? Where is Gyp?' Surely something must be amiss if the dog was not here in the forefront of the expedition.

'They are camped about six day's journey up river,' he told her, and then, blissfully unaware of her disappointment, he added, 'We have made a strike.'

'Gold?' she whispered, her throat suddenly constricted with excitement, 'You've found gold!'

'Yes, but keep it to yourself just at present. I must get into Dunedin as soon as possible to register our claim. Until that is done don't say a word to anyone. You understand?'

'Jessie and father, surely?' she qualified his statement.

'Oh, I shall tell them, of course, but not a word to anyone else.'

The waterfall was now a mere trickle compared with the foaming gush of water Ian had seen on his first visit to the village.

'I see that you have problems with the lack of rainfall, also,' he observed as they left the almost dry stream bed and made their way along the dusty village street.

'The water problem is very acute,' she told him. 'The river water has become polluted and is undrinkable and now even the feeder streams, further west, are drying up. Tomorrow morning the men are gathering to begin digging a well.'

'Do they know where to sink it? I might be able to help.'

'One of the Maori grey-beards has predicted that they will find water in the Johnsons' back yard, but I am sure the white men would be more inclined to participate if they knew that a mining engineer had confirmed the site.'

'It's not all that easy to locate underground water,' Ian told her, 'and I'm not familiar with the strata here about. What I can do however is to look at the Maori's site and see if there is any obvious reason *not* to dig there.'

'I'm sure that will help,' she said 'and if we say that father sent for you to confirm the position of the well, that will explain your returning here without the others.'

'You're a wise girl, young Catherine,' said her brother, admiringly. 'Some lucky fellow is going to get himself a very special wife one of these days.'

I hope so. Oh, I do hope so Catherine thought and again glanced back along the path in the direction taken by the prospectors wishing Julian had returned with Ian.

'What have you been doing up at the school?' Ian asked. 'I had the impression that friend Moodie spurned all offers of help in that department.'

'He has gone. One hopes, for good.'

'What, already?'

She told her brother the story of Matilda Brown and of how James Bantrie had made a citizen's arrest. Although he said little, Ian felt doubly justified in having made his own attack upon the unpleasant schoolmaster.

As it happened, the Maori had chosen well. Johnson's property lay to the east of the high street on a couple of acres of gently rising ground. Johnson, a gardener of many years' experience, had chosen the run for its light sandy soil, believing it was easier to build up a rich fertile loam using seaweed and rotted vegetation than to struggle with digging into the heavy clay to be found on most of the village plots.

On the evening of his arrival Ian went out, with Catherine acting as his linesman, and surveyed the area. He found the Johnson's property to be standing upon alluvial sand which had been deposited within a deep basin of impervious clay. Rain, penetrating the sand and finding no escape through the clay, should have collected over eons of time, saturating the sand and providing what is known as an artesian basin. With sand acting as a filter, Ian had little doubt that a well sunk here would yield good, clean water. What intrigued him was that the ancient Maori wise man, without the benefit of Ian's four-year training in mining science, should have know exactly the spot to choose.

The well was sunk during the next few days and very soon the initial gush of sweet clean water had been successfully controlled using Ian's engineering expertise. A pump was installed to raise the water to a high level and a holding tank erected from which the villagers could draw their drinking water without fear of contamination from the polluted river bed.

Ian had delayed his journey until the supply was established, the delay successfully disguising his real purpose in returning to Mapourika. There was little likelihood of anyone getting wind of the success of the prospecting expedition but when gold was the prize, no precaution should be considered too excessive. He set out for Dunedin one morning early in February, to file his claim.

*

The rain, the first in six weeks, began as Ian crested the rise above the Mackie's run and started the slow descent towards the suburbs of Dunedin. He had gone only a mile or two further along the road when his horse stumbled nearly unseating him and he was obliged to dismount and examine the animal's feet. The mare had cast a shoe. There would be no further riding for Ian. Night was coming on fast and he had no wish to spend it stumbling through deep puddles along the unmade track. Thinking he might find a stable for the mare and a pile of warm hay on which to rest until morning, he turned off the main track and led his horse to the door of the woman artist whose paintings and more besides, had so intrigued him on his first visit.

He hammered on the door, hoping to make himself heard against the howling of the wind in the trees. The strength of the gale was such as to cause many unusual thumpings and scrapings so it took Nellie Parker a few moments to realise that she had a real visitor and not another of those phantom callers to which she had been responding all through the wet autumnal evening.

O'Leary knew this was no false alarm. He stretched his long lanky legs, rose majestically to his full three foot six inches, at the shoulder, and stared at the door, his coat bristling, his back legs trembling. Whether this was in fear or anticipation it was hard to say. As Nellie moved to open the door, the great hound accompanied his mistress on stiffened limbs. He was ready to do battle to the death if need be.

William Mackie had presented Nellie with the dog soon after she moved in. Alice Mackie had been so adamant the girl needed protection from strangers that William began looking about for a suitable hound to keep her company. As a pup, O'Leary had been just a small bundle of soft grey fur. They had had no idea of his breeding and certainly no notion of the size to which he would grow.

William had found a litter of mewling puppies washed up on the river flats, close to the sea. The hapless creatures had been tied up in their sacking shroud and condemned to a watery grave. William, for all his great size and strength was a soft-hearted creature. He had carried the puppies home, fed them with warm milk and placed them in a box beside the stove to dry out. By morning, two of them were dead but the third sucked strongly when he was offered warm sugary milk from the blacksmith's fingers and within no time at all he had learned to lap from a saucer. He began to grow and showed himself to be a bright intelligent animal, responding exceptionally well to instruction. When he was satisfied the dog would conduct himself decently about the house, Mackie presented him to Nellie as a guard dog.

At this stage, other than his inordinately large feet, there was little to indicate his breeding. He was far too friendly to frighten anyone and the notion that he might become a guard dog made Nellie laugh. Unidentifiable as was he, she called her new pet Pup, and waited to see what he was to grow into before choosing an appropriate name.

She had been captivated at first sight by the animal's deep brown, bovine eyes, so expressive that he had no need of speech. She learned early on to understand his language. Requirements such as food, water, a walk, the need to go outside, each had its own short bark, look or stance and Nellie understood every gesture.

As the pup began to grow, it became evident that Mackie had not found her a lap dog. When he stood two foot at the shoulder on straight gangling legs, the dog was uniformly grey with a rough- haired coat and thin ratty tail. It was his long inquisitive snout however and the flopped over ears, which finally determined his breed. He was without doubt, an Irish Wolfhound.

Only when she had finally identified his breed, did Nellie give the dog his name, O'Leary, after an Irishman she had met aboard ship.

When Nellie opened the door a crack to see who was calling so late and on such a night, the dog snarled for good measure and Ian took two steps back.

'I'm sorry to bother you, Ma'am,' he greeted her, hesitantly. 'It's a while since I passed this way. You may have forgotten me. I am Minister Bantrie's son, Ian.'

'Of course, Mr Bantrie!' Fighting to hold the door open against the wind and rain she gasped, 'You'd better step inside.'

She experienced an unusual warmth in her cheeks and a sudden trembling in her limbs. Perhaps it was relief that this was not a stranger at her door. More likely it was remembrance of that sneaking little frisson of excitement which she had known when they had first met. These past few weeks she had felt much the same whenever the Bantrie name had been mentioned.

Frequently she had found herself hoping for a second sight of Ian Bantrie. Now he was here, in her very presence and alone, she felt completely tongue tied.

O'Leary was confused. Was this friend or foe? He did not recognise the signals his mistress was sending out. His low pitched, exploratory growl broke the silence.

'All right, O'Leary,' she said, catching the dog by his collar. 'This is a friend; Mr Bantrie.'

'Ian,' corrected the young man, stretching out a friendly hand towards the monstrous hound.

'If O'Leary may call you Ian, so shall I,' she declared, laughing at this formal introduction to her dog. 'And you may call me Ellen or Nellie if you please.'

'I know that this is an imposition Miss Parker, Nellie, but my horse has cast a shoe and I am of no mind to continue walking all the way into town in this rain. I wondered if the mare and I might shake down in you barn for the night?'

'The mare shall, certainly,' she replied, her eyes twinkling, 'but I believe I can offer you something a little more comfortable. While you are still wet, please take your horse around back. There's sacking to dry her and plenty of sweet straw in the barn. You will find a sack of oats tucked away amongst the gardening tools.'

While he was gone, she spread clean sheets on the chaise longue in her studio, a closed-in area of the rear veranda. She covered these with a pair of woollen rugs and a few cushions and then returned to the kitchen to boil water and check the rabbit pie she had been baking for her own dinner. Thank goodness there was enough for two and she had made a fresh batch of bread only that morning.

She laid a second place at the table and brought out from the corner cupboard made by Philip Mackie and presented to her on her birthday, a bottle of the wine she had made last season, fermenting the first crop of grapes grown from vines imported by Mackie, just as an experiment. It was perhaps a trifle harsh for some pallets, but she found it refreshing.

From Ian's point of view almost anything warm, wet and filling would have served, so tired and hungry was he. The meal was a banquet by anyone's standards. Nellie was a dab hand at pastry and her use of the herbs which she had grown in her own garden, made even the rabbit filling taste delicious.

'I didn't know the rabbit was indigenous to New Zealand,' Ian observed when he had cleared his plate for a second time.

'It's not. There were none before white people settled in the North Island. Someone thought it would be a good idea to let a few pairs loose in the countryside so that there would be some game to be hunted and a source of food but like the wild pigs, they are beginning to get out of hand. William Mackie lost an entire crop of cabbages a few nights ago. No matter what kind of fencing is used, it seems impossible to keep them out.'

At the word rabbit, O'Leary cocked an ear, thumped on the floor with his tail and looked expectantly at the door.

Ellen went out onto the veranda and came back inside immediately. 'The rain has stopped and the stars are out,' she said. 'Shall we take a walk down to the stream? O'Leary and I generally have a stroll at this time.'

Tired though he was, Ian had no intention of foregoing one moment of her company. The air smelt fresh and sweet after the rain. Weeks of accumulated dust had been laid to rest in a few hours and now the stars seemed brighter than ever in the clear air.

'It was like this some evenings on the islands, at home,' said Ian, thoughtfully. 'The stars seemed so close you could reach up and pick them out of the sky. Gazing up into the heavens at planets so different from those in the northern hemisphere, each explored private memories from that past life. Nellie could remember only tall buildings reaching to the sooty skies of London town, narrow cobbled lanes and rowdy bars with the all- pervading smells of rotting vegetation from the fruit market at Convent Garden. Only after she had joined Sir Tristram Wimborne's household and had served some years as a maid servant, had she found herself working at Sir Tristram's country mansion in Hampshire. It was then she discovered the existence of trees other than plain trees and dusty laurels. As a child, it had been only on rare occasions that she had seen open water from the banks of the Thames. Now, every day, she could stand on her veranda and see the Great Southern Ocean, a small silver triangle in the distance out there between the Otago Heads. There was little in this view to conjure up memories of home. She remembered only days of fog and rain, the chill easterly wind blowing up the Thames, the dirt and squalor of her native city and the cramped little house which was all her father, a porter in the fruit market, could afford for herself and her ten brothers and sisters. She blessed the day the Wimbornes had persuaded her to accompany them to New Zealand and was thankful that the fates had decreed that she should be her own woman in this new and unsullied landscape. She thanked Providence also for the gift of recording the sights around her and the means of making her own living in an environment which accepted no passengers. Her paintings sold well in a land bereft of the cultural aspects of a modern civilised society. She could live comfortably on what she could produce in her garden and what she could make from her work. Ellen Parker was dependent upon no one and that was how she intended to remain.

Ian traced with his fingers, the pattern of the Southern Cross in the sky and named those planets with which Julian Frawley had made him familiar. During their long nights in camp they had spoken of their hopes and dreams for the future and of what they would do with the great amounts of gold they were going to extract from their claim.

Julian had dared to seek Ian's advice regarding his sister, Catherine. Would she be prepared to marry a man whose work kept him from home for months, often years at a time? Should she give the least indication that she cared for him, he would propose marriage. Ian too, had spoken once or twice of the kind of girl he would want to marry and his description strangely resembled the elfin creature who stood beside him now on the little bridge above the sluice with her golden hair tumbling over her shoulders, her tiny turned up nose tipped with silver in the moonlight and stars sparkling in her light blue eyes.

For a moment, Ian was tempted to tell Nellie about the gold, but something held him back. It was not that he feared she might tell someone else. By noon tomorrow his claim would be filed and the workings officially their own. No, his hesitation stemmed from the hope that she might accept him for himself and not for the gold he was going to own. He hoped it was the mining engineer, not the successful gold prospector whom she would love. How dare he propose marriage?

This was only the second time they had met. What would she think of such impetuosity? If he delayed, the news would be out about the claim and he would never know if it was the gold or he himself that she was accepting. Thus tormented, he followed her back along an alternate path to the house until coming upon a stile, he preceded her so that he might help her over. O'Leary, who until now had closed in on them whenever Ian came near to touching his mistress, seemed to sense that the man's approach was acceptable for this time he held back. Even when Ian held out his arms for her to fall into them, the dog remained standing apart, nose to the wind, watchful but not alarmed.

No words were needed for what passed between them then. He buried his face in her deliciously scented hair and searched her face as though to memorise every minute detail of those finely chiselled features. Then, gently, he drew her mouth to his, his hand held lightly behind her head. Lips brushed softly together, her mouth opened slightly and his came down hard upon it, his tongue entering, searching, his hands wandering over breasts and buttocks until their two bodies were locked together in the moonlight.

A small sound from O'Leary which came from deep within his throat and emerged as something between a growl and a whine reminded them that it was late and time to go in. Hand in hand they climbed the steps to the veranda and, still reluctant to break the spell of that magical night, they sat awhile upon a low bench, looking out across the open country to the distant seascape.

'This is the perfect spot to live,' said Ian, 'but do you never get lonely?'

'My early life was so full of people, it was difficult ever to find a moment in which to be alone,' she replied. 'Now I have all the space and solitude that I need and for company, I have O'Leary. The Mackie's are very good friends to me.'

She glanced over in the direction of the blacksmith's farmstead and Ian recalled the young man who had been so anxious for her safety on that first occasion. What if Philip Mackie were also a suitor?

'The blacksmith's son seemed most solicitous for your welfare,' he observed. 'How will he view your giving me a bed for the night?'

'Philip? What has it to do with him who I chose to entertain in my own home?'

He wondered if her reassurance was not just a little too adamant.

'Philip is a boy; a lovesick puppy. I fear he holds a quite unrealistic vision of my beauty and charms. He believes himself to be in love as do all adolescents at some time or other. It is not me, but an ideal of womanly virtue which he worships and I, I can assure you, am no more virtuous than the next girl!'

Relieved that the way was open for him to pursue his own suit, Ian relaxed a little and tentatively placed an arm across her shoulder, drawing her closer.

'Can you imagine being able to love someone who is almost a stranger? Do you by chance, believe in love at first sight?'

'As in the two-penny novels we used to exchange aboard ship?' she asked, playfully. 'Well yes, one might always hope that it was possible.'

'And have you ever felt like that way about anyone you have met?'

'Only once,' she replied, teasingly. 'Of course, a girl on her own in the world without support must look hopefully at the first man who will give her a friendly smile.'

'But you have made a life for yourself now and it appears you have no need of a husband simply as provider. You are free to make a choice based upon love, and love alone.'

'Yes, I suppose that is the case,' she agreed, 'but what is love?'

'For my part, it is wishing to be with one woman and her alone, for all time. It is to recognise her instantly at a distance and to recognise her mood in step or stance. It is to be sensitive to her tone of voice, to know what she feels without her saying it. To be ever aware of her presence no matter how far apart you may be. That is what it means to be in love.'

'My, my, Ian Bantrie, how eloquent you are upon the subject. I think it cannot be long ago that you were in love yourself?'

'I never was, until some weeks ago, when I passed by this very house and met a fair young woman with a pert smile, a lively tuneful voice and a hand so skilled with the brush that I can remember every detail of those paintings which I saw.'

Suddenly the air about them had become very still. There was a tension between them which caused even O'Leary to raise his head and cock an ear to their conversation.

'Are you saying that it is me of whom you speak, when you talk of love?' she asked, her voice strained; breathless.

'I am. Tell me Nellie Parker is there any hope for me?'

She turned towards him so that the soft light from the oil lamp fell upon her face and he could see in her eyes the truth of her words.

'From the first moment I saw you, when I should have been fearful of you as a stranger, I felt that there was something special between us. I knew that I could trust you. Always hoping that you would pass this way again, I have watched the road for your coming day after day.'

Her tone changed from one of wistfulness to a bright cheerfulness as she accused him. 'Then, after all that waiting and longing, you arrive in the dark and the rain so I cannot see you coming.'

He took her in his arms and kissed her tenderly once again as he guided her inside the house. The rain came on again in the early hours of the morning and Ian and Nellie scurried about, tightening window fastenings against the wind and placing buckets and bowls beneath the spots where the thatch had been disturbed by birds during the long dry spell. A trickle of water gathered into a puddle beneath the couch on her studio floor but neither Nellie nor Ian troubled to mop it up before morning. The makeshift bed remained unoccupied throughout the night.

Chapter Twenty-Five

The doctor had given his evidence clearly and concisely. Yes, the child's injuries were consistent with a severe beating. Yes, he had no doubt at all that she had run away in fear of her life. Yes, she had admitted that she had dealt the schoolmaster a blow with his own ruler but only in defence of her little Maori friend.

Charged with assault and with intent to cause grievous bodily harm Moodie had once again fallen back upon his influential sponsors in the home country. His trial had been held up while an advocate of merit was brought out from Scotland to defend him. Money appeared to be no object where the man was concerned.

For their part, James Bantrie and Alexander Beaton had had to refer their case to the one lawyer in the province who had the necessary legal qualifications to prosecute it on their behalf. The Browns could claim neither sufficient funds nor sufficient standing in the community to mount a viable case themselves.

Once Moodie had been removed from the school, the children had begun to talk of all manner of cruelties and indignities, meted out by their teacher. So incensed were their parents by what they heard, between them they raised substantial sums of money to pay for a proper lawyer. Nevertheless, it would fall to James and Alexander to foot a large proportion of the bill, should their action fail.

The advocate for the defence was Sir Bertram Mountpleasant, a man held in the highest regard within the Scottish legal profession. He wore his wig and gown with the aplomb of one who had rubbed shoulders with the greatest personages in the homeland and was fully conversant with all aspects of the Scottish Law.

He addressed the doctor in a manner which Alexander later described as the mesmerising hiss of a cobra about to strike.

'You have given a very full and accurate description of the child's injuries, I am sure,' he paused just long enough for Alexander to nod in agreement and to relax the highly professional manner which he had maintained throughout the questioning of his own advocate. 'Tell me about the feet.'

'They were blistered and cut about by the stony path Matilda had trodden.'

'Oh? In your opinion, these injuries were not inflicted by Mr Moodie, wielding his…' another dramatic pause while Mountpleasant searched unnecessarily for the term, '… taws?'

'No, of course not, the child had been walking for hours through dense undergrowth without shoes. It was obvious how she had come by her torn and bruised feet.'

Alexander knew that he must not lose his temper but it was a struggle for him to maintain a cool outward appearance.

'Her feet were torn by the stony path but her legs were bruised by her schoolmaster. Is that what you are saying?'

Alexander nodded.

'Please answer the question,' the advocate snapped.

'Yes.'

'Tell us doctor, at what precise point on the child's limbs did the work of the rough pathway end and that of the schoolmaster, begin?'

'I'm sorry, I don't understand the question.'

'It seems simple enough to me, Doctor. Which of the bruises described, do you attribute to the branches and rocks stumbled into as the child made her way through the forest, and which to the taws?'

'On her legs, the marks below the knee might have been caused by sticks or rough stones along the path but above her knees, on her thighs and buttocks and particularly across her shoulders and chest, these could only have been applied with a lash.'

'Enlighten me, Doctor. You went to a Scottish Public School, as did I?'

'I did.'

'Were you ever chastised with a taws?'

'Not a taws, no, with another implement.'

'Ah…' He gave a long, drawn out sigh of satisfaction. 'A cane was used perhaps?'

'Yes.'

'And this implement raised a weal on the flesh, the arms, the buttocks?'

'I suppose so, yes.' Alexander replied cautiously, wondering where all this was leading.

'Canes are made from bamboo, are they not?'

'Yes.'

'Bamboos or other plants of similar disposition are to be found in most of the woodlands around the globe?'

'I suppose so, yes.'

'Well doctor, can you tell me the difference between the weal left on the skin by a cane in a schoolmaster's grasp and that left by a cane growing on a bush?'

There it was at last! That was his game.

Alexander turned towards the judge as he answered.

'A single cane leaves a single weal My Lord. A taws with seven thongs leaves seven marks each fanning out from the point at which the leather is bound to the handle of the implement. Make no mistake about it, My Lord the injuries were made by a schoolmaster's taws.'

Mountpleasant had clearly lost the round, but the match was not yet over.

'Doctor, were you present when these alleged, wounds were inflicted?'

'No, of course not,' Alexander replied angrily.

'How do you know that the wounds were inflicted by the schoolmaster and not by the child's father, for instance?'

There was an angry murmur from the body of the courtroom.

'Matilda told me she had been attacked by the schoolmaster and I believed her.'

'My Lord, this is hearsay evidence and should be struck from the record.'

The judge nodded and indicated to the clerk that this should be done. To Mountpleasant's dismay however he added, 'Nevertheless, I am interested in this line of questioning. Continue with it, if you please.'

Mountpleasant was clearly ill at ease as he continued. 'You believed the word of this eight year old child, against the word of a qualified teacher of long standing, when many of those who know her well, have already testified that she is a couple of coppers short of a shilling?'

'Please explain that expression, Mr Mountpleasant. I don't believe I have heard it before. What was it? A couple of coppers...?'

'The girl is mentally retarded, My Lord.'

'Oh, I see.' He glanced over the top of his reading glasses towards where Matilda sat, between her mother and Jessie Dundas. She had been scrubbed clean, her hair washed and neatly tied and her new pinafore was so spotlessly white and stiffly starched that she might have been a china doll, newly removed from her wrapping.

Contrary to all convention, the judge indicated that the child should be brought forward and as, rather uncertainly, Matilda approached the bench, he leaned down to her with a broad smile on his face.

'Come up here and sit beside me, my dear.' He indicated a little wooden stool which the clerk had placed at his side. When she was comfortably settled, he asked her: 'Tell me Matilda, why did you run away from school?'

'Because he beat me.'

'Who beat you, Matilda? Can you point the man out to me?'

'That's 'im, over there,' she pointed to the man in the dock. 'Mr Moodie what used to be our teacher.'

'They say that you tell stories, that sometimes you make up things which are not true.'

She warmed to this friendly, be-whiskered gentleman in his curly white wig and his funny clothes. Throwing aside her natural distrust of all strange men, she told him 'We...ll, no. I don't make things up, not really. I just get a bit muddled sometimes.'

'Muddled?'

'With sums and spelling an' that. I know what words I wants to write down but the letters come out all wrong and I can't always remember my times tables and when 'e shouts at me I forgets all together!'

'I'm not surprised, said the judge trying hard to disguise his amusement. 'I sometimes find sums very muddling, myself. Is that all your teacher did when you were unable to spell words or get your sums right, shout at you?'

'N...o! She drew the word out dramatically and looked at the judge disdainfully. How could anyone be that stupid?

'He whacked us with the taws.'

‘The day you ran away from school, what happened then? Had you got your spellings wrong again?’

‘Na… not me. It was my friend wot got wacked an e’s only little, like. I couldn’t let that great bully thump a little kid so I picked up the ruler and ‘it old Moodie with it, but it weren’t very ‘ard ‘cause ‘eh’s taller’n what I am.’

‘And what did Mr Moodie do then, Matilda?’

‘‘e pushed me down on the floor an’ ‘e ‘eld me there while ‘e whacked and whacked and wouldn’t stop.’

‘He hit you with the leather thongs?’

‘The taws, that’s what ‘e used.’

As she spoke the girl’s eyes filled with tears at the memory of those terrible moments and she began to snivel.

The judge gave her a minute or two to compose herself, even handing her his own clean linen handkerchief to wipe her eyes.

‘Now then, Matilda,’ he continued, ‘Tell me, where were you going when you met the doctor?’

‘He found me. I was awful sick. I’d seen the birds eating these berries and I thought if the birds could eat them, so could I. I was so hungry.’

‘I’m sure you were.’ The judge pursued his point. ‘When you met the doctor you were on the main track into Dunedin, did you know that?’

‘I thought I couldn’t miss it if I kept the sun behind me all afternoon.’ She seemed startled when he gave her a friendly little pat on the backside and said, ‘Go along, back to your mother. I think I have heard enough.’

The judge apologised in turn to both Dr Beaton and to Mr Mountpleasant.

‘I realise that it is a little unconventional to bring in a second witness when the first is still under examination, but since Dr Beaton’s testimony was indeed hearsay,’ he acknowledged the correctness of Mountpleasant’s intervention with a thin- lipped smile, ‘I felt it better to have the matter cleared up, at once.’

In an authoritarian tone, which defied any dissent, he addressed the jury, ‘I think there is no doubt that it was Nicholas Moodie who used the taws upon Matilda Brown.’

Mountpleasant, who had been completely thrown by the judge’s unconventional approach, struggled to gain the ascendency.

'But, My Lord, it is the child's word, the word of an imbecile no less, against that of a respected gentleman with an unblemished record, highly considered in his profession.' He waived a bundle of papers at the bench. 'I have here letters of recommendation and approval from fellow teachers and the noble parents of several of his past pupils.' He laid the documents before the judge.

Ignoring these, the judge addressed himself to the jury.

'I have examined the child Matilda Brown in open court and can find nothing in her responses to convince me that she has other than a complete command of all her faculties. You will therefore disregard those observations of the council for the defence which refer to her mental capacity.'

Then, to Mountpleasant, 'Do you have any further questions for Dr Beaton?'

'No, My Lord'

'Very well. Dr Beaton, you may stand down.'

Alexander, still fuming at the manner of the defence council's questioning, made his way to the benches at the back of the court unable to assess what weight had been placed upon his evidence.

Matilda's advocate was on his feet.

'My Lord, that concludes the case for the plaintive.'

'Very well, we shall take a break for luncheon and resume at two o'clock precisely.'

*

'What has become of James?' Alexander asked, as they all sat down around the doctor's dining table and Teri served a light luncheon of cold meats and salads.

'Once he had given his evidence, he had himself rowed across to the ship which docked at Port Chalmers this morning, ' Jessie explained. 'He seems to be most anxious to receive a letter from home… something to do with the trial, I think. He said he would join us here later.'

Alexander turned to the young advocate at his side, 'Well Arnold, how do you think it's going?'

Arnold Walker swallowed, chasing meat and potatoes down with an excellent white Burgundy which Alexander had broken out especially for the occasion.

Matilda's advocate had been only a few months in the province when James Bantrie had presented him with this case. It had been a risk for such a newcomer as himself to take the case on. The defendant was a man of some standing back home in Edinburgh, enough to give him status here in Dunedin as well. He was championed by those wealthy and influential local personages who, in the future, would be the most likely to engage the services of an up and coming young lawyer. Nevertheless, there had been something about the sincerity of both Bantrie and his doctor friend which had convinced Arnold Walker they were right to prosecute Moodie. Like the judge, Arnold had questioned Matilda and had found her to be open, honest and very far from the portrait of a mentally retarded, aggressive little creature which Mountpleasant had attempted to represent to the jury.

'How do you think the case is going?' Jessie asked anxiously. She had not entirely understood the complicated language of the advocates and some of the questions had seemed quite irrelevant. She had been most unnerved when the judge had spoken directly to Matilda, particularly as most of the child's responses had been inaudible to those in the body of the court.

'For what it's worth,' said Arnold, 'I think the judge has taken a liking to Matilda, but you must remember the jury is for the most part, drawn from the town's most upright and God-fearing citizens. Believing in strict discipline and themselves almost certainly at some time victims of the schoolmaster's heavy hand, they probably see nothing wrong with corporal punishment. These are people more than likely to be impressed by Moodie's long list of recommendations from the noble citizens of Edinburgh and Aberdeen than by any suggestion of his brutality.'

'I don't think so, not when they hear what is contained in this letter!'

James Bantrie's triumphant declaration startled them all. Flushed and excited, he had entered the room, quite unobserved. He slumped into a chair and pulled from his pocket a large blue spotted bandanna which he used to wipe the beads of sweat from his brow. It had been a race against time to get back before the afternoon session in the court but it had been worth the effort.

'Just arrived this morning, aboard the clipper standing off Port Chalmers. I knew Murdo McLeod would never let me down!'

He dropped the letter, already opened, onto the table in front of the advocate. Arnold took it up and read with increasing excitement:

Edinburgh, August 1855

My Dear James,

How good to hear from you at last and to know that all is well with your little venture in the backwoods. Your church sounds delightful. How I wish I could hear the Maori singing Mr Wesley's tunes to the harmonium. What a pity we Presbyterians do not exhibit the same degree of harmony as the Methodists!

Nothing changes much here. As you know, I have now retired from my former parish and am whiling away my time in the library of St Giles where they have been pleased to give me the honorary title of curator of the archives which is a good excuse for spending my latter days with my head in a book.

Your question about this fellow, Nicholas Moodie, immediately jogged my memory but it was some while before I tracked down the real facts of the case. The task was made the more difficult because people in the know, seemed reluctant to discuss the matter. A little persistence unearthed most of the details however. It seems that Moodie was taken on as master in Classics at the Tailors and Merchant's School in the Michaelmas term of 1848.

Arnold Walker read on, fascinated by the story and whistling softly when he found in it precisely the evidence needed to destroy his opponent's case.

He looked up at last and smiling, folded the letter and placed it with his court documents.

'Well done, Mr Bantrie! This couldn't be better.'

'Why?' demanded Alexander impatiently, 'What does it say?'

'No time to discuss it now,' said Arnold, leaving James to explain to the others. If he was to persuade the judge to accept this new evidence before the afternoon session, there was not a moment to lose.

*

Mountpleasant had taken Moodie carefully through his statement of the facts as he saw them. He had been more than lenient with the child, despite her difficult behaviour. Yes, he had spoken quite harshly to the Maori boy, but Matilda's reaction to this had been out of all proportion to the mildness of his rebuke.

'Did you use the taws at any time?' Mountpleasant asked, his features placid, but his eyes startlingly intense.

'I prepared to give Matilda the lash across the palms of either hand which is the customary punishment for classroom misdemeanours.'

'And what happened?'

'Before I could touch her, she ran screaming from the room and I never saw her again until she appeared in court this morning.'

'You did not throw her to the floor and hold her down by the neck while you lashed her body mercilessly with the thongs?'

'No.

'No further questions, My Lord.' Mountpleasant sat down, clearly more than satisfied with his own performance, and smiled encouragingly at his client.

'Would you call yourself a good teacher, Mr Moodie?' Arnold Walker's first question came as something of a surprise.

'Well, it's not for me to say,' Moodie showed uncharacteristic modesty in his reply. 'I have always had considerable success in my work. My pupils did well in Edinburgh, some of my best boys gained entrance to University.'

'Do you normally advocate corporal punishment as a method of getting children to learn?'

'Some require more persuasion than others, shall we say.' Moodie beamed upon the jury and some members were disposed to titter at his little joke.

'You yourself raised the question of your work in Edinburgh, Mr Moodie. Would you say that that period of your career was entirely satisfactory?'

A slight shadow passed across the schoolmaster's face at this question but he recovered his composure quickly and answered plainly.

'I do.'

'Would you then care to give us the reason for your very sudden dismissal on the… 'Arnold deliberately consulted the letter in his hand although he knew the date well enough… 'on the ninth day of November 1851?'

'There was a disagreement between the headmaster and myself.'

'Over a matter of discipline, I believe?'

''Yes.'

'One of your pupils was involved?'

'A charity child, yes.'

Arnold appeared shocked and surprised.

'Was there some difference between the punishment meted out to charity children and those of wealthier parentage?'

'The charity children generally required rather more discipline than their more highly bred classmates.' Moodie explained, patiently.

There was murmuring in the courtroom. The judge used his gavel to regain the attention of those present.

'Is this line of questioning relevant, Mr Walker?' he demanded.

'I believe it is, My Lord, if you will just bear with me.' Arnold returned to the defendant.

'You administered punishment to a charity child and this caused an argument between yourself and the headmaster?'

'That is correct.'

'He felt you had been too lenient?'Arnold enquired, artlessly.

'No, he felt I had been too severe.'

'He considered… and I quote from a transcript of the enquiry held at the school at the time… that to beat a child senseless and lock him in a dark, airless stationary cupboard overnight, was a bit over the top even for a charity pupil?'

Moodie had the grace to hang his head when he replied quietly, 'Yes.'

'I'm sorry Mr Moodie, I did not quite catch that. Will you repeat it for the jury?'

'Yes, that was the verdict of the enquiry at the school.'

'Are you aware that because of his terrifying experience, the child in question had to be confined to a mental institution where he lives to this very day?'

'I am.'

'Such an act might in some circles be considered criminal. Why were no charges brought?'

'It would not have been in the interests of the school, which is a most prestigious and highly regarded institution. The Board considered it best to keep the affair quiet.'

'You were dismissed and your influential friends arranged for your departure to New Zealand, where you could no longer be a threat to the well being of the Tailors and Merchant's school?'

'Yes.'

'It seems to me Mr Moodie that you are not at all the mild- mannered, benevolent mentor of the young which Mr Mountpleasant has painted for us this afternoon. I believe this letter supports in every detail, the story as told by Matilda Brown, of what happened earlier this year at the Mapourika School. I put it to you that you lost your temper with her, just as you did with this other child, that you held her down by brute force and delivered vicious blows to her body in excess of what might be considered reasonable chastisement. It is my contention, Your Lordship, that this is an out and out case of assault with intent to cause grievous bodily harm and that the defendant deserves the maximum sentence the law allows.'

With this final flourish, Arnold Walker took his seat and after a brief summing up from the judge, the jury retired.

*

'Six months' gaol for the assault and the loss of his licence,' Arnold announced to his wife, at the conclusion of the case on the following morning. 'Costs were awarded to the plaintive which must have been a relief to the minister and Dr Beaton.'

'And my clever husband has won his first important case.'

His wife flung her arms around the young advocate's neck and gave him a hug. 'I am so proud of you my dear. Now we shall get plenty of briefs.'

'As for that, I can't be too sure,' Arnold cautioned. 'It was touch and go with the jury. There were several of them who clearly considered that a schoolmaster is king in his own classroom. Most men have recollections of beatings at the hands of one sadist or another. Some even believe that such chastisement is a necessary part of growing up."

His liberal- minded spouse shuddered at the thought. She glanced in the direction of her infant son, lying in his cradle.

'If any schoolmaster dares treat my Matthew so, I'll kill him!' she declared.

'Let's hope you can find a decent advocate to defend you!'

She chased him out into the kitchen beating him with her feather duster all the while, until he grabbed it from her and she collapsed, laughing, into his arms.

*

Nicholas Moodie, incarcerated within the walls of the town gaol which had for so long been devoid of any permanent inmate, was treated almost like royalty. His meals were brought in from the Wharf Hotel. His cell was comfortably, if sparsely furnished with bed and chair, there was even a desk at which to write and shelves for the collection of books he had had brought in. For much of each day, he was free to walk in the garden, where, if he chose to, he might lend the gardener a hand. Had it not been for loss of face and dignity, Moodie might well have accepted his sentence gracefully and gone on his way. It was not in his nature however to accept that anyone should get the better of him. Those responsible for his present situation must be made to pay and pay dearly!

For six long months, during which he had little else to occupy his thoughts, he spent every waking moment plotting the downfall of his enemies. Although his stay at Mapourika had been a short one, there had been sufficient time for him to observe the people around him and to assess the relationships between them. Although the minister and the doctor were his prime targets, he was astute enough to have realised that the woman, Jessie Bantrie, played a vital part in both their lives. Injure her in some way, and both men would suffer.

He was not so stupid as to consider another physical assault, however. No, this time he would hurt them in their pockets and he knew exactly how to do it.

Chance had brought him to James Bantrie's door and coincidence had decreed that his path and Jessie Bantrie's should cross for a second time, twenty years after and half a world away from their first encounter at the Edinburgh Infirmary.

He and his fellow students had been down from Aberdeen for the match, as he recalled. They had, no doubt, drunk more than was good for them. There had been an exchange of derogatory remarks with the Glasgow boys resulting in a fracas in which Moodie received crushed ribs and a broken leg. That was how he came to be in the infirmary, lying alongside a young fellow from the Outer Isles who was dying from tumour of the brain.

Chapter Twenty-Six

Ian Bantrie had no difficulty filing his claim and in addition to Dr Beaton and his own father, he managed to enlist the financial support of Fergusson, the land agent whose name had been suggested to him by Ellie Parker. Having appealed to his backers to exercise the greatest discretion concerning the find, armed with their promissory notes, he visited those merchants who could supply the necessary tools and provisions. From Tobias Leny, he hired a small team of Chinese labourers and from William Mackie, transport to carry both men and materials to the gold camp. At Alexander Beaton's suggestion, he arranged with Wei Lin to supply foodstuffs for the new camp on a regular basis. Until a suitable road could be constructed, the Chinese was to leave what they ordered with James Bantrie at Mapourika.

So while Nicholas Moodie had lain in the town gaol, awaiting trial and Catherine Bantrie restored order in the village schoolroom at Mapourika, two heavily laden drays drawn by teams of four oxen apiece set out across country bound for the highlands to the west. With such a wild and varied terrain the wagons were difficult to handle and despite the help of the Chinese labourers, the journey took far longer than anticipated

The party finally arrived at the site of the miner's camp nearly three weeks after setting out from Mapourika.

The almost continuous rain which had begun soon after Ian's departure, ceased as they completed the final few miles to the camp. During Ian's absence, the river had risen and the alluvial pocket in which they had first discovered gold had been submerged. Unable to continue panning in the deeper waters, Julian and Teko had first converted the tented site into a small village of more substantial huts; one each for themselves and Ian and two further buildings to house any additional men that Ian might bring in. A substantial, windowless building in stone was designed to house the explosives they would require for constructing their dam.

Now that they knew where the gold-bearing alluvium was sited, it had not been difficult for the two men to estimate from the direction in which the river currents flowed where those materials washed away by the stream might be deposited. They had found other small pockets of gold bearing alluvium at intervals lower downstream. By panning each of these locations assiduously, they had amassed a further cache of between fifty and sixty ounces of gold dust, sufficient, in Frawley's opinion, to warrant a further expedition into town. Julian, determined to renew his acquaintance with Catherine Bantrie, had already decided that this time it would be he who would make the journey!

Once they had established themselves in their new and relatively comfortable quarters, the Chinese were set to work felling trees for the dam while Ian made a survey of the route which the new waterway would take. The object of the construction was to direct the main course of the river away from the mother lode to rejoin the main stream bed some half a mile below the camp. It was a task which was to prove both long and arduous.

The channel through alluvial soil was easy enough to dig but timber reinforcements must be constructed to prevent the sides of the canal from capsizing and blocking the stream. Very soon they found they had to cut through hard rock of a volcanic nature. Ian's knowledge of quarrying now came into its own for he was adept in the use of gunpowder and had an uncanny instinct to find just the right position at which to place his charges. When his explosions took place, the rock seemed to fall apart like loosely packed building blocks, splitting neatly along precise lines. These blocks could then be stored for later use as the masonry wall required for diverting the river into its new course.

Julian, smarting under a democratically arrived at decision to concentrate all their efforts on the new waterway rather than have one of their number make a second expedition into town, soon tired of Ian's painstaking method of digging out the rock and hoping to speed up the process, decided to try his own hand at laying charges.

Choosing an early morning when his partner and one of the Maori had gone off on a hunting expedition to replenish the larder, he persuaded

Teko to accompany him to the channel workings. Using the long auger which was operated by hand, he drilled his holes ready to receive their charges.

While watching Ian at work, Julian had not appreciated the degree of skill possessed by his partner who made the process of drilling the rock appear so easy. Julian struggled with the unwieldy auger for a long time but even after all his effort he had managed to penetrate the rock by only a few inches. Despairing of completing his self-allotted task before Ian returned, he sank the next boring into a ready- made crevice in a section of rock which had deteriorated through weathering. At this point the auger went into the rock like a knife through butter and soon Julian had a hole deep enough to thrust in his charges. Two further holes, approximately at the corners of the rectangle he wished to remove, were made in the same way, choosing the easiest path for his drill. Now he had attained a modicum of skill with the drill, he returned to the first hole and completed it to a satisfactory depth. He packed in the explosive and retired to a safe distance. With Teko at his elbow, he crouched down behind a pile of logs and lit the fuse. It spluttered into life and the flame skittered fast across the sand, appearing to fizzle out as it disappeared amongst the rocks. Unsure what had happened to the fuse, Julian sent Teko scampering across the open ground to rekindle the flame. The Maori might have reached the apparently burned out fuse in time to prevent what happened, had he not stumbled on the auger which Julian had cast aside carelessly once he had finished his drilling.

Scrambling to his feet once more, Teko came upon the end of the main fuse where Julian had connected the four short fuses together only to discover that far from being extinguished, all four would ignite simultaneously, in a matter of seconds.

The Maori had the presence of mind to fall flat on his face and cover his head with his arms before the explosion occurred. The loosely packed charges, instead of splitting the rock neatly into blocks, shattered it into thousands of razor sharp shards which flew in all directions.

When the dust cleared, Julian saw to his horror that Teko had not moved. The noise of the explosion had woken the rest of the camp so that by the time Julian reached his friend, men had come from every direction to see what had occurred.

They stood around the silent figure of the young Maori while Julian got down on his knees to look for signs of life.

Teko suddenly opened one eye and grinned. 'That a bloody silly thing to do, Chief. Might have given Teko a nasty headache!' He leapt to his feet, laughing. Apart from a few nicks and bruises he was quite unscathed.

White as a sheet, Julian sat back on his heels, relieved and yet angry at the Maori for his deception. 'You allowed me to think you were dead!' he said, trembling with pent-up emotion. He felt too weak at the knees to stand up.

'You think you kill Keto that easy?' his friend exclaimed. 'Me too young to die yet!'

While the younger man gambolled about, telling his friends of the white man's folly, Julian picked up one shard of rock which had lodged in the sand, inches from where Teko's head had been. Perhaps it would be as well not to show the Maori what a narrow escape he had had. With a flick of his wrist, he sent the shard crashing into the bushes narrowly missing Gyp who, alerted by the explosion came crashing into the camp at that moment with Ian close behind.

Laughing and joking, unaware of the narrow divide that had existed between safety and disaster, the Chinese were calling Julian *Lord of the Fireworks,* while Julian, recovering rapidly from his fright, began to enjoy his elevated position in the eyes of the workmen. His pleasure was to be short lived however for Ian, seeing the shambles created by his partner's careless work and inexperienced handling of explosives, turned upon him with bitter recriminations.

'What if you had killed Keto?' he yelled. 'This was no accident, it was sheer bloody carelessness. There are simple rules to be obeyed in handling explosives and you have chosen to disobey them all.'

This admonition, delivered within the hearing of every man on the site, left Julian feeling like the raw ship's apprentice he had once been. He recalled, suddenly, that other occasion when his impatience had led to a terrible epidemic aboard the *Albatross.* Acknowledging the justice of Ian's condemnation, he hung his head and wandered off down river to be alone with his thoughts.

Ian went to the explosives store and taking out a padlock he fastened the door and pocketed the key. He alone would use explosives from now on.

The mutilated rock was redrilled, the rubble removed and Ian continued to blast away at the new watercourse until eventually it met up with the river further downstream. Now a dam was constructed to divert the flow along the new channel but also to hold back sufficient of the water to form a deep pool whose exit could be controlled by sluices. This reservoir would provide a head of water which would produce sufficient pressure to hose the alluvium out of the dry river bed in preparation for panning. Once used to perform its task, the water would then be allowed to continue its original course to Mapourika and the sea.

Chapter Twenty-Seven

While James Bantrie had gone to great lengths to understand his Maori parishioners he had never come to terms with their ancient religious beliefs concerning the plants and creatures of the countryside around them. To the mountains and the rivers, the clouds and the skies, they attributed feelings of peace, anger, thanks and retribution. At the time of drought, the old men of the village had decreed that the river was angry with them and had sent its brothers the fish, to remind the villagers of their insignificance in the great scheme of things. When the waters flowed fresh and clean and in great abundance after the rain, the river was happy and sang in its bed, trickling over the waterfalls and dashing between the rock-strewn rapids. When for no apparent reason, the flow began to ease off yet again, the elders decided that there was something amiss with their father the river and scouts were sent upstream to discover what ailed their benefactor.

*

At the mining camp, at long last sufficient gold dust had been accumulated to warrant a trip into town and Julian, who had tried valiantly to make up for his misdemeanour during the weeks which followed his attempt at quarrying, was commissioned with the task of seeing the gold safely deposited in Dunedin. With Teko as his guard as well as his companion, he set out on horseback, his saddle bags laden with gold dust. Anticipating the renewal of his acquaintance with Catherine Bantrie, he insisted that since the road was now clearly marked and open all along the way, they should ride on through the night reaching Mapourika the following morning. They arrived a little before noon and while Keto reported to his father in the Maori village, Julian went straightaway to the manse only to be disappointed. Miss Catherine, he was told, now resided in her own house beside the village school. She would not be free to receive him before afternoon school was out.

At the creaking of the schoolroom door, Catherine set aside the pile of exercise books she had been marking without looking up from her desk. Anticipating a little mew of greeting from the ginger cat which shared her lodging and expecting to feel it's warm furry body winding itself about her legs, she murmured, 'All right Puss, I'll soon be finished.' Now she looked up and was startled to find that the intruder lurking in the shadows was a man. Staring into the gloom of that late Spring afternoon, she tried to make out the shadowy figure but until he spoke, she was unable to place him.

'Please Ma'am isn't it time we all went home?'

He had seated himself in one of the tiny desks and had raised his hand for her attention.

'Julian? Julian Frawley is it really you, at last?' She threw down her pencil and stood up to greet him.

'When did you arrive? Have you seen father yet? Is Ian with you? What of the gold. Are we to be rich?'

The words poured out one after the other even before they had had time to exchange the usual courtesies.

'Noon, no, no and hardly,' he replied to each of her questions, grinning.

'Oh you!' she laughed and ran into his arms as casually as she might have done when a child, aboard ship.

He caught her up and returned her peck on the cheek with a kiss on the lips. It was a kiss over which he lingered a moment more than was necessary. He would have continued to savour her nearness, the sweetness of her breath, the scent of her freshly washed hair, but she drew back, regarding him, searchingly.

'Have you missed me?' he enquired.

'Of course we have. We have missed all of you,' she replied artlessly. 'But to be honest,' she continued, smiling a little at his disappointed expression, 'I have been so busy picking up the reins now that Mr Moodie is not to return, that I have had precious little time to pine for any of you.'

'And I imagined that you, like Odysseus' wife, would be stitching away at some record of our adventures until we returned.'

'But you are not my husband,' she teased, 'and besides, embroidery thread is very hard to come by.'

'We have been away for nearly six months,' he reminded her.

'Really, is it so long? How the time flies when one is busy!'

Was there something in her expression? Something in those laughing eyes to tell him she was only playing with him, that she really cared?

'Come on,' he said, losing patience, 'confess it! You really did miss me!'

'Of course I did, silly man.' This time her kiss was placed firmly upon his lips. 'I have looked out for you every day for months past and when Ian appeared a few weeks ago, all alone, I thought I would die. There now, are you satisfied that you have been missed?'

'Catherine Bantrie you are a minx and a tease and I love you dearly,' he declared. 'There is only one thing for it, if I am ever to have peace of mind in the future, you must marry me!'

'La Sir, is this a proposal?' she enquired and he was not sure if the roses in her cheeks were a blush of excitement or the result of their exposure to the blustery spring breezes which greeted them as they left the schoolhouse and sauntered along the path towards her own accommodation.

'Do you wish that it were… a proposal, I mean?'

If she said no, he would throw himself over the cliff for certain.

Suddenly serious, she held both his hands in hers and gazed into his eyes. 'Julian Frawley I fell in love with you on the day we first met aboard the Albatross. Had you asked me then, I would have followed you to the ends of the earth and back.'

'Then you will marry me, gold or no gold, seafarer or landlubber?'

'Oh, I don't know about that.' She glanced away, unable to bear his expression of dismay.

'But you said you loved me once.'

'I was a child; an adolescent flower in bud. Girls of that age believe that every man they meet is destined to be theirs for life.'

'Could you not learn to love me once again?'

'Maybe, but I should have to get to know you first. I have seen what ill-considered marriages have done to my dearest friends and I propose to be much more circumspect in my choosing. Besides which, I am not yet ready for marriage. I studied hard for many years to become a teacher. Now I have a school of my very own, filled with delightful children and a comfortable little house which I designed for my own pleasure so, for the time being, I am well content.'

'You could continue teaching,' he said, doubtfully. 'At least while I remain at sea. I should make no objection to my wife working while I am away from home.

'But you would expect me to stop whenever you sailed back into port, is that it?' She demanded and her question was only partly flippant. In any case, the Authorities may not agree to my being married and a teacher. In Scotland, a woman must give up her post when she marries. That is the rule.'

'Perhaps things will be different in New Zealand,' he suggested, but hoped it would not be so. A man expected to keep his wife, not have her working for a living.

'As to the house,' he continued casually, 'I shall build you something bigger and better but for the time being, you may as well live here as anywhere. After all, I shall be often away at sea.'

'Ah, so you really do not propose to leave the sea and make your living on the land?' It was the question she had been asking herself all along. How could she be married to someone who would be away from home for months on end? What kind of life would it be always waiting for her man to come home; having to watch her children grow without a father's guiding hand upon them?

'I can leave the sea, if that is what you wish.' He did not sound convincing.

'But I would not care to be the one to keep you from your calling. I believe the salt water is in your blood.'

Julian, after so many weeks on land, had to confess that he still yearned for the open seas and the motion of a rolling deck beneath his feet. She was right. He would find it very hard to give up the life of a mariner.

'If we strike it rich, then I may buy my own ship and sail her only in New Zealand waters,' he suggested. 'I could come home to you every week.' Instinctively he felt he must abandon the subject of their marriage before she could give him a definite answer, for if she gave it now that answer would most certainly be NO.

It was Catherine herself who provided for his escape.

'Ian told you how Charlie has run away to be sailor?' she asked, steering him from the topic of their personal relationship.

'Yes. Were your parents very distressed?'

'At first they were, but I think Pa has at last come to understand Charlie's great desire for the sea and Jessie has persuaded herself that she had no part in my brother's decision, so she too can rest easy. She made a promise to our mother you see.' Perhaps he did not, but at least the conversation was now in calmer waters.

'Then they don't blame me?' Julian's question startled her.

'Why should they blame you?'

'Aboard the *Albatross* I told him so much about the life of a seaman; taught him things about the ship; encouraged him to think about a life at sea.'

'I am sure my parents have not laid any blame at your door,' she assured him. 'The truth is that Charlie was never cut out to be a doctor. He only accepted the role because father wanted it so. Now Tommy is to be Dr Beaton's apprentice. Like Jessie, he has a vocation for healing and a true feeling for humanity. He will make a fine physician.'

They had reached the porch of her little house.

'Won't you come in and take some tea?' she asked. 'It will only take a minute to get the kettle boiling. I keep it always on the stove.' Now that the moment for decision making was passed, she was reluctant to see him go.

'I must report to your father. There are some matters concerning the dig. Will you not come with me to the manse?'

'There are things I must do in preparation for tomorrow's classes,' she told him. 'You go and find my father. No doubt Jessie will invite you to stay the night. I shall come along later and join you all for dinner.'

Thus dismissed, Julian went on his way. Perhaps there was logic in what she had been saying. He must go back to sea and she still had some growing up to do. He would ask her again when the fresh bloom of her new teaching post had worn off a little and independence did not seem to hold such an exciting prospect.

Chapter Twenty-Eight

Phantom figures in the night move silently from bush to bush, tree to tree. Creeping across stony ground where only the occasional clump of silvery tussock grass provides cover, the silent shadowy forms approach the sleeping camp. A low croaking sound simulating that of the familiar weka bird, brings the curious dog towards the strangers and even as he realises his mistake, a firm hand clasped over the sharp black muzzle and a quick twist of the head ends any last hope that he might alert his masters.

They reach the dam, this man-made object which has changed the natural course of their father, the stream. They see how the white man has controlled the waters for his own advantage and they set about reversing the course. The wooden piles have been driven deep and whole tree trunks have been cemented together by mud and lime but the shadows are skilful. They attach their ropes to the great logs and with brute strength, move them aside until their sister the water, imprisoned in the lake above, assists them with her fearful strength. At last the barrier is dislodged. With a sudden gush, logs, stones and even the sandy bed of the dried out river with its horde of gleaming yellow metal, all are washed away, carrying with them tents, cooking pots, spades, shovels, Chinamen; everyone and everything in the river's path.

*

The meal lasted well into the evening. James, anxious to hear of progress made at the prospector's camp, held Julian's attention and prevented him from brooding over his earlier conversation with Catherine.

If Jessie noticed some coolness between the two young people, she made no mention of it, assuming Catherine would unburden herself when the time seemed right. Even when the two women had left the table and cleared away the dishes, nothing was said.

'The river has been diverted already,' Julian reported. 'While the water passing downstream has of necessity been restricted, we have done all in our power to see that a continuous flow is provided. The dam could even be described as an improvement for should a drought occur again in the future we shall simply stop working until the rains return and direct the stored water downstream in controlled amounts. In any case, I don't think you will notice the difference as far east as this. There are many other tributaries which are unaffected by our workings.'

'The Maori have already expressed some concern about the reduction in the river's flow,' James told him. 'I have listened to their speculations and felt guilty, knowing the cause and being unable to enlighten them. The village elders seem happy enough to accept the changes but some of the young bloods are agitating to send an expedition up river to find out what has happened to their water supply. Despite the alternative source of water provided by the new well, there are many traditionalists who see the river as the source of their well-being and are angry at any disturbance in the flow.'

Perhaps Ian should explain to them the object of the changes he has made,' Julian suggested. 'If Maori men were to be employed at the gold workings, maybe the villagers would be more ready to accept the changes.'

In the kitchen, Jessie studied her stepdaughter, thoughtfully.

'Well,' she asked at last,' has he proposed?'

Catherine looked startled, had she made her feelings so obvious?

'He has,' she replied, hesitantly.

'And?'

'I refused him.'

'But why? I thought you had been pining for him these many weeks.'

'Yes, I suppose I have but when it came to the point, I could not bring myself to give up my freedom so soon after it is won.'

Jessie might have felt insulted that her step-daughter should regard her move into the schoolhouse as a bid for freedom. Had she not always been at liberty to do exactly as she pleased? Wisely, the older woman held her peace, allowing the girl to voice her thoughts without interruption.

'I suppose that every young girl dreams of a husband, a fine house and babies. I know that I did, especially when, aboard ship the conversation in the women's cabin was about little else. Later on, I got to thinking more about all the women I know who have been married. When I was a very little girl, I watched my mother lose, little by little, everything which gave her comfort and happiness. She was a clever woman, quite capable of making her own judgements but no matter how incautious or inappropriate my father's actions might appear, she always accepted them without question. Once, when I asked how she could bear to give up her old life to go and live on that dismal island, she said, '*On my wedding day, I vowed to obey your father in all things.*' Well, I cannot make such a vow if it takes from me all ability to make decisions concerning my own life. Then Jessie, you, a woman whom I have always regarded as an independent spirit, you too subjected yourself to my father's will even though you didn't love him.'

Jessie gestured, registering her protest at the suggestion, but her stepdaughter continued,

'What is it about the man, that he can command such loyalty?"

'Your father is a good man, Catherine, with an important mission in life,' Jessie insisted. 'He needs a partner to lift some of the more mundane pressures from his shoulders. When your mother lay dying, she begged that I take on her role of wife and mother and I promised that I would. I have no regrets. This is a good life. There are many ways in which I may express my own personality and leave my stamp upon the situation. I have no complaints.'

'And then there is Mrs Beaton, locked into a marriage of convenience.' Catherine, once launched upon her subject, was not to be interrupted.

'It is clear, even after all these years that the doctor has eyes only for you. When we were aboard ship, it was common knowledge that the two of you were to be wed. How could you have refused him in favour of my father? How could he find it in his heart to marry someone else so soon after losing you? Are all men so fickle?'

'You must understand that there are more things in life than romantic marriage,' Jessie reasoned with her. 'You and Charlie needed a mother and James wanted a companion for his journey into the wilderness. How could I refuse him when my dearest friend had already extracted from me a promise to take care of you all? For Tommy, it was best that he be brought up amongst friends. He has benefitted greatly by being a part of your family so everything has worked out for the best, believe me.'

But Catherine was unconvinced.

'I shall marry for love or not at all,' she insisted. 'But that love must be unselfish, forgiving and understanding and if I may not have independence of thought and the freedom to pursue my own interests, whatever those might be, then I shall never marry!'

Jessie smiled to herself but made no further comment. For all her twenty-two years Catherine, shielded as she had been from many of life's worst exigencies, was still a little more than child. It would do no harm for the young couple to wait awhile. Who could say what would happen to them all, should the gold prove to be more than a short- lived excitement.

*

Water, a tumbling, foam-capped wall, carrying with it gigantic tree trunks whose stout branches tear at river-bank and boulder, hurtling all before it; water, trapped momentarily behind temporary barriers, piling up its energy to break free at last; water tearing away cliff and promontory; water rumbling through deep chasms, its giant voices echoing from wall to wall; water swirling in muddy whirlpools, spreading gently at last over sandbank and low lying flood plain.

Not a stick, not a blade of grass, neither a chick in its nest nor a vole in its river-bank parlour, nothing is secure, nothing is saved.

*

Tommy Bantrie was packed and ready to depart for Dunedin by dawn the following morning. They had been awaiting Wei Ling on his way back to town for new supplies but now the lad would be able to travel with Julian Frawley who was himself, taking gold dust in to town for banking.

Of all the white settlers in the township of Mapourika, Tommy Dundas was probably the most at ease amongst the Maori. He had grown up in company with the village children and learned early on to communicate with them. Now he was fluent in their language and having at the age of twelve years, reached his maturity in the eyes of the Maori, he moved freely about the village accepted without question as one of their number. This morning as he walked along the street he found many friends to whom he must say goodbye.

'Goodbye, Uncle,' to an ancient Maori warrior, tattooed liberally from head to navel, 'See you at Christmas!'

'Make sure you keep some cookies for Danny to bring me on his next trip to town, Mrs Sawyer!' to the woman whose husband ran the village bakery. He would never forget the taste of the Scotswoman's honey cakes.

Despite his great desire to become a physician, it was going to be a tremendous wrench for Tommy to leave the village to pursue his studies with Dr Beaton. His excitement was inevitably tinged with sadness at leaving behind so many whom he loved. He would miss Catherine's companionship and he would be separated from his mother for the first time in his life but he suspected that her devastation at their parting would be far greater than his own.

Taking the river road, he climbed the steps beside the waterfall for one last time and sank down on his knees when he reached the river bank alongside the schoolhouse. Above the waterfall, the pool seemed tranquil enough and the water, trickling over the rocky ledge and tumbling into the depths below, was clear, sparkling and full of fish. Tommy lay at full stretch upon the bank watching and waiting for the trout-like kokpura fish which were just as susceptible to being tickled as their British counterparts.

A group of children on their way to morning school caught his attention. Coming up on the far side of the river, they were making for the stepping stones above the waterfall a route taken by many of them when the water level was sufficiently low.

Tommy leaned over the bank for one further glimpse of fish he knew to be skulking in the shadows. This close to the water he could distinguish a low, rumbling noise; a steady pulse, whose sound was increasing even as he straightened his back and glanced up river towards the source of the disturbance. Expecting the children to have heard the sound and stopped before fording the stream, he was horrified when he realised that they had heard nothing and were about to cross.

He shouted a warning and began to run towards them but they continued on down the bank, the tallest boy stepping out onto the first of the line of flat stones which would lead him to the further bank. One after the other the children hopped to the middle of the river, the first and older child glancing back to see that the others were following.

The roar was getting louder now and Tommy, knowing something was terribly wrong, yelled to the stragglers to make haste. Soon only one infant, perhaps four or five years of age, was left stranded upon his rock, half way across.

Tommy yelled at him. 'Go back!' but the bewildered child, not understanding the reason for Tommy's command and wanting to follow his brothers, stopped where he was and began to weep, his little fists tightly clasped, covering his eyes.

Even as the child hesitated, poised precariously in the middle of the river, a monstrous wall of water, fed on its journey downstream by many tributaries all of them swollen by overnight rain, rounded the bend and came into view at last.

Tommy ran to the pebble strewn beach from where the stepping stones reached out across the water and leaping from rock to rock, he swept the child up in his arms and leaped on towards the further bank.

In seconds Tommy, together with his fragile burden, was engulfed by the wall of water and carried away. The two bodies, still clinging close to one another, were swept into the middle of the stream. The child struggled, impairing Tommy's movement. He yelled in his ear, 'get on my back and clasp your hands together, around my neck.' Somehow the infant managed to do what he was told. With his hands free, Tommy made better progress. Knowing he could not now avoid being swept over the waterfall, he swam to the centre of the stream and was swept over the waterfall at its deepest part where no rocks protruded. The pair fell into a deep pool locked together, rising to the surface at last breathless but unharmed. Carried along by the current Tommy found that he was being swept back to his own side of the river where trees overhung the bank, their branches dangling in the water. As the swirling current carried them past, he reached out making a desperate attempt to grasped one. The first branch broke off in his hand. He dropped it and reached again, in vain. Just as he was forced to accept that his last chance had gone a lower branch which had been completely submerged by the swollen river, caught him around the legs and prevented his onward drift. Ducking down below the surface, he grasped the thick limb and managed to get one leg across it. Locking his ankles together and holding on with both hands he began to crawl along the branch until both he and his burden were clear of the water. Heedless of the rough bark and broken twigs which tore at his hands and scraped the skin from his legs, he made his way inch by inch towards the bank. The child on his back had made no sound since they emerged from the water and had it not been for his tiny hands clasped firmly about Tommy's neck, the boy might have feared him dead. The slightest whimper and a word in his ear which sounded like 'Mama' reassured him.

'Hold on little'n,' he gasped. 'We're nearly there.'

When only a matter of yards from safety, Tommy felt his strength beginning to flag and knew that he would not reach the bank without help. The angle of the branch had increased so that he was crawling up a steep incline and he could feel the bark beginning to slip through his fingers. Resigned now to being swept away to his death, he began to pray in earnest for the first time in his life.

At that very moment, he felt a strong hand grasping hold of his hair, the pain of it dragging him back to his senses. A second hand reached down and took a firm grip on the shoulder of his jacket. Two strong arms were hauling him on along the branch until he saw below him, in place of the swirling water, green grass. Only then did he release his grip on the tree. Tommy and his burden fell in a heap onto the grassy bank.

With Tommy safe, James Bantrie, still clinging to the sapling which had supported him during the rescue, began to ease himself back from the river's brink. As he did so his support gave way, the sapling uprooted by the minister's added weight. He felt his feet slipping from under him. With a wild cry of desperation, his limbs entangled in a leafy trap, James skidded down the steep, muddy bank and into the foaming river. James, unable to release himself from the tangle of branches hurtled away downstream and was carried to his death, his body dashed to a pulp against the huge boulders which constituted a second series of rapids below the village.

On the bank, Catherine Bantrie, who with her father had witnessed Tommy's heroic attempt to save the child had waited downstream in hopes of rescuing him. With Tommy lying exhausted at her feet and the sobbing child clutched tightly to her bosom she could only stand helplessly by and watch as the disaster unfolded.

They found the minister hours later, washed up on the mud flats at the mouth of the river. He lay still, entangled in the tree which had been both his support and his undoing, surrounded by the wreckage of the Maori village which had been engulfed by the massive tide of water. Many of his flock had received serious injuries, nearly all had lost their homes but miraculously, no one other than James himself had lost their lives.

Chapter Twenty-Nine

Nicholas Moodie stood on the gaol house steps and sniffed the air of freedom. Six months! It had seemed an interminable time when the judge had pronounced sentence but with so many plans to occupy his mind, the time had passed quickly. In one single respect Nicholas's plans had been thwarted. Fate had already stepped in to take her revenge upon the Reverend James Bantrie. Still, the doctor remained and the woman.

With a determined air, the former schoolteacher descended the gaol house steps, shouldered his canvas knapsack and set out for Mapourika on foot. On this occasion, there was no question of his paying for a seat on one of the increasing number of wagons following the route. Every penny Nicholas possessed had gone towards bribing his gaolers into making his life in prison tolerable. Never mind, the long walk and a night or two under the stars would help him to adjust to his new-found freedom. There would be time enough to think about replenishing his resources when he caught up with Jessie Bantrie.

*

He had been walking for some hours when he heard a rumbling of wooden wheels upon the unmade road. Footsore and weary, he glanced back in hopes of seeing a friendly carter who might give him a lift along the way in exchange for his company. To his dismay, he recognised the brightly painted wagon belonging to Wei Lin, the travelling merchant. Knowing that the Chinaman would undoubtedly report his presence on the road to those at Mapourika whom he wished to surprise, Moodie leapt for the ditch at the side of the road and rolling himself into a tight ball he concealed himself beneath the feathery overhanging fronds of a giant tree fern. He lay quite still until the wagon was well past and then climbed cautiously back onto the path before continuing on his way.

*

James Bantrie's sudden death had affected the entire Mapourika settlement. With characteristic fortitude in the days immediately following James's death, Jessie had buried her grief in hard physical labour about the house and garden. When her neighbours called with their condolences she heard them out but found herself unable to accept any comfort from the gospels they quoted. James's God had failed her once too often.

Immediately upon receiving news of James Bantrie's drowning, Dr Thomas Burns, the Free Church of Scotland's senior administrator in Otago, had ridden in haste to the village to bring consolation to the widow and conduct a funeral service befitting a member of the church hierarchy. Having partaken of the customary funeral tea, the reverend doctor was at pains to make clear to Mrs Bantrie her changed position now that the settlement was without its minister.

'I fear that you must seek other accommodation in due course, Mrs Bantrie. The manse is, as you know, church property.'

Catherine, with her brothers and stepmother, had helped make the mud bricks for the building with her own hands. She had cut timber until her hands were too blistered to hold the saw and had worked, up to her knees in water at the river's mouth harvesting reeds for thatching the roof. Surely the house was the property of those who had built it? Indignantly, she challenged Dr Burn's assumption that it belonged to the church.

'But my dear young lady,' he argued, 'when your father negotiated the purchase of land from the Maori, it was on behalf of the Free Church of Scotland. Payment was made from church funds. There was an understanding with the Maori, that the land would be used only for church purposes. Someday soon there will be a new minister with a family to house. You cannot expect him to set to and build his own manse.'

'Why not? Wasn't that exactly what we had to do?' she protested.

'Your father's contract differed from those now issued to immigrant churchmen. The time for pioneering is past. The new minister will expect everything made ready for his arrival.'

'What of my stepmother? Who will compensate her for the loss of her home?'

'Mrs Bantrie's tenancy died with your father.' He sighed a little, indicating how tiresome he found having to make such an explanation. 'When a tenancy agreement comes to an end, all investment in the property reverts to the landlord. That is the law of the land.'

'And the church will make no reparations? No compensation whatsoever?'

'There will be a small widow's pension, of course, some thirty pounds per year, I believe.'

'A pittance; a pauper's wage for one who has given her life these past seven years, to establishing your church for you, here in the wilderness. For shame on you and your church!'

Unable to contain her temper, the girl stalked out.

'I am afraid your daughter is a trifle overwrought, Mrs Bantrie. But then, hysterics are to be expected of course, in the circumstances.' The reverend gentleman was inclined to be tolerant of all females in distress. 'It is a pity that your older son is not at hand to deal with matters,' he continued. Perhaps you will ask him to call upon me when he returns from his expedition? There will be certain documents to sign.'

Jessie nodded listlessly. She had paid little attention to what was being said. Initially she had been numbed by the shock of her husband's sudden death and had gone about her daily living like an automaton. Today's funeral service had held little meaning for her, just a jumble of words. Only as she had watched the coffin resting on its cords, her husband's parishioners gathered around the open grave to lower him, had she shown any spark of awareness. In that moment she had recalled just such another ceremony, the burial of her other husband, that strong, cheerful, kindly young man who had been Tommy's father. Standing today beside the grave, supported, on either side, by her son Tommy and Julian Frawley, it was as much for Dougal Dundas as for James Bantrie that she had wept.

'I shall of course, be writing to Edinburgh for a replacement for Mr Bantrie,' Dr Burns rattled on, 'but meanwhile, I shall draw up a rota of temporary preachers who will make occasional visits to the parish. We cannot have your husband's carefully nurtured garden of souls reverting to paganism.' He allowed himself a quiet chuckle. 'It would suit my purpose admirably, Mrs Bantrie, if you were to stay in residence for the time being in order to entertain such visiting clergy.'

Too absorbed by her own thoughts to pay attention to what was being suggested, Jessie made no response. Julian on the other hand, astonished by the man's lack of sensitivity, felt obliged to answer on Jessie's behalf.

Trying hard to control his anger he replied, 'Mrs Bantrie will be pleased to accommodate your visiting preachers until she has made alternative arrangements for somewhere to live. After that, I fear you must make alternative arrangements, Dr Burns. I shall be riding up-country before nightfall in search of Mr Ian Bantrie and will give him your message. Now Sir, as you can see, Mrs Bantrie is tired and I believe that she should retire to her bed. Perhaps you will excuse us if we do not offer you a room for the night. Arrangements have been made for your comfort at the Accommodation House in the village. Allow me to show you the way.'

Catherine, while still fuming about the injustice of the church's claim upon her father's house, was nevertheless ashamed of her angry outburst. As Dr Burn's darkly clad figure disappeared in the direction of the village, she joined Julian at the gate.

'I'm sorry,' she said, 'I just could not listen a moment longer to that insufferable man!'

'I fear it may have been a mistake to offend him,' Julian admonished, gently. 'Jessie's future income may rest with his decision.'

But it seems so unfair that she should lose her home in this way.'

'As Dr Burns explained, any buildings or other improvements made to a property while it is held by a lessee, revert to the land owner at the ending of the tenancy agreement. It would have been the same had your father moved to another parish or lived until he was in his dotage. At some time, he would have had to give up the house. It is unfortunate that you mother must find somewhere else to live but she will overcome this difficulty as she has so many others. She has Ian to support her and Tommy and yourself and,' he hesitated, uncertain of her reaction, 'Me too, if she will allow it.'

Catharine smiled at him, her eyes filled with tears of gratitude. She had treated his proposal so casually. Perhaps her dismissal had been more abrupt than he deserved. He had proved himself invaluable to them during the past few days. Her stepmother could not have hoped for a more devoted son-in-law.

'I have been foolish,' Catherine confessed and she looked so forlorn and contrite that he could not resist the impulse to take her in his arms to comfort her.

'I wish Ian was here,' Catherine sighed, remaining in his embrace just a little longer than was necessary. 'He would know what to do.'

'If you and Tommy feel that you can take care of things here, I shall set out for the camp this evening,' he told her.

'It will be dark in an hour or so. Won't you wait until morning?'

Although tempted by her obvious desire to detain him, nevertheless Julian declined her invitation.

'I can cover some considerable distance before sundown and the first part of the road is well enough metalled for me to travel after dark if I take a lantern. Riding your father's mare, I should reach the camp on the third day.'

'Shall I come with you?' Tommy asked.

The boy had been very quiet ever since James Bantrie's drowning. Once recovered from his ordeal in the river he had retired to the stable and remained there, tending the beasts rather than come to the house to meet those of their neighbours who came to give their condolences. He had not spoken to Jessie and had left untouched the food which Catherine had brought out to him. Only at Julian's insistence had he bathed and put on clean clothes that morning to attend his stepfather's funeral. Throughout the proceedings he had stood apart from the crowd as though a casual onlooker. It had been as though he had divorced himself completely from the family circle.

'I think you should hold the fort here, old chap,' Julian told him 'The women need a man about the place to look after things.'

Julian believed he understood what was troubling Tommy. With an appealing glance at Catherine to leave them alone, he led the boy aside while his sister retired to the house.

'You feel some responsibility for your stepfather's death?'Julian asked.

The boy nodded, glumly. 'If it was not for me he would still be alive,' he said, miserably.

'If it was not for you, a child would have drowned.'

'I didn't think. I saw the water coming and I just ran to the children. If I had known what would happen to Mr Bantrie I would not have done it.'

'I believe you would and I know that he would have expected it of you. Do you really suppose that he would not have wished you to save one of Catherine's pupils? He loved them all, dearly and would willingly have given his own life for any one of them.'

'But mother has already lost one husband. How can she ever forgive me?'

'Have you asked her? Have you told her about your feeling so guilty? Do you truly believe that she will blame you for James Bantrie's death? How little you know of your mother, Tommy. How do you imagine she would have felt had James Bantrie allowed you to drown? Believe me Tommy Jessie does not blame you for her husband's death. She is only thankful that you are alive.'

'But she curses God for what has happened. I have heard her crying out in the night. Her words haunt me. She has lost her Faith and it is all because of me.'

'Give her time. She will regain her belief in God once she has come to terms with what has happened.'

'Can't I come with you? Maybe if I am not there to remind her all the time, she will recover.'

'I think she needs you with her. Now more than ever.'

'But what of Dr Beaton? I should have joined him in Dunedin by now.'

'If I know anything of the good doctor, as soon as hears what has happened, he will be out to see what he can do to help your mother. But you should be here when he arrives. That will be the time for you to talk about the future. Now perhaps you will saddle the mare for me. I shall travel all the faster on horseback.'

'I will ask at the Accommodation House for a spare mount for you to take along with you,' said Tommy. 'You can both ride back together.'

'One of us will still have to remain at the camp,' Julian told him, 'but perhaps it would be a good idea all the same; just in case anyone needs to ride out of camp in a hurry.'

'While Tommy went off to prepare for Julian's journey, the man himself returned to the house to take his leave of the women folk.

Chapter Thirty

Catherine had re-opened the school after her father's funeral although she remained living at the manse to keep Jessie company at night. Tommy, fretting at the necessary delay in beginning his apprenticeship, looked out anxiously each day for signs of approaching visitors. Jessie had assured him that Dr Beaton would come as soon as he knew of her predicament and he would expect Tommy to remain with his mother while she had need of him. In her quiet moments, Jessie too allowed herself to think of Alexander Beaton. How she longed for the comfort of his presence, to hear the sound of his voice.

When, on the day following Julian's departure for the gold field, they heard the clatter of horse's hooves and the sound of a wagon on the road outside both Jessie and Tommy set down what they were doing and ran to the gate. It was not Alexander Beaton, however, but Wei Lun who commanded his mule to come to a halt and clambered down from his high perch to greet his old friends with his customary politeness.

'Wei Lun velly solly 'bout Mr Bantrie, Missie Jessie, Ma'am,' he told her in his charming broken English. 'If there is anything Missie Jessie wants, just tell Wei Lun. He bling.'

'You are very kind, Wei Lun,' Jessie replied. 'It is good to know one has such good friends to call upon at such a time.'

Over the years, Jessie had come to depend upon the kindly Chinese for so many things. He could always be relied upon to bring her regular supplies of essential commodities but he would also include some additional small luxury, landed recently in Port Chalmers or newly produced in one of the Otago settlements. There would always be something extra; a special bolt of cloth; sweetmeats or quality tea not in the normal run of goods carried from the Old Country; a small piece of exotic porcelain perhaps or unusual preserves from China. Wei Lun had always received the utmost courtesy and kindness from the minister and his family and in a country where the Chinese were considered generally as a necessary evil rather than welcome neighbours, he was honoured by the ready acceptance afforded him by the Bantrie household.

As he unloaded Jessie's box of supplies from the wagon to carry it into the house, he said to Tommy. 'That box has special gift for your mama, Mister Tommy.' He indicated a large flat box covered in red paper and tied with ribbon. 'Bling along, please?'

As Tommy lifted the box, Wei Lun entered the house by the kitchen door and spread his wares upon the bare scrubbed table. Jessie counted out the coins she owed him and Tommy began to put away the cases of dry goods in the pantry.

'You have arrived at a difficult time, Wei Lun,' Jessie apologised. 'With everything that has happened this past week, I have not prepared an order for you. Now I find that I must soon move into another house and there will be many additional requirements. My list will be much longer than usual. Will you be coming back through Mapourika on your return journey?'

'I can do, Missie Jessie. First, I must go some miles into the bush to visit new farm, but I can call in on my way back.' He made a quick estimate of the time and said 'Tomollow, next day, for sure.'

'I shall have a list ready for you.'

'This worthless gift is for you, Missie Jessie. Is good luck to wear red.' He handed her the prettily wrapped box. Jessie, so overcome by his kindness that she could find no words to express herself, smiled at him as she untied the fastenings and shifting aside soft white paper wrappings, took out a neatly folded garment in rich, red silk.

With a gasp of delight, she slipped her arms into the sleeves of the luxurious dressing gown. It was heavily embroidered in costly metallic threads with beads of precious and semi precious stones forming the eyes of lions and dragons which chased one another over the breasts and across the shoulders of the garment with a dragon's fiery breath forming the decoration on the stiff upright Mandarin collar. It was the most beautiful gown that Jessie had ever seen.

'Oh Wei Lun,' she breathed, 'This is too splendid a gift. I have done nothing to deserve such a thing.'

'Is humble offering to a good and beautiful lady, Missie Jessie. My sisters make it for you especially, in Canton. I send them size so it fit proper.' She did not have to ask how he knew her size, for over the years James had encouraged her to send items of disused clothing via Wei Lun, to the poor families of Canton whose men folk were obliged to come to New Zealand to find work.

'I feel like a queen,' she told him, laughing as she waltzed around the room parading the gorgeous garment to the astonishment of Tommy, who had rarely seen his mother so exhilarated. She flung her arms around the kindly Chinese and kissed him on his whiskery cheek. 'Thank you, oh thank you so much, Wei Lun,' she cried and her tears flowed freely in response to his kindness.

It was a lesson to Tommy to see how a generous and unexpected gift can lift the spirits of the most dejected of women.

Together, Jessie and her son waited at the gate while the old man gave a quiet command to his mule, turned the cart in the road and with a brief wave in farewell, made his way back through the village.

*

Slinking along through back alleys, creeping in the shadow of high fences, Nicholas Moodie managed to negotiate much of the village without being seen. He came upon what remained of the Maori village after the flooding and breathed a sigh of relief that few remained here who might recognise him. Tired, dirty, unshaven and starving, he was in no mood to argue with Mrs Bantrie. She would hand over the money he demanded. If she refused she would take the consequences.

He came at last to the manse and concealed himself in a thicket until he was satisfied the coast was clear. He noted with satisfaction that the boy Tommy was about to leave the house. From the wicker basket on his back and the rods he was carrying, Moodie assumed he was going fishing. Good, the boy's absence would give him plenty of time to complete his business with the widow.

His patience was rewarded at last when Jessie Bantrie emerged from behind the house and as on that earlier occasion, commenced to hang out the washing. She was so concentrated upon this task that she was quite unaware of the intruder until he was upon her. Well shielded from the road by a line of sheets billowing in the wind he caught her around the waist and held her firmly while he clamped his free hand roughly over her mouth to prevent her calling for help. Jessie was a strong, well built woman who was not going to submit without a struggle and it was all he could do to subdue her sufficiently to frog-march her through the rear door of the house and into the kitchen. Forcing her down onto her knees he hissed his warning.

'Cry out or attempt to escape and I will tie you up and gag you.'

He thrust her from him with such violence that she struck her head on the corner of the table. For a moment she lay stunned. In the few seconds before Jessie recovered her senses, Moodie locked both doors to the house and pocketed the keys.

Jessie stayed still, her eyes half closed. Fearing she would be no match for him if he lost his temper, she was nevertheless determined not to submit without a fight. She would hold her peace and await the first opportunity to make a bid for freedom.

Having checked out the house, Moodie discovered fresh bread in the larder and a large piece of cheese. Watching her closely all the while, he stuffed the food into his mouth as though he had eaten nothing for days.

She wondered if he had escaped from gaol. If so, surely the constable would be hard on his heels.

'What is your business here, Mr Moodie,' she asked him coldly. 'I have nothing to say to you.'

'Oh, but I have a great deal to say to you,' he sneered.

She did not like his tone. He seemed too sure of himself.

'If it is my husband with whom you have come to quarrel, you should know that James died a week ago.' Even her anger at this intrusion could not disguise the tears in her voice as she thought of James and longed for his protection.

'I heard.'

So, despite knowing of James's death, he had come to pester her. This knowledge alone filled her with foreboding. Nevertheless, she continued boldly.

'Well then, if your business is with me, kindly let me know what it is and be on your way.'

'You and your friends have destroyed my reputation and deprived me of my livelihood,' said Moodie. 'What else would I come for, but money? I need money enough to get me right away from here to somewhere where I am not known, Australia perhaps.'

'Yes,' she could not suppress a triumphant little smile, 'I am told that is where most criminals end their days.'

'Don't play with me madam,' he snarled, his temper aroused. Even in extreme danger, she seemed contemptuous of him. Well she would sing a different tune when the time came.

Jessie ignored his threat. 'As for your reputation, Nicholas Moodie, you destroyed what credibility you had before you ever came to this country. Any difficulty you find yourself in at this moment is of your own making. Do not lay the blame for your condition at my door or of that of any of those connected with me. It was my husband's duty to have you arrested.'

'You will not be so hoity- toity when you have heard me out,' he told her. 'Your past has caught up with you.'

'My past?' Despite her indignation, Jessie suddenly felt a chill of apprehension. What could Nicholas Moodie know of her past life?

'I did not recognise you on the first occasion when I called here. It was only while we were dining, on the evening before I began teaching in the school, that I remembered where I had seen you before.'

'I am not aware of ever having had the misfortune to set eyes on you before you came to Mapourika.'

Jessie made no effort to disguise her contempt for him.

'What if I were to say to you: Edinburgh Infirmary,1840, April, or was it May?'

Jessie gasped. How could he know about the Infirmary? She had told no one other than James and Alexander Beaton about her time as a nurse at the hospital.

'An old man as I recall, and a young man,' he continued, enjoying her discomfort. 'You nursed them both and with such devotion and skill, as I remember it, that they both died!'

'The older man was my father and it was because he was dying that I was working there. The younger man was suffering from a brain tumour and needed constant attention. They let me nurse him in lieu of payment for my father's care. There was no hope for either patient. All I could do was make them as comfortable as possible.' She paused, noting that the sneer of amusement on his face had not altered one iota. 'I don't know what you hope to make of this knowledge,' she continued. 'It concerned no one other than my first husband, who was the young man's best friend.'

'First husband, there has been more than one then?'

This was news to Moodie. It might provide him with even more ammunition. 'So, you were married once before? It seems to be a somewhat risky business taking Jessie Bantrie for a wife! How did they die, these husbands of yours? Did you help them as well, in the same way that you helped that poor fellow with the brain tumour?'

'I don't understand you,' she replied, but her tone was now more guarded. 'Both James and my former husband died as the result of an accident. I was nowhere near either of them at the time.'

She chose her words most carefully. Something in his arrogant manner warned her that everything she said would be stored away in his memory and used to her disadvantage when the time came.

'And those two in the hospital, do you claim not to have been near them at the time of their deaths?'

'I carried out my duties as appropriate to my patient's needs that is all,' she protested.

'All!' he sneered. 'Everyone knows what goes on in those places between the so-called nurses and their more, shall we say, virile patients.'

'I don't know what you mean,' she gasped. 'You never saw me behaving other than with the utmost propriety.' She thought she knew what he was suggesting but his accusations were groundless. Now he was making wild guesses, simply to intimidate her.

'Oh, no?' he queried. He paused for a moment to let his next words take full effect. 'What about the lad dying from a brain tumour? Do you deny helping him on his way, so to speak?'

Jessie gasped in surprise. At his words, she found herself re-living those dreadful moments. In her imagination, she saw again the silent plea for relief in those impelling eyes. She felt again the sharp edges of the little brown bottle she had held, clutched so tightly inside her apron pocket that the ridged marks remained in her palm for half an hour afterwards. Vividly, she recalled the moment when she had made the fatal decision.

She could still hear the patient's final sigh of relief and see the calm which settled on that tortured countenance once his agony had departed for the last time.

Now she thought about it, she did remember another young person in the adjoining row of beds. Yes, it was all coming back to her now. There was a fellow who complained perpetually of his pain, the food, the lack of attention, he could have been a younger version of Moodie. Now as he stood over her, a self-satisfied smirk upon his ugly face, she remembered him.

'What of it?' she demanded. 'What do you hope to make of this amazing piece of information?'

'What of it? Murder, that's what! You gave a dose of poison to a poor helpless individual who was too sick to know what was happening; that is what you did. I watched your every move!'

'Nonsense!' she cried, genuinely alarmed now by his accusation. 'Even if there was any truth in what you say, why would anyone accept your version of events? Since your trial, you have a strong motive to hate me and my family, a reason to blacken my name.' She paused momentarily and then proceeded with greater circumspection.

'Anyway, what proof do you have? Your accusation would never be listened to. It would be your word against my own. I am a respectable widow with a certain standing in the community while you are a convicted felon whom the good people of Mapourika have every cause to hate!'

'Maybe so,' he laughed menacingly, 'but imagine what will pass through the small minds of the good citizens of Dunedin, those who would form the jury at your trial. Would they not think it a trifle odd that you, who are known to have extraordinary knowledge of and access to all manner of potentially lethal potions, should have lost two husbands? Might it not seem worth investigating the fact that while in your care, both your father and a young man with all his life before him, should have met their end in mysterious circumstances?'

'What mysterious circumstances? There was nothing extraordinary about either death. Both were expected.'

He nodded, admiring the fight she was putting up, but he went on ruthlessly, 'Even were you to be acquitted, would not the seeds of doubt have been sewn. Do you really believe that you can expect to continue to be accepted in the drawing rooms of the ladies of Mapourika and Dunedin town?'

Jessie felt compelled to laugh at this. The one thing which had never concerned her at all was the attitude of the so called upper orders of society, either in her former home in Scotland or here in New Zealand.

For herself, Jessie would not have cared one jot what he said about her. Without proof of any kind he could not have her convicted, of that she was certain. Her character would become tainted however and more importantly, his story might reflect upon her family and friends. She could not allow that to happen.

'Very well,' she said, capitulating so suddenly as to surprise even Nicholas Moodie. You mentioned business earlier. Do I understand you wish to make some kind of a bargain?'

'So, you have decided to be sensible after all?' He gave an audible sign of satisfaction.

'I don't know what it is you expect from me. I have no money. My husband was a charitable man, seeking little comfort for himself and his family. He never accumulated wealth.'

'You have children of working age, influential friends. Your doctor friend will surely help out.' Suddenly he grabbed hold of her and tipped her head back roughly, holding her chin between the thumb and forefinger of his left hand. She turned her head away to avoid his foul breath and wrenched the muscles in her neck. He smacked her sharply across the cheeks, first with the flat and then with the back of his hand, his knuckles leaving white marks which quickly turned to red.

'Oh, I'm sure you will find sufficient funds to accommodate my modest requirements,' he leered. 'As for my other needs, why should I wait a moment longer? Six months is a long time for any man to remain celibate. I feel sure that a whore of your experience will have no difficulty whatsoever in providing satisfaction.' He began to fumble with his belt.

All this time Jessie had remained with her back tight up against the wall, her feet spread out before her. When she responded to this latest insult with a contemptuous smile, he hit her again, across the face. Anticipating his move, she brought her knee up into his groin and rolled to one side, scrambling to her feet. Moodie caught her by the wrists.

'If it's a fight you want woman, a fight you shall have.'

She tried to push him away by stretching her arms up and out, forcing him to release her. Then, thrusting against his shoulders she stuck her foot behind his heels and got him off balance, giving herself sufficient time to grab a small stool which she hurled through the window. Before she could clamber after it however, he was upon her once more.

He caught her by the wrists, this time forcing her arms back behind her. Turning her in his arms, he propelled her through the open door and into her bedroom. He kicked the door closed behind them and thrust her cruelly backwards across the cast iron bed end, holding her down so that she was unable to move. Then, bending his face to hers, he kissed her brutally on the lips, forcing them apart and thrusting his tongue down her throat so that she nearly choked. The pressure he applied was so firm she could not even bite the offending member as she would have wished. Again, she brought her knee up between his legs, striking him as hard as she could. With a roar of pain, he lurched away. She turned aside and fell off the bed and onto the floor with her head resting against the cast iron fender. While he nursed his bruises, she made a grab for the iron poker which lay in the hearth.

Aroused now to a point of unrestrained passion, Moodie forced her down on the bare boards, lifting her skirts high as he did so. He bore down upon her, groping and tearing at her undergarments. His breath, foul from the liquor which had been his major sustenance for days past, made her want to swoon but she continued to fight, her struggles only serving to arouse him further. Frustrated in his attempt to rape her, he reached for her throat and began to squeeze the very life out of her. He would most assuredly have killed her had he not received a sudden and vicious blow to the back of the head. He fell like a stone.

Chapter Thirty-One

Alexander Beaton, called away to attend a birthing at a small settlement on the Clutha River to the south of Dunedin, heard nothing of the flooding at Mapourika or of James Bantrie's death until after Dr Burns had already departed to conduct the funeral service for James Bantrie. Rumours of serious damage in the settlement abounded, but there was no one to give a first-hand report of the disaster. The Maori messenger sent to fetch the Reverend Burns, had returned with him. When Alexander announced his intention of going straight to Mapourika to see if Jessie required help, Teri begged to accompany him.

'Apart from the accident of James Bantrie's death, I have heard only rumours concerning other damage to the settlement,' Alexander assured her, knowing her to be anxious about her father and brothers. 'But if you insist.'

What cause had he to try to dissuade her? His wife had every right to visit her family and see for herself that they were all safe and well. He was aware that her prolonged absence from home and her infrequent contact with her kinsmen produced in her a form of depression which made her introverted and distant at times. Perhaps she should accompany him for her own peace of mind and for the sake of the children who took the brunt of her moodiness.

'What about the boys?' he demanded, in a last attempt to deter her.

'Nellie Parker will take care of them for a few days,' she assured him. 'I may be able to help in the village, Alexander. There may be injury, or sickness to attend to.'

While Alexander had never completely come to terms with his wife's amateur doctoring, since the occasion when he had been obliged to employ some of her healing strategies himself and had done so with spectacular results, he had held her knowledge in much greater respect. 'Come along if you like,' he said, grudgingly, 'Although I fear you may have a wasted journey.'

The following morning the Beatons set out well provisioned for a couple of days on the road, in a smart, well sprung carriage hired from William Mackie. While Alexander fretted at the delay occasioned by their travelling in this manner rather than on horseback, he was forced to admit that should it be necessary to bring Jessie back with them, her journey would be more comfortable in Mackie's chaise. Not knowing anything of Jessie's condition or the extent of Tommy's injuries, he took with him supplies of medicaments and bandages sufficient to supply a regiment of wounded soldiers.

Teri's motives for insisting upon accompanying her husband were twofold. Naturally she was concerned for the welfare of her own family. If there was anything she could do to help her people it was her duty to go. Her second motive concerned her husband and the state of their marriage.

Teri had no intention of allowing Jessie Bantrie's new situation to reflect in any way, upon her own life and that of her family. Although Alexander rarely mentioned the minister's wife, Teri had always suspected some special relationship between Alexander and Jessie Bantrie. During the time he had spent residing with the Beaton's, on more than one occasion Tobias Leny had let slip some remark which suggested that had she not married the widowed minister, Jessie might have become Mrs Beaton.

Teri had accepted from the outset that her marriage was one of convenience, arranged by her father to ensure a stable relationship between the Maori and the white settlers. As the daughter of an important tribal chief, she had been prepared from birth for just such a transaction. Love matches were rare amongst a people whose daughters were considered to be valuable assets for barter. In the circumstances, Teri's marriage to the doctor had been remarkably successful. They had two fine children, a good home and commanded a certain respect in the town. Now that this other woman was free, however, Teri feared a change in her position. She was determined to prevent Jessie Bantrie from coming between Alexander and herself.

To the outside world, Teri Beaton might appear to be a submissive woman of docile temperament but Alexander would be the first to admit that his wife was malleable only up to a point. Should her home, her children or her marriage be threatened in any way, Teri would fight like a tiger to preserve them. Whatever the thoughts which may have passed through Alexander's mind when he heard the news of James Bantrie's death, his wife was determined to ensure that there would be no question of Alexander filling the gap which the accident had left in Jessie's life.

*

The merry tinkling of silver bells and the rattle of horse's hooves upon the cobbled street brought the villagers of Mapourika to their doors and the children from their play. The Chinese salesman was a welcome sight at any time but particularly so at this site of devastation. Ignoring the growing crowd however Wei Ling continued through the village until he came to the manse. Before descending from his cart, he rang the old ship's bell attached to the roof of his cab to attract Jessie's attention.

Disappointed at the lack of any response to his signal, he reined in the mule, slipped down from his seat and secured the animal to the hitching post. He walked up the path expecting all the time to hear Jessie's call or to see her hurrying to greet him. She must have been expecting him. Had she not particularly asked him to call again before returning to Dunedin? Partly annoyed that she might have forgotten him and not a little apprehensive that something might be amiss, he skirted the front veranda and rounding the side of the house, made directly for the rear entrance.

To his surprise, he found the kitchen door hanging lopsidedly from its twisted hinges. The frame was shattered and the bolts torn from their fixings. It was clear that someone had broken down the door in great haste.

Silence hung over the house like a thick pall. Treading warily in the dim light, he entered the room and picked his way carefully through the debris left by Jessie's struggles with the intruder. On the far side of the kitchen he pushed lightly on the door he knew led directly into the Minister's bedroom. It swung open, very slowly.

There were three bodies.

At first sight he supposed them all dead and felt the bile rising in his throat at the sight of a great pool of blood which had flowed from beneath the entangled bodies of Jessica Bantrie and her assailant.

Tommy Dundas lay slumped against one wall, his eyes wide open but sightless. The boy showed no sign of any injury except for the streaks of blood on his hands and on the huge greenstone rock specimen which lay in his lap.

Wei Lun studied the boy closely, searching frantically for some sign of life. After a few seconds, he was rewarded by a slight movement under his hands. The boy's rib cage rose and fell very slowly but regularly. While Tommy was not dead as the Chinaman had first feared, he was certainly in a curious state, dazed, shocked, comatose perhaps. Whatever the cause of the child's condition, he was breathing and could safely be left while Wei Lun examined the other casualties.

Jessie's attacker was sprawled across her body, his head lying close against the iron fender. It had been battered to a pulp. The man was undoubtedly dead. The mess of brains and blood where his face should have been made him unrecognisable and it was not until Wei Lun turned the body to one side to free it from the prone figure of Jessie Bantrie, that he recognised the figure as the schoolmaster, Nicholas Moodie.

Unceremoniously, he dragged the body aside and knelt beside Jessie. He could feel no pulse. There was no sign of her breathing. In desperation, he bent over her and forcing back her head he placed his lips over hers and breathed into her mouth. The chest rose almost imperceptibly. He tried again. This time the response was more positive. Again and again he forced into her lungs his life- giving breath. Suddenly she coughed, painfully and then without his aid, took in a great gulp of air. The action clearly caused her great agony for she let out a groan and held her breath again until she could resist no longer. Her throat was covered in the livid marks of her near strangulation. Something within her throat seemed sharp, stabbing at her at each new intake of breath. She opened her eyes, staring around her as though trying to make out her surroundings. Suddenly conscious that she had been stripped almost naked in her last tussle with Moodie, she clasped ineffectively at the remains of her undergarments. Wei Lun laid a hand firmly upon hers, and shook his head.

'Not to wully Missie,' he said gently. 'Wei Lun soon see you all light.' When she recognised the well-loved face of the Chinaman, Jessie tried to smile.

Wei Lun worked quickly. His slender frame was deceptive. With very little effort he lifted Jessie and carried her to the second bedroom, normally occupied by Tommy. He covered her nakedness with all the blankets he could find. The shock caused her to shiver uncontrollably.

Returning for Tommy, he urged the lad to his feet and steered him into the kitchen where he sat him down in an arm chair beside the stove. The boy shivered uncontrollably so Wei Lun found an old woollen shawl to place around his shoulders. He stoked the fire, brewed hot sweet tea and made up a poultice for Jessie's bruised neck. From his cart, he brought in sleep-inducing powders which he added to both their cups before giving them the tea. Tommy although still silent, took the cup and clasped it tightly, warming his hands. Wei Lun was obliged to hold Jessie's cup for her but he managed to coax her into drinking sufficient for his potion to take effect. When he returned to Tommy he found the boy had managed to sip a little of the tea and helped him to swallow the rest. It was clear that he was traumatised and unlikely to recover for some time.

Wei Lun knew it was important to report the incident to someone, but who? The nearest constable was in Dunedin and James Bantrie, the natural leader of the white community hereabouts was dead. When eventually he found someone in authority, what account could he give them of what had happened here?

In his own mind, Wei Lun had already reconstructed the events which had lead to the gruesome scene. Moodie had quite clearly been intent upon taking his revenge upon the Bantries. When attacked, Jessie had resisted him, hence the damage to the kitchen. While he was in the act of raping her, Tommy had forced his way in, picked up the greenstone rock and hit the schoolmaster over the head until he was dead.

Wei Lun was not going to allow Jessie to suffer any more than she had to. Whatever Tommy had done, it had been to save his mother's life. He must not now be dragged through the courts for killing Moodie. He, Wei Lun, must take the blame. The judge would agree that Moodie had been killed to save Jessie. Surely, they would not hang him for defending a woman from certain death? If the worst happened and he was condemned for murder what did it matter? He was an old man at the end of his days. Tommy Dundas was a child with his whole life ahead of him.

Wei Lun sponged Tommy's face and hands, removing all trace of blood. Finally, he dropped the greenstone weapon on the floor beside the dead man and went out to his cart. Turning the mule in the road, he drove her down into the village to report to the Post Office clerk, the only representative of officialdom within forty miles.

He found the clerk in the village store in conversation with the owner of the Accommodation House. Together, all three returned to the manse and as they stood over the body of Nicholas Moodie, the two men listened to Wei Lun's explanation of what had happened.

'What about the boy?' asked the hotel keeper, studying Tommy carefully, attempting unsuccessfully to get him to respond to his questions.

'He has not spoken since he came in and saw his mother lying there. He must have thought she was dead.'

'Moodie died at once?' asked McPherson from the hotel.

Wei Lun nodded.

'Just as well if you ask me,' commented the storekeeper, whose daughter attended the school and who had led the villager's campaign to raise money to have Moodie convicted.'

McPherson glanced from Jessie, lying in a drugged sleep on the bed, to Tommy who had not moved from where Wei Lun had left him.

'It's still murder,' he replied, looking accusingly at Wei Lun.

*

Teko crouched in the barn listening for further sounds of disturbance. He had watched Tommy return from his fishing expedition expecting him to come running out of the house at once, looking for help. The boy did not re-emerge. Concerned for his safety, Keto was about to return to the house when he heard the bell rung on the Chinaman's cart. He knew the Chinese to be a good man and a friend of Mrs Beaton's. She and Tommy would be all right with him. As for Keto, for him there could be no hope. A Maori killing a white man, for whatever reason, would surely hang. He must get away. With his village destroyed and his family dispersed, he had nowhere to hide.

While Wei Lun was still occupied within the house, the Maori crept out of the barn, made his way up the slope towards the church and then slipped down the cliff to the river. Wading across the shallows he reached the further shore. Then, searching out a suitable landmark, he set course for Canterbury. He had heard that there was plenty of work for an English-speaking Maori on the sheep runs to the north.

*

By the time Alexander and Teri arrived at Mapourika, Wei Lun was already on his way to Dunedin, his signed confession in the pocket of his escort. With it was an affidavit from the storekeeper and McPherson, stating what they had witnessed at the scene of the crime. The Chinese travelling shop had driven past the doctor's chaise at some speed and Alexander had wondered at the time why it was not the Chinaman himself at the reins.

As they approached the manse, the doctor and his wife were surprised to find a small crowd gathered at the gate. When he stepped down, willing hands took the reins while he assisted Teri.

One of the onlookers could contain himself no longer. 'Mrs Bantrie's been attacked. She's in a poor way, doctor.'

The crowd parted to let him through as Alexander dashed towards the house, fearful of what he would find there. Teri followed more circumspectly, carrying his medical bag.

Catherine greeted Alexander with some relief and led him directly to the boy's bedroom where Jessie still slept under the influence of Wei Lun's opium.

Jessie's throat was now coloured a deep purple, the marks of Moodie's hands clearly defined. With gentle fingers Alexander traced the length of the wind pipe, discovering crushed cartilage as he did so. While he examined her body for further bruising, she stirred under his hand.

'Alexander?' she murmured.

'Hush, don't try to talk.'

'What happened?'

'Don't you know?'

Almost imperceptibly, she shook her head.

'Can't remember…'

'You will. Don't worry about it now.'

'Tommy?'

Alexander turned his head glancing inquiringly at Catherine.

'He is in the kitchen.' She would not elaborate in front of her stepmother.

He nodded and returned to his patient.

'How does your neck feel now,' he asked her.

'Sore. It hurts when I swallow.'

'When you say hurts, what kind of pain?'

'A stabbing sensation.'

It was as he feared. The trachea was damaged. He would have to operate.

He patted her hand and stood up, stretching his cramped muscles. To Teri standing at his side, he murmured, 'There is no damage to her from the rape. Jessie seems to have fought him off. The bruises and scratches will heal of their own accord but I shall have to perform an operation on her throat.'

Teri nodded. 'Tell me what you want and I will prepare the instruments.'

In silence, Alexander busied himself turning out his medical bag and selecting instruments. Teri made for the kitchen, intent upon boiling water to sterilise everything. The familiar routine made her feel she was needed. Even she could not deny the minister's widow Alexander's services at a time like this.

'What about Tommy?' Alexander turned to Catherine who, white faced and trembling, stood at the end of the bed gazing anxiously at her stepmother. She started at his question.

'He seems to be in some kind of a trance. He has not spoken to anyone since it happened.'

'I'd better look at him while we're waiting.'

He followed her into a kitchen milling with people. They were well meaning he had no doubt but what the household needed at this moment was peace and quiet. He addressed the entire company.

'I am sure that Miss Bantrie appreciates your concern, ladies and gentlemen but I have my duties to perform here and require room in which to move. I would beg you to leave. As soon as there is anything for you to know I will make sure you are told.'

With everyone gone except Catherine and Teri who was busy at the stove, Alexander turned his attention to Tommy. Crouching down beside the boy he spoke to him, very softly.

'Tommy… Tommy, can you hear me? It's Dr Beaton, Tommy. Everything's all right. You're quite safe now. I'm your friend, you can tell me…'

To everyone's surprise the boy responded at once, fixing his stare upon the doctor's familiar face.

'She's dead.'

'No Tommy, she's very much alive.'

His brow wrinkled as he struggled to remember.

'I saw her lying there… there was blood… he was on top of her… I knew she was dead.'

'Tommy, listen to what I tell you. Your mother is not dead. She is very much alive. Come and see.' He held out his hand, willing the boy to take it and follow him.

Tommy staggered to his feet and like a drunken man, allowed the doctor to guide him through into his own bedroom. From the bed, Jessie saw him and lifted her hand weakly in recognition. With a strangled cry the boy fell on his knees beside her and grasping her fingers none too gently he dropped his head to the counterpane and wept. With mixed emotions, Alexander watched them for a moment then closed the door silently behind him. It was a moment of intimacy in which he had no part to play.

'I think he will be all right now,' he said to the two women waiting anxiously in the outer room.

*

Alexander accomplished the operation to remove a tiny piece of splintered cartilage from Jessie's throat with infinite patience and skill, his earlier experience in tracheotomy aiding him in this delicate process. Jessie, still dopey from Wei Lun's administrations, offered little resistance as the scalpel was inserted. She lay still, aware that the slightest movement on her part might inhibit Alexander's actions. Tommy, whom Alexander had left kneeling at his mother's side, stood up as the doctor began his work and soon became absorbed in what was going on. Teri, seeing the boy so alert and interested, began to hand him the instruments to give to Alexander while she herself stepped back to allow the boy to see clearly what was happening.

By performing an upper tracheal tracheotomy, Alexander gained access to the crushed hyoid arch and could therefore reposition the damaged cartilage so that there was no longer any pressure on the surrounding tissues. He released the clamps on the major vessels and closed the gaping wound in Jessie's neck with horse hair stitches. Looking up for a moment, he caught Tommy's eye and as though lecturing to a student doctor, he said, 'horsehair is best in this case as we don't want to leave a puckered scar. If I had silk thread, I would have used that.'

It was the first lesson for his new apprentice. Tommy, who had followed every step of the operation with close attention and without once feeling faint, had passed his first test.

*

Ian Bantrie and his partner finished packing their personal possessions in the saddle bags and prepared to depart. They took one last look at the bleak scene of desolation and turned their backs on the prospector's camp. The alluvial drift which had promised such riches was gone, washed away by the flood and redeposited, who knew where?

Maybe he would return one day to pan for dust in the lower reaches but for the time being, Ian was determined to turn his attention to the more mundane process of quarrying stone. It was work he was well able to perform and one which would bring him a steady income in the fast-developing settlements of Otago. The days of quickly erected shacks made of thatched reed and tree ferns were now past. People were demanding more substantial structures and he had discovered the ideal stone for the purpose.

Ian and Julian had calculated that with the gold already deposited in the vaults of the Bank of Otago, together with that which had been amassed up to the moment when the deluge had washed away their hopes, they would be able clear their debts without recourse to the investor's money. It would take all the cash they had, but at least they would be starting off with clean sheet.

'What about you, Julian?' Ian had made it clear what he intended to do but his companion had remained silent until this moment.

'I shall return to the sea. There should be notice of a new appointment awaiting me in Dunedin.'

Ian nodded. Neither of them mentioned Catherine. She had already expressed her opinion of life as a seaman's wife. It would be a long time before Julian would be able to broach the subject of marriage again.

'And you, what of you and your little artist lady?' he asked Ian, pointedly.

'I have spotted an excellent outcrop of building stone which just happens to be situated on Mackie's run. If I can persuade him to sell me the land, her cottage will be within half a mile of it.'

'She might not care to have a stone quarry yards from her door,' observed Julian, mischievously.

'It will be on the far side of the hill, out of her view and besides, I don't believe she will consider it inconvenient, not one little bit.' Ian gave a knowing smile and walked the horse out of the valley and up onto the track for Mapourika.

*

The murder trial was a three-day sensation in Dunedin where petty theft and bar room brawls were considered to be major crimes.

Wei Lun had confessed to killing Nicholas Moodie and no matter what extenuating circumstances his lawyer might present to the court, the judge was obliged to try him on the major charge.

Jessie had insisted upon engaging in his defence, Arnold Walker, the advocate who had served them so well during Moodie's trial. Wei Lun had saved her life. It was the least she could do to help him, even if it took every penny she had.

The prosecution had shown that Wei Lun had on the 21st day of May in the year 1855, reported to the postmaster at Mapourika that he had killed one Nicholas Moodie by hitting him over the head with a piece of rock. In his statement, he had explained that the attack had been necessitated in order to rescue Mrs Jessie Bantrie, widow, of The Manse, Mapourika. Believing the woman to be in danger of her life, Wei Lun had struck Moodie several times, crushing his skull and causing his death.

Affidavits were then read out from the two men who had accompanied Wei Lun to the house. The scene described indicated that a struggle had taken place. Mrs Bantrie had been attacked. Her clothes had been stripped from her body and she was severely bruised about the body and particularly in the region of the neck. The body of Moodie had been moved aside in order that Mrs Bantrie could be carried to a bed and given attention.

At the request of the prosecutor, Dr Alexander Beaton gave his report to the jury, listing the injuries to Mrs Beaton including his statement that in his opinion rape had been attempted and that she had been strangled near to death.

'Do you wish to question Dr Beaton on his findings?' the judge asked of Arnold Walker.

'Just one question, My Lord.' The advocate for the defence addressed Alexander.

'It has been assumed that the weapon used was a large specimen of greenstone kept in the house as an ornament. Is it your opinion that the injuries to the deceased were caused by this implement?'

'The wounds to the back of the head were entirely consistent with such a weapon, yes.'

'The stone in question is here in the courtroom. Would you kindly take it in your hands and demonstrate how you believe it might have been held?'

The Clerk of the Court lifted the exhibit with some difficulty and carried it to the witness. Alexander held the stone in both hands and struggled to raise it to shoulder height.

'I see you are using both hands, Doctor.'

'It would certainly have taken both hands to administer the necessary blow.' Alexander explained, relieved to return the heavy piece of rock to the Clerk.

'Could you have administered such a blow?' Walker demanded. Alexander confessed that he did not believe so.

'It would have taken someone far stronger than me,' he declared.

Walker seemed satisfied with this reply.

'No further questions, My Lord.'

The case for the prosecution was quickly wound up. There seemed little reason to doubt that the Chinese had killed Nicholas Moodie. It only remained for Wei Lun's defence lawyer to make a plea for extenuating circumstances.

'I call Mrs Jessie Bantrie to the stand.' Walker had gained in stature since his success in prosecuting Moodie. He created an air of supreme confidence as he went about the job of saving his client from the gallows. As Jessie moved slowly towards the stand aided by the lawyer, Walker addressed the judge.

'Mrs Bantrie is still hoarse following the injuries to her throat, My Lord. I apologise in advance for any difficulty you may have in hearing her.' He glanced at the jury box. 'Perhaps you will allow me to repeat her answers for the benefit of the jury?'

His Lordship nodded.

Jessie was lead gently through the events leading up to Moodie's death, each of her answers repeated with emphasis by the advocate.

'Were you aware of anyone other than yourself and Moodie in the room at the time when your assailant was struck down?'

'No.'

'Do you have any reason to doubt that the man who killed Moodie, saved your life?'

'None.'

'None!' Walker repeated the single word triumphantly.

'How long was it before you realised that Moodie was dead and no longer a threat?'

'I don't know. I must have fainted. I remember nothing until the weight of his body was lifted off me and I opened my eyes to see Wei Lun standing over me.'

'Were you surprised to see him? Wei Lun was not a frequent visitor to your household.'

'I was at first, but then I remembered I had asked him to return to the house on his way back to Dunedin. Anyway, it was a good job he arrived when he did.'

'Why do you say that Mrs Bantrie?'

She looked at him as if he were daft. 'Because I would surely be dead had he not turned up when he did.'

'Because I would surely be dead had he not turned up when he did.' Walker made good use of every syllable.

'Thank you, Mrs Bantrie. My colleague for the prosecution may wish to have a word with you.'

The prosecutor shook his head and Jessie was allowed to stand down.

In his summing-up, Arnold Walker was careful to stress that there was never sufficient justification for taking the life of another.

'Nevertheless,' he stressed, 'We have heard how Wei Lun came upon a house in confusion, how he heard screams from the woman he regarded as his good friend and when he went to her aid, discovered her on the bedroom floor, the assailant on top of her apparently choking her to death. He grasped the first object which came to hand and despite his age and apparent lack of strength, mustered sufficient power to beat the attacker about the head until he let go his victim. I submit My Lord that my client's intention was to prevent the attack, nothing more. I submit that there was no intention to kill Moodie, only to save Mrs Bantrie. The fact that the blows were enough to kill the deceased was merely an indication of the extreme provocation of my client. I therefore submit a plea for mercy and a verdict of death by misadventure.'

They were all in court to hear the verdict. Alexander with Teri at his side, Jessie had her hand resting loosely in that of her son Tommy, Ian and Nellie Parker, beside them. The young people had announced their intention to marry in the spring and were happy to appear together in public. Further back Catherine and Julian sat with William Mackie and Tobias Leny, who was very anxious to hear what was to happen to his Chinese partner.

'Mr Foreman, have you reached a verdict?'

'We have, My Lord. We find the defendant guilty of manslaughter in extenuating circumstances.'

'That is a strange verdict Mr Foreman.'

'My Lord, we are not knowledgeable in matters of the Law but we do understand a little about Justice. Whatever may be the rules back home, here we are able to make a few of our own. Until a New Zealand

Judiciary is properly established, we maintain the right to make our own recommendations. We consider this homicide was justifiable and believe it would be inappropriate to pass a verdict which would require a sentence of death by hanging.'

The Judge looked from one advocate to the other and seeing there was no dissent, he placed his fingertips together and bowed his head in thought.

The courtroom was still. It was as though even the great Parliament clock on the wall above the bench, held its breath.

'Very well,' the Judge cleared his throat. 'Let the prisoner stand.'

Wei Lun, at a signal from his gaolers, rose to his feet.

'Wei Lun you have been found guilty of justifiable homicide. I cannot however allow the taking of a life, no matter in what circumstance, to go unpunished. The sentence of this court is that you shall be deported to your native land. Your licences to trade in New Zealand will be revoked and you will not be allowed to return to this country.'

The sigh of relief from all parts of the court was sufficient confirmation that the judge had made an acceptable decision. Wei Lun glanced across at Jessie and saw her raise one hand in congratulatory salute.

Tommy stared straight ahead, apparently unmoved by the verdict. It was something the advocate said about the stone, about it being too heavy to lift. He had always found that rock difficult to lift and knew that he could not possibly have used it himself to kill Moodie. But if it was too heavy for him, how could the old man have carried it as far as the bedroom, let alone lift it to hit Moodie.

With a lightning-like flash, the boy suddenly remembered everything. He remembered catching a glimpse of a familiar brown figure slipping behind the barn just as he himself ran up the path towards the back door. He recalled his concern when he discovered the door hanging lopsidedly on its twisted hinges. He remembered his horror at finding the kitchen in a shamble and having to navigate his way through the debris to reach the bedroom. He recalled the horrifying sight of his apparently lifeless mother entangled beneath Moodie's body. He remembered the blood.

The courtroom was fast emptying. Tommy turned to say something to the lawyer but found him in celebratory mood, shaking hands with Alexander Beaton.

Convinced now that Wei Lun had not killed Moodie, Tommy was uncertain what to do. Teko must have done the killing. He was the only one strong enough to have wielded that stone. For some reason the old man had taken the blame but he was not going hang. If caught, Teko would surely do so. All any of them wanted was to have Jessie safe. Perhaps it was best to leave things as they were.

'What happens now?' Alexander asked of the lawyer.

'Wei Lun will be kept under guard until the next ship sails for the Chinese mainland. Once on board, I imagine they will give him free rein. The Judge must show some recognition of the enormity of the crime, justified or not. Excuse me.' Walker moved across to Jessie.

'Mrs Bantrie, I have a message for you from Wei Lun. Whatever the outcome of the trial he asked that you call to see him before you return to Mapourika, you and Mr Leny.'

'Tobias Leny? How strange. What can Wei Lun have to say to the two of us?'

'I'm afraid I can't tell you that, Mrs Bantrie. Will you go? Tomorrow would be most convenient.'

'Of course,' she replied. 'I am sure Catherine will not object to delaying for a further day.'

*

Wei Lun's cell was clean, if sparsely furnished. He professed to having been well treated and thanked his visitors for coming. The warder found them places to sit and then there was an uncomfortable silence while Wei Lun appeared to be waiting for something or someone, to join them. At last Arnold Wallace appeared looking somewhat harassed and carrying a sheaf of papers.

'My apologies everyone,' he exclaimed, nodding thanks to the warder for the chair he was offered. He slumped down and shuffled his papers, apparently searching for a particular document.

'Ah, here it is.' He beamed upon the assembled company. 'Wei Lun has asked you to come here today so that he may distribute his assets in New Zealand to those he considers most deserving of consideration.' It was like the reading of a last will and testament.

'The situation is uncommon in that Wei Lun does not forfeit his property in New Zealand, although he is of course unable to continue to retain control of it himself. He has therefore drawn up this document which I propose to read.'

The lawyer cleared his throat, lifted his eye glasses the better to see the paper and read:

My Small Loans and Pawnbroking enterprise I leave in the hands of Tobias Leny, my partner in the provision of Chinese Labour. He is fully conversant with my policy in the matter of loans to those of my countrymen temporarily in financial difficulties and I trust him not to exploit them.

To Mrs Jessie Bantrie I leave all my other New Zealand assets including my warehouse and travelling shop. I am sure the enterprise will flourish under her hand and I wish her and her family good fortune in the future.

Signed by my hand this 18th Day of December 1855.

With a flourish, Walker spread the papers before Wei Lun, who signed several copies of the document, both in Chinese and in English. Both Leny and Jessie witnessed his signature.

Walker handed each recipient a copy of the declaration and the relevant certificates appertaining to the bequests.

Stunned, Jessie could hardly speak.

'Wei Lun, you did not have to do this,' she cried. 'The business could have been sold and the money transferred to you in Canton.'

'Hush Missie… you take shop. You get someone to drive van Soon, you open shop here or in Mapourika, perhaps all over. You do good business, you make Wei Lun velly happy.'

Unable to speak for tears, she kissed him, feeling the soft wispiness of his long white beard as it brushed against her still tender throat.

Leny regarded the papers he held in his hand with a quizzical look. 'I've never seen myself as a pawn broker and loan shark,' he muttered. 'A bookmaker perhaps but as for the other…'

'I know you will treat my people well, Tobias,' said the old Chinese. 'They cannot help gambling, but they always try to pay off their debts.'

*

Julian Frawley had been given a berth as first mate aboard the Canton Princess, bound for Hong Kong and ports in China and Catherine, grateful for the additional day in town, had come to see the ship sail.

Once again, she stood beside Julian on the deck, watching scores of albatross wheeling and diving around them as though impatient to be off.

'Will they come with you all the way?' she asked.

'I doubt it,' he replied. 'We sail too far to the north.'

'Then I shall ask them to report your progress when they return,' she decided, smiling broadly at him.

'I shall be back myself before you know it,' he insisted. 'Will you wait for me, Catherine?'

'I have no plans to go anywhere… yet awhile,' she teased.

'You know what I mean.' Despite his resolve, he could not hide his exasperation. 'You won't go and marry someone else while my back is turned?'

'No, that I can promise you.' Her smile was more kindly as she placed a hand gently on either golden epaulette. 'I will not marry anyone without your knowledge.'

With that he must be content. He kissed her lightly on the lips not daring to mar the moment of their parting with a display of ungentlemanly passion. There were members of the crew nearby and he had yet to make his mark with them.

As he handed her to the top of the gangway, two prison officers came on board with between them, Wei Lun. Dressed in traditional Chinese robes for the occasion, he was like an emperor reviewing his troops. Catherine stood aside while Julian welcomed the old man on board.

'I have to add my thanks to you for what you sacrificed to save Mrs Bantrie,' Julian told him. 'We shall try to make your voyage as comfortable as possible.'

'You will still be in touch with Tobias?' Catherine asked, as she too thanked him and bade him goodbye.

'I think it velly possible, Missie. Take care of Mr Tommy. He a good boy. Make fine doctor some day.'

'I will tell him you said so.'

As she was about to descend to the quay, she turned back, throwing her arms around the old Chinaman's neck. 'I am so sorry you are going Wei Lun,' she told him. 'We shall miss seeing you and your van travelling the roads.'

'No, you won't Missie,' he replied, smiling. 'Much plettier shoppee come your way, velly soon.'

Wondering what on earth he could mean, she hurried down the gangway. The two escorts from the gaol descended behind her, their assignment completed. Once again on firm ground Catherine turned to wave.

From the deck above, two hands were raised in farewell. The Chinese she might never see again but woe betide Julian Frawley if he did not give her good warning of his next arrival in port!

*

'You know Teri, I rather fancy myself as a professor,' Alexander settled himself on the porch and watched Tom Dundas gather up his books and depart to continue his studies in his own room. What would you say to setting up a school of medicine here in Dunedin?'

'I think I would like it very much to be surrounded by handsome young men all looking and speaking like you but then, maybe they would not all be such model pupils as Tommy.'

'First thing is a decent hospital of course.' Alexander puffed contentedly on his pipe. His eyes became brighter and words tumbled forth excitedly as he began to assemble his thoughts.

'Imagine it Teri, a great school of medicine as prominent and well respected as that in Edinburgh, but right here on our own doorstep!'

'I am sure that if it is what you want, you will get it, some day.' He glanced at his wife expecting to see on that broad, eloquent face an indulgent smile, amusement perhaps, but what he observed was an intensity as strong as his own.

'I mean it you know,' he leaned forward eagerly, anxious for her approval. 'I've been speaking with some of the other practitioners and with Dr Burns. We feel that between us we represent a fair cross section of medical expertise.'

'You had better hurry things along,' she said, as Malcolm came into sight swinging his school bag and kicking at pebbles in the roadway. 'Our boy should be one of your first students.'

Malcolm gave them a cheerful wave and darted round back in search of Tom.

'I do hope he won't make a nuisance of himself,' Teri worried. 'Tom gets little enough time to himself.'

'I shouldn't worry,' Alexander continued to puff, contentedly, 'They help each other out with their memory games. At ten years of age, young Malcolm knows the name of every bone in the human body, just think of that.'

She smiled happily at Alexander's undisguised pride in his oldest son and for a while they were silent, each deep in some private thought.

Absently, Alexander allowed his fingers to entwine themselves in her long hair, still luxuriant despite the touches of silver at the temples. She was a buxom woman right enough, but comfortable and he had reached the age when comfort was important. 'We might even incorporate some knowledge of Maori medicine,' he murmured, playfully.

Teri was never sure when her husband was being facetious. Her incredulous expression at this last suggestion made him burst out laughing.

'No, really, I mean it. I think it's important for young physicians working amongst the Maori to understand their beliefs and of course we both know that some native remedies have been proved scientifically to have real merit.'

'You used to call it voodoo,' she accused.

'I know. I was wrong.'

She nestled comfortably against him, enjoying the cool evening breeze. Lazily, they watched the bellbirds and tuis darting in and out amongst the clusters of red flowers on the Pohutukawa tree which grew close by the house.

That tree's getting too large, Alexander murmured. 'We'll have to have it down soon.'

'Oh, that would be a pity, the birds love it so.'

He smiled at this response which was so typical of her. Teri would hate to lose the tree herself, but it was the bird's loss which worried her the most.

It would soon be Christmas Teri thought, time perhaps to take a little trip to Mapourika to see her father. Alexander would protest that he had too much work to do but she knew he would never forego an opportunity to visit Jessie.

She glanced across at her husband. His eyes were closed. A smile played about his lips and those laughter lines which had seldom appeared a year ago, now seemed more prominent day by day. It was good to see him so relaxed and happy.

Tommy's presence had made such a difference to the household. The boy was so keen to learn, so willing to work and such a contrast to Charlie Bantrie who had been for ever wandering off to watch the ships in the harbour. She had noticed too how her own children responded to the boy's presence. Malcolm particularly seemed determined to model himself on Alexander's pupil. There would surely be another Beaton doctor in the house in a few years.

She smiled to herself. Fancy her ever thinking Alex might leave all this for the Scotswoman. As things had turned out he would have looked rather silly running after a travelling shopkeeper! Jessie had caused quite a stir when she first appeared on the street with Wei Lun's travelling shop. More than a year had gone by since then and it seemed that people had come to accept her in his place. Those in the more remote areas looked forward eagerly to her regular appearances. Teri had heard talk of a new store opening in Mapourika. The travelling shop must be doing well if Jessie could afford to go into business in such a big way. Well, good luck to the widow.

Alexander regarded his wife through half closed eyes.

Dear Teri. She had had to put up with quite a lot these past years. Thankfully the practice was on its feet at last. The house was just about as they wanted it and they could afford a maid to answer the bell and take down the messages. That was the trouble with being a doctor's wife. You could never escape from the job. It was time they went off for a few days to Mapourika. Tom could come too. They might get in a little fishing and they could call on Jessie.

His thoughts dwelt for a moment on that quiet face, those delicate features and the raven-black tresses now showing a little silver just like Teri's. Just for a moment he pondered upon what might have been

'Mum, Dad, Mr Mackie's here! He say's we can ride over with him to the farm. Philip has some new pups and we can have one if we want. Can we Dad? A collie's a good dog, easy to train. Mr Mackie says he'll help.'

Alexander could resist Toby's pleading no longer. How was it that this younger son could manipulate them so easily? Teri had spoilt him of course. He had been a sickly baby and she had had to give him more than his fair share of attention.

'Oh, very well,' the doctor said, defeated. 'But remember, you'll be responsible for his good behaviour and I don't want him anywhere near my consulting room!'